On Fridays We Dance

On Fridays We Dance

A MEMOIR

Pat Buysse

ISBN: 1453788123
ISBN-13: 9781453788127

Acknowledgments

The Author wishes to express her thanks for the use of the lyrics from the song, "I'm gonna sit right down and write myself a letter," to:
© 1935. Azure Pearl Music (ASCAP)/David Ahlert Music (ASCAP) Beeping Good Music Publishing (ASCAP)
Administered by Bluewater Music Services Corp. All Rights Reserved. Used By Permission.

* * *

Deep thanks to my husband for his faithful love and technical help in seeing me through this accomplishment.

In memory of my dear parents, who raised their nineteen children in the flat farmlands of Minnesota; who never stopped working, praying and loving the best way they knew how.

Thanks to our dear children, Ann, Terri, Sharon and Charlie, for encouraging me to turn this manuscript into a published work. Special thanks, also, to friends Shelly Troff, Debbie Foster, Katherine Ashe and Robin Underdahl for their positive reinforcement and practical input concerning this endeavor.

Contents

Introduction

This story is based on my life, written from my own perspective. It is written as a novel, in the third person, with names of people and places changed. Some events and characters have been compressed to improve the flow of the story. The conversations are related as I best recall them.

These events happened in a recent time in America, the fifties, before the women's liberation movement, Vatican II, and the advance of technology (especially e-mail and cell phone) changed much of how we communicate with each another. Convent boarding schools like the one Chloe attends flourished in the Midwest through the forties, fifties, and well into the eighties, supplying teaching nuns to Catholic schools.

As an adult I returned to college, earning my BA in English from the University of Maryland. (One day, while discussing *The Scarlet Letter,* a young student, exasperated with the angst of Hester Prynne, asked with a shrug, "Why didn't she just leave town?" That may be the thought of some readers while reading this story. To those readers I say: remember the times.)

We spend our years as a tale that is told.
—Psalms 90:9b

"What happened to your eye?"

"I ran into a door."

Chloe was schocked at how easily she had lied. She ducked down to search for a book in her desk. She had thought herself an honest person, but the lie had sprung up without her even planning it. But it wasn't right to tell on your dad. He had lost his temper, was all, and it was none of Sister's business what happened at home. She knew her brothers were rough. Let her think *they* had done it. Setting her elbows squarely on her opened book, she pretended to be intently reading.

* * *

CHAPTER 1.

Polowski Home

"It's seven thirty, time to leeeeeeve! Come on all your slowpokes! You'll be late for school!" Mrs. Polowski yelled up the enclosed staircase, and received an answering thump from the boys' room in return. Throughout the rambling two-story farmhouse children of all ages dawdled in various stages of dress. Joe Polowski, Daddy to all these children, sat at the kitchen table eating oatmeal and listening to WCCO's morning news broadcast blaring from the radio on top of the refrigerator.

At the counter, thirteen-year-old Chloe Polowski stood before a row of gaping black lunch-buckets, slapping a napkin into each one before she buckled them up. Today she would find out! A thrill shot through her stomach. For weeks now Sister Clarice, her eighth grade teacher, had been studying her, as though she saw something interesting in her. Often Chloe had looked up from her desk to find Sister's eyes on her.

Chloe hoped it meant she was being considered for a part in the class play, *Columbus*. Gary, the best-looking boy in class, would play Columbus, and she wanted to be Queen Isabella. With a flourish she flipped the metal buckles closed, grabbed all six dinner pails by their handles, three in each hand, and banged them down at the front door, yelling, "Don't forget your lunch-buckets!" to no one in particular.

Daddy raised his chin at her, but just then WCCO's 7:30 theme song, a lively tick-tocking melody, burst from the radio and frolicked through the house, merrily upsetting everyone as no shout or command could ever do. Cries of "Where're my shoes?" and "I haven't eaten yet!" and "Who took my catechism!" rose from kids dashing about like ants scattered when a rock is overturned. "We'll be late for school again!" someone wailed.

The round kitchen clock hanging over the stove told the time plainly. But because so many fingers had tampered with its hands, turning them first ahead, then behind, in efforts to get the family somewhere on time, by now no one believed it anymore. But everyone knew the radio didn't lie. It really was 7:30!

It was 1955 in rural Minnesota. The scene in the Polowski household repeated itself (with more or less mayhem) in other farm homes scattered over the flat frozen tundra of St. Eli Parish in the southwestern part of the state. Because no buses served St. Eli's, parents drove their children to and from school. The Polowski farm lay five miles east of St. Eli. It was not a pretentious farm, but for those who knew where to look, it showed signs of promise. Its many buildings; the barn, granary, pig shed, silo, and chicken coop were all in busy use. Groves of box elder trees sheltered the farm on two sides, shielding it from excess snow in winter and high winds in summer. A gravel road passed by their farm, and from it jutted their short driveway leading to a separate garage. From there the driveway curved down past past the machine shed, the windmill and the barn on its way out to the gravel road again. It was a great driveway for bike riding.

The old farmhouse stood alone, large and white, with many peaks and gables. Its front porch showed wear, sagging a bit toward the cement steps, where the broken sidewalk met it in humble submission to the many feet that trod it daily, in and out of the house, scraping off mud, kicking off boots. A white picket fence framed bright Zinnias in summer, and in winter revealed that it wasn't white at all, but dirty grey. Behind the lone garage an old oak tree tilted toward the brand-new machine shed that Daddy and his sons had built last summer. Arched in a semi circle, with sliding doors, it held two John Deere tractors and an orange Allis Chambers combine.

Chloe dove into a cardboard box to rummage for mittens. Yesterday she had forgotten them, and her fingers had nearly frozen during recess. The kitchen door opened behind her, sending a draft up her skirt.

"Shut the door, were you born in a barn?" Daddy bellowed. Chloe kicked back at the door, causing Momma to lunge for baby Warren, furiously crawling towards the morning light flooding the doorway.

"Chloe, be more careful!" she yelled, scooping him up just on time. But Chloe, two mittens in hand, had already dashed through the living room and halfway up the stairs where she collided with Brent, her fourteen year old brother, sauntering down. He pushed her aside and continued on, barefooted, dangling a sock in his hand. "Hey Ma, you got another sock like this somewhere?" he drawled.

In her room Chloe slammed the door. Fuming, with both fists clenched, she stared into the mirror. "Why hurry?" she asked. "The *king's* got all the time in the world!" She sat down on the bed, her mouth hard as she listened to WCCO's jolly theme song finish its romp through the house. She smoothed down her dress and picked off a drop of butter. Today she would meet with Sister during recess, up in the classroom. At a rumbling sound Chloe rolled across her bed and looked out to where the big yellow school bus from Chester High groaned to a stop in front of their mailbox. Michelle, already seventeen, stepped daintily aboard, disappeared inside and rode away to Public School. "Next year that'll be me!" Chloe said out loud. "What a life! No dinner pails to fill or little kids to wait for. Just me, myself and *I* to think of for once! Humph! Even the *king* will have to be ready on time!" She rose, lifted her mattress and reached way under it to retrieve a copy of the *Farm Journal.* She removed her homework papers, ruffling through them to make sure Brent had not found and copied them. Zipping them up into her briefcase, her hands shook from fasting. She was hungry, and her mouth was dry. But since she liked to receive communion at Mass, she had to wait to eat or drink anything until after Mass.

Had Brent done any homework? Chloe hated having him in her grade. It had been like this ever since an over-zealous nun had flunked him in third grade. But Michelle said that next year *everything* would be different. In public high she might not even see Brent all day.

Chloe fluffed up her brown hair, wishing she had yellow curls like her classmate, Lucy Fry, or a cute pert nose like Gladys Gehring. Momma said her blue eyes were her best feature; and her smile. Momma said anyone was pretty when she smiled. At the sound of the car horn Chloe grabbed her briefcase and flew down the stairs. Daddy, seated behind the steering wheel of the blue Ford station wagon, played the car horn as though tapping out a tune. The car filled up with kids as Chloe squeezed past Brent into the middle seat. Then, as the five-mile trip began, Daddy lectured, softly at first, then louder, as was his custom when he held his audience captive in the car. "Like I always say, but what you kids never seem to learn, is, 'keep moving in the morning.' If you don't want to be late, you've got to keep moving. Think! And remember what it is you ..."

The thick snow frosting the open fields reminded Chloe of the wide ocean Christopher Columbus had sailed upon so long ago, not knowing where he was going.

"The older should help the younger, it's so simple! No lollygagging. If you could just get it through your thick skulls ..."

As her father spoke, Chloe rose from her throne to address the kneeling Columbus, "Why insist on this reckless journey? Don't you know that the world is flat?"

"You bigger kids should look around—see what needs to be done. Then everything would go so much smoother. I think you'd find that ..."

They arrived so late that Daddy didn't drive up to the school, but stopped at the big stone church instead. His kids piled out, banging dinner buckets and slamming car doors before racing up the wide pavement and up the cement steps of St. Eli's. At the top they tugged at the heavy doors. "Shssssh," Chloe hissed as her siblings crashed their dinner buckets on the foyer floor before dashing down the church aisle, seemingly in the vain hope of joining their classmates in a pew before being detected by the nuns.

Chloe knelt down next to Lucy Fry, took a deep breath and let it out slowly. Her hands still smelled like the pickle sandwiches she had made that morning. Lucy turned toward her, pointing in her missal with a clean white finger to the "Agnus Dei." Chloe was mortified; Mass was half way over. It was almost communion time. They had *never* been this late before. Again she thought of next year. Public High. Hastily she recalled her morning; had so much as a crumb or a drop of water passed her lips? Her conscience clear, she rose and went forward to receive communion. Upon returning, she felt Sister's eyes on her.

During catechism class Chloe ate her breakfast self-consciously hunched over her lunch pail, chewing the thick homemade bread. She didn't like being the only one eating, but it was the price she paid for going to communion. Floyd Inderbitzen, standing beside his desk, was reading out loud. His deep gravelly voice made Chloe want to clear her throat. The way he paused at every syllable made her want to grab his book and read it for him. "He-who-serves-God-in-a-re-lig-i-ous-or-der-choos-es-the-high-est-most-ex-al-ted-way-of ..."

Thirsty, Chloe contemplated opening her jar of milk, afraid to spill, or worse, to slurp, and embarrass herself. Suddenly Sister Clarice stepped down from her platform and swept past Chloe, her black skirts swishing above the ponderous shoes. Floyd paused, his throat gurgling like an engine suddenly thrown into neutral. The sound of paper being ripped filled the room. Without looking, Chloe knew it was Brent. Her breakfast sat like a lump in her stomach, as from the corner of her eye she saw paper fluttering to the floor.

"That's all the good your homework is to me!" Sister said. "Now pick up every bit of this trash and put it in the wastebasket where it belongs!" Heavy heels rapped on the hardwood floor as she returned to her platform. Her whole being bespoke authority, from her stiff arched veil to the rosary beads rattling at her side. A large metal crucifix hung from the end of the rosary, half-hidden in the thick folds of her skirts, but continuously peeking out, showing the crucified hands of Christ. While Brent scrambled to retrieve the scraps of paper, Chloe felt guilty for being selfish.

"Floyd! Read." Sister said.

"Saint-Ben-e-dict-of-Nursia,-when-he-was-a-young-man,-de-ci-ded-to-fol-low-Christ- in-to-the-full-ser-vice-of-Al-might-y ..."

"Stop!"

Brent, on his way to the wastebasket, stopped, his hands cupped together, holding the paper scraps. His lips trembled. Thin and tan, he was not yet tall, but his legs showed potential. He was wearing a red plaid shirt and a pair of blue jeans, patched at the knees. Sister, her arms buried deep within her voluminous sleeves, stepped down from her platform and circled Brent, eyeing him with arched eyebrows. "How is it?" she began in a singsong voice, "That two people from the same family can be so opposite?" Chloe's heart lurched. "No sister! Please!" She tensed and prayed silently.

"Hmm?"

"I dunno," Brent said, making a quick dash to the wastebasket to empty his hands. As he clapped them together lightly someone on the seventh-grade side of the room giggled. Brent smirked.

"Oh, comedian, are you?" Sister grabbed Brent's ear and twisted it so that his head bent sideways. His face turned deep red.

"Who can figure it out? *One* in the family studies! The *other* cheats. One is smart! And the other?" Sister turned up the palm of her free hand.

Chloe stiffened as Sister pushed Brent down into an empty front seat with no desk. "Sit here today!" she said, "What does a monkey like you need a desk for?"

Brent's neck shone as red as his plaid shirt. For the rest of the morning, as Sister's strident voice filled the classroom, the seventh and eighth graders appeared listless. Surreptitiously glancing at the big clock hanging high on the wall, they waited for lunch and recess. Chloe burped several times. She watched as Brent balanced his books and papers on his lap. Tonight he would take it out on the rest of them. "Didn't Sister know that? Did she think she was helping? Had she been away from *family* so long that she had forgotten how they worked?"

On her way to the pencil sharpener, Chloe tried to appease Brent with a smile, but he only glared back at her. Lunchtime in the classroom was subdued as students gulped down their food, closed their lunch buckets, and waited to be dismissed. In the crowded cloakroom, as the seventh and eighth graders jostled each other for coats and caps, Chloe glimpsed Brent's scowl in the crowd. Bending over, balancing on one foot as she pulled on her boot, she felt a shove against a coat hook. She cried out in pain.

"Serves you right!" Brent said as he and Floyd spun on their heels and sped down the back cement stairs with a yelp like an Indian war cry. Hurt and embarrassed at fighting in public, Chloe grabbed her coat and flew down the opposite staircase, a wide wooden one leading to the front doors. Outside she ran; past the first graders playing "Duck-Duck-Goose," through a broken down fence, between two lilac bushes and around the back of Father Black's big white house.. There she paused to catch her breath. It was a familiar path. She often visited Jesus during recess. Out of sight, she trudged up a slope toward the church and tugged at a side door. Slipping inside, she passed the curtained confessionals and entered a pew, her footsteps echoing through the cavernous church.

For a long time she sat, her back pressed against the pew, until the pain subsided and her breathing slowed. She didn't cry, just gazed sadly toward the altar, where the tabernacle, a golden box with white curtains, stood at its center. Inside of it Jesus stayed. He lived in the white host that had been consecrated that morning at mass. She could feel Him looking out at her, listening. In a dark corner of the Sanctuary a flickering red candle testified to His real presence.

"Jesus," she said, knowing He heard, "Why are nuns so mean? And why do they hate big families?" As she pondered this sad conundrum, knowing she would not receive an answer, her eyes wandered to the left, where a statue of Mary stood enshrined in a blue arched niche. She was smiling sweetly as she held her baby, Jesus, perched on her arm like a bird. Sister said that Mary was everybody's mother and that she could ask her for anything. And Chloe had. But today she felt annoyed at the statue. Anyone who knew anything about babies knew that was no way to hold a baby.

Next her gaze flew to the stained glass circle high above the altar. Its bright colors glowed from the sunlight shining behind it, making it seem alive, as if God were ready, at any moment, to step through it and address her. "Dear God," she prayed, "how can your brides say they love you when they hate us so? And Sister's stupid! I hate to say it but it's true. Even *I* know that comparisons are odious." After a while, Chloe grew quiet, listening to the soft creaks echoing through the church. It was so peaceful here. Then, with a quiet thrill she recalled her secret; someday she would be a nun. God's bride. But she would not be a teaching nun. Oh no. Up in her room, hidden in her underwear drawer, she kept an ad torn from the *St. Anthony Messenger.* It spoke of a missionary order, the Maryknolls. On it there was a picture of a young nun in white leaning over a little African boy lying in a hammock. She was offering him a drink of water. Beneath the picture blazed the question: "How much can you love God's little ones?"

"And when I am a nun, I'll favor the kids from *big* families, and pick on the others for a change!" she vowed. At this, the round high window brightened again, sending its rainbow colors down upon the brown pews and cinder block walls of the church. Chloe felt answered.

Then it dulled, and with a gasp Chloe remembered her meeting with Sister. She jumped up and hurried from the church, forgetting to genuflect or say good-bye to Jesus.

"Oh, there you are!" Sister turned stiffly in her cumbersome veil towards Chloe, stepping cautiously into the classroom. "Were you in church?"

"Yes, Sister," Chloe said, panting heavily from taking the long flight of stairs two at a time. Sister held a sheaf of papers in her hands. "I've been looking over your work of the past weeks, Chloe, and I must say I'm very pleased with it. Keep this up and you might get an A in history." Sister beamed at her.

"Oh. That's good," Chloe smiled bashfully. So that's what this meeting was about, her grades.

"You are doing well in all of your classes. You wrote the Beatitudes perfectly. That took a lot of study." While Sister gazed kindly at her from over the silver rims of her glasses, Chloe squirmed. She was not used to praise and was not sure how to respond. For the first time she had really studied this year, and it felt good to have someone notice.

"You're *even* doing better in arithmetic, though it will never be your strong suit." Sister laid the papers down and leaned back in her chair. "All in all, I'd say you're having a very good year, Chloe Polowski!"

Chloe smiled shyly. She wanted to say that lately she even *liked* learning. But, not sure how that might sound, she kept still. Then she thought of Brent. Now might be a good time to put in a word for him. Sure, he was mean; she often hated him herself. But as Momma had often remarked, "If Sister would just work with him and try to get on his good side instead of his bad, she might find that he …"

"Brent can study too." She blurted out. "He was really smart when he was little and he …"

"I didn't call you here to talk about Brent." Sister's face had tightened. "It's you who interests me." Chloe fell silent. In a softer tone Sister said, "You're growing into quite a nice young lady, Chloe. I see a lot of potential in you."

Her heartbeat quickened. What, exactly, was potential? Was it a trait of Queen Isabella's?

"The other nuns have been watching, and they've noticed it too. We think that such qualities as you have been demonstrating should be encouraged and developed."

Chloe was stunned. "The other nuns? Watching her? Why and When? Most likely it was after school, when Daddy was so often late picking them up. Those times she would play with the little ones in the empty school yard or read to them, sitting on the curb. When it was cold she took them inside the church to wait, since the school was locked. Brent chose to hang around Pete's Gas station, with its pot-bellied stove.

"And there's something special about the way you love church. You do love church, don't you?"

"Love it?"

"Well, you're not bored with it, as so many of your age are."

"No, Sister."

"You seem to have a special affinity for spiritual things; an unusual gift in one so young."

Chloe squeezed her toes inside of her shoes and held them, hardly able to bear another word of praise, she felt so anxious and unsure of how to receive it.

"Chloe, tell me, have you thought much about your future? What you'll do with your life?"

Chloe blinked, remembering her secret, and shrugged in what she hoped was a careless, easy way. "I'm pretty busy just thinking about today." She said with a laugh. But sister stayed stern.

"Well, maybe now would be a good time to think about it. For instance, next year! Have you thought about that?"

"Sure. I'll go to high school."

"Where?"

"Chester High, like everyone else."

"You know what I think of that school, Chloe."

"Yes, Sister." It was a cesspool of sin. Sister had said that often enough. But it was the only high school around.

"You deserve so much better."

Chloe tried to look calm. So this was how it felt to be in Sister's favor. But everyone knew that the closest Catholic high school was twenty miles away. If Sister thought Daddy would drive her that far twice a day just for high school, she didn't know farmers. Michelle, her older sister, had had to beg Daddy for three days just to be allowed to go to Chester High. And Owen, her oldest brother, had not gone to high school at all.

"There's a special school for girls like you, Chloe, called Mater Dei, where girls can get an excellent education.

"Oh? Where is it?"

"In Magnolia. Have you heard of that town?"

"I think so." Chloe smoothed down the back of her hair.

"You'd fit in so well at this school, I just know it." As Sister rambled on about this faraway school, exclaiming and explaining how wonderful it was, Chloe's thoughts wandered. Nuns were mysterious creatures. They were women of course, but with so many secrets. They had no last names, didn't drive, and never ate or drank in public. No one knew the color of their hair. It was hard to tell their age. Lucy Fry said they shaved their heads. Brent thought their ears were cut off, but that was impossible, 'cause everyone knew nuns could hear better than anybody else. They never mentioned their families or their past. "In many ways," Chloe thought, "they are almost not human. They had left all for Christ, so they must be holy. And they were smart, since they were teachers, but sometimes they weren't very down-to-earth; like now, with Sister Clarice going on about this girls' high school as though she had half a chance of going there."

"Tell me, Chloe, have you ever thought of becoming a nun?" Sister asked, her steel gray eyes riveted on Chloe's, demanding an answer.

CHAPTER 2.

Barn and Recall

It was one of the first warm days in May, and a strong south wind blew through the open loft door hanging down like a giant tongue on the outside of the barn. From where they lounged on the bales, Chloe and Brent could see their father's fields all the way to Highway 69. Both of them had been kept home from school to help with the work.

"I hung out six loads of wash today," Chloe said, "and it's all dry already." Brent didn't reply as he opened his lunch-bucket and took out a sandwich of thick homemade bread. He peeked inside it before taking a bite. "Oh good, Spam!" he said, chomping down hungrily. "Well," he said between mouthfuls, "I've been cleaning the barn." Together they watched the Chester High school bus crawling along the blacktop of Highway 69 like a huge yellow bug. Brent gulped down his jar of lemonade and turned to Chloe. "Next year, that'll be us! No nuns. Whoopee! I'm sick of 'em, aren't you?"

Chloe nodded. Lemon seeds floated on the bottom of Brent's jar as he tilted it up. "The trouble with them is they're against anybody having any fun. It's gonna be so different next year. You can't even imagine."

Usually Chloe liked it when her brother talked to her. But today she was anxious to get back to the house to iron her blue skirt and polish her white flats. Tomorrow she was going to visit Mater Dei Heights with the nuns to see the senior class play, *The Mikado.* She dared not tell Brent.

Besides herself, Sister Clarice had invited two other eighth-grade girls, Lucy Fry and Gladys Gehring, to see the play. Lucy's dad had agreed to drive. They were leaving early the next morning and wouldn't be home until late at night. It would be grand. At the very thought of it, her heart leaped with anticipation. She would have liked to share her news with Brent, but she feared he would scoff or be jealous, so she kept mum.

Not that she had any hope of attending Mater Dei Heights! Impossible. She knew that. But it would be fun to see the place anyway. Sister made it sound so great. The farthest Chloe had ever traveled was to St. Paul once to attend the state fair with her parents. And never had she gone anywhere very far without them.

Brent cut her a sharp look. "I know those nuns think I'm dumb ... can't learn noth'n. But they're wrong. It's no use even trying with them. Next year I'm going to play football. Floyd's big brother, Jim, watched me play last Sunday, and he says the coach will have me all right!"

"School's more than football," Chloe ventured, hoping she didn't sound too much like a grown-up.

"I know," he said, holding up his hand to block a beam of sunlight spearing him from a crack high in the barn wall. "And I've been thinking. I got an idea." Brent's dark eyes shone into hers.

"What?" she asked cautiously, hoping she could approve.

He edged a little closer on the bale of hay, animated. "With both of us in the same grade, we could be a team. You can help me with homework and I could, you know, introduce you to guys. I hear Chester High gets rough sometimes. You're lucky to have a brother like me to look after you."

"Yes, I suppose." Chloe said, twisting a hay strand in her hand. The part about meeting guys sounded good, but the part about him looking after her made her want to laugh. "Well, I've got things to do," she said, gathering Brent's empty jar and the waxed paper he'd tossed and stuffing them into the lunch pail.

"Come on," he said, "let's shoot a few baskets. They can get along without you in the house for a few minutes." He jumped up, grabbed the basketball and dribbled it on a cleanly swept area of the barn near the open trap door. He made a jump shot and bounced the ball to Chloe. She deflected it with her arm, shaking her head. She knew he'd be mad at her rejection. He scowled, but she ignored it, inching toward the ladder. "No, really, I gotta go," she said. He dribbled the ball deftly, his hard muscles carrying him about the barn like a practiced athlete. Smoothly, in perfect control of the ball, he made a jump shot and then another, begging, "Come on, it's fun! Just one game of horse?"

"Ma needs me," she lied, backing toward the steps. She knew Momma liked to see them get along and would have encouraged her to play. But other things pulled at her today and, besides, playing next to the open door could mean trouble. As Brent made a long shot, his lithe, lean body leaping into the air, she quickly climbed down the ladder.

As she emerged outside, the basketball struck her head. Stunned, she staggered.

"Bull's-eye!" Brent yelled, pointing and jumping up and down in glee. Chloe, her head ringing, reeled and she stepped into a cow pie. "Eyaggh!" she yelled as the putrid smell filled her nostrils. Scraping her canvas shoe sideways on the grass she cried, "My brand-new shoes!" Brent doubled over with laughter from sheer joy.

"I hate you! I hate you! You're just like the devil!" she screamed, kicking his basketball toward a cow pie. It missed, and he laughed louder, calling after her, "I always thought you stunk, and now I know for sure!"

"It don't pay to be nice to Brent," Chloe exploded, stomping into the kitchen, her face beet red. Momma, surrounded by stacks of folded laundry, asked wearily, "What did he do now?"

"Threw a basket ball at me so hard he nearly knocked me out, that's what!"Chloe cried. When Momma didn't respond she shouted, "And then I stepped into a cow-pie besides!"

"Scrape it off, it's just a little thing, Chloe. "I'm sure he didn't mean anything by it," Mother said picking up a large stack of folded diapers and walking into the baby room.

"Oh, no, he just meant to kill me, that's all! Oh! I wish I didn't have any brothers!"

"Chloe! You don't mean that," her mother pleaded, "A lot of girls would give their right arm to have just one brother."

"Yeah, well they're nuts, whoever they are!" Chloe said, hurtling her dirty tennis shoe outside.

That night Chloe lay awake thinking about the next day. No one in the family had mentioned her trip. Chloe guessed that Momma was keeping it quiet so that the others wouldn't be jealous. Anyway, nothing would come of it. Chloe knew from reading novels that only rich girls went to boarding schools. She, Lucy and Gladys were each just simple farm girls going on a trip that Sister had arranged. Nevertheless, it was exciting.

Beside her little Julie slept curled like a kitten, purring softly. From the boys' room next door she heard her big brother, Owens's, radio crackling and fizzing from a fading station. He must have fallen asleep with it on. Sometimes Chloe would creep in to turn it off, but tonight she rolled over and relived, with a twinge, that conversation with Sister Clarice weeks ago.

"Tell me Chloe, have you ever thought of becoming a nun?"

To Chloe it felt as if they had strolled down a pleasant path together, admiring the roses when suddenly she stood at a precipice with Sister leaning over her.

She tried to sound casual. "Oh, I guess every Catholic girl thinks of that at one time or another."

"But you aren't every girl, Chloe. I'm talking about you!"

Chloe's stomach tightened as her mind scampered about for an answer that wasn't a lie.

"What do you mean, exactly?" Chloe tilted her head.

"I mean," Sister said evenly, "Have you ever thought, even once, of becoming a nun?"

Chloe's heart beat a muffled protest. The permanently frosted windows of the classroom waited in mute silence for her answer. "I've thought about it," she said, swallowing. She saw a flash, a gleam of triumph flicker in Sister's eyes. "What would Sister do with this information? Fearful, wanting somehow to erode her admission, Chloe added, "I want to be a missionary nun, with the Maryknolls."

"And what do you know about the Maryknolls?"

"They work with the poor."

"Do you know where their motherhouse is?"

"No, Sister, I ..."

"California ... How do you think your mother would like to see you leave for California, hmm? That's pretty far away. You've got to think of these things. Now our motherhouse is right here in Minnesota, just a few hours' drive. Don't you think you'd be much happier in an order closer to home, like ours?"

"I, I could never be a teacher."

"And you think you could be a nurse? That's what the Maryknolls are, nurses! And nurses have to take a lot of math. And you and I both know that arithmetic comes hard for you."

"Oh, well, I have to get through high school first anyway before I decide about anything," Chloe said with relief.

"That's where you're wrong, Chloe. Do you know how many girls have stood right where you're standing now, and said they wanted to be nuns?"

"No, Sister."

"Ten at least, over the last four years. And do you know where they are today?"

"No, Sister."

"Married, every one of them. Or engaged." Sister said sadly.

"Maybe they didn't have a real vocation."

"Or maybe they did, and lost it! Something happens in high school, Chloe, to the nicest girls, that makes them forget all her high ideals; their love for God. It makes me sad; girls like you, so devout and promising. They leave here with the best intentions, and by the time they graduate from high school they've lost it all."

Chloe blanched. She had not known a vocation was built of such fragile stuff. It would be sad to lose it before even knowing if it was real. But what could she do about it?

"Chloe, This school that I was telling you about, Mater Dei," Sister stopped to lick her lips, "is a girls' school; far away from the temptations of the world. And the girls are free to try out the life and see if they truly have a religious vocation or not. There is no requirement, no obligation to stay, but it's a great opportunity that I think you'd enjoy, Chloe, as a girl who. . ."

As sister talked, Chloe pressed her tongue tightly against her teeth. For years she and her brothers and sisters had come to this school and none of them had been favorites. The nuns liked to ridicule their greasy papers and they seemed annoyed at their patched up blue jeans. Chloe thought of her classmates, Mozelle and Louise, whom Sister had chosen for special tasks, like getting their mail or passing out art supplies. She didn't' count here, she knew that. And at home, with her big family, she worked harder than any of her classmates, she was sure. She'd never had a room of her own, and her big brothers badgered her and tried to copy off her papers. For her, life was a struggle just weaving her way through her brother's fights, her mother's moods, and her daddy's heavy hand. She was like a mom to the little ones at home, and yet, with all this, she had managed to get mostly B's, except in Math.

"They attend classes like any other high schooler and there's a separate building called the villa where they live, just like a happy home."

"Sounds nice," Chloe said, wanting to say that farm girls didn't go to boarding schools, that her family was not rich, and that her mother needed her at home. But Sister knew all that.

"I'd like to see you have a chance at this place. If you could just visit it once, I'm sure you'd love it. Do you think you'd at least like to visit the school if I could arrange it?"

"That would be nice," Chloe acquiesced. When the bell ending recess rang and the noisy voices of her classmates filled the classroom, Chloe felt strangely set apart. She seemed to float to her desk as she imagined a faraway place where girls like herself lived in harmony. For the first time she noticed how drab the classroom looked, and how mean her fellow students.

CHAPTER 3.

Visiting Mater Dei

Chloe had never been in a car with nuns before, but now she sat so close to them she could see the warp and woof of their black arched veils. When Mr. and Mrs. Fry had arrived at the Polowski farm in their station wagon to pick up Chloe, her friends, Lucy Fry and Gladys Gehring were already ensconced in the back seat, so the only place for Chloe to sit was in the middle, between the two nuns; for it wasn't right for a nun to have to straddle the hump.

Sister Clarice's starched veil rustled and scraped as she turned to Chloe and said, "I can't believe you're really coming, and pinched Chloe's arm playfully. To Chloe's left sat Sister Dorcas, the third-and fourth-grade teacher. She was young, with smooth slender hands resting quietly in her lap. A faint odor of soap emanated from her. She seemed to have been born a nun. "But no, she had once been a girl, like Chloe. But where had she grown up? And what had been her name?" Those secrets no one could pry from her.

As the trip got underway, Chloe noticed how differently the nuns behaved away from school. They laughed and talked like women set free, even joking and teasing one another. As the merry banter flew back and forth between the car's occupants, Chloe squeezed her hands together tightly in her lap. She felt shy, wanting to join in, but every time she thought of something clever to say she rehearsed it so often that by the time she was ready to speak the moment had passed, and she had lost her chance.

"Cat got your tongue?" Sister Clarice teased, elbowing her.

"Aren't you glad you're coming?" Sister Dorcas asked sweetly, twisting sideways to see Chloe, which caused her head-covering to pull away just enough to reveal an ear and a wisp of blonde hair.

"Oh, yes, Sister!" Chloe replied, looking away quickly. Sister's flattened hair had looked like corn silk. Chloe wanted to tell the other two girls in the back right away what she had learned, that Sister Dorcas was a blonde. But she had to wait.

In the pale May sky, watery clouds skimmed the horizon. On the ground, black plowed fields flew by on either side. Oats, planted early, had already popped into tender green shoots. Gradually the flat Minnesota farmland began to swell and dip, making hills and vales where sheep grazed, reminding Chloe of a child's picture book. The change in the landscape surprised Chloe; before today she would have sworn that all of Minnesota was flat as a pancake. But here Minnesota reared up in hills and stony cliffs jutting up from the earth as if breaking free of its hold.

"Not very good land for farming," Chloe remarked in the manner of her father, who always judged land on those terms. No one responded. When a sheer bluff rose up close to the road, Chloe bent her head to see its crest, where she glimpsed a gnarled and twisted tree that looked as if it had survived many a vicious winter.

"I always thought Minnesota was flat as a table." Lucy exclaimed from the back.

"They say a glacier passed through here long ago," Sister Clarice explained, "causing this rugged terrain."

"I wish a glacier had passed over St. Eli," Lucy quipped, "it wouldn't be so boring then."

Her parents in the front seat smiled at each other.

"And look at those black and white cows, how pretty they are. The only cows we have around St. Eli are plain brown!" Gladys piped in.

"That's 'cause this is dairy land and those are Holsteins. Where we come from, we raise cattle for beef." Mr. Fry explained.

Chloe tried to join in with, "I see they raise sheep." But Sister Clarice exclaimed, "Look! There it is! Mater Dei Heights!" She wagged a finger at some faraway hills, saying, "See, over there. Do you see something shining through those trees? That's the water tower!" Sister pulled in her starched veil to let Chloe see around her.

"I see it!" Gladys cried from the back.

"Me too!" added Lucy. But all Chloe saw were brown hills covered with bare trees. As they descended into the heart of downtown Magnolia, Sister Clarice leaned forward eagerly, giving Mr. Fry directions. Then the car left the city and began to climb up a winding road hidden on one side by sheer rock, and on the other by thick groves. All the way up, Sister Clarice pointed first to the left and then to the right, explaining, "The girls go hiking in those woods. And in the winter they go sledding over there on those hills!"

"Spring comes so beautifully to these woods," Sister Dorcas sighed with a smile. She seemed happy to be visiting the Motherhouse.

Chloe looked around, loving the trees and hills. "I'm changed already," she thought, "even though I'll *never* go here." Mr. Fry shifted downward and the car climbed higher until it emerged onto a level road. All was bright and sunny here. A shady lane led to a small city of brick buildings and neatly kept lawns. Sidewalks outlined the perimeters of the lawns, and here and there bloomed bright circles of red tulips. They parked in a large lot already abuzz with cars and buses. People milled about in clusters and in pairs; children followed their parents, and groups of students trailed after the nuns and priests like happy lambs. They had all come to see the class play, *The Mikado.*

The three St. Eli farm girls gawked at the large brick buildings set against the blue sky. It looked like a picture in a book. Sister Clarice continued to talk and to point. "That's the boarder's quarters, over there; see that tower on the end? And that long middle part with all the windows, that's the academy. That curved part with the dome is the chapel. And look!" she said, turning to the opposite side of the campus. "That's the villa where the aspirants stay." She pointed to a lone brick building, stout and square. It was three stories high and surrounded by lawn. It bore a front porch where chairs were set, and a beautiful front door. "And those must be aspirants!" she added. Some girls in uniform lounged on the steps. They wore navy blue jumpers with white blouses. Bobby socks and saddle shoes completed their uniform. A girl rose and approached them, smiling shyly. "Good morning!" she said, tossing a short mane of straight blonde hair away from her blue eyes. "I'm Lynn Dahlset, a junior here. This building behind me is our home, the villa."

Sister Clarice introduced her St. Eli girls by name, adding, "They're thinking of attending here next year." At this, the three glanced uneasily at one another, shuffling their feet, and pulling their feet a little closer together.

"I hope you do." Lynn said sweetly. "We just love it here. There's no place like it in the whole world. And wait until you meet Sister Damien, she's like a mother to us!"

When Lynn offered to show the girls around, Sister Clarice agreed, saying the sisters needed to eat their lunch in the convent. The others had eaten in the car, while traveling. Chloe, Lucy, and Gladys followed Lynn up the steps and through a beautiful wooden door with an oval window at its center. It opened on a bright entry with a fern glowing in the window. A round Persian rug with fringes lay on the floor, too pretty to step on, Chloe thought.

"Go ahead, it's for walking on," Lynn said as Chloe tried to step around it. Chloe was sure that any girl passing through this entry every morning on her way to school was bound to have a good day. Inside the villa it was dark, with high ceilings and narrow corridors and slick hardwood floors. A soft breeze wafted through the hallways. Everything was clean and orderly. A sign saying, "Office" hung at the door of a room lined with books, with a desk in front of a large window.

As they trudged up the stairs to the dormitories Lynn said, "You just can't imagine a better place to live, we have so much fun." The dormitories reminded Chloe of the hospital rooms where Momma stayed whenever she had a baby. The white bedspreads covering each bed were without wrinkle. Beside each bed stood a nightstand on which rested a basin and a cup. A white towel hung neatly on a side rack. Near the foot of each and every bed a plain wooden chair stood like a sentry. The golden floorboards gleamed in the sunlight. Dark green window shades pulled to exactly the middle of each window gave the dormitory a quiet rested look.

"Where are the mirrors?" Lucy asked. Lynn explained that they were in the bathrooms. As they clattered down the stairs a nun stood in the doorway of the office; a petite precise figure with a pleasant face and freckles sprinkled over her nose.

"I'd like you to meet Sister Damien, our mistress of aspirants," Lynn said to the girls.

Sister clasped each girl's hands in both of hers, repeating their names and smiling into their eyes as she laughed and talked with them, inquiring about their hometown and their families. Chloe noted in her a gracious femininity so lacking in Sister Clarice. "Even Brent would like her," she thought.

"Sister Damien's tops with us, "Lynn said as they descended to the basement where they saw the showers, the study rooms, and a small kitchen. "Here's where we bake all kinds of goodies for our Friday night parties." she said.

Lucy and Gladys glanced at one another with dawning gleams in their eyes. Chloe liked the showers. At home, because of the constant water shortage, Daddy had disconnected the shower because it wasted water. They could take just one shallow bath a week. For the first time Chloe wondered what these girls had said or done to get their parents to allow them to come to this school. Lastly Lynn threw open two double doors revealing the recreation room, a large homey room furnished with stuffed chairs and couches. It had a fireplace. "Here's where we have all our fun!" Lynn said.

"What do you do?" Lucy asked.

"Oh, we play games, cards, crafts, and read—anything we want." She opened a cupboard filled with games and puzzles stacked high.

"I see a phonograph," Chloe said. "Can you play records?"

"All kinds!" Lynn said, "And on Fridays we dance."

"Dance?" Chloe exclaimed, "With boys?"

"Oh, no!" Lynn said, smiling, "with each other. You know, for exercise! We learn all kinds of new steps and just goof off. We have a ball!"

Chloe was glad her father wasn't there to hear all the emphasis on "fun." He'd like more to hear about work and duty. Soon it was time for the play to start, so the girls assembled in the gym on folding chairs and sat back for the entertainment.

Much later, as the weary group started for home the sun was low, a golden orb dropping through the boarders' trees. Sister Damien appeared to see them off. “And how did you like the play?” She asked, her pretty lips puckering quizzically.

“Very much, Sister!” the girls replied together.

“Maybe we’ll see you next year?” she asked.

Lucy shrugged. Gladys murmured something unintelligible.

“I-I-I’m just visiting,” Chloe stammered, feeling Sister Damien’s glance at her like a motherly hug.

It was pitch black by the time Chloe stepped through the gritty porch and into the kitchen. The supper dishes were still scattered on the table, with greasy leftovers dried on them. Hungry, she picked up a T-bone lying at the edge of a plate and bit off a piece of steak someone had missed. Then she followed the sound of her mother’s humming to the baby room, where Momma was scrubbing the collar of a boy’s white church shirt. Little Peter played at her feet, pushing a truck loaded with blocks around and making loud noises with his lips.

“How come he’s still up?” she asked irritably.

“Oh, you’re home! I didn’t hear you come in,” Momma exclaimed, wiping her hands on her apron to give Chloe a quick hug. “He’s not tired I guess; had a long nap, fell asleep in the parlor. I thought he was sick, but now I’m not sure.” She reached down to feel Peter’s forehead. The front door opened and men’s voices filled the kitchen. Chloe grimaced.

“They worked late,” Momma said, “haven’t had supper yet.”

Cupboard doors slammed. Daddy belched; then heavy footsteps brought him to the baby room. A milk mustache frosted his upper lip. “Oh, Chloe, could you fix me and Travis something to eat?” he asked, looking momentarily puzzled at her skirt and blouse, as if trying to remember where she had gone. “We’ve just chased a bunch of cows in from all over creation. They got loose in Huffiker’s grove,” he said.

"Okay," Chloe replied, removing her sweater and throwing it over the baby crib.

"I might have to get you kids up early before church tomorrow morning to look for strays," Daddy added.

That night Chloe knelt by her bed and thanked God for the day. "Oh dear Jesus," she began, resting her head on her arms while the sights and sounds of Mater Dei swirled through her head, "it's so beautiful." She heard the German nun in the grotto saying, "Velcome! Velcome!" and saw the flecks of light dancing in Sister Damien's eyes. She saw Lynn Dalset's earnest look as she said, "I think you'd love it here."

An hour later she woke up and crawled into bed, her legs numb and tingling.

CHAPTER 4.

Pressure from Sister

"Chloe, have you made up your mind about next fall yet?"

"No, Sister. But you know I'd like to go."

"Well, what does your father say?"

"I haven't really asked him."

"He's a good Catholic. He would be honored. Do you want me to speak with him?"

"No, Sister. That's all right. I will."

"The deadline for applications is July first."

"Yes, Sister."

All morning Chloe had carried her application in her back pocket (waiting for a time when her mother wasn't busy or Michelle wasn't around, or Peter wasn't crying and the big boys were outside), to talk to her. She wanted to go to Mater Dei Heights. Ever since her visit the desire had grown until she thought of little else. She knew she didn't deserve to go. It wasn't fair to leave Michelle with all the work. But if she had a vocation, sacrifice was necessary. Anyway, Warren was walking already, and Momma wasn't pregnant again.

Chloe followed her mother to the baby room where she was changing Warren's diaper. "Mom, I have to talk to you," she said, as Momma stuck a safety pin in her mouth and wrestled with the baby. Chloe held down his shoulders while Momma cleaned him, laid a clean diaper beneath him and sprinkled his bottom with cornstarch. Little Peter shouldered his way between the two, sucking his thumb.

"Mom, have you and Dad talked about Magnolia yet?"

Momma's quick fingers pulled the blue rubber pants over the diaper and pulled the squirming baby to his feet, pulling off his T-shirt, which was soaked. "Some. Why?"

"I ... well, do you think? It really is a great school, and I was wondering if you, have you discussed my going there?"

Momma lifted Warren and hugged his soft little body to herself, nuzzling his cheek before putting him down. "Chloe, we have a good enough high school here. And besides, you're so young to be leaving home." Chloe clicked her tongue impatiently. Leaving home would be an adventure. And as far as being *young*! Mothers were so stuffy sometimes. "I know it costs money," she said with a pout. "And we have a big family."

Momma answered sharply. "Chloe, don't ever use our big family as an excuse for not following your vocation. Your daddy and I would never stand in God's way. You know that. I just think it's a big step at your age."

Chloe suppressed a sigh. "Sister said she would talk to Dad about it if I wanted."

"No! Sister's said enough already" She turned and looked squarely at Chloe. "Do you really want to go, Chloe?"

"Oh, yes, Momma! I do. It's all I think of. If you could just see it, you'd know why. I'm not afraid to leave home. I mean, I'd miss you and all, but Sister says I would be with girls just like me. If I could just try it, that's all, and see if I really have a vocation. I just want to try it. Then I'll know if it's the right place for me or not."

Her mother studied her, looking sad and a little tired.

"Mom, I know you need me here and it's not fair to the others."

"Pshaw!" Her mother waved her large rough hand. "That's not the reason. I've got Michelle. I just don't want you getting talked into something you can't get out of."

"I'm not!" Chloe declared. "Sister said I can quit anytime. I just think it's worth a try, to see if I really have a vocation."

While her mother stared into space, Chloe babbled on, barely able to suppress her impatience with her mother's caution and hesitance. "Why couldn't she appreciate this opportunity? What would it hurt to try? Even if she didn't become a nun, she would still get a top-notch education. There didn't seem to be any way to think of it but positively." But the only indication her mother gave of hearing her was a tightening of a muscle in her neck.

After a while Momma said quietly, "Maybe you should be allowed to try it."

"Oh, Momma!" Chloe exclaimed, "That would be wonderful!" She wished Momma would look at her, but instead she picked up Warren who had returned to her, and turned toward the window. "Just don't ever say I made you go," she said.

"I won't!" Chloe cried, hugging herself while jumping up and down on her tiptoes.

"You have to ask your Dad."

"But when? There's never a good time. The boys are usually around, and at night he's so tired and crabby."

"He wants his lunch brought to him today in the field," she said. "He's cultivating the north forty. Why don't you carry it out to him? You'll have all the quiet you need. And don't forget the checkbook."

All the way down the gravel road, through the clover and across the narrow creek, Chloe rehearsed her words. Daddy spotted her a long way off and waved.

While he ate, sitting on the metal seat, she stood on the axle and sat back against the tractor tire. The young green corn rustled softly in the breeze. All around them in every direction lay a flat rich land resplendent in growth. For dessert she handed him a huge oatmeal cookie.

"Big, just the way I like 'em," he said approvingly, turning the cookie over in his hand. "You make 'em?"

"Yes," she said, sliding the application form out from her back pocket.

He heard the paper rattle. "What've you got there?" he asked.

While he polished off the cookie, she told him. He wiped his mouth with the back of his hand.

"Sister thinks I probably do have a vocation and, well, the deadline is coming up and I was wondering …" Her voice trailed off.

Resting his fists on the steering wheel he sighed and looked out over the wide expanse of fields to where the earth met the blue sky. The new crop of corn stood in straight green rows before him. "You think that's quite the place, don't you?" he asked with a kind of resignation in his voice.

"Oh, yes, Daddy!"

He removed his straw hat and ran his hands through his thick black hair. His face was cracked and dirty where the fine black dust had blown into the creases. "Your mother will miss you," he said, taking the paper and positioning it on in the middle of the steering wheel for signing. The pen made a scratching sound. A meadowlark lilted nearby, and Chloe wanted to hug Daddy's big wide back. But instead she smiled and repeated, "Oh, thank you Daddy, thank you!" She handed him the checkbook. "They want fifty dollars up-front," she said, and thanked him again.

Walking home through the rows of young corn, the young leaves tickling her ankles, Chloe fixed on a joyous thought: by the time this corn was tall and tasseled out, with ears ready for picking, she would be gone—away to a brand-new world of happy people with high ideals and wonderful plans for her life.

Above her the sky arched like a large blue bowl without a cloud.

July was hot and windy. It hadn't rained for weeks. Yesterday, at supper, Daddy said that unless they got rain soon the entire corn crop would burn up. Chloe's room felt like an oven. She could only open her window a couple of inches. Her skin felt sticky with sweat as she sat on her bed opening a letter from Mater Dei Heights.

"Dear Chloe," it started. It was from Sister Damien, welcoming her to the villa, the "Aspiranture of the Humble Handmaids of Mary." Enclosed was a typewritten list of the clothes she would need.

"2 regulation uniforms (see details in letter)

7 pair underpants, white, cotton

7 pair socks, white

4 brassieres, white, cotton

7 hankies

2 slips, white, cotton

2 pair nylons and garter belt

2 pair winter pajamas

1 housecoat

1 pair bedroom slippers (soft sole)

1 pair saddle shoes, black and white

1 pair tennis shoes, white

1 pair dress shoes, black

1 pair boots

1 sweater

1 coat

1 scarf, no hats

2 pair jeans with shirts

1 black suit (no flecks, not charcoal) with white blouse

3-4 skirts and blouses for weekend wear

1 dressy dress

2 sets of towels and washcloths, white

1 comb, brush, toothbrush, bar of soap, shoe polish, sanitary napkins and belt.

This list is adequate for your needs. If you bring more, we cannot promise you convenient storage, as we have reached maximum enrollment at the villa. Mark all of the above with indelible ink or sewn-on name tags (not iron-on). *Do not* bring seasonal changes, as you can switch wardrobes during Christmas and Easter vacations. --You may bring jewelry, but not in excess. Space is at a premium.

-Our laundry is not equipped to handle anything dry-cleanable."

Chloe's hands dropped listlessly to her lap. A defeated feeling closed in around her as she felt the power, the precision of those strange nuns from across the miles invading her hot close room. She could feel them through the letter, seeing her unmade bed and her dusty room, and condemning. It was not too late to stop. But at the thought of that her heart nearly failed, and her face grew pale. Everyone was counting on it. The only sound was the moaning of the hot wind blowing around the corner of the house, whispering at her window. Even the usually noisy house below seemed stifled, laid low by the unrelenting heat and the hot gales.

And now, added to this misery came this letter from Mater Dei, telling her what to wear, as if they owned her already. She didn't like it. "Had she acted too hastily?"

Sluggishly, Chloe pulled open her underwear drawer and rummaged, first holding up her panties, ragged, pitiful things with loose elastic, then her bras, gray and stretched out. Her slip was Michelle's old one—okay for home, but not for where people in the laundry would see it. At least her pajamas were new from Christmas. But she needed a second pair! Unheard of! She bit her lip. What would Daddy say? It already cost two hundred dollars a year just to go there; and now all new clothes besides? It wasn't fair to the other kids. And fourteen dollars for uniforms! That was more than Momma ever paid for one of Michelle's dresses. And she needed two! And where would she find a pure black suit?

Chloe had never had a suit, but she liked one in the Sears Catalog, a yellow one with the new boxy cut. Now her first suit would be a black one. "Oh why, why, did I ever tell her …" she groaned softly, glancing into her mirror, noticing her limp, straight hair, her greasy face, and her deeply tanned skin. Momma was right. She was too young to know what she wanted, to take such a step. Maybe it wasn't too late to change her mind. Slowly she crumpled the letter in her hand and dropped it into her wastebasket. This didn't have to go any further. She could stop it here. She was still her own. Free.

"Chloe! Chloe, are you up there? Come down if you are," her mother yelled. Chloe thumped slowly down, supposing Momma wanted her to fold the wash or change the baby. But, to her surprise, Gladys Gehring stood in her living room, smiling shyly. They were not close friends. Ever since the trip to Mater Dei they had hardly spoken to each other. But here she stood looking almost cool with her jet-black hair pulled back in a ponytail. She had on yellow shorts and a polka-dotted top that tied in the front. Her white canvas shoes shone brand new.

"Oh, hi Gladys!" Chloe said, wondering nervously what came next, for few guests came to visit farm kids, and she wasn't sure how to act. She noted with relief that the living room floor was swept. "Good old Momma, she keeps working even in the heat," Chloe thought gratefully.

"Hi, Chloe," Gladys said with an awkward gesture. My dad's buying seed from your dad and said I could come along for the ride."

"Oh!" said Chloe, not sure if she should invite Gladys into the dusty parlor or up to her hot bedroom. Momma rescued her by saying, "Why don't you girls get a glass of water and sit out on the back porch? It's shady, and the wind don't blow so hard there."

There were no chairs, so the girls sat on the warped wooden floorboards, holding their glasses of water, their backs resting against the wall.

"You'll be leaving soon," Gladys said, putting her red lips to her glass.

"Yeah, I guess so." Chloe had always admired Gladys's clear white complexion and the natural pink blush on her cheeks; like Snow White, she often thought. Gladys's mom was a quiet woman who walked with a limp since she had survived polio. She had one other child, a boy, who was retarded. Chloe had seen their farm once, and it was lovely; with a huge red barn and a pretty house.

"I wish I were you," Gladys said.

Chloe's eyes widened. "You do? Why?"

"Because your mom is letting you go to Mater Dei, and mine isn't."

Chloe was shocked. Her first question was, "Do you want to be a nun?"

"Sister Clarice says I don't have to know for sure to go there, but Mom says she needs me to help take care of Jimmy, and she won't even let me talk about it."

As Gladys talked, Chloe remembered a conversation her parents had had one Sunday after Mass about the Gehrings.

"That Mrs. Gehring's a nice woman," Daddy had said to Momma as she stir-fried potatoes on the stove with one hand and held Warren on her hip with the other. Peter, who was sick, clung to her legs. "How so?" Momma asked.

"She's such a trooper and always smiling."

"Well, I'd smile too if I was as lucky as she was!"

"Lucky? How can you say that when she's had polio, and she limps?"

"She's also got an exemption."

"From what?"

"What do you think?" Momma glared at him. "Take a look around you."

"Oh, you should be ashamed!" Daddy chuckled, coming near and placing his hands around her waist.

She shook him off. "No, *you* should," she said, not looking at him.

"Me? What do I have to be ashamed of?" He spread his hands innocently, mocking. He was smiling, but Chloe felt tense.

"Oh. No reason!" Momma said, tossing the potatoes so hard in the sizzling pan that a couple flew out onto the floor. "I'd say more, but cornfields have big ears!" Her dark eyes were snapping.

"You're terrible, and in front of the kids!" he chided, still chuckling, but some of the mirth had drained from his face as Momma's face grew darker. "Oh! I'm terrible, am I?" she said with a strange huskiness in her voice.

"So, will you pray that my mother lets me go?" Gladys was pleading. Chloe jerked back to the moment. "Sure Gladys. But, ah, do you, are you sure you want to be a nun?"

"It's a testing place, remember?" Gladys said.

Chloe nodded. "That's what Sister said." With a sudden longing she wished that her own mom would say right out that she couldn't go. How easy it would be then to withstand Sister. The whole question of her future could be postponed until after high school. Hiding her ungrateful thoughts, she said, "Maybe you shouldn't beg so, Gladys. If your mother says she … needs you, well …"

"Your mother needs you too." Gladys said, glancing back toward the screen door through which they could hear the children squabbling and Warren bawling.

"He's got heat rash," Chloe said by way of explanation. "And I'm pretty sure I have a vocation."

"Well, so might I!" Gladys cried. "Oh Chloe, you're so lucky, and your mother is so giving and unselfish."

The next day during a lull in the housework, while Warren was sleeping and the little ones were playing outside the sandbox, Chloe showed the list to her mother. She had retrieved it from the wastebasket and smoothed it out, feeling guilty for not appreciating what Gladys was praying so hard to possess. Her mother cast a quizzical glance at the wrinkled paper before reading it. While she read Chloe whined worriedly, "What's Dad going to say? I need so many new things. Maybe he won't let me go."

"Is that all you're worried about Chloe?" Mother laughed, rattling the paper. "Dad knows you need new things. And some of these you already have." She smiled at Chloe as she folded the letter.

"I don't feel right getting new stuff when there's so little money and the crops are bad. The boys will be jealous. And poor Michelle, she'll have to work all the harder with me gone, and you will too!"

"Chloe, the boys get new stuff when they need it. I see to that. And about the work, maybe everything won't get done just so with just Michelle and me, but we'll manage somehow, we always do. I've learned by now that crop prices rise and fall." Momma smoothed Chloe's hair. "If you really want to go, we'll make a way." She tucked the list into her apron pocket. "Besides, we don't have to show Daddy the list," she added gaily.

CHAPTER 5.

Pregnant

Chloe sunk her fist into the soft white mound of bread dough and heard the gas escape. She repeated the motion, each time folding the moist dough over onto itself until it was ready to set and rise again. As she spread a fresh kitchen towel over the huge mound, Momma walked in with Warren in her arms. "Oh Chloe!" she exclaimed, "look at you, baking bread! How early did you get up, anyhow?"

"I couldn't sleep. Guess I'm getting excited," she said, pleased with her mom's reaction.

"I'm going to miss you," Momma said, setting Warren in the high chair and clamping his metal tray in place.

Beaming at the praise, Chloe nevertheless felt guilty for leaving home when her help was so obviously needed. It was humid and hot. August had brought little rain, slowing the furious pace of farm work. Ahead lay harvest when Momma would be feeding the crew three times a day, for weeks. And Chloe would not be here to help.

Chloe hoped to go shopping today. Her new cotton slip from the Sears Catalog had arrived, along with five new pair of underpants and socks. But there were still many items on the list to buy.

"Mom, do you think Michelle could babysit while we go shopping today?" Momma was reaching up to tuck the kitchen curtain high and away from Warren's grubby reach when Chloe saw her open side zipper.

Momma looked fat. Chloe's stomach went hollow. Momma turned, her big shirt dropped over her waist, and she went about her work. But Chloe knew. Grabbing a dishrag she began to scrub vigorously at the dried flour on the counter. Her hands shook. All joy, all ambition for the day's activities had vanished, and she felt a blinding rage, like an added heat in the already stifling kitchen. It was unbearable. Tossing the dishrag into the sink, she left the house. Her mother called after her solicitously, "Chloe, what were you saying? Where are you going? Did you have breakfast?"

Chloe charged down the yard toward the grove. As she passed the trash a swarm of flies rose up then settled down again. Trotting down the sun-dappled path, she passed beneath a low-hanging branch and a mother dove sitting on her nest, startled, rose up with a cry, knocking down one of her eggs. Chloe looked at it, a small white egg, lying cracked in the dirt. She could see the yellow veins of a half-formed bird pulsing against the opening. "It was her fault!" She looked up at the dove's nest; a flimsy flat pile of twigs so poorly built it looked as if the wind had accidently built it. "Serves you right, you stupid bird!" she cried at the frantic mother, "Build a better nest next time!"

She ran on, across the tractor path and over the fence into the next grove, not thinking, not seeing, just wanting to get away from everything; the farm, home, and the ever-growing brood of brothers and sisters. Arriving at her favorite tree, or rather, cluster of trees all growing out of the same center, she stepped inside. Encircled by tree trunks, she leaned back against one, and looked up into the leafy roof. It felt like a cathedral. The hollow place in her stomach was now a storm of tears that raged but would not fall. "She should have told me," she muttered angrily. "Why does she treat me like a child?" There flashed into her mind a night this summer when she had come down the stairs to go to the bathroom, after saying good night to her parents. As she passed her parents' bedroom, she heard, "She's just thirteen!" explode from her mother's lips. Daddy's voice rumbled something, and she snapped back, her voice lower. Back and forth they argued before her mother shouted, "How is it different? Why can't it wait?"

"Some things can't wait. Be reasonable, woman," Daddy's voice was louder now.

"Reasonable? You're a fine one to talk about being reasonable."

"Why?" When am I not reasonable?"

"When *you* can't wait! That's when!"

"Oh … that … well, you …" Daddy's voice dropped too low for Chloe to hear. They continued; Momma's voice urgent, staccato and hot with muffled retorts bordering on tears; Daddy's firm, deliberate and sure.

Chloe tip-toed to the bathroom and stayed a good while. When she crept back upstairs all was quiet. That must have been the night that Momma knew she was pregnant. "If she wanted me to stay home and help, why didn't she say so?" Chloe wondered, pounding her fists on the rough, scratchy bark of the strong unyielding trees. Chloe didn't understand much about life. Sex and reproduction were subjects veiled in mystery. Whenever she was pregnant, Momma didn't draw attention to herself or talk about the coming baby. And after it was born, it was all formula and diapers and preparing for the big baptismal dinner. Carrying a child was a sacred duty that came to married women. How it came, exactly, Chloe did not know. She would find out when she was older, Momma had promised. But if she became a nun, maybe she would never have to know.

"It would have been a perfect excuse to give to Sister Clarice," Chloe wailed to the trees. "And I wouldn't have to leave home now, even though I want to go. I do." Her voice fell to a whine as she saw her own ambivalence and despaired. 'What was wrong with her? She hadn't been a fickle girl before. She had always known what she wanted.' "Oh, God," she cried, confusion settling like August's mugginess in her soul. Questions and ideas fumbled through her mind. She knew God heard them all. But she also knew He didn't always give a clear answer.

The next Sunday at Mass, Chloe followed along with the priest in her missal. Her older brothers, Owen and Brent, sat in the side pews with the other young boys of St. Eli. Chloe slid her eyes toward them, looking for Gary Bates. Last week at the county fair, he had asked her to ride on the Ferris wheel with him. She had, and when their bench rocked in the evening breeze he had wrapped his hand over hers, pretending to be as frightened as she. Other boys in the side pews looked bored, even haggard, as though they'd been out all Saturday night. But Gary was seriously following along in his missal.

Chloe felt pretty in the white sundress that Aunt Zita had included in her box of cast-offs. It hadn't looked like much when she pulled it out, all wrinkled and stuffed in a box. But after Momma had washed, ironed, and sewed a row of white rickrack over the little holes in the bodice, it looked almost new. The square neckline was cut lower than any of her other dresses, but it showed off her tan neck very nicely, she thought. She had spent much of Saturday starching and ironing can-cans to wear under the full skirt.

Mass over, the people filed out slowly and in silence, dipping their fingers in the holy water to make the sign of the cross on themselves. Chloe saw Gary pacing himself so that he would arrive at the fount at the same time as she. They both dipped their fingers into the stone bowl at exactly the same time and smiled at each other. In the vestibule, where talking was allowed, Gary was about to say something to her when she felt a tug at her elbow. Chloe! Chloe Polowski!" She turned to see Sister Clarice's white wimple a few inches from her face.

"Can I see you for a minute?" Sister steered her gently into the small baptismal room and closed the door. "I'm leaving for retreat today, and I want to say good-bye. Are you getting excited?"

"Oh, yes, Sister!" Chloe answered. Sister's eyes took in her lipstick and her bare brown neck, and her mouth tightened. "Do you have your uniforms and all?"

"Yes Sister, I'm nearly packed."

"Good. Are you going to bring this dress, too?" she asked, flipping a hand at the flouncy skirt, making the can-cans rustle.

"I don't know," Chloe said, "it's kind of summer-y."

"Yes, it is." Sister reached into her roomy sleeve to extract a package loosely wrapped in green tissue paper. "I've got something for you, Chloe; a going-away gift."

"Ohhh!" Chloe said, shyly, surprised that nuns gave gifts, being under the vow of poverty as they were.

"Open it," Sister urged.

Chloe unwrapped a white plastic statue of Our Lady of Fatima. "Oh! It's beautiful!" she crooned, turning it around in her hands, wanting to sound properly grateful. "Thank you, Sister." Through the door window she glimpsed Gary lingering in the vestibule.

"It glows in the dark," Sister said, "and the bottom comes off, here, just … pull it … there!" As Sister Clarice removed the base, a large wooden rosary fell into Chloe's hands. "My, what a big rosary!" she said. The colorful wooden beads reminded her of a baby's toy.

"It's from Rome. It was blessed by the Pope."

"Oh my gosh, was it really?" Chloe fingered the smooth wooden beads, feeling unworthy. "Thank you, Sister, I really like it," she crooned, "It's so beautiful!"

Sister cleared her throat. "Don't mention this to Lucy, I only have one, and I decided to give it to you."

"Oh. Yes Sister," Chloe said, feeling special, "Thank you so much!"

After Sister left, Chloe looked for Gary, but he was gone. In the car Brent, listening to the radio, said to her, "He got tired of waiting for you!" Chloe ignored him as she showed the kids her statue. Julie asked to open it, and Peter put the rosary around his neck. "When we get home we'll take it into the closet and see Mary glow in the dark," Chloe said, more gaily than she felt.

"Whoopee!" Brent said, slouched down in the seat, waiting for Owen. "What'cha going to that stupid school for? You nuts or something?"

"It's a free country!" Chloe retorted. "Besides, I'm just trying it." Heat rushed to her face. "It was bad enough to leave home, but why did he taunt her? He should be proud that his sister might be a nun." "Lucy's going too," she said, sniffing.

"Yeah, I heard!" Brent drawled. "She'll last a week." He turned up the radio so he couldn't hear anything she said back to him.

Chloe partly agreed with Brent, but she wouldn't admit it. Lucy didn't seem the type - too pretty and a little spoiled, with all those stylish clothes her mother bought her. But her daddy was strict. Maybe she wanted to get away from home. "But who am I to question God?" Chloe rebuked herself. "He calls all kinds of people to the religious life. Besides, it would be nice to have her there." Chloe was still praying that Gladys too might be allowed to go. Every time she saw her in church, Chloe remembered how lucky she was to have parents who wouldn't stand in the way of God's will.

CHAPTER 6.

Sunrise

It was still dark as Chloe rose, slipped on her clothes and tiptoed down the stairs and out of the house, carefully stopping the screen door from slamming. She crossed the gravel driveway, passed the arched machine shed, and arrived at the chicken coop. Stepping on an overturned pail she boosted herself up on to the roof, and climbed to its peak, where she sat, facing east. She had done this many times, to watch the dawn. But today was her last day on the farm until Christmas vacation.

"I'll be different when I come back," she thought, though she couldn't imagine how. Her movements had awakened the chickens below her, and they clucked softly. The pigs in the pig yard banged their metal feeders, lifting the lids with their snouts and letting them drop, much like little Warren banging his fist on his metal high chair when he hungry. The grove behind her rang with the songs of many birds.

Gradually the purple darkness turned lavender. Then, as though the sky had sprung a leak, red seeped through an opening near the horizon and oozed like blood around the edge of the earth. Next pinks and purples rose and spread across the sky, wondrously punctuated by streaks of gold. As the light increased in intensity, the tree trunks began to glow red. Leaves held the light. For a little while the whole farm, lit by the sidelong rays of the rising sun, lay like a new land before her. Every blade of grass was singing.

Sister Clarice had assured her that she would be allowed to watch a sunrise at Mater Dei, *on occasion.* Chloe hoped this was so. Finally, resplendent white clouds tinged with pink puffed out like airy mountains in a heavenly landscape.

"Magnificent! Thank you, God!" Chloe said, clapping. She took it as a going-away present. By the time she had jumped off of the chicken coop the farm had returned to normal. Only she knew the secret of its morning glory.

As she stepped up the front step, the smell of burnt oatmeal greeted her. Daddy had made breakfast again.

Chloe sat between her parents in the front seat. Warren lay fast asleep in her lap, his heavy head wet with sweat. Her new gored skirt would be all wrinkled by the time they got to Mater Dei. Chloe's shoulder touched her mother's, and she was glad Momma didn't pull away as she often did when she was pregnant and the weather was hot. Howie, Travis, Julie, and Effie were being very quiet in the back seats. As they reached Magnolia, Chloe's stomach started to twitch. "What would tomorrow morning be like at home? Who would rescue Warren from his crib?" Chloe swallowed so often she wondered if something was wrong with her. Her mouth went dry as the big blue station wagon climbed the road to Mater Dei Heights. By the time Daddy stopped the car in front of the villa, her throat ached as though a rock was lodged in it. The little ones clambered from the car. Howie and Travis each grabbed a suitcase out of the back. "Where to?" they asked, grinning.

The petite, erect figure of Sister Damien glided toward them. "Chloe Polowski! How nice to see you!" She exclaimed, grasping Chloe's hand warmly in hers. Chloe smiled, but her heart was pounding strangely as

Sister greeted her family in a musical voice. "Mr. Polowski, I understand you have quite a large family!" She smiled into his big broad face.

"Yes, Sister, you might say that!" Daddy said, casting a proud look around him at his troop.

"And you're going to have another!" Sister purred, turning her attention to Chloe's mother, tugging at her wrinkled maternity top. Momma smiled tiredly and nodded.

"Baseball team, plus two on the bench!" Daddy crowed, tousling Travis's hair.

"I know you'll want to get Chloe settled in and take a look around." Sister Damien took little Julie by the hand and led the family toward the villa. They trooped through the beautiful door with the oval window, across the Persian rug and up the stairs. On the second landing Sister stopped to explain, "We put the freshmen on the fourth floor. It teaches them discipline."

"How so?" Daddy asked between puffs.

"Well, after a few times of running back up four flights of stairs for something they forgot, they learn to remember their things."

Daddy chuckled approvingly. Momma lagged behind, clinging to the railing.

On the fourth floor Sister led them into a sunny dormitory with seven beds. Howie, groaning and lugging the suitcase, swung it up onto a bed so vigorously that it slid off on the other side, hitting the dresser and sending a basin clattering to the floor. Sister jumped. Chloe ran to pick it up.

"Howie, remember you're not throwing around a bale of hay there!" Mr. Polowski chided. Then turning to Sister he said, "My boys don't know their own strength!"

Momma entered panting. She reached for the nearest chair. The little ones looked about, staring at the dormitory. "Oooh!" Agatha crooned, stroking a white bedspread with both hands, "You're so lucky, Chloe!" Chloe waited for her mother to say something nice about the dorm, but she was holding her hand to her chest. Each bed stood exactly one foot from the wall. Wooden dressing screens with curtained panels stood neatly folded in a corner. Sunshine splashed golden squares on the hardwood floors.

"This is Chloe's bed and nightstand. We put Lucy here, and Gladys right next to her." Sister said.

"Gladys?" Chloe burst out. "You mean Gladys Gehring?"

"You didn't know?" Sister's eyes shone as she gave the happy news. "Yes. Her mother finally relented. It was quite a battle. I've been corresponding with her all summer, so I understand the special problem it was for all of them."

Momma looked away.

"It's an answer to prayer," Chloe breathed.

"Three from little St. Eli! It's a record!" Sister said, dashing to stop Warren, pulling on the cord of a radio set inside a windowsill.

"We emphasize people more than things here," she said, unplugging the radio and tucking the cord up and away. "Very few of our girls have radios, and they only play them on weekends."

"Nothing but worldly music on them things anyway," Chloe's father said.

"I'm going outside," Howie whispered hoarsely to his mother before clattering down the wooden steps. Travis and Agatha tagged behind him. While the grown-ups talked, Chloe inspected the names posted on the door; there were six girls in this dorm and half of them were from St. Eli! It made her feel good. The walk-in closet offered each girl two feet of space to call her own, which included the shelf, the rod, and the floor beneath it. Chloe read the other names: Lena Betters, Kay Wakely, and Sue Gallant. Now Chloe felt excited. It was going to be so nice here. She was sure to love it.

A howl pierced the quiet, followed by rapid footsteps pounding up the stairs. Agatha rushed headlong into the room wailing between gasps, "Travis hit me!" She was holding her arm.

"He did?" Momma asked in a tone of amazement. "Why?" But she received no answer, as Agatha spun on her heel and rushed from the dorm. Sister continued, "We find that girls from big families do very well at the villa."

"Is that right?" Daddy squinted as he pondered this fact.

"Yes, because they are not spoiled. They're more used to sharing."

"My kids know how to share, that's for sure," Daddy said, nodding toward Chloe.

Later, Chloe led her parents around the Heights, her brothers and sisters making a ragged circle around them as they walked. But her parents were tired, and it was getting late. Before they left, Chloe walked between them in the apple orchard. The grass beneath their feet was soft and green. The apple trees hung thick with ripening fruit. Chloe noticed that every one of her siblings was hungrily munching on an apple. She hoped they had found them on the ground.

"It's pretty here, Chloe," Momma murmured, hugging her daughter's arm. "And the nuns seem nice. But if you ever want to come home, don't be afraid to tell us."

"Now Mother, don't go telling her about quitting before she's even started!" Daddy chided with a snort.

"I'm not talking about quitting," Momma answered. "It's just that she's never been away from home before, and I thought . . ."

"You're putting ideas into her head."

"Ideas?" Momma sounded exasperated. "Chloe, was I putting ideas in your head? Was I? Tell me." Chloe, dumbstruck that her parents were arguing now, right before they left, shrank into herself. Was this the way they wanted her to remember them? But she knew them both so well. Patting her mother's arm she said, "I'll be all right, and I'll tell you if I don't like it."

Her mother's face stayed hard.

"I'll give it a good try, you know me!" she said softly to her dad.

"Yup, I know you will," he said, laying a heavy hand on her back. The children, a moment ago swinging lustily on swings and twirling madly on the merry-go-round, came running, saying they were hungry. Momma unpacked lunch while Daddy spread out a blanket. Chloe poured cherry Kool-Aid from the large thermos.

Before they left, Julie had to go to the bathroom, so Chloe took her inside the villa. While they waited outside the bathroom door, Chloe heard someone sniffling in the kitchen. A girl with long red braids was hugging her mother and sobbing on her shoulder, while her mother kept repeating, "There, there, now darling, there, there, everything's going to be all right."

Back at the car, Momma stared moodily out of the car, oblivious to the noisy children bouncing in the seats behind her. Chloe wished her to smile. She kissed her on the cheek and was surprised how soft it was. Then she went around to her father and kissed his rough cheek. It felt like sandpaper. It was the first time she had kissed either of them. Smiling broadly so everyone would believe how happy she would be here, she stepped back onto the sidewalk and waved until the car disappeared around the bend.

She stood alone. Behind her loomed the brown brick villa, solid and square. As she turned toward it her stomach clenched. So she walked, instead, toward the grotto, where she could be alone with the sound of trickling water and the statue of Mary.

"Chloe! Chloe Polowski!" It was Lynn Dahlset, her guide from her first visit last May. "Come on in! We're all in the rec-room having a get-acquainted party before supper."

"Oh, do I have to?" Chloe shrank back. "I'd like to be alone for a while."

"Alone?" Lynn's eyes were wide with shock. She took Chloe by the arm saying, "Come on! I'll introduce you to my best friend, Teela!"

Chloe glanced back at the empty curb where her family's car had been parked. If, for some reason, it would return, she would jump in and never look back.

CHAPTER 7.

Mater Dei - Home Away from Home

The aspirants' dining hall rang with the laughter of girls reunited after summer vacation. While the older girls renewed acquaintances, the new girls watched with wide-eyed stares and awkward movements as they partook of their first meal at Mater Dei Heights. One girl from each table was assigned to serve, and now those chosen girls bustled back and forth from their tables to the serving window carrying pitchers of milk, plates of garlic bread, and steaming pans of a hot dish that Sister called "lasagna." Chloe felt like a queen, sitting and being served. She didn't have to jump up once to serve another. All the tables in the long dining hall were spread with white tablecloths and set with white china dishes. A glass of water, with ice, stood near each plate, as well as a dessert plate holding a thick square of apple pie, juicy and golden, and all hers. Her place card read: "Welcome to the villa, Aspirant Chloe Polowski!"

Though Chloe felt unworthy, she liked it here. No more standing at the kitchen counter to eat because there wasn't room at the table for her. No mashing potatoes and cutting up meat for the little ones before she could eat. And best of all, no spilled drinks running onto her lap.

Here things were refined. At home Momma had often, after setting the meal on the table, disappeared to her bedroom for a quiet cigarette.

Sister Damien, the mistress of aspirants, sat at a small wooden desk at the back of the dining room silently reading a book while keeping an eye on her charges. A small bell stood near at hand. When Sister shook it, its silvery notes silenced the dining room instantly. No one even whispered or finished her sentence, except the new girls. Sister smiled. "Girls, I can tell you're getting acquainted fast, the way the noise level is rising." A ripple of girlish laughter greeted this remark, rising and falling as if directed by some unseen hand.

"There are eighty-three of you this year, and thirty of you are brand new." At this news a lusty applause broke out. Sister beamed back at her girls. Some girls wore a blank expression, and Chloe guessed that they, like her, were new to these lively responses to announcements. Lynn Dalhset gazed at Sister with rapt attention. Her wavy blonde hair was cut boyishly short, with a lock drooping over her right eye. Her chin was firm, but not sharp. Her pale blue eyes and full lips softened her boyish look. Chloe wished to know her better. She especially wanted to know why she wanted to be a nun, and if she had ever regretted her decision.

"Girls, I want to tell you about a very special event we have here at the villa. It's called "instructions.'" A collective sigh, as of joy, escaped the older girls, which made Sister's green eyes glow. "The older girls know what a *treat* instructions are; and so will you, in time. It's a special hour once a week when I meet with *just* your class to talk about whatever is on your minds! It's like a mother-daughter time, though I know I can *never* take the place of your mothers. I don't want to! There are way too many of you for that! A trickle of laughter rose and fell. But here at the villa you are my spiritual charges, and we live so close to one another that I often feel like a mother. We truly are a family. You have lots of new things to learn, and I have so many things to teach you that this special time we spend together becomes the most precious hour of our week, doesn't it girls?"

As if on cue the dining room full of girls burst out with "Yes, sister!" There were shining eyes all around.

"And if you new girls are anything like the rest, you'll come to look forward to instructions as the highlight of your week!" The older girls' heads bobbed in agreement.

"Tonight, for starters, will be the freshmen's first instructions; and to celebrate because it's their very first time, we're going to have coconut snowball treats."

Amicable cries of "No fair!" rose up while a pert smile played on Sister's lips. She shook the bell again and just as the Red Sea once rushed in to close the gap behind the Israelites, the young female voices rushed in to fill the void, drowning any doubts or thoughts of home that might be swimming inside a new girl's giddy head.

The freshmen still wore their name tags as they gathered in the recreation room for their first instructions. Chloe sat next to Gladys, whose calm demeanor put her at ease. Lucy looked pensive. Chloe noticed Sue Gallant, the girl whom she had seen crying in the kitchen, sitting alone on an overstuffed chair, twirling one of her long red braids in her hand. Sister Damien greeted them all warmly while distributing mimeographed copies of their daily schedule. "To help you get oriented," she said, smiling at her new charges. Chloe chewed her inner lip as she read:

Week Day Schedule for Aspirants: The villa, 1955

6:00: Rise, keeping Grand Silence, span sheets, wash, dress

6:20: Prayer, Meditation and Spiritual reading (in recreation room) led by Sister Damien

6:40: Make bed, clean, go directly to chapel

7:15: Daily Mass and Holy Communion

8:15: Breakfast in Aspirants' dining hall (break Grand Silence)

8:45: Report to Academy homeroom

9:00: 1st Period Class

9:45: 2nd Period Class

10:30: 3rd Period Class

11:15: 4th Period Class

12:00: Noon meal in Aspirants' dining hall (and clean up)

12:30: Visit to chapel, report to homeroom.

12:45: 5th Period Class

1:30: 6th Period Class

2:15: 7th Period Class

3:00: Dismissal by homeroom (day students first)

3:15: After-school snack at the villa, outdoor recreation (keep uniforms on)

3:30: Study hall

5:00: Supper (and clean up)

5:45: Visit chapel, outdoor recreation

7:00: Evening Study hall (or Instructions)

8:00: Snack, talking

8:15: Rosary

8:30: Prepare for bed (no talking)

9:00: Lights out, Grand Silence observed

As Sister elaborated on the schedule, Chloe squirmed. Lucy was blinking rapidly. Gladys listened with her pretty lips slightly parted. Sue Gallant squinted at the paper as though she suddenly needed glasses.

"A schedule is merely a tool to help you navigate your new surroundings," Sister said, eyeing her freshmen. If we don't have rules, we won't have order. And order makes our days more fun, you'll see. I'd like to talk about the second point, 'prayer and meditation' for a bit." Sister began. Chloe stared straight ahead, feeling as though a sharp pin had been poked into her balloon of expectations. Her hands lay in her lap. Her jaw was set. The schedule came as a shock to her. It felt like a net thrown over her day, capturing and ordering every minute of her waking hours, and her disappointment could not be hid. She knew her face was hard, but she didn't care. She liked to walk in the woods after school, or read a book, or just be alone. This list left no room for any of that.

"Chloe, is something wrong?" Sister asked, arching her eyebrows pleasantly.

"Yes. I expected more free time," she said, meeting Sister's gaze boldly.

"Such as?"

"After school," she said, flicking the paper with her finger. "This keeps us busy right up to bedtime." Someone tittered, and Chloe felt a rush of heat all over her body.

"Girls, Chloe is being very open and honest in her reaction. Tell me, what would you like to do that's not on this schedule, Chloe?" Sister asked.

Chloe shrugged. "Read. Be alone. Walk in the woods. Maybe visit the farm." Her stomach jumped as her new classmates observed her.

"Chloe, it just so happens that we do have a hike planned for this Friday night! It was going to be a surprise, but I'll tell you now so that your week won't seem so long. As for the farm, it's off-limits I'm afraid. I thought you knew that." Sister turned up the palms of her finely tapered hands, saying, "It's not my doing. Farmer Gene put a stop to girls visiting the barn long ago. He says it upsets the animals."

Chloe kept her scowl. Not only was every waking moment dictated, any hope of holding a cat or petting a horse was also dashed.

In soft, sweet tones Sister said, "Girls, these rules may seem arbitrary and demanding at first. But believe you me, if you give them a chance, you will find they are your friends. This first week will be tough, and you might feel frustrated and even feel like crying! But this is your chance to show what you're made of, whether you want to be a grown-up or a baby! Maturity, girls, doesn't happen overnight, it happens one choice at a time, as we learn to handle disappointment in a grown-up way and not like a baby, kicking and screaming.

"Girls, change is difficult. But, believe you me; we are doing everything humanly possible to make it as easy as we can for you. If you persevere, I promise you, in a few weeks this schedule will be like second nature to you." Sister's green eyes swept the girls in her gaze. And though her lips were curved into a smile, and her voice soft, her eyes like daggers warned Chloe with a glance, "Blunt complaints will get you just so far here, girl."

Each day at Mater Dei Academy became a blur of new faces, places, and rules. Bells rang, announcing every classroom change, every meal, recreation hour, study-hall hour, snack, and bedtime. Chloe often got lost. Wandering about in corridors she would peek into classrooms and see strange girls in uniform staring back at her. Between classes, streams of girls wandered the hallways like sheep in search of pasture. Seniors, stationed at the crossroads like guards, Repeated, "Silence, please, girls. Single file!"

By the second day Gladys had mastered her schedule. Often as Chloe arrived, breathless and late for literature class, Gladys sat calmly reviewing her books. Chloe soon found out that aspirants were not the only students attending Mater Dei Academy. Boarders and day students wearing the same uniform as the aspirants attended the classrooms. No one wore makeup or carried a purse. Their shoes were all black and white saddle shoes, and they all wore the emblem of the school, MDA embroidered in white on their front right shoulder. The boarders lived across the campus from the villa, and the day students went home every day on a bus.

"Be friendly to the boarders and day students, but not friends," Sister warned in instructions. "They are of the world; you are not. Some of the boarders come from rich families where their parents have no time for them, so they send them up here while they travel to Europe. The boarders' tuition is twice as much as yours. That's why they are not required to work in the laundry or the garden or the kitchen, as you are. But don't envy them. Many of them struggle so with loneliness. They are completely on their own to make friends and to do their homework. They miss the close family ties that we enjoy here at the villa.

"And the day students are girls from downtown Magnolia whose parents are paying for them to have a good education. Don't envy them, either. You, each of you, have the most precious thing a girl can ever have; a religious vocation. There is nothing, absolutely nothing that can compare with that! Is there?"

Each weekday at three o'clock the day students boarded the blue school bus they called "The Swan" and rode home. The boarders disappeared to their side of the campus, and the aspirants reported at the villa for their after-school snack; a doughnut or a cookie or an apple. A senior was posted to see that no one took more than one. Dieting was not allowed. If a girl was concerned about her weight, she was advised to stay active during recreation hour. At three-thirty, the bell rang for study hall, which lasted until supper. This schedule and these rules were not learned at once, but little by little, as Sister Damien, in her lilting, encouraging voice, promised the girls that by the second week all this "rigmarole" would come as easy to them as breathing.

Chloe didn't cry. But at night, curled up gratefully between the fresh crisp sheets, she pondered Sister's words: "Girls, your vocation is a rare and precious gift. You may not think so now, or feel that this is true, but give it time. Give yourself a chance to learn the routine and make friends, and I am absolutely sure that you will come to love and appreciate what you have here. Don't give into discouragement. The devil would certainly want that. And don't discourage others with your complaining. Come to me with any questions or difficulties you may have. Or better yet, wait until a few more days have passed, and things will become clear to you. I guarantee it! Also, it's only right to remind you of the great sacrifice your own parents have made for you to be here. Don't be quick to disappoint them. You may never have a chance like this again."

Before Chloe could examine the depths of her questions, she had fallen asleep. She awoke to the vigorous ringing of the hand bell by Sister Ruth, Sister Damien's assistant, at 6 a.m.

By Friday Chloe cringed at the sound of bells. "Bells for rising, bells for eating, bells for praying, playing, sleeping," she muttered as she crossed the campus alone in the early morning on her way to Mass. But the week was almost over. She looked forward to Saturday, when she could do as she pleased.

But on Saturday the same harsh bell woke her up, though a half an hour later. And she had to don her school uniform for Mass. Later she could change. The boarders attended Mass in their regular clothes, sporting the latest styles and the cutest shoes. During Mass Chloe smelled the aroma of coffee wafting through the chapel, and it reminded her of home. A physical ache welled up in her heart. Today she would take her novel out to the woods and read alone.

After a breakfast of pancakes, syrup, and two slices of bacon, Chloe savored her last drop of coffee as the little silver bell as Sister's desk rang. A thick set of papers was handed out. Chloe stared in unbelief at the Saturday schedule: cleaning time, study hall, Saturday instructions, and sewing class. The entire day was planned. A hollow space yawned inside of her. She couldn't react again. She folded the paper and tucked it into the pocket of her uniform without a word.

Two hours later she emerged from the villa into the bright sunlight, wearing a cotton skirt, a blouse, and tennis shoes. She was happy to be in her own clothes. Her hair was up in rollers with a bandana tied around it. The morning hadn't been so awful, after all. Angie Zimms had turned on her radio, and the dorm rocked to music while the aspirants changed their sheets, polished their shoes, bathed or showered, and set their hair in pin curls or rollers. All with permission to talk! Lena Betters, a freshman, received a box of fudge in the mail for her birthday, which she shared with all her classmates in the kitchen.

But now it was time for study hall. As she crossed the campus Chloe saw two boarders sitting idly on swings, talking. Did they have a Saturday schedule? Chloe looked at her watch. She was ten minutes early. The woods beckoned to her. There was time for a short walk. Circling back around the grotto, she struck off toward the woods, moving hastily lest anyone seeing her call her back.

Sunlight flickered through the quiet, cool woods. Some leaves had turned a crimson red. She picked one up and held it. Birds twittered overhead. Weeds brushed her legs. The narrow path she followed led her on so that by the time she stopped and turned around she could not see even one brick building. This made her happy. "I need this," she said, with a skip. How fresh the air smelled! How good it felt to run and be free and alone. Following the sound of distant water, she came upon a creek. The water was low, but it was flowing and swirling around rocks and over fallen trees, making a pleasant scene. Chloe sat down and watched it for a while, letting all thoughts of rules and schedules and instructions slip away from her until she felt at last a core of peace and quiet settle down in her. "If I can come here once a week, I might last," she thought.

As she entered study hall late, Sister Damien strode toward her purposefully, grabbed her arm and led her out into the hallway. Chloe's heart beat rapidly.

"Where were you?" she asked anxiously.

"Walking in the woods."

"With whom?"

"No one. I had time. Am I late?" Chloe glanced at her watch, surprised that she had been missed already. Her stomach leaped, and her chest was heaving, but she tried to appear calm. Sister's face softened. She took a breath, and then said calmly, "Chloe, if every aspirant disappeared every time she took a notion, where would that leave me?" Chloe's blood pounded in her throat as Sister questioned her further, explaining how it was her duty as mistress to eighty two girls, to know where each one was at all times. It was her love for them and a regard for the parents who had entrusted them to her, that made her seem anxious and upset. By the time she finished Chloe felt heavy with guilt. She had not realized any of the things that Sister had said to her. She had only thought of herself. At home she was used to disappearing for hours without anyone questioning her. Here it was different. Chloe apologized. She didn't like to disappoint Sister. Back at her desk, Chloe stared at the words in her book, her eyes swimming, her heart pounding and her inner being stricken.

CHAPTER 8.

Sue Gallant, Kay Wakely

Supper was nearly over when Sister Damien shook the silver bell, silencing the chatter instantly. Sister was pleased. Last night's instructions to the freshmen had focused on prompt obedience in small things. "Girls, I have an announcement," She said.

Chloe was savoring a chunk of juicy pork chop, thinking how she liked the way the nuns cooked with spices. At home, because of Daddy's stomach ulcer, Momma's cooking had to be bland.

"Some of you have probably missed seeing Sue Gallant around. She went home this morning."

Chloe stopped chewing. The pork turned dry. The dining hall fell still. Sue, the redheaded, pigtailed girl with the sad eyes was gone? Chloe's eyes darted about. Lynn stared down at her hands.

"I know you feel badly. I do too. Sue had an extreme case of homesickness. I told her it would pass, but she just would not believe me. Girls, that child has turned down the greatest opportunity of her life. We need to pray for her and for any other girl who might be tempted to run home the moment she feels the first sign of homesickness." A sympathetic murmur of assent rumbled throughout the dining hall.

"Girls, please! I can't stress this enough! If you're feeling homesick, come to me! Homesickness is the most natural thing in the world. It's a good sign, actually, because it tells me that you come from a good home. You miss it. But you stay because you have a higher calling, and you're willing to give that a chance. Girls, I know that each and every one of you comes from a good home, or you wouldn't be here, aspiring to the highest, purest calling a girl can have: to be a bride of Christ. Think of it! There is nothing, nothing, nothing more precious that God can give to a young girl than that.

"So, please, I'm begging you, come to me if you need to talk. Don't go to another girl and jeopardize her vocation. You could, without meaning to, bring her vocation down. And I know none of you would want to be responsible for such a thing."

Sister smiled, and a shiver seemed to ripple through the dining hall full of girls. Then, in a lighter tone she added, "And one more thing. Please! I can't stress this enough. I am asking that you *do not* discuss Sue Gallant. I'll go so far as to say, don't *even* say her name. She has made her choice, and she is no longer one of us. Mother Euphemia wants it this way. She is a wise mother who knows that idle conversation about absent girls only leads to no good. Concentrate on the friends you have here in the villa. I don't think God would have it any other way? Do you?"

Soft "No, Sisters" echoed each other down the rows of tables.

"Can I hear that a little firmer?"

"No, Sister!"

"Thank you," Sister said, touching the bell for the girls to stack the dishes and bring in the dish pans in silence.

That evening, as Chloe and Kay Wakely strolled toward the nuns' cemetery, touches of pink laced the eastern clouds, as faint reflections of the sunset shone on them. As the two laughed and talked, their eyes glanced away from each other, then back again, as if they both wished to speak of what they must not. Last night Chloe had heard someone crying in her bed. She knew it was Kay. She wanted to go to her then, but because of the Grand Silence she had not. She wanted to encourage Kay, but she didn't know how.

Kay was a thin, gangly girl with an angular figure and skin blotched with sloppy freckles, even on her arms. She was not athletic, and she couldn't catch a ball or even throw one well. When playing hopscotch she easily lost her balance, and in jump rope she was positively awkward. But she had a gay, infectious laugh that drew Chloe to her. Her easy acceptance of everyday life charmed her. Kay was not pretty, with her rather long nose and buck teeth. But she could laugh at herself. And she was a good listener. When Chloe spoke, she felt Kay's full attention. And she didn't talk about herself the moment Chloe was finished. Kay's gray-blue eyes spoke words to Chloe without a sound. One day the two realized that they had a lot in common. They were both from large families, and they both liked little kids. Kay was an aunt already, and she talked about her nieces and nephews as much as Chloe talked about her younger brothers and sisters.

"I miss them, don't you, their sweet little faces, the cute things they say?" Kay said, and Chloe nodded. She wanted to hug Kay and tell her not to leave. She racked her brain to think of something she could say about Sue Gallant without breaking the rules. Finally she said, "We'll have more room in our closet now."

"A lot more," Kay answered, sliding Chloe a meaningful look.

"I saw her crying the first day we arrived, in the little kitchen," Chloe went on, hoping Kay wouldn't stop her.

"Everybody cries sometimes," Kay replied lightly. "It doesn't mean they're leaving." She broke into an awkward trot. "Come on, let's run. We need exercise, remember!" As Chloe followed, a sob caught in her throat. But why? She hardly knew Sue Gallant. Outrunning Kay, she arrived at the nuns' graveyard first. Puffing heavily, she leaned against a tombstone and laughed as Kay gamboled in, panting, red-faced and laughing, to plop down on the grass. Standing beneath the white marble crucifix, they bowed their heads in a quick prayer for the dead. When they looked up from their prayer their eyes met and held. "Let's be bosom buddies," Kay said.

"What does that mean?"

"It means two people agree to be best friends."

"All right." Chloe said. "Bosom buddies, I like that."

"Dear Mom and Dad and all." Chloe started her first letter home, trying to say only cheerful things, as Sister had instructed. All outgoing and incoming mail would be opened and read by Sister Damien. This was necessary, she explained, so that, as their mistress she would know what was going on in their lives. "Why, you might get bad news from home, and I would know nothing about it! Or someone might write challenging your life up here, and you might get confused. I can't help you if I don't know what you're going through."

"I am fine. I like all my classes." Chloe bit down on her pencil, thinking of Sister Gerard, the pinch-faced Latin teacher who insisted that all Latin homework be done with a fountain pen.

> "Could you send me money for a fountain pen? Or rather, buy me one and also a bottle of ink? My Latin teacher forbids ballpoint pens because they smear. We had such a good time on Friday. We hiked through the woods and had a picnic in the orchard. That was fun! I have a new friend, Kay Wakely. She's an aunt already. Sunday we watched one hour of television."

Chloe paused, thinking of how badly Brent wanted a television at home. So, to avoid making him jealous, she added,

"We watched Bishop Sheen's sermon on *Christ's Incomparable Self."*

Chloe read over her letter, hoping that the part about the fountain pen didn't sound too negative. She concluded her letter with: "The food is good and I sleep well," even though she knew that Momma didn't care about eating and sleeping well. Those things were givens. What Momma wanted to know was, "Are you happy?" or "Do you want to come home?" But Chloe couldn't write about those things.

"P.S. School's hard, "she added, in case Michelle envied her life up here. Confident that she would not be asked to re-write her letter, Chloe placed it, unsealed, in the basket on Sister's desk.

CHAPTER 9.

Want to Leave

Every Friday the Blessed Sacrament was exposed on the altar all day for adoration. The large round white host was framed in a sun-shaped golden monstrance that stood on a golden stand. From its center, Jesus in the host looked out at her. Fixing her eyes on Him, Chloe declared, "I'm leaving." She said it just as though she were confiding in a friend. "I've been here three weeks, and I hate it." The white circle at the hub of golden brilliance looked back at her. Chloe believed she looked into the very eye of God. "It's not what I thought it would be. It doesn't even seem like high school! Every minute is scheduled. We do everything in groups. And yesterday on that hike, we sat in a circle and sang, "Rinky dinky do, datt's what we learn in da school, yahoo!" Humph. It's so babyish; not at all what I expected. The others seem to love it here. But I don't. I don't belong, and I'm going home."

The fragrance of incense still hung in the air from the morning's service. The deep hush of the chapel calmed her. Sunbeams filtered down like gold dust from the windows way up high. The burning candles caused the golden prongs of the monstrance to quiver with light.

Chloe heard: "I agree. Go home. It's all right." she felt the words, like warm liquid in her head and in her soul. There was no condemnation. She was free to go. He would not hold it against her. Years from now, when she was older, she could enter the convent. Chloe felt a glad leap in her stomach at God's sweet understanding.

But almost immediately the thought of facing Sister Damien stabbed her soul. She would not agree. She would not believe that God had given His okay. Chloe wished she could write to Momma, but Sister read every letter. She did not know any day-student well enough to risk asking one to mail it. What if she got caught! Chloe blanched at the thought.

The villa's only phone stood on Sister's desk. But she had once seen a pay phone on the fourth floor of the academy, where the schools' sewing rooms were situated. How many quarters did it take to make a long distance call? Chloe pictured herself running out of coins while trying to call her mother. "Hello Chloe? Is that you? What do you want? Is something wrong?" Her mother would worry and probably call the villa. Oh dread!

The villa supply store was open on Saturdays. She had a few dollars, but if she asked for two dollars' worth of change, Sister might get suspicious. And what if a nun passing by stopped to listen? Chloe paled at the thought. She could call collect. People did that in emergencies. But it was expensive, and Daddy would not like it. And Momma got scared when she got a collect call.

Sadly Chloe looked toward the altar again, this time with reproach in her eyes. "Why didn't God perform a miracle for her as He had for Philip in the Bible, whom He whisked from one place to another?" She closed her eyes and pictured the big living room with the fireplace and the baby room off to the right where Momma stayed up late at night washing and mending and ironing clothes. When she opened her eyes the prongs of the brilliant monstrance winked merrily back at her. "I shouldn't have to convince anyone, if *You* agree!" Chloe said fiercely. But without coming to any conclusion, she left the chapel, making a double genuflection on both knees before leaving the exposed presence of the Lord.

"Boy, I wish I could pray like you do. What were you praying for so hard?" Kay teased Chloe after the two girls had left the Silence Zone.

"Oh, just my family," Chloe lied, avoiding Kay's eyes. As the two girls stepped outside for recreation, evening shadows stretched before them. At home Michelle would be drying the dishes while the little kids ran outside chasing fireflies before dark. Home: how delicious the mere sound had become in just three weeks! Never before had she felt its warmth or its pull as she did now, from over here.

"I think about my family more than I ever thought I would," Kay confessed. Chloe nodded, seeing in her new friend's eyes the same longing she that she knew.

The next morning, as Chloe tilted back her head to receive Jesus on her tongue, she told Him, "I've got a plan." It was a sin to chew the host. Carefully she tried to dislodge it from the roof of her mouth with her tongue, but it was stuck. It was a sacrilege to touch it with her finger. "I'll stay until Chicken Dinner Sunday" she told her divine guest as He gradually became free to slide down her throat. "It's just four weeks away. I'll pack ahead of time. And when they come I'll jump in the car and say, 'Take me home! I can't stand it here.'" A thrill walloped her stomach. She would be able, once again, to squeeze and stroke baby Warren's fat smooth little legs. Leaving chapel Chloe tossed a happy glance back at the tabernacle. "I still want to be your bride, but later, when I'm older and out of high school," she said gaily.

Chloe's plan brought such relief to her that the constant bells no longer vexed her. "Go ahead, ring!" she sneered at them. "I'll soon be rid of you." Instead of studying she read her novel, *A Tree Grows in Brooklyn*, by Betty Smith. Lena Betters, seated next to her, glanced curiously at her as she herself studied her Latin. Chloe wanted to tell her that where she would be attending school soon, Latin wasn't offered. At the dinner table Chloe suddenly possessed a new wit. She no longer felt shy and inhibited. She didn't care if she said something outlandish.

"What's got into you?" Lynn remarked one evening at supper as she dabbed away tears of laughter at some irreverent quip Chloe had made. Chloe felt almost giddy. Humor lurked in every subject. Happiness lay latent in every observation, just waiting to be discovered. In just a few more weeks she would not be sitting at this long, white table full of girls, or marching in line with them in silence. And how easy it all was! Freedom, still so far away, brightened today. "Oh, everything's just so funny," Chloe exclaimed between giggles, her face flushed from laughing.

Sister Damien, strolling past her table, stopped to ask, "What's so funny?"

"Chloe is full of jokes tonight!" Lynn said, still shaking from laughter. Faint smiles lingered on the other girls' faces, too. For an instant Sister's eyes narrowed, as though she saw something written on Chloe's forehead. Chloe, suddenly sober, almost choked. If Sister guessed her plan … but she must not! Chloe coughed, all humor gone. Her hand shook as she reached for her glass of water and took a long drink.

The next day when Sister announced a "name contest" for the freshmen, Chloe listened intently. Cooperation would diffuse suspicion. "We are one big happy family here and the villa is our home. So it only makes sense that we all know each other's names." So far Chloe only knew a handful of girls' names. But upon hearing about the contest, she determined to win it. It would dispel any suspicions Sister might have. She had two weeks to learn the names of the eighty-one aspirants who lived at the villa.

The campaign absorbed her. She drew up a list filled with notations. "Mabel Sappe (frizzy hair, thick glasses, grandma-like), Aimee Sikes (shy, five sisters, all nuns), Teela Rodriguez (Spanish eyes are smiling)." She reviewed it constantly while standing in line or marching in silence and even while waiting for a bell to ring. At night she fell asleep putting names to faces.

On the night of the contest the aspirants filled the villa's recreation room, standing and lounging about. Chloe trembled as Lucy Fry volunteered to go first. She named all the freshmen and a few sophomores. Sister thanked her for trying. Kay Wakely, able to name all the underclassmen, nevertheless stumbled on the juniors, and clapped her hand over her buckteeth before returning, red-faced and laughing, to her seat. Lena Betters, a round-cheeked girl from South Dakota, asked to go last. Gladys, her brown eyes calm and confident, named all the underclassmen and every junior. But at the seniors she paused, shaking her head and smiling sweetly before sitting down. Sister Damien led a round of applause for her.

Next it was Chloe's turn. She started in a rush before her voice cracked. She cleared her throat and began again, naming all her classmates and every sophomore. She saw looks of wonder on girls' faces and pleased surprise on Sister's. Her legs shook as she started on the juniors. "Mary, Evy, Lori, Kathy." She paused at a petite Spanish girl sitting cross-legged on the floor. The girl grinned coquettishly, tossing back her glossy black hair. But her name eluded Chloe. "I know you're Lynn Dahlset's friend, but you've got me stumped. I'll get back to you later," she said, winking. The Spanish girl winked back, and everyone laughed. Chloe's stomach jumped with emotion as she continued naming all the rest of the juniors and the seniors. Applause broke out wildly. Chloe's head reeled. Then the room hushed. The pretty Spanish girl, still unnamed, rolled her brown eyes mischievously. "Teresa?" Chloe guessed timorously. The crowd groaned. Chloe had lost the contest.

Lena Betters smiled humbly as she rattled off her classmates' names as if reciting the rosary. Then she named each sophomore as if they were family. Lena's pink flushed cheeks made her look beautiful as she approached the juniors. "Teela," she said, pointing to the Spanish girl, and Chloe groaned. Without a pause, Lena ticked off the other juniors' names, not stopping until she finished the seniors' names as well. The room burst in applause. Girls patted Lena on the back and praised her. Chloe was forgotten, but she didn't mind. She had achieved her goal of looking sincere and allaying any possible concerns in Sister's mind.

Now she only had to wait until Chicken Dinner Sunday.

CHAPTER 10.

Instructions

"Girls, this isn't just a high school. If you think *that*, you're missing the whole point of your being here. Now, for your classmates, the boarders and day-students, it is just a high school where they are getting a top education. But for you aspirants, it's more like a home. God has chosen you, think of it, out of hundreds of girls, to be his bride." As Sister lectured, Chloe recalled Sister Clarice speaking of a "testing" time to happen at Mater Dei. So far no one had referred to such a step. Angie Zimms raised her hand and asked, "Sister, how can we be sure that we have a vocation? Angie was a slim athletic girl with a radiant smile that crinkled her whole face and made her eyes crease so tightly shut that Chloe wondered how she could see.

"Girls, in all my years as mistress of aspirants I have never met an aspirant who didn't have a true and genuine vocation. Those who are not sincere don't make it this far."

Chloe raised her hand. "Sister, my eighth-grade teacher said that you ... that we ... that there would a test or something like that to help us know if we have a true vocation."

Other heads nodded. Sister rested her pretty chin on her entwined hands and said, "Girls, this may come as a surprise to some of you. But hear me out. I don't know what all you heard about the villa before you came here. No doubt some people have mistaken ideas about what goes on here, even the nuns. But you've been here long enough now to know some things firsthand. One thing you know—we seek to please God. You came here, each one of you, for that express reason. Maybe you weren't sure if you had a religious vocation, yet you were willing to come and find out. It was your decision. No one dragged you here, did they?" A whimsical smile played on Sister's lips as she looked at the faces of her freshmen girls. "It seems to me each and every one of you came here of your own choosing." Then in a more serious tone she said, "You're here because you answered a call, no matter how weak or uncertain you felt about it at the time. You took the necessary steps to get here. And in the short time that you've been here, God has done marvelous things in you. Girls, I believe that I know each one of you well enough now to say, unequivocally, that there isn't a one of you sitting before me today who does not have a true, genuine, religious vocation!"

Chloe's heart fluttered. No one breathed. In the stillness, Angie asked, "But how do you know that?"

Sister explained how she had been mistress of aspirants long enough to spot a phony within the first week. Chloe heaved a great sigh. Was it settled then, that pretty Gladys would never, should never gaze into a husband's eyes? And that Angie would never smile on her own baby? Lena Betters, well, she was a natural, she already acted like a nun. Mabel too, with her odd grandma way of walking and her thick glasses, would make a fine nun. But pretty Lucy? And laughing Kay? Were they *for sure* destined to wear black and white for the rest of their lives?

"So, you're saying the testing time is over," Chloe blurted out, crossing her arms on her chest. Sister looked coolly over her flock. "Girls, you've heard the Scripture, 'He who puts his hand to the plow and looks back is not fit for the kingdom of heaven.' You each put your hand to the plow when you came here. That may sound like an oversimplification, but it's not. A religious vocation is not a mysterious thing. It is simple and easy to detect. And it's a precious, precious gift, and the heart of it lies in your will. Angie, you first heard of the villa from your aunt, did you not?"

"Yes, Sister."

"And you were interested?"

"Yes, Sister."

"That's the first sign. And when you wanted to come did anything prevent you?"

"No, Sister."

"That's another sign. Tell me, did you have doubts along the way, fears?"

Angie nodded.

"And yet here you are. God called you. You answered. Many are called but few are chosen. To go back now only means you're turning your back on Him."

Lucy raised her hand timidly. "But people change their minds," she said.

Sister placed the tips of her delicate fingers together. "And God is a gentleman. He doesn't force Himself on anyone. He leaves the choice to us. But let me warn you, rejecting God's call is the epitome of ingratitude. In a way it is like slapping Him in the face."

That night, Chloe awoke in the middle of the night. She arose and stood on her bed to look out of the window. Far below, the city of Magnolia bustled with lights and honks and the buzz of traffic, all oblivious to holy callings and yeses that could not be revoked.

Chloe first wanted to be a nun in third grade, when she fell in love with her teacher, Sister Willomena. She wanted to be just like her when she grew up. And because that desire had never completely disappeared, Chloe was sure that she had a vocation. It was gratifying to know she had been chosen, but part of her wished she had been chosen a little later in life.

CHAPTER 11.

Open Weekend

Sister's sharp bell cut short the dining room din. In the sudden silence that followed she announced, "Girls, tomorrow night starts our first open weekend." Screams of joy pierced the air, followed by vigorous clapping. Every girl's face, it seemed, beamed back at Sister.

"This means (for you new girls) that the boarders will be going home for the weekend, and we will have the entire Heights all to ourselves!" Another round of clapping erupted. Girls looked excitedly from one to another, poking and hugging one another in glee.

"Many people have worked long and hard to make this the most fun-filled open weekend you will ever have. Now do your part! Throw yourself into the activities, and you won't have time to be bored. And please, please, don't look down on any of the games as childish. Just remember, we're a family having fun together."

Softball tournaments, with the winning team playing the postulants were arranged, as well as relay games, a scavenger hunt, a hike, an amateur hour, and a slumber party in the junior's long dorm. Everyone was required to sign up for three activities. Special treats of food and drink were promised, and even a walk downtown to a movie theater was hinted at for Sunday afternoon. Excitement ran high. Sister reminded her girls that when playing softball with the postulants they were not to speak one word to them of conversation, just baseball talk, or they might not be able to play them again. "And now … I've saved the best surprise for last!" Sister said, pausing. "The novices …"

A girl gasped. It was Aimee Sikes, looking as though she were in ecstasy, her eyes closed, and her mouth open in a silent scream.

"… Will give us a half hour concert of sacred music on Saturday night in the gym!"

Aimee jumped up and down, her clear young face staring trance-like at nothing. Sister smiled indulgently. "Please excuse Aimee, girls. Her sister, Margaret, is a novice this year, and Aimee hasn't seen her since July. For those of you who don't know, novices do not see or speak to any of their family for a whole year. They are in seclusion in preparation for vows."

Just as Sister had promised, it was busy weekend, with no spare moment. With the boarders absent, the aspirants enjoyed a new freedom on the Heights; they could use the boarders' playground with its swings, roam the park with the pavilions, and play on their baseball field, which had real bases and a fence backstop. But best of all, they were allowed to take their meals in the boarder's dining room. Far different from the aspirants' sparse white room, this one was circular, with bright cheerful table clothes and matching curtains. A bouquet of flowers adorned each table. The smooth pink-stoned floor bore sparkles beneath its sheen.

Every one was glad that they didn't have to wear their uniforms once during the entire weekend.

"I wish we didn't have any boarders!" Chloe remarked to Kay as Sunday evening drew to a close. The sun was setting behind the boarders' trees, shining golden through the leaves like the glittering pieces of a faraway kingdom.

"But they help pay our bills," Kay offered.

"How so?"

"Remember, they pay twice as much as us for the same education."

"But we work twice as hard! They don't clean or work in the laundry or anything!"

"Who works twice as hard?" Sister Damien asked, coming up behind them and tousling Chloe's hair. Even Sister seemed more relaxed during open weekend.

"We work more than the boarders," Chloe said.

"That may be so, but we are a family and families work and play together," Sister explained.

"They don't have vocations either," Kay said piously.

"Well, some of them might," Sister said, cocking her head. "They just don't know it yet."

When the open weekend was over, the boarders returned in time for evening benediction. With satisfied looks they filed into their pews, tired but happy. Some had hair cuts or new perms. Almost all looked smart in a new dress or suit. And some wore lipstick, Chloe noted. This whole "open-weekend" the boarders had been home. Lucy elbowed Chloe. "They must have spent the weekend shopping," she whispered. Suddenly Chloe saw the aspirants' open weekend, with its games and plays and skits, for what it was: a diversion from real life. While the aspirants were learning how to be happy children, obediently joining in on whatever activity was planned for them by someone else, the boarders were learning to be women. Some of them may even have gone on dates.

As the organ played and the girls sang "Veni, Veni Adorato," Chloe tried not to pout. She knew she should rejoice that she was a chosen one. But some of the boarders might be chosen too, Sister said, yet they were allowed to grow up first before committing themselves.

CHAPTER 12.

Chicken Dinner

Chloe's eyes flew open at five a.m. It was Chicken Dinner Sunday. Pure joy washed over her at the thought: "I'll see my family." How Brent would scoff, if he knew.

She had not packed her suitcase. Weeks ago her furtive plot to leave on this day had weakened and fallen away like the dead leaves of summer. There were too many obstacles. She could not pack without the others seeing her, and without her suitcase would Daddy take her home? He did not like waste. He would say she must pack, and then Sister might see her and ... oh, the embarrassment of being caught sneaking away! Also, the letters from home spoke of how much the little ones looked forward to this day. She couldn't make them turn around as soon as they got here. Since the dinner tickets were bought and paid for, Daddy would want to use them before whisking her away. She might leave at the end of the day, but how could she do that, with all her classmates standing around saying good-bye to their families? No, instead, Christmas vacation would be a much more convenient time to quit. She would already be home. Just a phone call from her mother would settle it, and she would not have to face Sister Damien.

When the 6:30 a.m. bell rang Chloe sat up, exclaiming with her dorm mates, "Praised be to Jesus Christ!"As they rolled back their covers. She dropped to her knees and together they all recited "Hail Holy Queen, Mother of Mercy. Hail, our life, our sweetness and our hope. To thee do we cry, poor banished children of Eve, to thee do we send up our sighs, mourning and weeping …"

Chloe dressed behind the wooden screen pulled securely around her. She eased up her nylons, buttoning them to her garters, slipped on her petticoat and buttoned up her white cotton blouse, which had grown a little tight across the bust. Next she put on the black suit that Momma had bought from Milly's Attic. It was an old style, with wide lapels and a fitted jacket. Her black flats would pinch her feet all day.

During Mass Chloe tried to concentrate, but her thoughts ran about like unruly children. No sooner had she sternly focused her attention on the priest's movements at the altar, than her thoughts were at home; watching Momma putting slippery nylon dresses over the little girls' heads while the little boys chased each other through the house until one of them got hurt, and then Daddy would yell, "Do you want to stay home?" They would shake their heads and creep away while Warren in his crib, his diaper sagging wet, would cry for someone to release him from his prison.

The sharp ring of the consecration bell yanked Chloe back to attention. She struck her breast three times, praying, "Mea culpa, mea culpa, mea maxima culpa," while Father Schlick lifted both arms high above his head, holding the host aloft while pronouncing the words that changed it into God Himself. Transubstantiation.

"My Lord and my God!" Chloe said, and then added, "Let them be on time Lord, please!" As soon as the host was on her tongue, she peppered Jesus with unspoken questions. "Who's all coming? Will Michelle be along? Or Brent? Someone has to stay home for chores. Sister says we aspirants have to clean up when the dinner's over! It's so unfair! To make us work while our families are still here. Why can't the day students clean up? They see their parents every day! Or the boarders ... they've been home twice since school started, and we haven't seen our families once! Oh! Why didn't I sell Momma early tickets, like Lucy did, instead of two o'clock tickets?"

After Mass and breakfast, even though no visitors were allowed until 10:30, Chloe's stomach jumped every time she heard a car approach. They straightened up their dormitories and then waited in study hall for their parents' arrival to be announced. Sister Ruth sat at the teacher's desk, her wide plain face trying to look stern as she gently urged the girls to make good use of this study time, "because you'll be too tired to study tonight!"

Chloe purposed to concentrate. "The Sherman Antitrust Act of 1890 was one of the first steps taken to control corporations and to oppose monopolies ..." Reaching the bottom of the page Chloe realized she had not taken in a word. She started again. "The Sherman Antitrust Act ..." Angie Zimms was chewing on a pencil, and Gladys Gehring was reading a comic book placed in front of her English book. She looked very calm. Lucy was twirling her blonde hair while staring blankly at a textbook. Only Lena Betters seemed intent on studying; bent over her algebra, her pretty forehead puckered in concentration. She was not getting visitors today. Her family lived too far away, in North Dakota, to visit, so she would not see her family until Christmas.

At the crunch of car tires outside, every head except Lena's turned. The thud of car doors sent Chloe's heart pounding crazily. She listened closely to the voices and laughter floating into the room through the half-opened windows of the study hall. A senior entered, leaned toward Sister and whispered a name.

"Angie Zimms," Sister called, and Angie burst from her seat, knocking a book to the floor as she fled the room, her eyes so tight shut with smiling that Chloe wondered how she found the door. As the door closed behind her, the girls in the study hall heard a squeal followed by joyful cries. The students pulled their books closer to themselves. Lena studied as though she were deaf. For the next hour, as one by one, girls were called out of the study hall, Chloe tried to concentrate: "The Northern Securities Company was a consolidation of the Hill-Morgan and Harriman railways, which included the Northern Pacific, Great Northern, and the Chicago, Burlington, and Quincy systems." But the noises outside grew more and more distracting. Children's cries and the deep resonance of male voices stirred up anticipation. Chloe could hardly sit still. Once she was sure she heard Peter's voice. She waited expectantly, her heart still, to be called. But no, it was someone else, and a sob caught in her throat. Surprised, she tried to calm herself, planting both feet flatly on the floor, staring at the print in her book. Lucy was called, then Gladys, and Kay, and Mabel Sappe. Only a few girls remained. Her family was late again. In place of sweet longing there now lay a hot impatient pain. She must be stoic. "It was not such a great thing, after all, to see your family."

Gripping her history book Chloe suddenly felt her whole body tingle. They were here. Something, a voice or a sound tossed in the mix of other voices, had pierced the walls and touched her soul. She knew. Calmly she put her books inside her desk, folded her hands and waited. When her name was called, she rose with great composure and left the room. The hallway buzzed with families and aspirants, all laughing and talking at once. Mabel held a fat baby in her arms. A hefty woman was dabbing at her eyes with a hanky.

Chloe stepped past them into the brilliant October day. Turning the corner, she saw the car. The long blue station wagon was parked at the curb, with Daddy at the wheel. She tried to hurry, but her straight suit skirt prevented big steps; her knees banged against the fabric, forcing her to take little mincing steps when she wanted to gallop. She ran as if she dreamed, forever, before finally reaching the car. Once there she threw her arms about her father's neck and cried. Great huge sobs rose up from deep inside of her as she hugged her father's big wide shoulders. How good it felt, to cry. Her mother was watching her curiously, as were the little ones in the back, with wide eyes. When she stepped back she felt lighter, as if a great weight had been lifted from her, and she could almost fly. She wiped her eyes. "It's so good to see you!" she squeaked, feeling clean all the way through. "Agatha! Julie! How you've changed!" Opening the car door she motioned them out as they smiled shyly at her. Howie and Travis scrambled out of the back door and took off running. "I'm so glad you brought the kids," she said to her father, clearing her throat. "I wish you could have brought them all."

"They all wanted to come," he replied. "It was hard to decide."

"Except Brent and Owen!" Chloe said, laughingly.

Daddy shrugged. "They're boys, you know," he said, chuckling. Chloe walked around to her mother's window and reached in to touch Warren, who buried his face in Momma's shoulder.

"It's Chloe, Warren, don't you remember her?" Momma asked, trying to turn his head. But he refused.

"Mom, you must be tired of sitting," Chloe said, opening the door, "Come on. Stand up."

"Sitting's something I get too little of to get tired of!" Momma said, pushing Warren from her as she struggled to get up. She was big. Her maternity top had a small rounded collar, like a choirboy's top, that made her look like a little girl. She smoothed out the wrinkles and straightened up with a sigh.

So began Chloe's first visit with her family. Daddy smiled expansively at Sister Damien's praise of the "The St. Eli girls."

"Cream of the crop!" she said, extending her small white hand towards his big brown one. But Momma was quiet, walking way too slowly for Chloe, who was eager to show her every nook and cranny of the Heights. All through her tour, as Chloe chattered at her side, Momma moved like a snail, her head cocked to one side as if listening to another voice, one carried on the wind, and saw things other than what Chloe wished her to see.

That night in bed Chloe's feet throbbed with pain. A new corn ached on the top of her toe, where her wretched Sunday flats had rubbed. All day she had run, it seemed, serving tables, cleaning up, covering the campus with her family and chasing the kids around the orchard. Her jaw clenched as she remembered how the day students had skipped out on cleaning. "While my family waited for me to finish washing all those dishes!" she thought, regarding the day-students coldly in her heart. As in a kaleidoscope she reviewed the visit; her mother's lovely profile, her daddy's portly shape. She had forgotten how bright children's eyes were; and how unruly boys could be. Howie and Travis had shimmied up fruit trees, breaking branches and plucking apples. They even entered the forbidden barn.

"Howie, where did you get that kitten?"

"In the barn."

"You're not allowed in there! No one's allowed."

"I didn't do nothing, just found this here cat."

"Why is the barn off-limits?" her mother asked, "You like barns so."

Staring into the dark dormitory now, hearing the deep steady breathing of her dorm mates, a tear rolled down her cheek onto her pillow. The day had gone so fast. Her mother had seemed listless and uninterested in the classrooms or the villa. One special time they had slipped into a restroom, with the kids following, and Momma had shooed out the little ones saying, "Stay with Daddy a while. We'll be out later." Then she eased herself into the white wicker chair in the corner of the lavatory and opened her purse for a cigarette. "Let's rest," she said, "I'm tired. You sit there, in that deep windowsill." Momma struck a match and lit her cigarette. Chloe hopped up to the window sill and sat uneasily, eager to continue her tour. Visiting time would soon be over.

"Chloe, are you happy here?" Momma asked, inhaling deeply.

"Yes Momma, very happy," Chloe replied, a little surprised and chagrined. Hadn't Momma heard or seen a thing all day?

"Chloe, if you're not happy here, you can always come home," her mother persisted, exhaling a puff of smoke that curled up between them.

"Of course I'm happy here, why wouldn't I be?" Chloe snapped. Her mother shot her a sharp look. Chloe winced. Sister was right; a mother might not understand the most precious gift a girl could have.

"Oh, I don't know, it's just that, this big place, so far from home, I worry about you and wonder." Her mother cut her a searching look.

Chloe was glad they were in the bathroom and no one could hear them. This wasn't what her mother was supposed to say. Why couldn't she be like Dad, basking in the glory of the day, the praise of the nuns, enjoying everything?

"Mom, I'm happy." she said, trying to sound patient, clenching a fist tightly at her side. "I belong here. The nuns are nice, and I have good friends. The food is good, and we get plenty of sleep and ..."

"Then why did you cry like that?"

"Oh!" Chloe waved her hand, but her stomach sunk with a wallop. "I, I don't know. It, it surprised me too. Just happy to see everybody, I guess." She spoke lightly, but her voice choked at her own words. She swallowed. A thin white line of smoke snaked up from the cigarette wedged between her mother's fingertips. A chasm stretched between them. This was no time or place to talk about leaving. She had been through all that, alone, and today she just wanted Momma to appreciate her efforts, maybe even praise her for how well she was doing.

"Come on, let's go," Chloe said, jumping down from the window-sill, "I'm worried what the kids will get into in the classrooms with Daddy watching them."

Slowly Momma crushed her cigarette into her small metal ashtray that she carried in her purse and struggled up from her chair. At the sink she rinsed out her ashtray, tapping it on the edge and drying it off slowly before dropping it into her purse. Through the mirror she smiled at Chloe, a sad resigned smile full of knowing. But she asked mo more questions.

After that, the joy seeped out of the visit for Chloe. Her cheeks ached from smiling, and her feet screamed for rest. When, at last, her family was seated in the car with the motor running and everyone waving wildly to her, she felt a great distance between them and herself. And when the car pulled away she felt farther from them than she had ever felt before. It was a distance of experience. Could she ever feel one with them again?

She turned toward the villa. It was her home now. Maybe it wasn't what she liked exactly, with its rules and regulations, but she could study here. And she had friends; but most of all, she had put her hand to the plow and must not look back.

CHAPTER 13.

Advent

"Girls, next week is the first Sunday of Advent. I can see by the gleam in your eyes that you're already thinking of Christmas and going home."

Chloe's stomach jumped at the words "going home."

"Three months is a long time to live away from home, and you've done just beautifully, every one of you. I'm very proud of you." Sister Damien beamed at her freshmen, whose cheeks glowed from playing outside in the first snow fall. A fire crackled in the fireplace. Tonight was the first of a series of instructions called, "Advent."

"It's a time of preparation for Christ's birth, not for going home. Put those thoughts of home out of your mind, as much as you can. It will be a sacrifice, but in the end, I promise you, you will experience the best Christmas you've ever had if you put Jesus first."

A log in the fireplace shifted, sending showers of sparks up against the blackness. At home the mantle would be hung with stockings close together. Last year Peter had insisted on hanging two, because, he said, "I've got two feet, haven't I?" But Brent had yanked the second one down.

"Here we put aside the worldly trappings of Christmas to emphasize the spiritual. We will not sing Christmas carols until the last day before

Christmas break. That means no radios. You might as well put them in the attic for the month. Sister Ruth will help you. Yes, Angie?"

"How can we get into the Christmas spirit without music?"

"Right here in the heart, where joy originates," Sister said, tapping her wimple. "You'll see. It's a spiritual process. Also, we do not exchange gifts. It's easier all around that way. You don't get downtown to shop anyway, and if you did, you would not find it edifying to be among the crowds. Like Mary, you have chosen the better part, and it will not be taken from you."

A sigh of falling ashes was heard, and a fresh flame leaped up in the fireplace.

"I don't know if I need to mention this, but it goes without saying, that we do not give any gifts, not even a candy cane, to any boarder or day student. Remember our motto, 'friendly, but not friends.' Mother Euphemia wants you to be very conscious of our separation from those of the world."

Also, no visiting Sunday this month, remember? Most of you just saw your parents at Chicken Dinner. And you will see them at Christmastime. You will be allowed to write home once, on Gaudete Sunday, but there will be no mail call on weekdays." A murmur arose, and Sister's eyes glittered as she said, "It's a small sacrifice to commemorate the coming of the King of Kings. And one more thing, we will keep our black suits on all day on Sundays."

Chloe groaned.

"What's the matter Chloe?" Sister said archly.

"I hate my black suit," she said.

"Why is that, Chloe?"

"It's not very comfortable, and my shoes hurt."

Sister smiled. "Then that would be a very special sacrifice for you, wouldn't it?" Hands shot up all around Chloe.

"Sister, what if a letter comes after Gaudete Sunday? Do we have to wait 'till Christmas to get it?"

"Sister, can we send Christmas cards?"

After Sister had answered all the questions Chloe asked, "Sister, will you tell me when my mother has her baby?"

"Of course, Chloe! As soon as they write, I'll let you know. Now, some of you have such long faces, I think it's time we call in junior, Lynn Dahlset, for a special announcement. Every Advent, the juniors take it upon themselves to design a project specially suited to fostering the Christmas spirit. This year I think they have outdone themselves." Sister raised her voice. "You may come in Lynn!" Lynn walked in smiling shyly. She held a small manger made of Popsicle sticks. She stood before the freshmen and explained, "This manger represents our hearts, empty and hard. Not a very soft place for a baby." She tapped it with her fingernail. Then she reached into her navy blue letter-sweater pocket and pulled out a wisp of straw. "But just as a little straw softens the crib for him, we can do acts of self-denial or kindness to prepare our hearts for Jesus on Christmas day." She laid the straw in the crib.

Lynn explained how each class would be given a popsicle-stick manger for them to soften with straws. "Every time you deny yourself some small pleasure or perform a good deed for another, you can place a straw in the crib."

Chloe bit her lip. "We're not little kids," she wanted to say. "How could Lynn present this project with a straight face? She was so smart; an excellent writer, and a whiz in chemistry. And she could play the piano like Mozart. Popular with the boarders and day-students, she had been elected to be class president this year." Chloe watched Lynn's face for any sign of embarrassment. Once, when she flipped a yellow lock of hair out of her eyes Chloe thought she spied a look of uncertainty there. But it could have been her basic shyness.

After Lynn left the room Sister, beaming at the freshmen, asked for suggestions on how they might earn straws.

"Smiling when you feel grumpy?" Angie Zimms suggested, and everyone laughed because she was never grumpy. Mabel Sappe said they might deny themselves a drink of water when they were thirsty. Sister nodded. Lena Betters said she would deny herself all thoughts of home. Then Sister said, looking straight at Chloe, "Girls, this project may seem simple on the surface, maybe even a little childish, but let me warn you, that is exactly what the devil wants you to think! Jesus said that unless we become as little children we will not enter the kingdom of heaven. I promise you, if you put your whole heart and soul into this Advent project, you will have peace and joy this Christmas such as you have never experienced before!"

That night in her bed Chloe lay awake long after the others' even breathing told her they were asleep. She watched the gray shadows of the trees move like sticks on the wall. If she were home now, she would slip outside and go walking over the hard snow in the moonlight on her daddy's farm. The manger project rankled. But she knew it was pride. She was sorry to disappoint God. She wanted His blessing. Pressing her lips together tightly she acquiesced. "I'll do it, if it's what *You* want," She prayed. Then with sudden fierceness, added, "But after Christmas I'm not coming back. I'm not coming back. I'm not."

CHAPTER 14.

Each and Every One

"You're not the same girls you were when you came here. There isn't a one of you that hasn't changed. You've matured. And I'm so proud of you." Sister's lively gaze included all of the freshmen in its warm embrace. "And as Christmas vacation draws near, there is something that bothers me. And that is, well, I don't know if you know how dear you have become to me, each and every one of you; and how vitally important your presence in our little family really is."

The room grew suddenly still. Not a muscle twitched.

"If just one of you were missing after vacation, our family would not be the same." Sister Damien leaned back, her eyes hooded as she toyed with her pen, slipping it back and forth through her fingers. The smallest furrow wrinkled her smooth, pale brow. She pursed her lips as if she were struggling with a strong emotion, and then went on. "Girls, I'm going to say this right out, so that there can be no doubt. If anyone here is not completely resolved in her mind about her vocation, if you are not absolutely sure that you belong here, please, I beg of you, come see me. Don't go home that way. If ever there was a time you needed to be free of doubts, it's now, on your first visit home.

"Let me tell you a story. Once we had a freshman, a lovely girl, just like each of you, who decided she was not going to return to the villa after Christmas. Of course, she kept this a secret from everyone.

While she was home, her parents showered her with gifts and gave her a big party. Then, on the last day of vacation she told them she wasn't going back. I tell you, her parents were heartbroken. They called me so shocked and saddened, but there was nothing I could do. That girl had been a model aspirant. I never would have guessed she was capable of such low-down trickery. It was the epitome of cowardice, really. But when Satan gets a hold of our hearts we lose our shame. And the reason that girl gave for not returning? She missed her friends and wanted to be with them."

"Did you ever hear from her again?" Lucy asked breathlessly.

"No, but I did hear that she was never able to be in the same class with any of her friends anyway. Exams at Mater Dei are after Christmas break, so, being she did not complete her semester, she lost all the credit she might have had, and had to repeat it. She graduated a year behind her friends."

Somewhere in the room a sigh escaped. The freshmen stared with long faces at their mistress. Chloe's ears flamed. She dared not touch them, but she was certain that Sister Damien could see them burning red. During the remainder of that night's instructions a heavy sadness pervaded her soul. Evidently there was no way out of the villa for her, now that her foolish plan had been portrayed as wicked. Furthermore, there was no one she could confide in honestly, except Jesus, and He didn't talk very much that she could hear.

On Gaudete Sunday morning, thick snow swirled about the silent aspirants as they crossed the white campus for Mass. Today was mail day. Christmas was near. Wasn't Momma's baby born yet? Poor Momma, so long overdue, she must be miserable. Chloe's excitement, already at fever pitch, was heightened by the muffled quiet of the snow. She wanted to shout and run. Instead she kicked at the snow, joy bubbling up inside of her like a fizzing soda pop. "I bring you tidings of great joy." She scooped up handfuls of snow and tossed them into the air. Kay, passing her, smiled knowingly. She too was excited about Christmas and going home. Chloe jogged to the cloakroom door and held it for the others, smiling boldly even though during the Grand Silence they were not supposed to even look at one another. Merry Christmas. Home. Though no one said the forbidden word, she saw it sparkling in other's eyes as they glanced nervously at her, choosing rather to submit to the restraint of the Grand Silence than sin by returning her smile.

At mail call Chloe took her letter and instantly knew there was a baby. Her address was written in Daddy's handwriting. That meant Momma was in the hospital. Chloe's hands shook, and her stomach warbled as she slid the letter from the already opened envelope. Why hadn't Sister told her? "It's a girl! It's a girl! It's a girl!" Chloe yelled, jumping up and down with the letter flapping in her hands. Tears of rage filled her eyes. She was shaking all over. The baby was already two weeks old. Sister Damien looked concerned as Chloe exploded, "Why didn't you tell me? You said you'd tell me!"

"Chloe!" Sister raised her hand. "Look at the postmark."

Chloe looked. "Yesterday," she mumbled.

"It arrived yesterday, and I only read it last night after you were in bed. I had no chance to tell you. Congratulations!"

Chloe blushed. "Oh," She said, seeing it was her family's fault. "I see. I'm sorry, Sister," she mumbled, her trembling stomach settling into an awful ache at her uncalled for accusation.

"What did they name the baby Chloe?"

"Gretchen Elizabeth, seven pounds, eight ounces."

"Come to me later, and I'll give you a special card for you to send to your parents."

"Oh, thank you, Sister!"

* * *

"Girls, remember that I said last week that you've changed? Well, others have changed too while you've been away. Can you think of whom I might mean? Kay?"

"Our families?"

"Yes, in that they've learned to get along without you. But I was thinking of people outside of your family, whom you were once close to. Mabel?"

"Our friends?"

"Exactly. Most of your friends have gone to public high schools, and that experience has already affected them. For instance, you might find your best friend is now boy-crazy. She may want to do things that aren't right for an aspirant to do. Can you think of some examples of what some of those things might be? Angie?"

"Ah, dating and ah, some parties?"

"Dating goes without saying. If I ever found out that a freshman dated, she would be dismissed at once. I'm glad you said 'some parties' Angie, because it puts things in perspective. A family party with adults in charge—fine! Laugh! Play games! Have fun! But stay away from parties where there is no chaperone, where things might get out of hand. Girls, don't put your vocation in jeopardy, in places where you might be asked to compromise the high standards of your vocation.

"Sometimes half the battle is just being ready. That's why we are talking things over now, before the temptation arises. Take it from me;

I've seen too many sincere freshmen excited about their vocation, committed to God, go home expecting their friends and family to understand and rally round them in safeguarding their precious vocation. But they don't. How can they? They don't have the spiritual understanding that you do. An aspirant who goes on Christmas break putting too much hope in her old friends might find some bitter disappointment. And it takes a lot of work to get her back to where she was before the break. That's why we don't go home very often."

Chloe raised her hand.

"Yes, Chloe?"

"Can I go to the New Year's Eve dance?"

Sister raised her eyebrows. "Hmm, I didn't expect that question from a freshman. Would your parents allow it?

"They always said I could go once I was in high school."

"And do you think your parents will be disappointed if you don't go?"

"They'd be surprised, 'cause they know how much I've always wanted to go."

"I see Chloe. This might be your chance to show them you've changed. Those dances are usually just a lot of wild drinking anyway, aren't they?"

"I don't know. I've never been," Chloe said, lifting one shoulder. She knew she wore an insolent look on her face, and she tried to mollify it; but ever since she had heard about her new baby sister a wild flame of recklessness leaped inside of her that was hard to contain. And it seemed these long lessons about their pending vacation only stoked the fire's flames.

The next day as the aspirants filed silently out of the dining hall at noon, Sister Damien beckoned to her with her small white finger. A dash of fear skipped through her as she stepped aside. "Yes, Sister?"

"Chloe, can I see you after school, in my office?" Chloe blanched.

"You haven't done anything wrong; I just want to touch base with you on a few things."

"Yes, Sister," Chloe said, cocking her head. "Are my mom and little Gretchen all right?"

"Ohpht!" Sister dismissed her question as foolish. "They're fine."

At three o'clock Chloe knocked on Sister's half-opened door. She had never been in Sister's office, but had passed it daily, situated as it was, at the hub of the villa. Its two doors opened on to the two corridors much traveled by the aspirants. It was a large square room lined with wooden filing cabinets and bookshelves full of books. Sister's large desk stood before a bay window through which the late afternoon sun cast golden hues into the room. The only other color came from the healthy green fern in the windowsill, pointing its delicate fronds in all directions. It seemed lit from within.

"Chloe, I just wanted a few minutes with you before your break," Sister said, turning toward her from where she sat at her desk. She motioned Chloe to a nearby chair. "You're excited, aren't you?"

"I guess." Chloe tilted her head.

"Do you think you'll have any problems with the things we talked about in instructions?"

"No, Sister."

"That New Year's Eve dance, will all your friends be going?"

"My friends are Lucy and Gladys now," Chloe answered pertly.

"Good! I'm glad to hear you say that. So will you be chumming around with them quite a bit?"

"We all live on farms. We'll mostly be home. And with Mom recuperating, there'll be a lot of work for me."

"I see." Sister Damien gave Chloe an odd look. She spoke very slowly. "I just feel for some reason, Chloe, that you are upset about something, anxious maybe. I'm trying to figure out what the message is that I'm getting from you. You aren't angry with me, are you?"

"No, Sister. I can't wait to see the baby, that's for sure."

"Hm huh, yes, I suppose you are. It's good timing for your momma, to have you around. I'll be praying for you."

"Thank you, Sister."

"Your parents are so proud of you, Chloe, do you see it?"

Chloe smiled wanly. "I guess."

"They are, Chloe, especially your father. Your being here means more to him than you will ever know. I think the younger ones look up to you, too. You have a great responsibility as their big sister."

Chloe looked down at her hands twisting in her lap. Sister did care about her; she saw that. She was ashamed now for her brash attitude during instructions.

"Chloe, you are one of the bravest freshmen I've seen."

Chloe looked up in surprise. "I am?"

"You handled your transition here like a real trooper. You didn't shed one tear that I ever saw. And I know it wasn't easy. You have a good share of inner strength in you."

Chloe pursed her lips and looked steadily at Sister. The attention and the praise felt like a warm blanket wrapped around her. She didn't feel so alone anymore.

"And you wait, after Christmas it will be like a whole new start; but without the homesickness. All that's behind us, and everything goes smoother. I see it every year. The girls pick up right where they left off and really become a team. Then we really start doing some exciting things."

"Sounds good."

'It really is." Sister reached over and patted Chloe's knee. "Things will be a lot different after Christmas, you'll see."

"Yes, Sister. I'm looking forward to it!" Chloe said, rising and smiling. She left Sister's office with warmth glowing inside of her. She was just beginning, she realized, to appreciate how much this woman loved her. Responsible for so many, she was still able to treat each one special and to make her concern personal.

CHAPTER 15.

Going Home

"I'm going home. I'm going home!" The car wheels rumbled beneath her, carrying her away from the Heights, through the slushy streets of Magnolia, toward home. Chloe wished them to go faster.

Why did the shoppers look so grave? It was Christmas! Just this morning the entire student body had sung their first Christmas carol of the season and Father Schlick had passed out candy canes. Chloe fingered the crinkly paper in her pocket. She had asked for extras for the kids. They would be thrilled. Finally, the green Pontiac carrying the three aspirants broke free of Magnolia's traffic and skimmed the black topped road. Telephone poles flew by, each one a friendly cross marking Chloe's progress toward home. Home! The mere word tasted like candy in her mouth. Just being there with Momma would be Christmas enough! Two weeks of it! To drink coffee with her while the little ones played around them; to see her own room again and hold the new baby; to walk the farm and the groves! "I'll visit every shed and barn and chicken and pig!" she vowed. "I'll even sniff the silage in the silo."

"They must wear you out up there. I've never heard three girls so quiet!" Mr. Gehring remarked, turning on the radio. Gladys, seated next to her father, looked up at him and smiled. Lucy and Chloe, in the backseat, laughed and returned to their private thoughts.

For the four weeks during Advent, Chloe had obediently suppressed thoughts of home, marking each victory with a blade of straw placed in Jesus' manger. In the end, her class had won the contest. The freshmen's popsicle-stick manger was literally buried in straw. "You have learned to love Christ as a little child." Sister had cooed to them. Privately, Chloe believed she had single-handedly won the contest for her class, so often had she quelled thoughts of home. But three days ago she had given up, releasing her grip on her thoughts and letting every fond, forbidden thought of home flow through her mind like a cool, refreshing drink. The experience made her dizzy with joy.

When they finally reached Red Branch, the halfway mark, the girls sat up and searched the streets. But they saw no one they knew. They were still too far from home. "You girls hungry or do you want to keep going?" Mr. Gehring asked.

"Keep going," they replied as one. In Morgan Town, their hungry gazes fell on familiar storefronts; Mike's Repair Shop, the Farmer's Co-op and Milly's Attic, where Chloe had finally found her black suit. She recalled how the clerk had suggested, "Wouldn't you rather have a navy blue suit than a black one?" And when Chloe had told the reason for wanting black, the lady had looked at her in grave admiration.

They sped on, oceans of frozen snow spreading out on either side of them. Farms lay nestled in depths of snow. Snow streaked across the highway 69, threatening to block the road if it got any worse. At every small town the car slowed down, and then sped up again. By the time they rolled through the quiet towns of Delton, Fairview and Mazel Run, it was dark. The strong yellow beams of Mr. Gehring's headlights pierced the blackness as they hurtled toward St. Eli, now a tiny light off in the distance. At last they stopped beneath that light, at its only intersection. Snowflakes swirled in its yellow glow. How small and deserted

St. Eli looked. On one corner the square brick schoolhouse loomed in the darkness. Across from it, Ray's Food shone a weak interior light, and Jake's saloon bore a lighted sign above its door, advertising "Pabst Blue Ribbon." A lone car was parked in front of it. Lastly, Pete's gas station was closed. They turned at this intersection and rolled through town unnoticed. Chloe wished that at least one person from St. Eli would be standing outside to wave and welcome them. But the streets were empty. The looming church was dark. The convent too, showed no light.

Lucy's farm came first. Her dad, Mr. Fry, a thin, red-haired man, stepped out of his house, slapping his long arms around himself for warmth. He hugged his daughter, and then shook hands with Mr. Gehring, thanking him for bringing Lucy home before he hurried inside with her. Watching, Chloe wondered briefly if Mr. Fry had any idea what kind of a life his precious girl had lived for the last four months.

On the road again, Chloe pressed her forehead against the icy window, searching for her farm. One of those twinkling lights lying on the horizon like a fallen star was hers. She zeroed in on one, fastening her eyes upon it until at last, like a miracle, they were parked beneath it. Her heart felt like it was leaping inside of her. All around her in the outer darkness of the farm loomed old familiar shadows. To her left stood the house, every window lit up with small faces flying past them excitedly. The porch door opened. Howie stood in the yellow light, wearing an oversized coat. With long sleeves flapping he bounded toward them.

"Hi, Mr. Gehring. How you doing?" Chloe noticed that Howie's voice had deepened. Next Daddy appeared, smiling and booming "Merry Christmas! Welcome home!" he greeted them, squeezing Chloe's shoulders with one arm while scooping up her suitcase with the other. Following him up the front steps, Chloe felt like she had traveled around the world and was back again to a familiar, lovely spot.

"Watch that step there," Daddy said, "It's got a chip in it." Chloe resented the reminder. "Did he think he was talking to a stranger?" The kitchen door opened and there stood Mamma, her frizzy black hair making a halo around her head. She turned, uttering softly, "Chloe's home!" Drying her hands on her apron she stepped forward, a wistful look on her face, and hugged Chloe briefly around the shoulders. Bashful children hid around doorways, peeking at the scene. To Chloe they looked like little ragamuffins, wild and unkempt, their clothes baggy and worn. The radio blared from the top of the refrigerator, and a musty greasy smell met her nose.

"Well Chloe, how does it feel to be home?" Daddy bellowed. Chloe was staring about in shock at the walls, wondering what was different. This was not the home she had remembered all fall, with its big rooms, high ceilings and that sweet airy breeze blowing through it. This was a shabby resemblance, for sure, but something had changed. She turned about, trying to guess what it might be.

"It's different," she said, squinting, "smaller." Darker too, she thought, hoping that soon Daddy would explain that a lamp had broken or an extra wall had been put up. Eventually she had to ask, "What did you do to the house?"

"Not a thing!" Daddy boasted.

"Come on, you're kidding!" she insisted, wandering into the living room with a dazed gaze. Even the huge brick fireplace that had dominated the living room like a giant had shrunken to a quite normal size and its fine golden bricks looked worn and soiled. She looked up. "Had they lowered a ceiling? Couldn't have. Pulled in some walls? Done some clever trick that they were just waiting for her to discover?"

"You did something!" she persisted.

"Nope," her father said, "it's the same sweet home it always was. You just forgot."

Forgot? Her lips quivered. Not one day had passed that she had not remembered every inch of this home. She tried again, a bit plaintively, "Did a light break?"

"No. No light broke."

"You didn't lower the ceiling?" The blank faces of her family stared back at her.

"Chloe, you've just grown used to those big hallways and the bright lights up there in that school," Daddy boomed, touching her shoulders. "Take off your coat and stay awhile. It'll feel like home soon enough." As Daddy hung her coat on the kitchen wall of hooks already bulging with coats, she ran over exclaiming, "Wait! I've got something for the kids." Reaching into her coat pockets she retrieved the candy canes, and at the sound of the crinkling wrappers the children inched nearer. "Everybody sit down in a row!" she directed, holding the candy high above her head. Instantly they obeyed, crowding the couch, legs straight out, hands in their laps, with eager, expectant looks on their faces. At least they hadn't changed. The older kids, Howie and Travis and Agatha, stood awkwardly on either side of the couch watching furtively as Chloe placed candy canes into the younger ones' hands. Chloe heard her father in the kitchen say something to her mother about some things never changing, and they both laughed heartily. She had enough for everyone. Father Schlick had been generous. While everyone licked their candy canes, Chloe suddenly felt awkward. Michelle had come down the stairs and was standing in front of the fireplace, her back to Chloe, as she fiddled with a knickknack and watched Chloe through the large fireplace mirror. The big boys weren't around.

Chloe's letdown over the size of house still bothered her. Timidly she broached the subject one more time. "Did you get more furniture?"

Daddy waved her words away, saying, "Chloe, the only thing new in this house is in the baby room. Come meet your new sister!" He took her by the arm. "She's a doll!" He lifted the white receiving blanket from a miniature sleeping face with rosebud lips still bubbling with milk as if the bottle lying near her had just dropped away from them.

"She's beautiful!" Chloe breathed.

"No need to whisper," Daddy declared, "she sleeps through anything. Best baby we've ever had."

"You say that about all of them," Chloe bantered as she gave little Gretchen a kiss.

Later, trudging up the stairs toward her room, Chloe's sense of alienation grew worse. These stairs had never been this narrow. She knew! She had dashed up them a thousand times; the same for this puny hallway with its battered railing. "It used to be wide and elegant. Was everything to be a caricature of what it had once been?" The children followed, licking candy canes and watching her with big, fascinated eyes. When she stepped inside her room her disconnection became complete. Her lovely room where she had been boss, where she had studied and ranted and raved and looked out of the window at Hufficker's grove, had shrunk to a dark, stuffy closet. Chloe eased herself down on the bed. "Nothing was the same; nothing." By some strange science that no one could or would explain, her whole home had shrunken, grown darker, and lost the luster from last summer. And no one noticed it but her.

"Who sleeps here now?" she asked softly.

"Effie and me!" Julie said brightly.

"Effie and I," Chloe corrected her.

"Yeah, you while you're home!" Julie agreed cooperatively, "I'll sleep on the couch."

"Are you kids rough in here? Do you have a lot of fights and stuff?"

"Oh no!" Effie's eyes grew big with earnestness. Julie was shaking her head vigorously.

"Do the boys come in here?"

"No. They stay in their own room."

"Hmm. Maybe you don't clean it very often," she said, talking more to herself than to them. "Who scratched the dresser?" Chloe pointed to a line swooping down across two drawers.

"Effie did!" Julie said promptly.

"I did not!" Effie cried, hitting Julie's arm.

"Well, let's not talk about it now," Chloe said. She wished to go to bed, but it was still early. She wasn't sure what to do with herself. Hopefully, by morning everything would feel normal again, and she'd feel at home.

She awoke to the smell of burnt oatmeal and heavy footsteps downstairs. Daddy was up and had burned the oatmeal, as usual. In the blue shadows of morning the old familiar furniture of her cramped room seemed ashamed of itself. She ignored it and ran downstairs to see Momma. The downstairs looked even worse in daylight than it had at night. The pungent smell of diapers soaking in Hilex water emanated from the baby room. The floor felt gritty beneath her bare feet, and everywhere she looked she saw work; dirty dishes, soiled laundry, and crying babies. Everything in the kitchen felt sticky to the touch. And overall, an old sweaty smell!

Then it dawned on Chloe! The house needed a good cleaning! How could she have been so dense? While she was living like a queen at Mater Dei, Momma had been slaving away, pregnant and burdened with a hundred kids to feed and clothe. She couldn't keep up! Guilt struck her full in the face. She hoped her mother had not noticed her disappointment of last night.

After breakfast Chloe marched up to the boys' big bedroom and began to clean; scooping up clothes, sorting, folding, and stuffing them into drawers. She worked fast, tugging gray sheets from the beds and tossing them on a pile. Soon a curious band of siblings gathered at the doorway to watch, flinching as she raised a broom over their heads to swipe away cobwebs on the ceiling, wincing as she dashed it against the mop boards, jamming its frayed edges into corners, digging out dirt. She yanked beds away from the walls, pulling out papers and trash and long-lost toys and swept them into a pile. The kids rushed forward to retrieve forgotten treasures. Chloe leaned on her broom, resting. "At least here you see what you're cleaning," she thought with satisfaction.

Next she seized a mattress, flipping it head to toe, then front to back, shouting orders to the children as though she labored against a pressing deadline. "Julie, find me a big box for that trash, will ya? Travis, bring me a pail with soapy water and a good rag, please. Veronica, ask Momma if there are any clean sheets." Then she invited Agatha, the oldest of the bunch, to help make the beds. "I'll teach you how to span sheets and make square corners," she said, as though offering her a treat. And while she worked she sensed all the other rooms waiting to be cleaned. "Tighter! Tighter!" she screamed, as Agatha tried to master the art of spanning a sheet. Chloe stomped over, grabbed the sheet from her hands, and yelled, "Like this!" and tucked the sheet in as tightly as she could. "And this is how you make square corners, see!"

When Agatha tossed a pillow back at Travis after he threw it at her, Chloe shouted, "If you're going to play, get out of here! Don't you want things clean?" How good it felt, to be in charge and to boss others around. Finally she chased everybody out of the room scolding, "Out! All of you, out! I can work faster without you."

Lastly she took the pail of sudsy water that Travis had brought, knelt down on a towel, and beginning in a corner, scrubbed the dull linoleum floor of the boys' room. When she at last reached the worn threshold, she leaned back on her heels, breathing hard, surveying her work. The green plaid floor shone cleanly now. Beds stood smoothed and straight. Even the thin plastic curtains looked better now that she had trimmed their ragged edges.

"Chloe!" her mother called from the bottom of the stairs, "come down for dinner. You can't do it all in one day."

"No wonder nothing gets done—with such an attitude!" Chloe thought self-righteously as she rung out her rag. The water in her pail was black and cold; nails scraped the bottom, and corn kernels floated on the top. Here was true reward for her work.

"You shouldn't have to work so hard the first day you're home," her mother said as Chloe lurched through the kitchen carrying the pail to the bathroom where she emptied it down the toilet, making sure to hold back the nails. "We haven't had a chance to sit and talk yet. I know that upstairs looks awful. Michelle and I have all we can do to keep the downstairs clean. So we ignore the upstairs. Have to. The kids will just mess it up again."

"They could be taught *not* to!" Chloe snapped. She felt Brent watching her; his feet propped up, a toothpick in his mouth. As she sat down to eat the meal of steak and boiled potatoes, she slowly became aware of the poor table manners about her. The children took their meat in their hands to tear at it with their teeth. But they were little. They would learn to use forks and knives when they were older. Grease shone around their mouths. They looked happily oblivious to the need for napkins.

She knew that Daddy said paper products were a waste of money. When the children buttered their bread slices whole, before breaking them in half, she tried not to look. But when they laid their used knives on the table instead of placing them on their plate's edge, she was ready to speak. Daddy was reading his mail. Mother was not present. All around her boorish and unkempt children chewed and gulped and burped without any knowledge that there were rules governing how to eat. "Take your elbows off the table!" Chloe ordered Howie. He obeyed quickly, shooting a grin at Brent.

"He can put his elbows on the table if he wants to," Brent growled. "Put them back, Howie." As he obeyed, Brent glanced coolly at Chloe.

"The table manners at this table are abominable!" Chloe announced to her father. He looked up. The children slid their eyes from Brent to Chloe to Daddy.

"There's nothing wrong with learning a few table manners," he said to Brent. Then to Chloe he said, "Remember, this ain't no convent."

"You don't have to tell *me* that!" Chloe countered hotly. Then, mortified at her own insolence, she bent over her food and ate. Her father chose to ignore her outburst. "Pass the meat," he muttered, and Chloe obeyed him quickly.

Chloe's first week at home flew by like an engaging dream. She rose early and worked hard, finding joy in seeing her efforts make a difference. The kitchen windows sparkled. The cupboards shone, and the floor was clean. The house even smelled better. But it took constant work to keep it that way; and how soon it all needed to be done again! Besides all that, every night all the bottles and nipples had to be sterilized and the water boiled for formula. Also, it amazed Chloe how fast food disappeared. A cake, hot from the oven and not yet frosted, was gone in minutes, and all the golden loaves of bread that Mother pulled out of the oven, hot and steaming, lasted just two days.

"Where is Michelle?" Chloe asked irritably one night as she lifted the steaming baby bottles with the tongs and set them on a clean towel to drain. "Does she live in her room?"

Momma, punching open a can of evaporated milk with a butcher knife, said softly, "No, she's usually a great help. I think that with you home, she's decided to kind of take a vacation."

Chloe understood. It was only fair to Michelle, she supposed, but still it felt like a punishment to her. The next day, after another day of housework, Chloe took the stairs two at a time as she ran up to her room. At the top of the stairs she stopped. The afternoon sunshine lay like a golden doily on the hallway windowsill. A pang shot through her. Another precious day was closing, and she had not yet watched one sunset or taken one walk in the grove. Her time at home was melting away like snow on the sunny side of the house.

That night she awoke to the new baby's cries and heard her mother's footsteps padding through the house. It angered Chloe that a helpless baby could pry a tired woman from her bed. Sister Damien's sleep was never interrupted. Now she understood why nuns could not marry. Why, they'd never get anything important done if they had to raise kids!

The second week of vacation, Chloe thought of a way she could help her family even after she was gone; by baking ahead. With ambition she took down her mother's stack of cookbooks and studied them. Then she began to assemble ingredients for cakes and cookies and brownies. She mixed these up it double batches, one batch for eating now and the other to freeze for later. Soon the aroma of chocolate cookies and spice bars permeated the house.

"Hmmm! Smells like a bakery in here," Brent exclaimed as he swooshed into the house from the cold, stamping his feet and scooping up a mitten full of cookies from where they lay cooling on the table. He stuffed them into his mouth.

"You could ask, don't just take," Michelle said, who was filing her fingernails by the light of the kitchen window.

"What? Haskh her?" Brent spoke with his mouth full, "Phlthere notph her cookies. She don't even liffe here."

"Oh, shut up Brent. Be nice to her, she's been cleaning your room. You ought to thank her." Michelle said.

"Humph! She should thank me. If it wasn't for *me* she couldn't even *go* to that fancy school."

"How so?" Michelle asked.

"Who brings in the dough around here? The men!" Brent thumped his chest. "We do the real work outside that pays the bills."

"Oh yeah? You don't call changing diapers and making meals real work?"

It was an old argument—the girls against the boys. Chloe pressed her lips tightly together so as not to jump into the fray.

"You girls got it made! Get to stay in the warm house, while we …"

The front door opened. Dad stood there, appraising his son coldly as he peeled off his thick gloves. "So here you are," he remarked, "I wondered what happened to you. Better get going, there's work to be done."

"Just thawing out," Brent said, grabbing another handful of cookies before fleeing the house.

After Daddy had gone outside again and the kitchen was quiet, Chloe asked Michelle, "Where's Momma? Sleeping again? She sure sleeps a lot, don't she?"

"Course she does. Wouldn't you?" Michelle said, spreading out her fingers and surveying her work. After a while she asked, "Why do you work so hard when you come home?"

Chloe blinked, not sure that Michelle could understand what it was like for her to be home again, next to Momma, after being away for so long; or what a thrill it was to just be helpful, or how cute and loveable the little ones were to her.

"I miss the cooking and the baking," she said. "We don't get to do that up there."

"Must be nice," Michelle said, tossing her head. Chloe wanted to say that if, by some miracle, she could stay home forever she would be glad. But instead she leaned over the cookbook searching with her finger for another recipe requiring basic ingredients that were sure to be in Momma's cupboards.

That night fresh snow fell, transforming the farm into a hilly white playground. The children left their Christmas tractors and dolls for the winter wonderland outside while Chloe helped them in and out of their coats, boots, and scarves. Finally, toward evening, as Momma stood at the stove turning the sizzling hamburgers for supper, Chloe bundled herself in coat, scarf, and mittens, pulled on her boots and slipped out the front door. The cold struck her hot face like a cool fan. She breathed deeply of the fresh air. All around her snow glowed in the moonlight. As she trudged through the groves her steps were the only sound in the frozen world. Its stillness calmed her spirit. She felt happy; supremely happy. She was home. And this was one thing she had missed, being alone outside. The wind was God's own breath, the moon His bright eye. The naked trees with their stark branches reaching toward the sky were her quiet, uncritical companions. "Oh God! It's so … so You!" she exclaimed, kicking happily at the white fluff. Then, with a mental thud she remembered her daily prayers and the chart hanging in her room. Every day the same spiritual duties nagged to be fulfilled: meditation; reciting the rosary and spiritual reading. I can meditate out here, she thought, and say the rosary on my fingers. It's too bad spiritual reading can't be done out here as well.

She tramped through the groves and beyond into the open fields covered with snow. Here the sun had melted the surface before it refroze, forming a brittle crust that almost, but not quite, held her weight. With every other step her legs sunk knee-deep into the snow. Chloe traveled on, enjoying the exercise, and trying to concentrate on reciting her rosary as she walked in the moonlight on her daddy's farm.

CHAPTER 16.

Daddy!

It was good-bye time. The little ones played, happily unaware that this alien sister who had popped into their lives, scrubbing and scolding and cuddling them for two weeks, was leaving. Chloe sought them out to say good-bye at the breakfast table, on the couch, in their rooms. Hugs, squeezes, cheek pressed to cheek, her hand clutching their small sturdy arms, Chloe rushed from one child to the next. Their clear bright faces smiled up at her. She hadn't had enough of their firm little bodies and their cute faces. She wanted to see them every day. It was her right, wasn't it?

"We best be going," Daddy said, handing Gretchen back to Momma. "Lucy and Gladys will be waiting."

"Good-bye, Chloe. I'm sorry you had to work so hard while you were here," Momma said. "Things aren't always this bad. But with the new baby and all, you saw the worst of it I'm afraid."

"I'm glad I could help," Chloe croaked. Michelle, leaning against the doorway, waved lethargically, a sardonic smile on her lips. Brent and Owen were outside, doing chores. As Daddy backed out the car, small faces pressed against the living room window, continuing to wave. Chloe squinted against the bright snow, tears welling up in her eyes. As the car pulled forward past Huffiker's grove where she had so often played alone, the tears fell. Suddenly every feeling she had known since

September rose up and joined in a swell that she could not suppress. She cried silently, tears rolling down her cheeks in big droplets as she saw in her mind's eye the Heights, the sisters, and the villa toward which they now drove. And none of it gave her any joy. It felt good to cry! To be real.

"Daddy, I don't want to go back!" she said. Her world cracked. She had said it! Like a cork wrenched from a bottle, a fresh flood of tears accompanied this spontaneous cry. "Turn the car around Daddy! If you knew what it was like. If you only knew!" As Chloe sobbed a picture formed in her mind, symbolizing all the misery and control of Mater Dei that she couldn't express: the sugared figure-eight doughnut. Fresh, fat, and exquisitely delicious looking as it sat on a tray along with eighty more of them; it waited for her every day after school at 3:15 sharp. She must neither deny herself one nor eat more than one. Someone always seemed to know who had not had one, or who had taken two. Any discrepancy was looked into; inquiries were made: was someone dieting? Or in a place she shouldn't be? The guilty person was always ferreted out.

No glad bursting out of school at three o'clock, knowing that the rest of the day was hers. No part of any day was hers. Instead, duty and responsibility or planned recreation lay in waiting. There was no freedom after school.

Like rains held back for a long time, Chloe's sobs rose up from a place deep down, gushing out and washing her clean as she told the truth. "If you only knew, if you only knew," she finished, shaking her head as if even she could not believe Mater Dei as she saw it now. But soon her agony would be over. No going back now. Immensely relieved, Chloe blubbered on while Daddy drove. He had listened without moving his head. Soon now he would turn the car around, and they'd go back home, and he'd tell everyone that Chloe had changed her mind; everyone would be so very happy and surprised. Chloe saw her mother's face as they reentered the house, asking, "What in the world?" but there would be no mistaking her approval.

Snowdrifts blocked the first field driveway. He passed it up. Chloe watched eagerly for the next one. It was partly cleared, but he passed that one up too. Then she understood that Daddy was wisely waiting until he got to the highway, where he could turn the car around more conveniently without getting stuck. When they reached that smooth blacktop Daddy slowed down, turned left, and kept on going. In shocked disbelief Chloe stared at the back of her father's head. She sat stock-still. Farms were flying by.

Eventually he spoke. "It's hard leaving home, Chloe, I know. I can see that you appreciate your home more than all the others put together. That's because they've never been away from it, as you have. If, after you're back up there you still feel this way, let us know. But think it over, Chloe. Don't do anything rash."

By the time they reached Lucy's farm, Chloe's tears had dried. Lucy and Gladys waved gaily from the porch where they stood waiting. Lucy wore a new red coat. Chloe's Daddy gripped the steering wheel in his thick brown hands. He was right, of course. In his own immoveable way he had saved her from herself. She should be grateful. But she felt oddly betrayed. The wild, gushing sobs that had accompanied her outburst lay quiet now, sunk deep and lost in some underground cavern where they could not be heard or seen. And in their place, a hard, dry surface, devoid of feeling and of tears had formed. Chloe smiled wanly at her two companions as they started back to Mater Dei.

CHAPTER 17.

Back

They were back. The girls who had been so loud and unmanageable before Christmas arrived with new hairdos and new clothes that made them look older and wiser than before.

"Merry Christmas, Chloe!" Kay hugged Chloe clumsily, her blotched face all smiles. "I missed you. Did you have a good time? Tell me everything you did!"

Chloe smiled. "No, *you* tell me!" Kay obliged, prattling on about her nieces and nephews. Chloe fingered the calluses on her hands. They had started as blisters on her first day at home and were now toughened scabs on her palms. By the time Kay stopped to insist, "And what did you do?" the bell rang and the girls filed back to study hall. That night Chloe turned back the crisp white sheets of her bed with a genuine appreciation for order and cleanliness. She slipped between the fresh folds and fell instantly asleep. She opened her eyes to the clang of the hand bell, rolled back her blankets, dropped to her knees and recited the opening prayer of the aspirant's day. "Hail Holy Queen, Mother of Mercy, hail, our life, our sweetness and our hope …"

Soon the traces of lipstick and eye shadow that had lingered on some faces faded, along with the cigarette smoke that clung to their clothes. In uniform again, with their jumpers dry-cleaned and their blouses freshly washed, ironed, and mended, the aspirants settled down to their studies. Winter and exams lay before them. In the morning as they crossed campus, their breath made frosty clouds in the air. Sister shortened evening recreation to allow for more time for study. And after exams, school, uninterrupted by any holidays, was followed by six weeks of Lent with no visiting Sundays. Sister Damien resumed instructions. Easter was a long way off.

Little by little, Chloe's calluses softened and disappeared. Sister was right, adjustment was easier the second time around. She was not homesick, nor did she chafe at the routine, but accepted it as a necessary guide to her success. It was nice to be able to study without crying babies around, fighting brothers and the radio blaring. Between classes, while the girls marched from classroom to classroom, the aroma of the next meal wafted through the corridors, filling everyone's nose with enticing smells of roast beef or chicken pot pie. And these creature comforts, Chloe saw now as a blessing and a privilege that was hers because of her vocation. She was called. She was chosen. This truth, impressed deeply on her mind, squelched even the tiniest bit of guilt she felt at leaving her mother and Michelle at home with all the work.

One noon, after lunch, Chloe asked for permission to go to the villa. After leaving the dining hall she ran across campus, entered the villa and dashed up the four flights of stairs to her dorm, taking the steps two at a time. Puffing heavily she collapsed into the wooden chair near her bed and looked about. It was red dot day: senior inspections would take place in the dormitories. Anything the least bit askew or unclean would receive a red dot, which then counted against the dormitory's "clean" score. Last month her dorm had failed, and it had been her fault. A hair had been found in her hairbrush. As Chloe looked about she learned to her joy that the seniors had not yet been there. She was not too late. Not one red sticker glowed on any bed or dresser. She rushed to the closet. No red dots there either. She sighed with relief.

Her morning had been hectic. First her shoestring had busted, then, as she bent to fix it she got a nosebleed. Precious time had been lost while she held her head back in the bathroom, holding a cold washcloth to her forehead. By the time she arrived at her cleaning spot, Gladys was finished and she swished by with her dust rag. Chloe was late for meditation and had to climb past the seniors to sit with her class. After that came Mass, then breakfast and school, with no time to return to her dorm.

Relieved that she could still redeem herself, Chloe scrubbed out the ring in her basin and thoroughly dried her cup and toothbrush with her towel. Her hairbrush was full of hair. No time to clean it now. Where to hide it? Seniors' eyes searched everywhere. Chloe dropped it into her uniform pocket, where it caused a bulge. Next she opened her nightstand to check on her underwear. Bras and panties and stockings were folded and stacked in wobbly lines. It would never do. Quickly she refolded each item. But the bras, with their unruly straps, refused to lie flat. It was ridiculous to fold bras. At home she just threw them in a drawer.

A picture of home flashed before her eyes. She recalled the bathroom floor, strewn with towels, none of them white. The black lava soap the boys used for their farmers' hands left scum in the sink. The tub was filled with dirty laundry, and the toilet often stayed not flushed to save water. A dark brooding sorrow washed over her. What was she doing here, worrying about hair in her hair brush?

Sunshine gleamed on the hardwood floors. Beds stood in perfect rows, with dressing screens folded and tucked into a corner like sentinels of neatness. Next to each bed a wooden chair stood, perfectly straight, not touching the white bedspread. Dark green window shades hung at precisely half-point. Chloe wrung her hands. Guilt that had been mere pinpricks before now throbbed like wounds and seized the day. Chloe sat down on a chair. "Cleanliness is next to Godliness." Sister said. If that were so, then why wasn't she home, helping Momma live a more godly life?

Chloe rose and descended the stairs, automatically kissing her fingers before touching them to the bare toes of the Infant of Prague statue. "Jesus, Mary, and Joseph" she whispered, thereby gaining for herself a three hundred-day indulgence. The first time she had seen this ritual performed by the others she had recoiled and said she'd never do it. It looked silly, she thought. But now she did it without thinking, mouthing the same ejaculation that everyone else did, thankful that, by so doing, three hundred days of burning were automatically removed from her future punishment in purgatory.

Poor Momma had no statue to kiss to gain an indulgence. Was that fair? Didn't she need indulgences as much as the nuns did?

"What a strange life you've brought me to, little Jesus," she said to the Infant's painted eyes. He wore a stiff golden robe, with a jeweled crown on his head. His hair was curly blond. In one chubby hand he held a globe. With the other hand two pudgy fingers were extended in the sign of peace.

"Is cleanliness really next to godliness?" The Infant stared straight ahead with his round hard eyes. She returned to the academy feeling unsettled. Her vocation no longer carried the day. It was still a precious gift from God, but did it require abandoning her mother? Many girls living at home and attending high school right now would graduate and enter the convent later. Why not she? The idea made sense, like tossing bras in a drawer.

These thoughts were not new. But with the demand of classes and the joy of friendships, she had pushed them away. Now they had a toehold and stayed and grew. Studying, praying, recreating, or eating, she felt their pressure building like bothersome brothers, demanding her reaction: give up this life of ease and go home where you belong. Her throat felt dry, so that she swallowed often. She decided that she must speak to Sister. Surely Sister would see that leaving was the right thing for her to do.

* * *

"Yes, what is it, Chloe?"

As Sister Damien rose gracefully from behind her polished desk, a wave of regret washed through Chloe. She was sorry she had come. "I'd like to talk with you," she said weakly, "If you have time."

"Yes, come in Chloe. What's it about?"

"It's about when I was home, Sister," she said, swallowing hard.

"Yes?" Sister raised her fine curved eyebrows. Her green eyes brimmed with warm attention. Chloe wished to sit down, for her knees were trembling. "Well, it's just that, well . . ." Blinking furiously she locked her clammy hands together as if in prayer. "You know we have a big family, with lots of boys and kids," she took a breath, "and now the new baby."

"Yes, I know Chloe," Sister nodded sympathetically, "I admire your parents very much."

"I helped out all I could when I was home. There's so much work, you can't imagine! It seems all I did the whole two weeks was work. And well, I've been thinking that my place is there, with Momma. It's not right for me to be here, enjoying a life of luxury while everyone at home has it so rough."

"Chloe, what a vacation you must have had!" Sister's gay laughter brought a wan smile to Chloe's intense face as Sister took her hands in hers and squeezed them. "And while you were home, doing all that work, these thoughts naturally came, and you've been pondering them ever since, is that right?"

"Well, sort of, I, it's come to me," Chloe gulped. "Sometimes Momma stays up till all hours, just getting the daily chores done." Relief washed through Chloe's tight stomach as she shared the anguish of home with Sister Damien.

"Chloe, you should have come sooner. When the devil tempts us it's always good to get reinforcements."

"The devil?"

"Why yes, Chloe! Who else would be so clever as to tempt you in just this way? Don't you see how he's using your love for your mother to get at your precious vocation?"

"I'm not leaving my vocation, I still want to be a nun, but later, after I graduate." Chloe said, jutting her chin out.

"Sit down, Chloe," Sister said, smiling. "I don't doubt for a minute, Chloe that you sincerely love and cherish your vocation. But the devil has other plans and once he gets you home he's free to work on them. Don't you see?"

Chloe bit her inner lip at this new twist. She had not imagined that Satan was interested in her. But she could see where he might have influenced her thoughts. She needed to go slower, think things through. Sister seemed so sure it was the devil. They talked more, even laughing together at funny incidents from home as Chloe recounted them. Eventually Sister said, "Tell me Chloe, did you mean that when you said this was a life of luxury?"

"Oh yes, Sister. It is! The good meals and all the time to study in peace and quiet." Her eyes grew big as she thought of the fresh sheets too. But she shrank from denigrating her home or dear Momma who worked so hard, and said no more.

"Chloe, some aspirants complain that they work too hard at the villa, and that the food isn't good."

"Pshaw!" Chloe snorted. "They're spoiled! The food's the best, and the work is nothing compared to …" A sad look shadowed her face.

"And that's exactly why we need girls like you here in the villa. You are like salt, flavoring the whole group." Sister reached over and tilted Chloe's chin up gently so that she must look into Sister's eyes. "Chloe, I think you deserve a little luxury in your life. Did you ever think that maybe God gave you this place away from the distractions of home so that you could discover and develop your own character and talents?"

It was a new thought, not without comfort. "Was it really all right for her to stay? Had she overreacted?" Then Sister's beautifully freckled face so full of love and understanding grew serious. "Chloe, were you able to keep up with your prayers during your vacation?"

"Yes, Sister. I did them all."

Sister clamped her lips as though holding back tears. Her green eyes were pools of compassion as she murmured and nodded. "That's how you survived." She rose and took a few steps around the office, then, facing Chloe she asked softly, "Would you mind, Chloe, if I mentioned your story to the upperclassmen? I won't use your name. They need to know how one freshman was faithful to the little things in the midst of so many needs of her own."

"If it would help someone," Chloe said weakly. By the time Chloe left Sister's office she felt washed clean as she often did after going to confession. Sister's words had eased her guilt and calmed her fears. She was free. Strange, she thought, how just sharing her heart with her mistress had such a calming effect, like putting a few drops of oil on a pot of boiling water. Nevertheless, as she breezed into study hall ready to do battle with Latin once again, she paused. “Had her deepest thoughts been plumbed and given a hearing”? She had been so sure of herself before. “Were all of her ideas so fraught with deceit that she couldn’t trust them?” Chloe shrugged. “Sister was the mistress of aspirants. She knew about vocations. And wasn’t her first duty as a good aspirant to trust and obey her superior?”

* * *

Chloe was walking across campus reading a letter from Michelle when she noticed, written in the margin with a red pen, “This girl needs prayer!” It was Sister Damien’s handwriting. Heat flashed through her. She must tell Michelle to be more discreet.

“Chloe! Are you deaf?” Kay Wakely grabbed her by the shoulder, “I called your name three times!” She was puffing.

“Look at this.” Chloe pointed to the scribbled notation. Kay whistled. “What did your sister write to deserve that?” She asked.

“Oh, just about boys and going to Lake Cochrane for a beer.”

“Just!” Kay said teasingly.

“It’s okay for her. She’s not going to be a nun.”

“But remember what Sister said about those of our own household being our enemies.”

“I hardly think my sister is my enemy!” Chloe said stiffly.

“I know. But she *is* of the world.” Kay admonished. “Remember Sister saying that? Oh, it’s cold out here! Come on! Let’s run to the cemetery so we can get back to where it’s warm.” The girls broke into a trot. They had become close friends since Christmas. Kay had coached Chloe in Latin for hours in the small piano room that Sister had allowed them to use. At one point Kay, reviewing Latin declension, exclaimed to Chloe, "It's almost like you've been skipping class, the way you're so behind!" Chloe did not tell her how she had stopped studying before Christmas thinking she would not be back. "I hate Latin," was all she said.

Now as they trotted along, Chloe glanced at her friend's long nose, the half-opened mouth with the buckteeth protruding, and loved her. She wondered if girls like Kay were spared the usual interest in boys. "Or did she too long to date boys and drink beer just once? Or did God purposely make some girls ugly to help them stay true to the end?"

CHAPTER 18.

Particular Friendships

"Girls, I would be remiss in my duties if I didn't bring up a certain subject," Sister said, glancing down at a notebook before her. A natural bluish shadow on Sister's eyelids made her prettier than usual tonight, Chloe noted. Her lips were a deep wine color that made her face look more charming than any lipstick ever could. Chloe could almost picture Sister without her veil, her light brown hair falling gently about her face. "She would be easy for a man to love," thought Chloe, a woman as kind and as wise as she. "Had a man ever loved her? Was he sorry to see her go to the convent? Surely there must have been one man drawn to those expressive lips."

"There are many kinds of friendship," Sister was saying, bringing Chloe back to the instruction at hand. "Many of us have a best friend, a girlfriend to whom we feel close, maybe because we share interests, or have certain things in common. Or it could just be because our personalities fit together, complimenting each other. It's very natural to enjoy one person more than another. Anyone who has a best friend is lucky indeed.

"But tonight I want to warn you about 'particular friendships.' These are *very* different from what I just described, and they can crop up almost before we know what's happening. That's why I find it necessary to talk very openly and honestly with you tonight." Sister tented her fingers and then folded them, pursed her lips and, leaning forward, said in a serious tone, "Particular friendships tend to be exclusive, almost like a boy-girl relationship, where the two girls want to be alone much of the time."

As Chloe listened intently, Kay's face sprang into her mind.

"Girls, God meant for a man and a woman to enjoy an exclusive relationship in marriage. When girls get to be your age, they naturally start taking an interest in boys. God made you like this. And as girls get older, they date in preparation for marriage; all perfectly natural for those who are called to the marriage state. But for girls like you who have received the high calling of a religious vocation, it's different. Your affections are directed toward God. And yet, because we are human, that natural feeling for a boy's attentions, if we are not careful, can be so strong that we mistakenly direct it toward another girl.

"This may surprise you. But I've been in this job long enough to know it's true. It does happen, and when it does, it always hurts. Two girls start to find all their enjoyment in each other's company. They seek each other out at almost every opportunity, and very soon they are spending so much time together that others begin to notice and to feel left out. This hurts everyone involved. Then, when that particular friendship gets stale, as it is bound to, since it is an unnatural friendship to begin with, the two involved get sick of each other. Suddenly they find themselves without friends. Loneliness sets in. I've even seen girls lose their vocations over such a silly thing as a particular friendship. I say 'silly' but it is also very, very serious.

"Girls, on a happier note, someone once said that aspirants are 'going steady with Jesus.' Now I see some of you are smiling at this, but it is a creative way to look at your lives during this time of growing up. You want to become nuns, and that is the highest and most beautiful goal a girl can have. Truly it is. But meanwhile, while you are being trained up to become mature in your vocation, this is one of the most important things to learn: to love everyone the same, as much as is possible. If you learn this now, while you are young, it will help you so much in the future, when you are nuns. Believe you me, I can't tell you enough how valuable that lesson will be to you as brides of Christ. Girls, you will never, ever regret one lesson you've learned here at the villa in preparation for that great day."

"You can have friends. You can even have a best friend. But please, please, for your own sakes, don't ever let a girl take the place of that special love that is meant for God alone."

Chloe mused on her friendship with Kay. Sister added, "In case some of you are wondering if you might have a 'particular friendship,' here are some of the signs: If you can't enjoy a recreation hour without that person next to you, if you must include her in whatever activity you are engaged in, be it softball or walking to the cemetery, and no one else will do, then, girls, you are in great danger of having a particular friendship."

Chloe let out a slow sigh of relief. She felt none of those things for Kay, and she was sure Kay did not feel that way about her. Sister was still speaking. "Our goal should be that no one should ever guess who your best friend is. This is possible, if you work at it. Choose a different companion at every recreation hour. Then I can assure you, you won't fall into the trap of a particular friendship."

Chloe felt something like a stone settling in her stomach. Though she was sure her friendship with Kay was not a particular friendship, a needling worry said it might appear so to others. It seemed, that night, as the aspirants filed out of chapel to recreation that none dared look at another. They walked with eyes downcast. Chloe held the door open for the others, and then she smiled at the last one leaving and asked, "Want to walk to the cemetery with me?" The girl nodded. Later Chloe met Kay laughing and talking with another girl. Their eyes met in a mutual search, as if each were looking for confirmation that their friendship was all right.

"Girls, summer vacation is just six weeks away. And summer vacation is very different from your Christmas and Easter breaks. Really, they don't compare at all."

Chloe surprised herself. Before Christmas she had been delirious with longing for home. Easter vacation too, had glimmered all through Lent like a light at the end of a tunnel. But now, facing a summer of three whole months at home, no elation stirred her. Instead a deep calm possessed her.

"I know you're looking forward to all the fun you're going to have, picnics and trips and family reunions and all. And I'm glad. I want you to have fun this summer. But I'd like to say a word of caution."

A tan from the spring sunshine had brought out the freckles on Sister's nose, enhancing her beauty, Chloe thought, as she watched Sister's dainty but sure hands press together at the fingertips, a mannerism she used whenever she wished to stress the earnestness of her message.

"Some girls go home and forget all about the disciplined life. They neglect their prayers and let their correspondence with me lag. They want to get back in with the old crowd.

"Girls, all the fun in the world isn't worth losing your precious vocation for. Fun always starts out innocently enough, some party or get-together where one questionable thing leads to another until things get out of hand. That's why I warn you girls: 'The devil goes about like a roaring lion, seeking whom he may devour.' There's no one in the world he'd like better to devour than girls like you who aspire to a high calling. You have so much potential for good. Don't throw it all over for a few moments of fun."

Sister's cheeks glowed pink. Her green eyes swept the girls' eyes longingly. Chloe felt a bond in the room between Sister Damien and her charges; a bond of loyalty and of love. It was a new and bracing sensation for her, to belong to something bigger than herself or her family. She would miss Sister's instructions and the villa.

"I can always tell when the girls come back, who has brushed too close to danger. It shows on her face. It takes so long for her to feel at home here again. Please girls, I can't say this strongly enough, don't put yourselves through that! It's so much better the other way."

Then Sister passed out a stack of blue booklets, explaining they were meant for keeping track of their prayers while they were home. Chloe leafed through the booklet, admiring Sister's handwriting. She hoped her own handwriting would look that smooth by the time she was grown. She lacked other skills, such as a quiet spirit, and musical ability, and of course math. But for now there was summer, lying before her like a vast, uncharted ocean. Sister gave each girl a mimeographed copy of everyone's address so they could write to each other. "You may attend two wedding dances this summer, preferably those of a relative."

"Can we dance with boys?" Angie asked.

"Yes, that is permissible," Sister said, "though not with the same boy twice. I think you can see the wisdom in that rule."

CHAPTER 19.

Home for the Summer

"Whoever eats their soup without spilling one drop gets a prize," Chloe stood at the long table filled with her younger siblings eating lunch. Baby Gretchen sat in the high chair with towels stuffed around her to keep her from slumping. Chloe had found some paper napkins in the back of the cupboard and passed them around to the children, showing them how to keep it on their laps. "Before taking a drink from your water glass, dab your mouth like this," she was saying when the deep voices of her brothers were heard outside.

On rainy days farmers couldn't get into the fields, so they went to town. So today Daddy and Momma were shopping in Morgan Town. Michelle had gone along, saying she needed new clothes for school. Before they left, Chloe heard Daddy giving orders to the big boys to clean out the barn and to the younger boys to clean out the chicken coop. Chloe was babysitting. She had spent the morning cleaning the kitchen. She looked forward to making Peter's birthday cake while the babies were napping. He was five today.

At the slam of the screen door, irritation stabbed Chloe. She needed more time to teach the children table manners. The boys, loud and pushing one another, scraped their muddy boots on the gunnysacks in the porch before bursting into the kitchen, asking, "What's to eat?" Brent swung his leg over a chair to sit down.

"Yeah, we're hungry!" Howie said, mimicking his older brother's action. But when his leg failed to clear the chair back, he tipped it over with a crash. Little Peter giggled into his hand. This made Julie giggle, which made her cough, which sent a spray of soup from her mouth across the table.

"Eauh! You spit on me!" Travis cried, reaching across the table to shove his little sister in the shoulder.

"Leave her alone," Agatha said, "she didn't mean it."

"I said, 'What's to eat?'" Brent bellowed, banging his fist on the table. Soup bowls jumped, and so did the little ones. Gretchen, in her high chair, puckered her face and let out a wail.

"You're scaring the baby!" Chloe scolded, lifting Gretchen from the high chair.

"Yeah, Brent, take it easy," Owen chided, father-like. He stood at the counter, sawing a loaf of homemade bread and knocking crumbs to the floor. Brent turned the radio up and music blared through the kitchen.

Chloe tensed. Outside a soft steady rain streamed down upon the farmyard, making everything muddy. Inside, the house was dull and gray. She wanted to get the children out of the boys' way. A mangy cat had followed the boys inside and was hungrily licking the floor beneath the table. Brent kicked it with his boot and the cat screeched, scooting into the porch. "You hurt the kitty!" Peter cried.

"Don't take it out on the cat just 'cause Cindy turned you down for a date," Owen drawled, buttering a thick slice of bread.

"She didn't turn me down. She's at her grandma's for the week."

"Yeah? That was some grandma she was with at Ben's Ballroom," Owen said, smirking.

Brent sprang from his chair to shove his older brother. But it was like shoving a steer. Owen's arms were thick and swarthy, his legs like pillars.

"Truth hurts!" Owen said coolly, about to take a big bite out of his bread.

Brent rammed his arm with his shoulder, knocking Owen's bread to the floor, face down. Owen picked it up, his blue eyes cold and bright. Chloe, with Gretchen in her arms, began to urge the little ones to leave the table. "Come on now, you're done eating, let the big boys eat." She said, but the children didn't budge. Splat! Owen's slice of bread landed on Brent's cheek and stuck there. The little kids laughed out loud. When Brent swatted it to the floor, Chloe cried, "My clean floor!"

"Shut up, you old nun!" Brent said, grinding Owen's bread into the floor with his heel.

"Is that necessary?" Owen asked. Brent charged him like a bull and grabbed his arm, twisting him to the floor. But Owen took Brent with him, and a great grunting and heaving and swearing followed as arms and legs flailed against the chairs, knocking them down. The boys' hard boots hit against the white metal cupboards.

"Come on kids! Out! Let's get out!" Chloe yelled, tugging at little arms. But they seemed mesmerized by the fight and wouldn't budge. "Come on! Let's go ride on the train!" She shouted louder, and they moved cautiously, their frightened eyes fixed on their cursing, grunting brothers splayed out on the floor.

"Go down to the silo. Don't mind the rain, it won't hurt you! I'll be right behind you." With little Gretchen bouncing on one hip Chloe grabbed Peter's hand and ran jerkily after the others. Julie followed, carrying the mangy cat, while Agatha brought Warren.

Once inside the feed shed Chloe comforted the little ones, hugging and reassuring the ones who were crying. Get up in the train, I'll give you a ride," she urged. The "train" was a strong wooden wagon the size of a bathtub that hung from a track in the ceiling. Daddy had built it to make moving the silage along the length of the feeding barn easier. After filling it at the silo, it could be pushed along the entire length of the barn for handy unloading for the steers. It made a great ride-on toy. The children scrambled aboard, sniffing and wiping their noses with their shirts. "Choo-Choo! All aboard for St. Paul and Minneapolis!" Chloe sang as she pushed the loaded cart to the other end of the barn. It rumbled and swayed, giving the children a thrill, and quieting the babies until all were laughing and happy, their bright tears still sparkling on their little cheeks. The steers watched with solemn eyes as back and forth they rode. Eventually Gretchen fell asleep, nestled on Veronica's lap.

After a while Chloe sent Agatha back to the house to see if the boys were gone. "Sneak around through the grove and listen at the back door!" she advised. Agatha came back saying the house was empty. "There's no one around and it's as quiet as a mouse! But you should see the kitchen!" she said, rolling her eyes. "It's a mess!"

By the time Michelle and Daddy and Momma walked through the door with their packages, Chloe was seething. She had cleaned up some, wiped up the butter and picked up the chairs, but the floor looked as if she had never washed it. The little ones cried the moment they saw Momma. The table was still cluttered with soup bowls, and Peter's birthday cake had not been baked. Luckily Momma had bought lollipops, which satisfied the children immediately. Dad set a large box of groceries on the table, and Michelle poured herself a drink of Kool-aid, saying, "Chloe, did you know Gladys isn't going back?"

Chloe felt as though a softball had struck her in the stomach. "Who says?"

"Lucy Fry. She said Gladys is all signed up at Chester High." Michelle regarded Chloe through half-closed eyes while she downed her Kool-aid. Chloe sank into a kitchen chair. This news, coming on top of the dreadful afternoon sucked all the joy from her heart. "Satan truly does go about like a roaring lion, seeking whom he may devour," she thought. Chloe glared at Michelle as though she were a co-conspirator with him. But Michelle couldn't know the impact of her words. She was of the world. What was just gossip to her was devastating news to Chloe. A precious vocation might be lost.

Momma, already sifting flour for Peter's birthday cake, chided, "Michelle, tell Chloe the whole story. It's getting harder for Mrs. Gehring to walk, and she needs to be in a wheel chair. She can't handle Jimmy by herself, so she said Gladys had to stay home for the next three years. But she plans to go back to the convent after she graduates."

Chloe breathed easier. Gladys's vocation was still intact.

"Yeah, Gladys begged and cried, but her mother wouldn't budge," Michelle added. Chloe fled to the quiet of her room. She took out her little blue notebook and checked off her prayers for the day, chagrined that her fifteen-minute meditation was yet undone. That was the hardest duty to keep. It was almost impossible to think holy thoughts for that long a time, and yet, every day, she had to try. She opened *Exploring the Holy Life*, and tried to read. The hubbub of family life drifted up to her; a baby crying, pots and pans clashing, Michelle's and Mother's voices together in happy unison. And above it all, laughter of children glad to have their world returned back to normal again.

Chloe pictured Mrs. Gehring in her quiet house, seated in a wheelchair while Gladys set the table and poor vacant Jimmy stared straight ahead.

The following Sunday at Mass, Chloe watched for Gladys, expecting her face to be red and swollen from tears. But instead, her calm demeanor and her clear brown eyes smiling sweetly, made Chloe doubt the news. After Mass, as the three aspirants met together, Gladys confirmed the news; she was not returning to the Heights. Jealousy and awe made Chloe stare at her as she tried to picture meek, pleasant Gladys walking the halls of *public school*. It was like throwing a lamb to the lions. Would she date? Would she keep up with her prayers? How would she preserve her vocation?

"Does Sister Damien know?" Chloe asked.

Gladys nodded. "She talked to Mom. I talked to her, too. She says this is my cross." Her lips quivered, and her Adam's apple bobbed in her pretty white throat. "I told her I'll be back. In three years we'll all be together again—as postulants!" Gladys's eyes glistened as they glanced from Lucy to Chloe. Chloe rode home silently from church, replaying over and over again Gladys's brave words. She felt ashamed. She knew that if she had the same news she would not grieve. She wanted to go to Chester High, live at home and taste the world before putting it all behind her. But Gladys's cross was not hers. She carried a different one.

Fall came and Mr. Fry drove only two girls back to Mater Dei. Lucy had a stylish new haircut and was wearing a new skirt and sweater, with a matching bandanna around her neck. Chloe wanted to ask her if she was glad to go back. She wanted to ask her how she felt, how her summer had been. Lucy broke the silence. "I bet Gladys will be popular at Chester High."

"Not too popular, I hope," Chloe replied. Lucy turned blue eyes on her, saying, "Her vocation will just get stronger there."

"If that's true, what are we doing at Mater Dei?" Chloe remarked dryly, rolling her eyes towards Lucy, ready to discuss further this subject of vocations and persevering. But Lucy dropped her eyes to the floor. "Oh, it was just an idea I had, didn't mean anything," she said, stretching her legs and yawning before settling back in her seat, her face turned to the window.

Ahead, a few brilliant clouds hung suspended in a bright blue sky. With the humidity gone, the air was clear, and they could see for miles, except for where the tall fields of corn blocked their view for miles on end. Hints of orange tinged the edges of the trees. As the car wound its way steadily back to the Heights, a great empty space yawned inside of Chloe, full of questions she couldn't ask.

CHAPTER 20.

Harvest Letter

"I like being a sophomore," Chloe wrote home in mid-October. Had she been permitted to seal her own letter she would have added, "Sister Damien doesn't treat us like babies this year." For instance, she and Kay had been allowed to skip mending class one Saturday to help the boarders make centerpieces for the annual Chicken Dinner. Last Saturday, she and three other aspirants had been allowed to walk downtown to choose fabric for their home-economics project. True, they had received strict instructions not to accept a ride from any day students they might meet, or to enter any store other than Sears, and to be back by two. But still, it was a thrill to go to downtown Magnolia at all.

One noon at mail call, Chloe heard her name called, and her stomach tingled joyfully as she pushed forward, hand outstretched, to receive her letter. Just seeing her mother's large scrawl on the envelope gave her joy, a feeling of being loved. The envelope, already slit open, revealed the folded letter inside, enticing and promising, written on the scented lavender stationary. But she was learning this year to deny herself legitimate pleasures so that she might grow in self-discipline. Sister called it "the habit of sacrifice." So instead of reading it, she tucked it into her uniform top to read after school. All day it sat there, close to her heart, like a promise. Then she forgot about it until the Grand Silence bell had rung and she was undressing behind her screen. It fell to the floor.

Behind the privacy of her screen she read her mother's words, oblivious to the usual noises of her dorm mates preparing for bed; water splashing, shoes dropping, wooden screens scraping and softly padded slippers sliding on the floor.

> "Dear Chloe,
>
> How are you? We're in the middle of corn picking and I've been feeding about six (extra) men a day, three times, plus the kids. It's a lot. I barely get done washing the dishes from one meal and it's time to turn around and start all over again. Michelle stayed home from school all last week to help me. But this week she has tests. Travis was sick with a high fever and delirium and I had to check him constantly. I don't know what it was. Tonight I'm so tired I could drop. This harvest will go on for weeks. We have such a good crop, for which I'm thankful, and I don't mean to complain, but ..."

The next morning Chloe awoke with a weight on her heart. She reached under her pillow and felt her mother's letter. All night it had troubled her dreams. The corn picker was chasing her mother up and down the rows. With the dawn she saw clearly. Here she was, performing small acts of self-denial while ignoring an obvious need: Momma needed her. Why had she not seen it this summer? It would have been so easy to stay home, as Gladys had done. A decision, a few phone calls, a letter, and it would all have been settled. Regret plagued her. She felt ashamed for so easily using her vocation as an excuse to escape the drudgery of home. What had the apostle John written? "Whoever sees his brother in need and shuts up his heart from him, how does the love of God abide in him?" There was only one thing to do. It would be hard, but she must not delay.

"Are you okay?" Kay cast her friend an anxious glance as they left the cloakroom and breathed in the late afternoon air. Songbirds twittered all about the campus. To the west the setting sun behind the boarders' woods glittered like a brilliant jewel broken into a million pieces. She would miss this place and Kay. There would be no good-byes, just a terse announcement, and her name would not be spoken again.

"You're not listening to a thing I've said!" Kay protested. "Do you feel all right?"

"I feel fine. I've got a lot of homework," she lied. She felt queasy at the thought of what she must do. The next evening during study hall she watched for a chance to talk to Sister Damien, her stomach jumping and twitching until it turned to liquid. She hurried to the bathroom and returned to her seat. Then, her hands clammy, she rose and approached Sister Ruth's desk to ask permission to see Sister Damien. Her mouth felt so dry she could hardly speak.

Approaching Sister's door, she steeled herself against the arguments that were sure to come. Spasms pierced her stomach. As much as she hated this, she must do this for Mamma's sake. She knocked. In one hand she clutched the letter like a weapon.

"Come in. May I help you?" Sister's pretty eyebrows arched questioningly.

"Yes, Sister, do you have a few minutes?"

"Yes, could you wait a few moments, please?" Chloe nodded and waited an agonizing few minutes outside the door, dreading lest another girl pass by and wonder about her. When Sister said, "Okay, Chloe, come in," Chloe burst into the room clumsily. Sister continued making notations in a book. When she looked up at last she asked sweetly, "What may I do for you this evening?"

"Did you read this letter from home?" Chloe burst out, clasping it to her breast like a shield.

"Was there bad news? Did I miss something?" Sister looked alarmed.

"Well, not bad news exactly. It's just that, well, things are getting bad at home. I've never heard my mother go on like this. There's so much work. Sister, I've been thinking, I mean I know, ah, I've decided that I must leave the villa. My mother needs me, and it's the only right thing to do." Chloe ended in a strong voice, looking boldly into the green eyes of the mistress of aspirants.

"What did she write?" Sister's voice was flat.

"Well, it's harvest time, and the corn-pickers are there, and Mom has to feed them all and it's so much work. She needs help! She says she could get it all done if someone were there to help with the kids. I know it must be getting her down, or she would never have written a letter like that. She might even be pregnant for all I know."

Chloe placed the letter into Sister's outstretched hand, and she read it silently, concern written in every line of her fine features. Finished, she lifted her green eyes to Chloe's and seemed to meet her at her very center. "From this you have decided to abandon all the good work you've started here?"

"Yes, Sister." Chloe straightened her shoulders. "I can't bear knowing she is suffering, doing all that work. I believe my place is there beside her."

Sister squinted as though trying to recall something. "I thought … you had an older sister … Michelle, is it? Is she not living at home?"

"Oh, yes, Michelle," Chloe waved her hand, dismissing her sister. "She's a cheerleader this year, and all she thinks about is boys. She's really not much help." Shame at exaggerating her sister's faults lapped at her conscience like flames, but she needed to show the strength of her conviction. Sister Damien looked concerned. "Harvest time will be over soon, won't it?"

"Yes, but the situation won't change much. Farmwork never lessens, it just keeps on coming."

"I see." Sister nodded. "Even in winter?"

"Oh yes, on the farm there's always work to do, especially for women."

"Chloe, do you like it here?"

"Yes, Sister, you know I do!"

"And what, exactly, do you like about it?"

A hot flush roared over Chloe's body at these questions obviously meant to dissuade her. She answered politely. "Well, my friends in the villa, the studies. You. I like the neatness and the order. That's what I like."

Sister pressed two clean white fingers to her lips. "Now Chloe, forgive me for questioning you, but I need to understand everything you are saying to me. This is a crucial step you are taking. You are willing to give up this orderly life here for the work and chaos of home?"

"Yes Sister. For my mother."

"But you still want to be a nun."

"Oh, yes Sister. I'll come back after high school, like Gladys," Chloe said, blinking.

Something, a flicker of irritation, a slight change in Sister's jaw, told Chloe she should not have mentioned Gladys.

"You realize that you would be giving up the very best education that you can get anywhere in Minnesota?"

"Yes, Sister. But I can't be selfish. You said yourself that love demands sacrifice."

Sister sat very still. When she spoke she sounded weary. "Chloe, I'm sure that you would be a great help to your mother. And you might do well in your public school. You are a sincere girl with high ideals. But we are all weak. You said yourself that your own sister is worldly. How long do you think it would be, Chloe, before your vocation would start to weigh on you? If you insist on making this sacrifice, as you call it, I am, frankly, worried for your perseverance."

Chloe looked intently at Sister. Her stomach started churning again. To insist she could persevere would be boasting, as Saint Peter had boasted before his denial of Christ. She must remember her main truth. "I love my mother, and love demands sacrifice, you said it yourself!" Chloe said, realizing she was repeating herself. She kept her jaw strong.

"You have a lucky mother, to be loved that much. Tell me, Chloe, does your father love your mother?"

"Why of course!" Chloe blinked at this sudden change in the subject.

"And where does *his* sacrifice come in?"

Chloe frowned. Sister didn't know much about farming if she thought *he* should help with housework! "Oh, he's way too busy to help in the house. We have a big farm with lots of land and buildings to keep up, and the machinery is always breaking."

"I know what farming is like." Sister interrupted.

"Well then you know how busy Dad is." Chloe replied.

"But he has time to make your mother pregnant, doesn't he?"

Chloe's mind reeled. She felt caught off guard. Never had she talked about such things with anyone and for Sister to bring it up here, now, was shocking. All her hot arguments fell in a heap as Sister's words went on to pierce her heart like ice picks. "You speak of sacrifice, Chloe, and love; all well and good. But I think the one who ought to be sacrificing is your father. Where is his love? Why must his daughter sacrifice her vocation because of his big family? I think you know, Chloe that such things are in his control."

Chloe nodded dumbly, groping feebly in her mind for a response. She felt oddly protective of her father. Also, Sister must not discover her ignorance on the subject of sex.

"That's not my concern," she said stiffly.

"Then why make the *result* your concern?"

Chloe knew she was defeated. She did not wish to continue with this unexpected twist of the conversation. She wished with all her heart that she had never come.

In a kinder tone Sister said, "Chloe, be careful that you don't step in with a sacrifice where God wants obedience."

Chloe felt weary. The room had become very warm. As they talked on, Chloe agreed that perhaps she had been hasty. She had not thought things through. She cried a bit and listened, sniffing and nodding in agreement as Sister spoke in a modulated tone; serene, understanding, and correct. Finally Sister asked, "Can you trust God for that Chloe?"

"For what, Sister?"

"To take care of your mother. And the babies. He made them, after all."

Chloe nodded. "Yes, Sister."

That night Chloe dreamt she was lost in a cornfield. The sun was hot, and she couldn't see where she was going. No matter how high she jumped, she couldn't see above the tassels. She started to climb a cornstalk, surprised that it held her. "Why didn't I think of this long ago?" she cried. But just as she reached the top the stalk broke and she dropped to the earth. She awoke in a sweat and kicked off her blankets. Then, shivering, she pulled them on again. Her whole body ached. Curling up, a gnawing sickness closed in on her. By morning she had a high fever, and she knew she had caught the Asian flu that was presently raging through Mater Dei Heights.

Chloe was sick for a week. Since the infirmary was full she stayed in her own bed. Each evening Sister Damien came to take her temperature and give her medicine. The first three days she slept, waking only for Kay Wakely's cheerful "Chow time girl, get your tray!" She would nibble her food and fall back to rest again. She had never felt so weak. Just lifting the fork to her mouth tired her.

On Sunday night, Angie Zimms, her merry eyes squinting mischievously, smuggled her radio wrapped in a towel, into Chloe's dorm. "Here, this will keep the days from being so long," she said, hiding it in Chloe's nightstand. The next morning, after the last door had slammed and the villa had fallen silent, Chloe plugged in the radio and set it up near her pillow where the sounds of the world could flow into her ear. It was almost as good as being home. The music, the humor, the newscasts, even the advertisements transported her to another place where life was easier and fun, where, instead of solemn reminders to be holy, there was a zest for living that made her want to sing and shout. The afternoon sun shining through the trees cast lazy shadows on her walls. Chloe dozed and woke to the three o'clock "hit parade." Love songs, so poignant they squeezed her heart with sadness, serenaded her on the airwaves. Though she had never been in love, a wistful craving for that experience possessed her. She wished to hold the hand of the boy crooning "A white sport coat and a pink carnation." "The world, what did she know about it? She had been a child in eighth grade, when Sister Clarice had first urged her to come here. But it was too late now." "They who put their hand to the plow and look back are not worthy of the kingdom of heaven."

Footsteps downstairs and a door slamming jerked her to attention. She snapped off the radio. Someone was climbing the stairs to her dorm.

It was Kay, carrying an armload of books. "You're falling behind, kid!" she said, dumping the textbooks on Chloe's bed. "But don't worry, girls are dropping like flies, and the whole school's closed till Monday!" Kay's eyes slid along the cord running from Chloe's bed to the wall socket. "Sister's coming with the medicine," she said, "let me help you clean up a bit, huh?"

By Friday night Chloe felt well enough to sit up and thumb listlessly through her textbooks. She was frowning over her Latin book when Sister Damien entered the dorm, smiling. "God must love you a lot!" she said, dropping a letter on Chloe's lap. Her green eyes held a bright expectant look. It was a letter from home. Chloe slipped the letter out of the opened envelope and read:

> "Dear Chloe, things are looking up here. I must have written that last letter to you when I was down. Dad surprised me with a clothes dryer last week so now I can dry the diapers inside. They come out so nice and fluffy! (But we still hang the other clothes outside to save electricity.) I don't want you to worry about us here. We are all fine. God will take care of us. Here is some spending money. (Dad got a good price on a load of cattle.)"

Chloe's hand closed around a ten-dollar bill. Never before had Momma sent so much money! Jubilation made her speechless. God was taking care of Momma. She smiled up at Sister Damien as they shared the moment. God had honored her trust and rewarded her obedience.

After Sister was gone, Chloe snuggled under her blankets and let relief spread through her whole self. No longer did she question where her duty lay. Free from guilt, she sighed deeply and slept sweetly all through the night.

CHAPTER 21.

Teela

As the sophomores gathered in the villa's recreation room, waiting for instructions to begin, Chloe flopped on the couch next to Kay. The two giggled over a silly remark. Through the basement windows they could see dead leaves sliding along the sidewalk. Winter was coming.

"I'm happy!" Chloe realized. Life at the villa pleased her, and her classes this year challenged her to new levels of learning. She still missed home, and sometimes her longing for Momma hurt like a hunger pang. At such times she took out a ragged snapshot of the whole family seated on the couch, and stared at it until she could almost hear her mother's voice and feel her big chapped but gentle hands touching hers. There were other longings too, strong and urgent, making her want to ... do what? Have fun? Something more; to know the big world beyond and explore . . . what? Often her own thoughts confused her. Just when she felt steadied by her strong faithful potential, something else, quite the opposite, rose up in rebellion and rattled her peace. But she was determined. Nothing must interfere with her vocation.

This fair evening, with her friend, Kay, beside her, and everyone chatting away cheerfully, Chloe knew happiness. This was her family, all aspiring to a high goal. Yes, it demanded sacrifice, but that was the price one paid to become a bride of Christ.

"You're getting it!" Mabel Sappe shouted between laughs as she watched Angie Zimms make a pom-pom from yarn. Angie's merry eyes squinted happily as she wound the red yarn.

"Don't wind too tightly," Lena Betters chided. Lucy sat with Jay Preston, a new, athletic-looking girl with short hair who played basketball like a boy. Jay had made the school team. Her lithe moves on the court had endeared her to the day students, so that they had voted her team captain - a "first" for an aspirant, Sister Damien said. Chloe admired Jay's quiet confidence. Her boyish good looks and her finely chiseled features held an aura of calm strength. "Why had she left her public school? Had she dated? Mater Dei must be a drastic change for her." Chloe wished to ask Jan about these things, but it was a worldly concern that must not be broached.

Another classmate, Aimee Stokes, was built like a twelve-year-old. Small and pale, she wore her straight brown hair in a page cut. Chloe thought she even acted like a child. Extremely bright in math, she irritated Chloe with her always agreeable remarks and her perpetual smile. Aimee came from a large family that had so far produced three priests and two nuns. Sister said that her parents would each get big crowns in heaven for their sacrifice of children and potential grandchildren. But Chloe suspected that Aimee was being pushed into becoming a nun. But again, she dared not ask such an unedifying question.

Sister Damien glided into the recreation room, her face glowing pink against her white head wrapping. It was 7 p.m., time for sophomore's instructions. After praying, Sister smiled at her sophomores and said, "Before we get started, I have an announcement."

Suddenly all went still. Each girl braced for the impending news.

"Teela Rodriquez left today." Chloe's heart lurched. Kay's mouth dropped open. Angie clapped her hand to her mouth; her eyes squeezed tight shut against this painful news. Aimee blinked blankly. Only Jay, the new sophomore, seemed calm. Since she had hardly had time to know Teela, she did not share the tremors passing through her classmates.

Teela was a senior, a petite Spanish girl with shiny black hair and a fetching smile. Everybody liked her. Chloe's mind flew back to last Friday's dance in the recreation room, when Teela had been teaching her classmates a new step, "the calypso." Her hips swayed, and her dark Spanish eyes laughed as she demonstrated the steps. Chloe loved how her silky black hair swung back and forth.

"She was fun," Aimee said.

"The life of the party," Chloe added.

"We're all going to miss her," Sister nodded sadly. "She's been with us since her freshman year."

"She would have made a wonderful nun!" Lena said. In the silence that followed Sister said, "It's always hard to lose a senior. We've invested so much in a girl by that time, so much love and time and care."

"What happened?" Kay's voice cracked.

Sister Damien folded her delicate hands together and rested her chin on them. With a look of exquisite tenderness she began: "Teela had a rough summer. As some of you know, her family is poor, and her dad had been out of a job for some time. Teela wanted to help out so badly. I advised against it, but she got a job as a waitress for the summer, and, well, she fell in with a bad crowd. Girls, it can happen so fast." Sister snapped her fingers. "Soon she didn't have time for prayer and meditation. Once a girl lets those things slip, it doesn't take long."

"But she came back!" Chloe cried, deeply moved. Sister's green eyes brimmed with tears as she said, "Yes, and that's what gave me such hope. But I didn't realize how far she'd fallen. She was ... deeply discouraged about ... certain things she did last summer, and she became convinced this life was not for her. Her classmates noticed the difference. Even her best friend, Lynn, could do nothing for her."

That evening as the girls ate their usual snack before bedtime, the chatter was noticeably subdued. Shock and sorrow still showed on everyone's face. When the bell rang for the Grand Silence to begin, the weak chatter faded easily, as though the girls were relieved to be left alone to absorb their loss in silence.

Undressing behind her screen, Chloe reached beneath her mattress and removed her diary. She scribbled, "Dear Mary, Teela's gone—Teela Rodriguez, with her laughing eyes and her bright white teeth. She was such a riot. I can't believe it. We're all gonna miss her. Lynn looks so lost. Remember when I couldn't recall her name in the contest last year? Now we're not allowed to speak her name. Why Mary? Why? She had such devotion to you. Remember the Spanish song she taught us: 'Oh Maria, Madre mea.' Help her Mary! Good Night. Chloe."

The next day all traces of Teela had been erased. Her name was removed from her dormitory door, and the cleaning duties list was retyped, minus her name. In study hall, instead of an empty desk where Teela had sat, there was no desk. It had been removed, and the others shoved together as though hers had never been there. Places at table were reconfigured so that no one faced an empty chair. But though her name had vanished, Chloe saw Teela everywhere; in chapel, in corridors, outside standing at bat, feet apart, cap askew. "She cut a cute figure," Chloe thought. One day she saw Teela's signature on the library card of a book. She stared at Teela's signature, trying to find in it a hint of the disturbance that Teela had known at home but that she hid so well when she lived at the villa.

During class Chloe daydreamed, picturing Teela as a waitress, flashing her warm smile as she set down a tray of Cokes. Once she thought she heard Teela's laugh. When she began to dream of Teela, Chloe got concerned. She felt guilty. But the more she tried to banish Teela from her thoughts, the more brightly her brown eyes laughed, intruding on Chloe's prayers and mocking her studies, until she finally decided to go to Sister for help.

But that night, after supper, Sister Damien asked the sophomores to stay behind after the tables were cleared and the dishes washed. Then, in the semi-darkened dining hall, against the comforting clank of pots and pans being washed by the novices in the outer kitchen, Sister said, "Girls, Teela came to the Heights today."

The girls stared dumbstruck, for they knew that once you left the Heights you were not allowed back for a visit.

"She begged so hard that Mother finally permitted this exception to the rule. It would have been cruel to refuse her."

"What did she want?" Chloe asked, her stomach churning.

"To see her true home, is how she put it." Sister's lip trembled. "If you could have seen how that girl cried! She literally threw her arms around me and sobbed. Her parents looked so sad. Oh girls! Don't ever think that you can bring your parents joy by abandoning God's perfect will for your lives. It just isn't so."

Chloe ached to comfort Sister. Before today she had not realized the depth of Sister Damien's love for her girls. Now she felt it deeply and wanted to give back just a bit of that love to her.

"Then I did something I've never done before: I let her visit her classmates."

Chloe started. Sister's eyes flared. "I won't say I'd do it again. It was very hard on the seniors. By the time it was over they were all sobbing. And do you know what Teela told them? That she would give anything—anything—to wake up to the villa bell again." A slight smile played on Sister's lips as she explained, "You maybe don't know this, but Teela used to get so mad at that bell! She'd ask why it couldn't ring a little softer; she'd get homesick too, so very homesick. But now she says she misses the villa ten times more than she ever missed her home."

"That's because she's lost more than just a home. She's lost a … a way of life." Chloe said in a husky voice.

"Exactly, Chloe. I couldn't have said it better myself."

Chloe was embarrassed by her own outburst, though she meant every word. She felt the others' eyes on her as she basked in the joy of Sister's approval.

"Why can't she come back?" Aimee asked, tilting her head inquisitively. "Stupid child," thought Chloe. But the mistress of aspirants answered Aimee patiently. "If it were up to me, I would give her another chance. She could be an influence for good now that she sees what the world has to offer. But Mother won't hear of it. Once a girl walks away from all this," Sister waved her hand, "she's pretty much walked away from God."

In the evening gloom Sister said in a lighter tone. "Girls, Teela's suffering may all be worth it if just one girl settles it with the Lord tonight. If you haven't done so yet, embrace your vocation with all your heart. Thank God for it; ask Him to preserve it at *all costs*. You will never regret it. For you can never, ever out-give the Lord."

That night Teela waltzed into Chloe's dreams, smiling and carrying a tray of beer bottles. She tripped and the bottles crashed to the floor. But upon inspection, none of them were broken. "See what happens when you pray!" Teela crowed, picking them up one by one with a sly smile.

"Let's show Sister!" Chloe cried, sure that this "miracle" would convince Sister to let Teela back. But the morning bell rang, jarring Chloe from sleep before she could do it.

A few months later, on a rainy Sunday afternoon as Chloe was crossing the campus, thankful that her obsession with Teela was fading, she saw a couple on a motorcycle. Chloe was thinking of Teela's friend, Lynn, who had gone to the hospital for an emergency appendectomy. The man was tall and slim, with his black hair slicked back. He was wearing a black leather jacket. The girl seated behind him had a ponytail and big golden hoops in her ears. She wore tight blue jeans and a leather jacket. The girl was Teela. Chloe wanted to turn around, but it was too late. Her heart jumped into her throat. The man's hand rested on Teela's waist. How pretty and svelte, how totally worldly she looked.

Chloe felt dowdy in her black Sunday suit with her sagging nylons and scuffed flats. Should she say hello? It was not allowed. But should she be rude and ignore her? Her conscience jumped back and forth as she drew closer. "Did Teela remember how it had been to live like this, like a child weighing every tiny thing against a rule? By now she must have made decisions far more important than whether or not to greet someone."

"Hi! Teela!" Chloe blurted out, bravely including the man in her smile. She could make up her own mind and decide what was right to do in social situations.

"Hi. How ya doin?" Teela's brown dyes appraised Chloe coolly from beneath her arched eyebrows.

"Fine. How are you?"

"Oh groovy, just groovy!" Teela's lips twisted into a wry smile. Chloe kept walking, glad to move on, glad she had greeted her. 'Had anyone seen her?" She glanced up at the windows of the villa. Then she remembered about Lynn. She spun around. The couple was getting ready to leave, the man's foot ready on the motorcycle's pedal.

"Teela!"

The thick ponytail swung around.

"Lynn's in the hospital, downtown. She had an appendicitis attack," Chloe shouted, forgetting her embarrassment, caring only that Teela knew about her friend.

"Is she okay?"

"Yes, she's in the hospital."

"Hillside or Catholic?"

"Catholic."

"Thanks." Teela flashed her white teeth in a smile.

"You're welcome." Chloe felt breathless, as if she had just run a race. As she slipped inside the villa door, she heard the motorcycle roar away. She leaned against the door with a feeling of satisfaction. She felt grown-up. She had accomplished a mission and done the right thing. She had broken a rule, yes, but she had kept another, of love, and she felt good about it. "Thank you, God!" she breathed as she trudged up the stairs to her dormitory, where the voices of her girlfriends playing a Sunday afternoon game of charades drifted down to her.

A few weeks later, walking through the corridor leading to the dining room, someone suddenly grabbed her arm. Chloe looked into Lynn Dalhset's gray-blue eyes. "Thanks Chloe, it meant a lot to me," she said.

Chloe started. "Did she visit you?"

Lynn put a finger to her lips, nodding.

CHAPTER 22.

Interpersonal Problems, Jealous of Lena

When Chloe's parents wrote saying they would not be coming up for Chicken Dinner this year because "The harvest is late, and we have to work every day and night before the snow flies," Chloe was thankful for the extra day of study. A Latin test loomed, a world history report was due, and Sister Bruno wanted a sonnet written for English class. Suddenly Chloe noticed her own thoughts and marveled. "I must be maturing, to prefer studying to my family's visit!" This year she would be like Lena Betters, whose family never came for Chicken Dinner Sunday.

But when the day came, Chloe found studying difficult with the Heights swarming with visiting families. Though she smiled, a knot of resentment growled inside her. By the time she and Lena were called to join in on the after-dinner cleanup, Chloe was smoldering.

"How can you stand it?" she exploded to Lena the minute they got outside.

"Stand what?" Lena asked, turning a sweet face toward Chloe.

"Not seeing your family!" she exclaimed.

"I know they can't be here," she said, shrugging, "and that settles it."

"Just like that?" Chloe asked, incredulous. Lena nodded and Chloe burned. "What made her so demure and submissive?" It maddened Chloe. "Why, a chair could fall down on top of her and she wouldn't let out a peep!" Chloe complained later to Kay as they took their evening stroll to the cemetery.

"What's wrong with that? It shows self-control," Kay chided, "and isn't that what we're always taught, to control ourselves?"

"But it's not natural!" Chloe cried.

"No, it's supernatural," Kay said, "Isn't that what we're striving for, to live supernaturally and not naturally?"

Chloe knew Kay was right. She should rejoice at Lena's self-control, not rail against it. That Thursday afternoon in the shadows of the confessional, Chloe crossed herself and said, "Bless me Father for I have sinned, my last confession was a week ago. Since then I have hated someone twelve times." When she was through confessing, Father Schlick cleared his throat and bent his face close to the screen. Chloe could feel his warm breath and hear him lick his lips before he whispered, "When we hate someone it's often because we are jealous of her."

Back in the brightness of the chapel, Chloe recited her penance; five Our Fathers and five Hail Mary's, and remembered Father's words. He was right, she was jealous of Lena because no matter how hard she tried, she could not be as good as her. When she thought a rule was stupid, she complained. For instance, what was the harm in talking in the bathrooms? It seemed like just another silly rule to squelch them. But when she expressed this complaint to Lena, Lena just smiled and said, "They don't want us hanging around in the bathroom, that's all."

Besides feeling guilty for hating Lena, she envied her contentment. So, to make herself feel better, she doubled her penance and prayed an extra Hail Mary for Lena.

Soon the sophomore school year was over. It was May, and once again the aspirants swarmed over the campus with suitcases and boxes, saying good-byes to one another and "See you next fall!" and shouting "You better write!" across the busy campus. Chloe and Kay hugged and looked deep into each other's eyes. "You better come back!" Kay admonished.

"Of course I will!" Chloe mumbled. Did Kay doubt her?

"You better!" she shouted before running back to the villa for her other suitcase.

"And you too!" Chloe called after her.

CHAPTER 23.

Sophomore Summer—Max

"Just think! We'll be juniors next year!" Chloe said to Lucy. Sister Damien, the villa and the Mater Dei routine seemed far away on that perfect summer's day at Dawson Park. The sky was positively the brightest blue she had ever seen. And the sun was hot. A big crowd had turned out for the Farmer's Union Fourth of July picnic. From where Lucy and Chloe sat on the hood of Mr. Fry's car, they could see the circle of grown-ups sitting in the shade, talking and guarding the tables full of dishes and food covered with white towels to keep away the flies. Babies toddled under their mothers' watchful eyes. To their left a large swimming pool glittered and rang with the cries of many children.

The two aspirants combed their wet hair and set it in bobby pins. Chloe tingled with excitement. All afternoon two boys from Dawson had pestered them, following them around and asking them their names. Then in the pool the same two boys had splashed them until they screamed. They dared Lucy to go off the high dive, which she did, dropping like an eagle to the water, while Chloe watched from below. She felt giddy with joy. So far, this was the best summer of her life—and she had not compromised her vocation once. She was glad Sister had said, "By all means, be friendly to boys. You don't have to be stuck-up." But the two boys in the pool were small fish compared with what was coming tonight. Tonight Chloe had a date with Max.

It wasn't exactly a date. Aspirants didn't go on dates. The two aspirants were just going to the movies with two guys who were just riding along with Brent and his girl. It didn't mean a thing. They were going to have "good clean fun" as Sister always said they should have. Chloe hadn't explained everything to her mother exactly the way it was going to happen. Ever since Sister Damien had written that letter to her parents asking them to "guard the precious vocation of your daughter with the same diligence as we do up here," Momma was asking more questions than she had before. So Chloe had made the evening out sound like a night out with her brother, which it was, in part.

"With Brent?" Momma had looked surprised, "Brent's taking you to the movies?"

Chloe tried to sound casual. "Yes, we made a deal that if I washed the station wagon for him, he'd take us along."

"Us?"

"Yeah, me and Lucy. And a couple of Brent's friends, as long as Brent does chores first," Chloe said airily, her stomach fluttering. She felt like a naughty teenager, planning an evening based on half-truths.

"Well," Momma said, "I'm glad to see you and Brent getting along. I always knew you could if you'd just give each other a chance."

Chloe had bit her tongue and dashed away before her mother asked any more questions.

"I hope my hair's dry by tonight," Chloe said, noticing how Lucy's blonde hair curled even when damp. Her own hair fell straight as a stick. They spread a blanket on the grass and lay face down so the sun could dry their hair. Every now and then Chloe glanced up to check if the station wagon was still there. She didn't quite trust Brent to stick to his half of their agreement. He might leave without them. Satisfied, she shut her eyes and stirred luxuriously on the sun-warmed blanket. Sister Damien could say all she wanted to about the emptiness of worldly joys. She had never been happier or felt more fulfilled than she did right now. And she knew it was mainly because of the boys in the pool and her own wildly racing heart every time she thought of Max.

Max, a town boy from Chester, had a long droopy face and a sad-sack smile. He worked at the Red Owl Grocery Store, and he was Catholic. Chloe liked the droll way he told a joke, with a cigarette hanging loosely from his lips. He made her laugh.

Lucy would be paired up with Floyd, an old friend from their eighth-grade class, and Brent was picking up his protestant girlfriend in Morgan Town.

This sophomore summer Chloe had discovered how fast time could fly just being with kids her age, doing nothing more than talking and laughing. So far this summer Chloe had gone to two dances and she was allowed one more. There were so many to choose from. Every Friday or Saturday night some couple's wedding dance was held at Ben's Ballroom in Fairview. For fifty cents anyone could attend, and the ballroom was always packed with friends and relatives from miles around. It was the perfect place for boys and girls to meet.

Thanks to the villa and its Friday night dances "for exercise," Chloe knew how to dance. She could waltz, fox-trot, jitterbug and polka. Plus she had discovered to her great delight that boys liked her. When one leaned over her in the booth, just behind her parents' heads, to ogle her, she felt as if she had arrived. Some would even dare to ask her for a dance. And, once out the dance floor, they would ask such things as, "Where have you been all my life?" or "How come I've never seen you before?" but she knew how to be coy. She skirted their questions and kept to her rules. She didn't dance slow dances or let anyone kiss her. Also, she did not dance with the same boy twice. That would be inviting temptation. When she introduced a boy to her dad, he always wanted to know his last name. That alone gave her father a background, a family, and often a religion to judge the boy by.

Of course she could not let a boy take her home. Sister Damien had made it plain in instructions that that was forbidden. So when a boy asked, "Can I take you home?" Chloe answered that her dad didn't allow it. But she would never say that she was studying to become a nun!

But afterward, seated between her parents' car in the dark, skimming toward home over the black straight roads, she had felt hot tears of regret. It wasn't fair. Other girls, younger and duller than she, were right now seated next to a boy with the radio playing and his arm around her. Maybe he was offering her a cigarette. And when they arrived at her home he would walk her to her front steps and attempt a good-night kiss.

Tonight Chloe would experience something close to that. Exactly what, she didn't know. No kisses, for sure, because she had resolved not to let that happen. But she would enjoy everything else, the jokes, the banter, the flirting. She might even languish in Max's long and lanky arms for just a few minutes. Surely there was nothing wrong with that.

"Yes, God, you have my heart. But today I'm going to take this one thing for myself," she prayed, her face hot against the blanket. "It's not a real date because I won't be alone with him." Chloe opened one eye as two boys strolled by. She did not know how to act on a date. Did Lucy? She had tried to broach the subject, but Lucy had closed her eyes and preferred to sleep. Was this her first date? Did she like Floyd just a little? Would she let him kiss her? Chloe had wanted to ask Michelle what to expect, but she didn't want to be found out. Chloe thought they ought to have a plan in case the boys wanted to park, but every time she tried to bring up the subject, Lucy either didn't catch on or didn't respond. Chloe sighed. Once again she must find her own answers and work her own plan.

CHAPTER 24.

Forbidden Feelings

"Hey, you girls! You still coming? We gotta leave now for chores!" Brent swaggered by with his buddy, Floyd. The girls scrambled off their blankets, gathered up their things and ran to the car. Chloe had brought her good clothes along to the picnic so she wouldn't have to go home to change. The boys kept to themselves during the long ride to Lucy's farm. There they dropped off the girls at the house, saying they would be back in a couple hours. "Floyd's got six cows to milk and we got ten new steers to feed, plus that load of sows," Brent said. "Then we gotta get Max in Chester," he added, winking at Chloe.

Lucy's home was clean and quiet, so different from Chloe's cluttered home. And since Lucy's family was still at the picnic, there was no one around. The kitchen floor gleamed, and the counters were cleared of everything but a row of red canisters with glass knobs with blue powder in the knobs. When Chloe asked Lucy what that was for, and she said it kept the contents fresh. Then she opened a canister and pulled out a cookie, giving it to Chloe. "See how fresh and crisp it still is?" she asked. Chloe nodded, thinking that at her house cookies didn't have a chance to get stale. Lucy's living room reminded Chloe of a magazine picture. Two lovely end tables with matching lamps stood on either side of the flowered couch. A low, modern piano stood against one wall with framed photos of the Fry family members displayed on top of it.

A large bay window to the west allowed a view of the lawn, the road, and the acres of cornfields beyond. A cloud of dust still hung over the road where Brent and Floyd had made their exit from the driveway.

Two hours seemed like a long time to get dressed. Chloe was used to throwing clothes on in a hurry. She wasn't used to primping before the mirror.

"We have two bathrooms," Lucy said, "so I'll take the upstairs one."

"Has it rained lately?" Chloe asked.

"What? I don't know. Why?"

"Is there enough water for a bath?"

"As much as you like," Lucy said easily, "We have two cisterns." As Chloe luxuriated in the bathtub with the warm sudsy water swirling up around her shoulders, a sweet effusive feeling came over her. At home baths were rare, because of the water shortage, and at the villa they were forbidden. Only showers were allowed, and they were limited to three minutes so as to avoid temptation to thoughts of impurity. After what seemed like a long time, Chloe got out of the tub and dressed. She had on a pink checked blouse with a boat neckline. It was tucked into a blue gathered skirt that she had made of polished cotton. Soft pleats fell from the tiny waistband. She felt pretty. On her feet she wore her white church flats. She wandered down to the living room and sat on the flowered couch. She could hear Lucy splashing in the tub upstairs. A television was pushed into a corner of the living room. She pushed a knob. After a few minutes the screen lit up. The picture was snowy with a static sound issuing from it. Chloe shut it off and sat waiting.

Bored, she kept looking out of the big picture window, but the road stayed empty. After leafing through a woman's magazine she looked through Lucy's stack of forty-fives, neatly tucked in a wire rack. She chose one and played it on the phonograph. Then she danced to the music, moving gracefully around the coffee table, keeping an eye on the driveway.

"I'm gonna sit right down and write myself a lettah,

And make believe it came from you.

Gonna write words—oh so sweet,

Gonna knocka me offa my feet . . .

A lotta kisses . . ."

Gratitude for this house, this clean, quiet house in which to dress for her first date, almost overwhelmed her. God was kind to let it happen like this. But she didn't want to think too much about God. Why would He want to bless her first date, anyway?

Lucy descended the stairs wearing a white dress with a can-can rustling beneath the skirt.

"Wow! You look great!" Chloe exclaimed.

"Thank you," replied Lucy, flouncing into the living room. "You look nice too. Did you want to use any of my makeup?"

A horn tooted. The girls rushed to the window and saw three boys seated in the front seat of the station wagon. Brent was at the wheel, Floyd next to him, and Max's narrow droopy face at the window, staring toward the house. He greeted Chloe with a wry smile as she bounded outside to greet him. He got out of the car, stretched his long legs and opened the back door. Her heart beat furiously as she climbed into the third seat. He followed close behind her. Lucy and Floyd sat in the middle seat.

Brent adjusted the rearview mirror saying, "I'll have to keep an eye on you lovebirds in the back!"

"Ah, shut up!" Chloe retorted, more vehemently than she intended. She felt instantly sorry, because Brent grimaced. She knew she had embarrassed him. An awkward silence followed as the car bumped over the potholes in the Fry's driveway. Brent's date lived in Morgantown, thirty miles away. Chloe sensed her brother's nervousness keenly and racked her brain for something smart to say, something that would show him that she was as relaxed and as clever as anyone else in the car. Lucy sat with her hands in her lap, clutching her small white purse.

Max finished his cigarette and patted his pockets for a match. Chloe, seeing the unopened cigarette pack in his shirt pocket, slipped it out, saying pertly, "I'll open this for you." She had never opened a pack of cigarettes before. When he saw her open the seams, he let out a vicious, "Damn you!" and grabbed it from her. "That's no way to open it," he said, shaking a cigarette out and jamming it into his mouth before trying to close the pack where she had ripped it.

"Here, I'll put back the cellophane," Chloe offered feebly, catching Brent's glare through the rearview mirror. He would never take *her* out with him again. She wanted to sink through her seat to the gravel road below. Brent turned the radio up loud, but all they could hear in the backseat was the wind rushing in at the open windows. The orange sunset in the western sky was muted, as though veiled by a thick layer of gauze.

In Morgantown, Brent drove up and down the unfamiliar residential streets looking for the right house. He continually checked a slip of paper in his hand, swearing as he made his second U-turn and headed down the same street again. He jabbed his cigarette in the ashtray, then lit another. At last they stopped in front of a neat white house with red trim. A sprinkler watered the grass. Flowers bloomed near two little white wrought-iron chairs. A little girl in shorts skipped towards them from the house and invited Brent inside. "Sherry's not ready yet," she said.

"That's all right, I'll wait," Brent said, getting out of the car and leaning against it. He bent toward the side view mirror, combing his slick black hair. He tucked in his shirt and glanced repeatedly toward the house. At last Sherry emerged, a pretty brunette in a green suit and high heels. She swung a large straw purse with a giant daisy tacked on the front. Brent jumped into the car and waited for her to get in. "Took you long enough!" he said good-naturedly as he turned the key and revved the motor. Sherry looked back toward the others and smiled, but no introductions were made. Brent had said Sherry was home from *college*. She was studying to be a teacher. Chloe stared at the back of her beautiful hair and wondered if she knew what a poor student Brent had been. He was handsome, maybe that's all that mattered to her.

As darkness approached Chloe felt less tense. She felt the others relax, too. Max cracked a joke. She laughed. They grinned at each other in the shadows. She wished Lucy would say something, but she was unusually quiet, gazing out at the cornfields as if they held great interest for her.

They arrived at a drive-in theater where a big sign announced, "One Dollar a Car!" Chloe's heart plunked like a stone into her stomach. Father Schlick had warned the day students continually against such places. "Going to a drive-in with a boy is the same as walking into a bedroom with him. And, anything that happens there is *your* fault for permitting it" Chloe glanced at Lucy who was searching in her purse for something and didn't look up.

Floyd and Max each dug in their pockets and gave fifty cents to Brent, who then maneuvered the behemoth station wagon to a spot where he could unhook a speaker and hang it on the window glass. This done, he slid out from behind the steering wheel and sat closer to Sherry. Darkness was falling fast. Max said his legs were cramped and would Floyd slide over toward Lucy so he could turn down the end-seat for leg room. Floyd complied gladly, and they all settled down to wait for the movie to start.

The big screen lit up with Woody Woodpecker streaking across it, laughing, "Ha ha ha ha ha!" over and over again. Max's long arm dropped from the backrest, where it had lain throughout the long drive, to Chloe's shoulders. An unexpected thrill shot through her, leaving her weak.

She could not follow the plot of the Western. As cowboys larger than life swaggered through dusty streets, she wondered what she should do if Max tried to kiss her. But he was enjoying the movie, laughing and smoking one cigarette after another. He offered her one, but she declined. He folded his lanky body out of the car once to get her a large bag of popcorn. As they munched it together she would occasionally look up at his sallow face, his hooded eyes, and he would slide his gaze from the cowboys on the screen to her and smile that charming downward tilting smile, almost like a sneer, that made her feel as if something were melting inside of her.

In the dark his face came toward her and he kissed her. Those thin, slightly pouting lips pressed hers ever so slightly, and her whole body tingled. His hand on her shoulder tightened, pulling her closer, and it felt heavenly being so close to him, feeling his warmth, smelling his cologne. She had never felt so alive or so happy. But she looked away coolly and asked, "Is the popcorn all gone?" Brent and Sherry in the front seat were slumped so low they could not even be seen. Floyd had his arm loosely around Lucy, who looked bored. Lucy is a good aspirant, Chloe thought. She hardly dared to look at Max, so strongly did her body react to the mere meeting of his eyes. "Father Schlick was right. Sin was easy." He said boys were beasts, with uncontrollable urges, and that girls are the guardians of purity. "How was she doing? Temptation alone was not a sin. But how many kisses made a mortal sin? Just one kiss had caused a sweet deluge to leap to life in her. What would happen if he kissed her again?"

Suddenly, without warning he leaned forward, pressing incredibly soft lips to hers. A shuddering sweetness engulfed her, and she wanted more, to kiss him again and again, to wrap her arms about him and feel his great lean chest against hers for a long time. Shocked at herself, she pulled away, pretending sudden interest in the Western movie. The pleasure galloping through her body slowly subsided. In its place crept a gnawing guilt. "Now you've done it!" she heard almost audibly and felt Father Schlick's eyes, like blue fire, on her.

"I tried not to sin, really I did!" she argued silently, while laughing outwardly at the movie with the others. But her heart curdled with fear. She, Chloe Polowski, who loved Jesus, and prayed and kept silence and performed acts of self-denial, had led a boy on. "Please God, take me back!" she pleaded, slipping her left hand to her side and pinching herself hard.

"Why so quiet?" Max asked in a feathery voice, inching closer, his sweet breath on her neck.

"Huh? Oh, this movie's boring," she said, "let me out for a while. I want to see if any of my friends are here."

"I'll go with you," he offered.

"No, that's all right," she said abruptly, shaking her head and fleeing, stumbling toward the bathroom. She blinked in the neon light, locked the door to her stall and took her rosary from her purse. She laid it on the toilet lid and knelt on it for penance.

"Hail Mary, full of grace, the Lord is with thee ..." Silently Chloe prayed while the sharp beads bit into her knees. Mortifying the flesh was the only way to conquer it. When the outer door opened she jumped off, flushed the toilet and stuffed her rosary into her purse, murmuring fervently, "Blessed Virgin, keep me pure."

For the rest of the movie Chloe sat with her knees up under her chin. Her skirt covered her to her ankles. She wouldn't mock God by praying for one thing, then indulging the other. On the way home she moved to the other side of the car, still holding Max's hand, but pushing him away whenever he tried to kiss her. At first he reacted to her mood by asking if she was mad.

"Why do guys always think a girl is mad at them just because she's tired of kissing?" She asked flippantly, fighting off the terrible pull of his chest so close to hers. He fell silent after that and they were quiet all the way to Morgan Town, where Brent walked Sherry to her door. He was gone for a very long time. Lucy and Floyd sat close together, saying little. Chloe made a few attempts at conversation, asking Max about his job at the grocery store. She asked so many questions that he finally said, "I'm tired of talking about my job, I'd rather talk about you," and pulled her toward him. His little-boy pout made her feel sorry for him, so she let him hold her hand and prayed for Brent's quick return. Dangerous sparks of feeling radiated from his touch, but she kept up the meaningless chatter, glad that Brent wasn't there to hear her. She wondered what Lucy thought of her.

Only when Brent returned and they were on their way again did she relax and move closer to Max, hoping she might enjoy the ride home. She wanted Max to like her. Outside, the brilliant stars punctuated the blackness like diamonds, and the moon was a silver sliver following them. Just as Chloe was wondering if she should permit a good-night kiss she realized that Max wouldn't be walking her to her door because he was staying at Floyd's house tonight. Soon it would be just her and her brother in the car.

Max didn't try to kiss her until one mile from Floyd's farm. Then his soft lips pressed hers, and she felt their tenderness but nothing more. She kissed him again, and it was victory. To her relief, all feeling was gone. The Blessed Mother had answered her prayer.

Monday morning dawned wet and gray. A fierce wind mixed with rain shook the trees in Huffiker's grove, sending leaves swirling through the air and plastering them against the windows. It was wash day, and the house smelled of Hilex. Chloe, on the porch, knelt over a mountain of dirty wash, sorting clothes; darks there, lights here. There was hardly room to walk. The two washing machines grunted sluggishly, "Rugga-rug, rugga-rug." The diapers, soaking in a large basin, gave off a bad smell.

To Chloe, it was as if the damp foul air had seeped inside of her. The drab sky mirrored her soul. Sometime during the night it had become clear to her that she had sinned mortally, and this conviction weighed on her like a wet blanket. Distant thunder warned her of God's wrath, growling at her from up there. She was out of grace. If she died before confession, she would go to hell. But Saturday confessions were a week away. Until then she must plod, downcast and dammed, begging God to spare her. But did God hear the prayer of the lost? She did not blame Max. He was only being natural. It was she who knew better, who was responsible. And now, for further punishment, she was in love. Max's slack jowls haunted her daydreams, and all last night while she slept his small pouty lips had floated toward her, threatening to arouse again those forbidden feelings. But with prayer and light sleeping she had been able to overcome, crying out, even in her dreams, "Jesus, Mary, and Joseph help me!"

Brent slept late. When he got up he sought out Chloe in the porch just as she was dumping a load of rinsed (but still stinky) diapers into the washing machine. She stiffened when she saw him. "Technically he was in mortal sin too, wasn't he? But maybe he didn't fully understand, in which case, was he excused?" "To whom much is given, from her much shall be required." She recalled. She dare not poke at the speck in his eye when she had a beam in her own.

"Have a good time last night?" he asked, his dark eyes friendly.

"Well, I would have preferred going to a theater instead of a drive-in movie," she said archly, dropping down to the stack of blue jeans and overalls to check the pockets for nuts, bolts, and nails that might get caught beneath the agitator and cause it to screech.

"Why? Did Max get fresh?" he asked.

"No," she answered quickly. "It'd just be more classy, that's all, instead of staying in a car all night." She finished her sentence with more staccato in her voice than she intended.

"Oh, you're too good for a drive-in movie, huh?" Brent's boot scraped on the wooden floor. "Well, that's because you women don't have to pay a red cent when you go out. You're all alike, want a good time and don't give a damn if the boy has enough money to pay for it." Brent turned on his heel, kicking her hand as he left. She didn't cry out. In the state her soul was in, she needed punishment. She heard him banging doors in the kitchen in search of breakfast.

"I'm always disappointing him," she thought. "Just when he tries to be friendly I go and get smart with him." As she was already on her knees, Chloe prayed silently as her hands roamed quickly in and out of the dirty pockets, ferreting out forgotten treasure and tossing it into a bowl. She found a dime and a nickel and put them in her pocket. But even as she prayed she knew the sinking feeling of being separated from God. She had never felt this way before. The pleasure she had enjoyed last night had plunged her soul into darkness. She had never looked forward so eagerly to Saturday night confessions as she did now.

The rest of the summer was lonely for Chloe. On balmy nights she wandered the farm looking up at the moon. She sat on the barn's lean-to and looked toward the lights of Chester, thinking how nice it must be to live in town and be able to walk uptown, meet friends and order a soda at the corner café. All that would all be innocent enough; and it would be enough. Max had not come back. But his face was as clear to her as the face in the moon, and hovering just as insistently in her mind.

On a hot summer day as Chloe and her mother drove through Morgan Town, her mother parked on Main Street saying, "I need you to run into the Red Owl for some bread." Usually Chloe loved to run errands while Momma waited, but now her stomach lurched in alarm. Max worked there.

"You just baked bread," Chloe said.

"Yes, but did you notice how fast it's going?" Momma handed Chloe a five-dollar bill. She felt nauseous getting out of the car. Vagrant pains, like needles, probed her stomach as she entered the store. "I can say 'hi,'" she told herself bravely, her throat suddenly going dry. She would obey her mother; she headed toward the bakery aisle. Then she saw him, his lanky body leaning over a grocery box, removing cans and stacking them on a shelf. The needles jabbed her full force in the stomach. She ducked down another isle while a deep, sudden pain spread upward to her chest. Panicked, she hurried from the store. Without looking back she jumped into the car, saying, "I can't get the bread, Momma, I'm sick." She lay down on the front seat, groaning as she held her stomach. “You must have the flu,” Momma murmured sympathetically as she drove home without the bread. But by the time they reached home Chloe’s stomach ache was gone. Her mother’s worried look subsided as Chloe hopped from the car. “It must have been the heat,” Chloe lied. It gets me like that sometimes.”

CHAPTER 25.

Junior Year

"Mom, can I order two new uniforms for next year? The ones I have are so worn and the blouses are frayed at the cuffs!" Chloe shouted over the rattle of the sewing machine where her mother sat, mending overalls. All around her stood large cardboard boxes dragged out from storage, each overflowing with overalls and blue jeans that needed mending.

"Oh, sure! And order that pink housecoat you liked. Crops look good this year." Momma smiled at Chloe, seated at the living room table with the Sears Catalog open before her. Then Momma whispered, "Oh, look!" pointing to little Gretchen, nestled between the two large boxes. She had burrowed her little head into a pile of overalls and fallen asleep. "She needed a nap," Momma cooed, straightening out a little bent leg and covering her with a nearby white T-shirt.

"Looks like she just keeled over while crawling!" Howie whispered, chuckling. He was sitting half clothed in the rocking chair with a towel over him, waiting for Momma to patch a pair of jeans for him. Early that morning Momma had pulled the big boxes out from the closet under the stairs, saying, "I need to get at this patching while you're still home. Without someone to do the cooking and baby tending I can't keep at it like I need to."

"You always have Michelle," Chloe said, clamping her teeth on her pencil.

"Yes, but she's lost a lot of interest in helping me. Maybe you've noticed. With boys and football games on her mind, who can blame her? She works harder at home than any of her friends, and I don't want to nag her to do more."

Chloe paused. She had not lost interest in helping Momma. She loved tending the babies and playing with the toddlers. "Coming home from school every day to this house would be like heaven even on rainy days," she thought. The screen door slammed. Brent leaned into the doorway of the living room, a scowl on his face. He was bare back, and his brown skin glistened with sweat. Chloe tensed. She couldn't resist putting her finger to her lips and pointing toward the sleeping child. "Shhh"

Brent grimaced. "Almost ready Howie?" he said to his younger brother. "It ain't gett'n any cooler out there!" He spoke in a low even tone, hard with authority. His boots scuffed authoritatively on the linoleum.

"He'll be ready in a minute!" Momma said, leaning her knee into the lever while her expert hands steered the denim fabric into the path of the chattering needle. All conversation ceased for a while. "Brent would be handsome," Chloe thought, "if he'd ever smile. Nobody likes a crab. But maybe he wasn't crabby around girls like he was at home." He looked taller. Summer's work of stacking bales had sculpted and carved his body into a lean taut image bulging with muscles. But his disapproval of her hurt like a bristle brush. Ever since the night of the drive-in movie he hardly looked at her, as if her very presence galled him. It was true what Sister Damien said, "Your enemies will be those of your own household."

"AHhhmm!" Brent exclaimed, glancing out of the window. "Max is here." He cocked a quick glance at Chloe, who froze, unable to move due to the panic surging in her breast.

"You go out and see him," she pleaded.

"No, you go!" he said, pushing her shoulder. Then in a friendlier tone he said, "He just wants to say 'hi,'"

Chloe backed away from the window as familiar pains gripped her stomach. "You go, Brent, please. Tell him I'm not home."

"Oh, lie, will you?" Brent sneered as Chloe dashed up the stairs. He had reason to despise her. But what Brent or anyone thought of her mattered little when her stomach hurt so. She threw herself across her bed. "Was it her appendicitis? Would she die?" She curled up, kneading her stomach and moaning, wondering what was wrong with her.

She heard a car leave the gravel driveway, but she did not rise up to look. Quickly her stomachache subsided. Later Brent said to her, "You're strange." His jaw was set tight in disapproval. "Or stuck-up. What's wrong with you, anyway? You can't even say hello to a guy?"

"I don't have to if I don't want to!" Chloe turned away to cover up her shame. Far better that Brent think her stuck-up than learn the truth: she wasn't normal. Normal girls didn't get a stomach ache around boys. Normal girls laughed and talked and joked with boys just as they did with their girlfriends. As Chloe resumed filling out her order in the Sears Catalog, she felt a deep sadness. This sickness confirmed that she was on the right path. Being a nun was all she could ever be. This knowledge, heavy though it was, was not without relief. "Momma, can I order these pink quilted slippers that match the housecoat?" she asked.

"Yes," said Momma, tossing a pair of patched blue jeans to Howie and whipping another pair from the big box, resting it on her bulging stomach as she studied the torn knees, planning her attack. "And then start dinner, will you? There's hamburger thawed and some corn left over from last night. Get Peter to run out and pick some tomatoes. He's good at that."

Soon summer was over, and the air had a chill to it in the morning that felt like winter. It was Daddy's turn to drive the girls back to Mater Dei Heights. Lucy and Chloe sat in the middle seat. Daddy listened to the news on the radio. Chloe's two little sisters who had begged to go along played quietly in the backseat.

Chloe had wanted her mom to ride along, but she had to stay home with the little ones. Tall rows of corn zipped by on both sides of the road. It was a clear September day with a few brilliant clouds floating in the sky. Chloe wished her soul were as white and as clean as the clouds. But her sin of the summer had left a gray film on her soul. She had gone to confession, but the feeling of guilt still plagued her. She hoped Sister Damien would not be able to detect a change in her.

Lucy was reading a book. Chloe had seen little of Lucy since the night of the drive-in movie. Lucy was as much of an enigma to Chloe as she had ever been. Though Sister said they were not to question another aspirant's vocation, Chloe often wondered about Lucy's. She was so noncommittal, so pretty, and she had an easy way with the boys. But she was glad to have her here, sitting beside her today.

"Just two more years and we'll be there for good," Chloe remarked.

"What?" Lucy looked up, her face blank. "One year at a time please," she said, returning to her book.

"This year we'll get marriage instructions," Chloe pressed on, intensely curious about her friend's knowledge of secret things.

"What? Oh yeah, from Father Schlick. That should be interesting," she said, hunching over her book. Chloe winced at her own lack of knowledge about the facts of life. She should know by now. But Father

Schlick's marriage instructions would change all that, and her private disgrace would be over. She was glad Momma had agreed to let her take the class. At first she had objected saying, "Why do you need marriage instructions if you're not going to get married?" But in the end she signed the permission slip, saying "It won't hurt you to know something about marriage. I wish I had."

"Chloe's mother with nine of her children
in 1948. "Chloe" is fourth child from the left.

Summer time on the farm; "Chloe's" siblings in 1952.

“Chloe,” age 18, in her postulant’s garb in 1959.

“Chloe,” age 18, as a postulant, with her mother in 1959.

“Chloe,” age 19, as a novice on her reception day, with her father in 1960.

"Chloe," age 19, as a novice on her
reception day, with her parents in 1960.

"Chloe" home on the farm, holding a baby sister.

CHAPTER 26.

Leaving Attempt Three

Chloe hadn't been back at the villa for long when, slowly but undeniably and with a smothering dread, she realized, again too late, her mistake. She should not have come back. She must leave. And, as odious and paralyzing a prospect as it was to tell Sister Damien her conviction, this time she was sure. Her mind was made up. In evening study hall Chloe's hands felt clammy. She kept rubbing them on her uniform skirt, clenching and unclenching them. She despised herself. "Why *now* did she see so clearly where she belonged? Why not last summer, when she was safely home and free from all of Sister's arguments?" Her stomach hardened in hurt, agreeing with her. She tightened her thighs. "Time was running out. Just two years left of high school." She wanted to attend school with boys, come home every night to Mom, and be free. "Soon it would be too late. She would enter the convent without knowing what a normal high school experience was like. Unthinkable! She must seize the moment and claim what was rightfully hers. She owed it to Mom and to herself."

Swallowing hard against her dry throat, her heart racing uncontrollably, she rose, nearly tipping over her chair. As she grabbed and righted it, Mabel Watts, ever kind and unassuming, threw her a scrutinizing glance, and Chloe wondered if Mabel had ever tried to go home. As she squeezed through the rows of chairs she felt eyes on her, guessing her mission. "How many times had she been through this?" It appalled her. "But this was the last time. She was older now and wiser! Sister could not talk her out of it. She would not let her."

"May I see Sister Damien please?"

Sister Ruth nodded, glancing briefly into her eyes.

In the wide cool hallway Chloe walked around the corner to Sister's office door and knocked. The sound struck her as profoundly soft for such a momentous moment. "By tonight all would be done. Settled. She would be free."

While she waited, her stomach turned to liquid. There was no answer. She glanced about, and then ducked into the restroom. Holding her clammy fingers under the running water she prayed, "Oh God, let her be there when I come out."

Opening the door she saw Sister Damien descending the wide staircase. Her stomach turned summersaults. A golden sunset framed her like a vision. Chloe lunged forward, "Sister, may I see you please?"

Sister, having just reached the bottom of the stairs, paused, reached beneath her stiff white wimple and extracted her little black watch. After consulting it, she tucked it back up into the folds of her bodice, saying, "Certainly Chloe, if you'll wait one minute."

Chloe twisted her hands together, wishing Sister would hurry. Sweat trickled down from her armpits like water. When Sister returned she swept into her office, motioning Chloe to follow her. Softly she closed the door to her office and turned to Chloe. "You look troubled Chloe."

"Sister, I've decided that I must go home. I've thought about it, and prayed about it, and I've decided that my place is there, at home with my family, helping my mother. I know we've talked about this before. But things are different now. And I've made up my mind." Chloe swayed at the import of her own strong words. For a moment Sister's face receded into the distance, like a faraway moon. She looked shocked and hurt. Chloe's ears rang. She inhaled the sweet clean scent of Sister's soap and revived enough to continue her speech.

As she spoke of Momma, pregnant again, and Travis, who had hurt his hand in an auger, which demanded extra time from Momma, Sister's green eyes regarded her patiently. Chloe told about Howie failing in math, and Agatha needing an older sister to take an interest in her. She didn't tell everything. She held in reserve, in case it was necessary, the sorrier details of her family's life: details that would make Sister see, once and for all, how desperate things were at home.

When Chloe stopped talking her rush of words seemed to be still swirling about the room, bumping and crashing with no place to land. Chloe straightened her shoulders. She had done well. Mary, mother of Jesus, had helped her.

"Are things getting worse at home?"

Chloe, struck by Sister's astuteness, nodded grimly.

"And you feel that your presence there would help things?"

"Yes, Sister."

"But you still want to be a nun, a bride of Christ?"

"Oh yes, Sister, I just want to give my mother some help in these two years that I have left before I enter the convent."

"Sit down, please, Chloe," Sister said, motioning her to a gray wicker chair with a bright yellow cushion. Sister rested on a window ledge that looked out on the lawn and the orchard. A potted fern, thick and green, glowed on the deep windowsill as if it had a light inside it. Sister's habit gleamed white about her face.

"Chloe, you've come to me in the past with similar concerns, and I've never doubted your sincerity for a minute. It hurts to see you struggle with this temptation all over again."

"This isn't a temptation!" Chloe snapped, wary of Sister's ways. She knew all the arguments and was ready for them. She would go home, soon, and Sister couldn't stop her.

This time her passion and resolve would see her through.

Sister Damien flinched and Chloe was instantly sorry that she had hurt her, for she loved Sister Damien like a mother. But her real mother came first, didn't she? "I know what is required of me by now; the prayers, the rules, and I think I can keep them the same way I've kept them during summer vacation. You saw how I kept up with all of them in summertime."

Sister nodded.

"Then, after I've graduated from high school, I can enter with a clean conscience, knowing I have given my mother at least two years of my time when she needed it most."

Sister moved slightly. The faint scrape of her starched wimple against her stiff veil was the only sound in the room. "You're right, Chloe, you are older now, and it's not my job to dissuade you from a carefully thought-out intention. I know you well enough to appreciate all the energy you have invested in this plan. But, if I may, I'd like to ask you one question."

"Yes, Sister?"

"Didn't your junior class elect you to an office this year?"

"Yes, Sister. Secretary."

"That's quite an honor. It shows you've won the respect of your peers. And you deserve it. And it's precisely because you've shown such uncanny ability to tough it out—to persevere despite all odds, that you are recognized as a leader."

Chloe listened guardedly, her jaw set. Flattery would not win today.

"But all that aside, let's talk about your family that needs you so much. Whenever I see them they look to me like a very happy, good-natured bunch. Instead of this drastic step of abandoning your vocation, maybe a little talk about pitching in would help. You've heard the motto, "Many hands make light work."

Chloe pressed her tongue against her teeth hard. Her heart was thumping, and she felt hot all over. Why did people insist on painting rosy pictures of big families? How could she convince this pristine nun who had not lived in a real home for years, what it was like in hers? Must she divulge family secrets? She took a deep breath. "Sister, my family is not a happy one." Chloe looked off into a corner of the room as she spoke. "Maybe I shouldn't say this, but there's a lot of hate and anger there. There's so much fighting between everybody. I know it's a terrible thing to say about your own family, but it's true Sister; sometimes it's just not Christian! If you could see the way the boys treat Mom! No respect! They don't care how hard she works, they just make more demands, and she keeps on doing for them. Like a saint! But she can't go on like that, being so mistreated! Sometimes they make her cry, and they tease the little ones. It's almost like they want everybody to be miserable."

A tremor passed through Chloe's body at this, her first revelation of her home life to an outsider. She covered her face with her hands, and to her amazement, felt real tears.

"But where is your father while this is going on?"

The indignation in Sister's voice encouraged Chloe. She had really heard her this time.

"He's away a lot. He goes to cattle auctions and sells feed and seed to make ends meet."

"And your mother? Can't she stop the boys' behavior?"

"She tries, but, well, I think she's given up," Chloe's voice squeaked.

"Chloe," Sister's voice was exquisitely tender as she asked, "What kind of a man is your father?"

"Daddy?" Chloe stiffened, recalling the dangerous subject his name had triggered the last time they had talked. She would not betray her father and tell how he lost his temper, mostly with the boys. She cleared her throat and wiped away a tear, resolving to portray him with the same exact words Momma had so often described him. "He's a good man. He works hard. But he's not very patient. He gets mad at the boys, and sometimes slaps them instead of talking to them." She waited while Sister absorbed this awful truth.

"And how does he treat your mom, Chloe?"

"Oh, he's good to her, in his own way. He's just not very sympathetic, and he expects her to be as tough as him, even when she's pregnant. She has to bake bread, and plant a garden, and can vegetables, and we're always running out of water." As Chloe spoke she saw the whole miserable picture of her sprawling, fighting, sloppy, unkempt family, and she shook with an inner horror at it all. She had betrayed her family and confessed her father's faults. She noticed she had no more tears.

"Chloe, I'm so glad you came to me with this whole thing. To know this about your family in no way lowers my opinion of you. Rather, it raises it. I appreciate more than ever the brave attempts you have made to fit in at the villa. Why, no one would think you came from anything but the most normal happy home! But Chloe, from what you just told me, how long do you think you'd stay the sweet loving girl you are now if you went home? Picture your life: a public school with no talk of God; a home with an overworked mom, brothers who are bullies, and a father who isn't as sensitive as he could be. How long, realistically, do you think you'd keep your high ideals? Why, in just a few months you'd be a much different girl, I'm almost certain. If Satan tries you here, in the green wood, what will he do in the dry?"

Chloe felt understood as never before. Sister moved aside from the window and pointed to the magnificent sunset spreading its last colors over the darkening world. "I am convinced, Chloe, beyond a shadow of a doubt, that the same God who created that beautiful scene out there also wants you as part of it, up here. And I think you know it."

Chloe was almost convinced. There was something peaceful about believing Sister, and accepting the comfort she was offering. But no, this decision was not about her comfort. She shook her head. "No," she said softly, and the very sound of her own voice strengthened her resolve. "I must leave, now."

"There is one more thing, Chloe," Sister said sweetly, "that I think you should know. If you would leave now, in your junior year, Mother Euphemia will not let you come back to the convent."

Chloe reared back in surprise. "Why?" she asked, blinking. Other times Mother Euphemia's name had been mentioned to strengthen a rule, or to explain a dress code. And Chloe had always felt irritated at this distant, unseen nun's intrusion into their daily lives at the villa. Or? A tiny doubt reared its head like a weak worm just for a moment, Was Sister Damien just saying this to strengthen her stance?

"Because you've come too far, Chloe. You're a junior, after all, and you know the score. To leave now would show instability, not a desirable quality in anyone, much less in a bride of Christ. Mother would probably say you are too attached to your family and this trait would not bode well in the years to come. You are free to go home, Chloe, but I think it's only fair to tell you that when a junior leaves, she leaves for good."

Sister's words struck Chloe like a slap. That she could not have two years at home without abandoning God came as a great shock to her. Chloe had held nothing back, had betrayed and exposed her family in order to play her best card. But Mother had trumped her. Sister's voice had taken on a steely quality, and her demeanor changed as she spoke for a higher power than her own with perfect submission. Chloe hung her head. Her carefully planned words fell away from her. It was too late. Somewhere in the deep recesses of her mind she heard a door close.

"It may sound harsh, but that's the way it is. And from what you said, you're not ready to make that leap away from God's will for your life, are you?"

"No, Sister." Chloe answered in a kind of dreamy far-off voice. "That does sound harsh," she added tiredly.

Sister squeezed her arm, her lips pursed gently again. Deep green eyes met hers in her pain. "But you weren't meant to suffer it, I feel certain Chloe. God so wants you here, to cherish you and nurture you to become the very best nun you can be."

Confused, Chloe blushed. "Thank you, Sister," she murmured, feeling weak from the tumult of emotions she had endured for the last hour; of resolve and retreat, resistance and compliance, hope and despair. She wandered back into study hall and took her seat. Opening her Latin book she bowed her head over it, seeing nothing but the cruel crush of truth upon her hope. She saw clearly now. Mother Euphemia, Sister Damien, her next two years of high school, her precious vocation, and her God were all tightly woven together in a web that had already closed her in.

Two days later, as Chloe was walking down the academy hall, Sister Bruno, the jolly rotund journalism teacher whom Chloe had liked last year in English literature, stopped Chloe with a big smile. "Hello!"

her cheeks shone red like a clown's. Her blue eyes, buried deep in her chubby cheeks, twinkled roguishly as she asked, "How would you like to work for the *Heights' Herald* Chloe? We don't have an aspirant yet on our journalism staff, and we like to have one girl, at least, from each of the three groups; boarders, day-students and aspirants. I think you would represent the villa perfectly. "Oh!" Chloe exclaimed, flustered with delight, "I didn't think aspirants could take journalism!"

"No reason in the world why not," Sister Bruno said, rolling her eyes. "I've also asked Angie Zimms, since she is also a good writer."

That night when Chloe and Angie told Sister Damien the wonderful news and asked for her permission to join the journalism staff, Sister Damien gave Chloe a meaningful look as she nodded her head. Then she solemnly reminded the girls not to consort with the boarders and day students any more than was necessary as they worked on the school paper.

"Never forget that you are aspirants first and staff members second. Observe the 9 o'clock curfew. There is no deadline more important than keeping up with your family in the villa," Sister warned.

"Yes, Sister," the girls nodded eagerly. This opportunity was a prize, a plum offered to few. Once again Sister Damien had been right; God must love her a lot. Just when she was about to throw in the towel He had a sweet surprise for her.

Chloe soon found that taking journalism was more like joining an elite club than attending a class. First of all the staff room, situated in the bowels of the basement, did not resemble a classroom but rather, a cozy relaxed room with couches and throw rugs, a refrigerator, a kitchen with a stove and running water, and a phonograph. Stacks of record albums stood on a counter. Instead of desks, the girls sat at a U-shaped table and discussed writing with Sister Bruno in a friendly and informal way. Colorful Curtains gave the room a homey feel. And when deadlines were near and they had to work late they listened to music and drank soft drinks.

Journalism quickly became Chloe's favorite class, for there, for the first time, she felt on a par with the boarders and day students. Having Angie there too assured her of having a friend. One evening as Chloe sat on the couch in the journalism room counting the words to her *Heights' Herald* article, "Music to Warm the Soul," about the coming piano recital, Patti Pruitt, a day student, sat down next to her cupping a mug of hot chocolate in her hands. She was a tall, leggy girl with thick black hair that fell in waves about her pretty face. Pattie had not been especially friendly to Chloe before, but now she wanted to talk.

"Hey Chloe, I was wondering, do aspirants date?"

"We're not supposed to," Chloe said, pretending a casual look.

"Aha! But do you?" Pattie asked, crossing her long legs and eyeing Chloe over the rim of her cup. Her eyes were almost as black as her eyebrows.

"I'd guess you'd have to ask each individual," Chloe said uneasily. She was glad to be included in conversation, but she didn't like being singled out. Other day students and boarders gathered around, curious. Neither Sister Bruno nor Angie was present. "How did you know you wanted to be a nun?" a boarder asked. "Have you ever been in love?" a day student inquired. Chloe bantered with her classmates, wishing Angie was there to join in. When she said that she wasn't sure what being in love meant, but that she had written a lot of love poems, Patti begged to see them.

Half reluctantly, half pleased at the attention, Chloe pulled her notebook from her briefcase and handed it to Patti, begging her "Read silently, please."

As she read, Pattie murmured, "Oh, nice!" and then, leaning close, she whispered, "I think you know something about love." Chloe glowed.

She glanced at the clock and jumped up. It was half past nine. She stood in danger of losing her privilege. Sweeping her papers and books into her briefcase, she asked for her notebook back. To her surprise Patti was dabbing at her eyes with a tissue. "I want a copy of the one called 'Loves Me Not,' she said. "It describes my boyfriend to a T."

"Oh! Okay." Chloe promised hastily as she left and hurried across the campus to the villa. She felt thick with pride. Her poetry had made a day student cry! Maybe she did know something about the world after all. And about love!

CHAPTER 27.

Marriage Instructions

With a collective "whish" the library full of junior girls rose from their desks, saying with one voice, "Good morning Father Schlick!" Father's round youthful face broke into a smile as his vivid blue eyes glowed with a brief intense stare. Chloe thought he looked cute in his long black priest-dress with the wide belt at his middle. He wore the Roman collar around his neck. Father bowed his head and led them in the Lord's Prayer. Then, while the girls seated themselves, he smiled again, flashing his white teeth while a bright blush crept up his neck and over his ears.

Today was the sixth week of marriage instructions, and today's lecture was entitled "The Marriage Act."

All morning a muscle in Chloe's right arm had been twitching. And now as she felt its steady jerk beneath her blouse, she hoped no one would see and guess her anxiety. Older girls, while never divulging any details, had raved about this class for years, saying how wonderful and informative it was. Chloe was so excited she could hardly sit still. For five weeks she had sat patiently, taking copious notes on "prohibiting impediments", "diriment impediments" and the "Pauline Privilege." Her notebook was scribbled full of notes on wifely duties, a husband's responsibilities, and the care of children. She had a whole page of notes under the title, "Reasons for Refraining from Marital Relations until Marriage."

But what were "marital relations" exactly? Chloe was not sure if her curiosity was proper for someone who would be a nun. But, shouldn't a teacher know all she could about being human? She fidgeted, hoping today's lecture might be more enlightening than the booklet Father Schlick had given them titled *Tips on Dating*. She had read it closely, only to find out that "When a girl languishes in a boy's embrace, sits on his lap or kisses him for over a half a minute, it leads to overstimulation, which can quickly lead to indulgence in the marriage act."

"Today we are going to discuss 'marital relations,' Father Schlick announced, rubbing his hands together. His blue orbs cut a look to his all-female audience before he turned to the board and wrote, "The primary purpose of marriage is the procreation and education of children," in his large uneven scrawl. The girls copied it down.

Slowly he laid the chalk in its place, stepped back and regarded his writing. Tilting his head back, he studied the ceiling. Then he spun around, fixed his gaze on a girl in the front row, and thundered, "The greatest gift a girl can give her husband on her wedding day is her virginity." His arm shot up. He wagged a finger in the air. "I do not mean just her physical virginity. I'm talking about her heart, about what happens between a boy and a girl the days and months and years before she walks down the aisle in a white dress and veil."

The room fell still. Not a shoe scuffed or a pencil scratched. All three groups of Mater Dei students, the boarders, the day students and aspirants, sat like statues. Chloe's muscle twitched steadily beneath her blouse's fabric. Father clasped his hands behind his back and began to pace. Back and forth across the front of the library he walked, his shiny black shoes ringing on the hardwood floor. He was frowning. "You *can* be worthy of wearing white on your wedding day. But it's hard. The flesh is weak, and the passions strong. That is normal. But what is *not* normal," Father swiveled and thrust out his jaw, "is for a young girl who *should* be the guardian of her purity to become instead a temptress. Such a girl violates her own virtue, betrays her future husband and robs her children-to-be of the joy of a pure marriage." Father's voice had grown so loud that Chloe was sure the younger girls out in the hallway could hear him.

"A boy's passions are like quicksilver." He snapped his fingers. Then he dropped his voice to nearly a whisper. "And a girl who makes a game of arousing him with her flirtations - is not worthy to wear white on her wedding day. For only if her conscience is clear about every single date, every embrace, every kiss, is she worthy to wear white."

Father's eyes were moist. He turned his back to the girls and stared at the blackboard for a long while. Then he began to write furiously, his chalk jabbing at the board as he filled it. As he reached the bottom he stooped lower and lower, squeezing unintelligible words under his other written words. Girls scribbled madly in their notebooks. But Chloe stopped. She laid down her pen and a sense of loneliness washed over her. Her twitching muscle kept time under her blouse. When Father finally straightened up and faced them again, he said in a normal voice, "The marriage act is the most mutually satisfying experience a man and a woman can know. It is a sacred thing. It can be a prayer, a preparation for Holy Communion, an act of forgiveness, or an act of thanksgiving."

A titter escaped a day student, but she covered her mouth daintily without Father taking notice.

"It is much too sacred a thing to be done in haste, in the backseat of a car. When the marriage act is engaged in out of wedlock, it sears the conscience and stains the soul. It damages one emotionally. Dear ones, the couple that engages in premarital sex is in danger of hellfire! If they should die in a car accident before confessing, they will burn in hell forever. And if they don't die, I can tell you as sure as you're sitting here that a different fire will burn inside them— the fire of lust, which is the hardest fire of all to quench. Such girls are never beautiful again." Father stopped, looked over his audience of girls with eyes brimming with emotion and said, "On the other hand, those girls who come to the altar with a clean conscience are the most confident, happy brides you'd ever want to see."

He resumed pacing. An electric bell buzzed in the hallway, but no one moved. "And yet, as great a sin as premarital sex is, there's something even worse." Father's neck was bright red next to his round, white collar. "I'm talking about the use of contraceptives. Contraception thwarts the primary purpose of marriage. It makes a mockery of the marriage act. It is an outright denial of life. Think of it! Limiting God's creative power! Any couple that uses contraceptives is living in sin and puts its marriage in jeopardy. How long do you think love will last grounded in such selfishness? The Scriptures say you can't mock God and get away with it."

Once again the bell rang, and this time the girls stirred as if awakening from a deep sleep. They knelt, as was customary, for the blessing, bowing their heads as Father raised his hand over them in the sign of the cross.

Chloe shuffled to world history in a daze. Immensely disappointed, she sat glumly watching Mrs. Morse, the only lay teacher at Mater Dei, stomp into the classroom in her high- heeled shoes, crash her books onto the desk and hoist herself heavily onto the teacher's platform. She looked grim. Chloe caught a whiff of her rose perfume and decided she preferred Sister Damien's honest smell of soap to that false odor.

Without a word of greeting, Mrs. Morse opened her textbook. After staring at it for a while she slammed it shut and clamped her hands on top of it. She looked like a bulldog ready to attack. Suddenly she barked, "What is this world coming to? I thought Mater Dei girls were a cut above the rest." She leaned forward, resting her double chin on her hands, and said in a conspiratorial tone, "I think it's time we talked—woman to woman! Milly, will you close the door please?"

For the next hour Mrs. Morse and her students, instead of discussing the Diet of Worms and the Council of Trent, discussed the dating habits of Magnolia's teens. The day students contributed to the discussion, naming lovers' lanes they knew about, places with names like "River Heights" and "Thunder Falls." Milly Haatch, who was the police captain's daughter, told of police raids on these trysting places. Others told of shotgun marriages of their girlfriends.

Chloe listened, doodling "Maria Goretti" in fantastic letters in her notebook. As the history hour dragged on, she shaded in the name of the saint who had been killed resisting a kiss. Clearly, something was going on at Mater Dei. This morning in homeroom the public address system had crackled to life and Sister Phyllis, the principal, had announced crisply that from now on each school day would begin with a prayer to Blessed Maria Goretti—for purity. Then new comic books about this Italian teenager, who had died a martyr for her purity, were distributed. Chloe knew Maria's story. Maria was alone in the house because her whole family was working outside in the fields. The hired man came in from the fields and asked Maria for a kiss. When she resisted, he stabbed her twenty times, killing her.

To Chloe "purity" was avoiding any interest in the naked body, your own or anybody else's. To want to see or touch such was wrong as well.

That was why Saturday baths and showers at the villa were kept to just three minutes long.

Chloe's date with Max last summer had taught her another aspect of purity, deeper and scarier than just touching yourself. She remembered her fright and her pleasure that night now as Mrs. Morse demanded of her class, "Is that all today's teenager want, is fun, fun, fun?"

Chloe scowled. Marriage instructions had failed her. And now history class made her angry. "Aspirants don't date, why do I have to listen to this?" She thought bitterly to herself.

That evening in dining hall the sharp ring of Sister Damien's silver bell sliced through the chatter, bring silence at first stroke. Sister asked that the juniors come to study hall fifteen minutes early. When they had assembled Sister began, "I don't know how many of you know day student, Pattie Pruitt, but she is pregnant and has been expelled from school. I believe she will be getting married soon."

At the word "pregnant" Chloe gulped. She remembered Pattie's beautiful legs. Then she remembered how Patti had asked to keep her poem about love.

"Naturally, the faculty is upset. This reflects very poorly on our school. Pattie had planned to go to college, but now she has ruined everything. Her family is extremely disappointed."

Chloe took out her notebook and found the poem Pattie had said reminded her of her boyfriend.

"I love you, but I hate you
You are good, but you are bad,
You are full of life's frivolity,
And yet you make me sad.
You are all, but you are nothing,

You are kind, but love me not
You would just as soon embrace me
As see me die and rot."

Chloe felt sorry for Pattie. She wished she could talk to her, but she'd never see her on the Heights again. What kind of a boyfriend fit that description? And now she had to marry him! "What had he done, exactly, to make her pregnant?" Chloe, disgusted at her own ignorance, turned over in bed and slept a fitful sleep, full of raging women and long lists of marriage instructions that, try as she may to read and understand, she could not decipher.

CHAPTER 28.

Prom

Winter came early and hard, with blasts of ice and snow that sealed the hilly Heights in a cocoon of white wonder. During evening recreation the aspirants flocked to the skating rink to skate until their ankles ached. On Saturdays the upperclassmen were allowed to skip mending class to go sledding without a chaperone on the hills of Mater Dei. Lucy Fry, Kay Wakely, and Chloe piled onto a wide piece of cardboard and slid down the hill sideways, screaming and laughing as they tumbled together in the snow. They played till their fingers were stiff and their feet numb.

As Chloe's junior year settled into a happy cadence of work, study and play, she earned rewards. Writing for the *Heights' Herald* won her Sister Bruno's praise as well as the begrudging respect of her classmates. Even the boarders and day students complimented her on her writing. "I'm fitting in", Chloe thought happily, "with the best and brightest of my class."

One night, after working late on the paper, Chloe, with a light heart, crossed the cold dark campus, returning to the villa. As she stepped inside, prepared to creep up the back stairs quietly, Sister Damien met her. Smiling, Sister beckoned her into the kitchen and softly closed the door, "So our voices won't float up the stairwell," she said, and proceeded to pour Chloe a cup of hot cocoa. She urged her to sit down at the little metal table, and then sat down across from her. Chloe felt embarrassed at the special attention. There had been many an instruction in which the girls were warned against wanting to be an exception to the rule; and she had already been "an exception" by working late on the *Herald*. Sister proceeded to ask Chloe about school, her friends, and about writing for the *Herald*. Then, clasping Chloe's hands warmly, she said, "Chloe, aren't you glad now that you didn't throw all of this overboard for Chester High?" Her soft green eyes gazed lovingly into Chloe's. Her first response was that she had not wanted to "throw everything overboard" for Chester High, but for her mother! However, in the face of Sister's gaze, brimming with holy gratitude, Chloe just nodded. "Yes, Sister," she said.

* * *

Chloe pushed open the cloakroom door, surprised at the balmy breeze that met her. It smelled of rain. How green the campus looked! When had the trees leafed out like that, and when had that circle of red tulips burst into bloom? Feeling suddenly cheated, Chloe regretted volunteering to head up the junior-senior banquet. Over the last two weeks she had spent every recreation hour in the basement, while outside spring had sprung. While she had been cutting out paper flowers, the real ones had bloomed. While she shaped cardboard birds and fake bees, the real birds and bees had been busy.

Tonight was the aspirants' junior-senior banquet. The tables were set, and the flowers arranged in the villa recreation room. Fuzzy little bumblebees swung from invisible string amidst a garden of tissue-paper flowers. A statue of the Blessed Virgin stood in the center of the garden. Father Schlick was invited to attend the banquet, and he had a seat at the head table. He would be the only male there, and since a priest had no restrictions about eating in public, as the nuns did, he would enjoy the girls' meal with them while the nuns served and ate later in the kitchen, behind closed doors.

Across campus, the boarders were also preparing for a big night; the prom. Shades were drawn as they primped and fussed over their hair. The campus was quiet and empty. No basketballs bounced or voices pierced the playground. The underclassmen had all been ushered away to the gym for popcorn and a movie. Soon the unusual spectacle of boys driving cars would be seen on the Mater Dei campus. All day in school the boarders and day students had buzzed about the prom with an excitement they could not conceal. Sometimes Chloe caught a furtive glance thrown her way, as though they pitied her for being an aspirant and missing out. Conversations had hushed until she was out of earshot. This behavior enraged Chloe. Though she would love to go to the prom, she didn't want to be pitied.

The banquet was the aspirants' "prom." Their theme was "Honeycomb." The shades in the villa were drawn too, as the aspirants donned their best dresses and jewelry. No, they wouldn't be picked up by boys in cars, but they each had a "date," a girl whom they had asked to be their "partner" for the evening. They would dance in the recreation room, all beautifully decorated and softly lit in a garden theme. Sister Celeste had made corsages for the juniors to give to their senior partners. Chloe, in rebellion at the idea, had delayed asking a senior to be her "date." And because she had waited, she got the last pick, a shy new senior who hardly spoke a word.

When Sister Damien was first told the words to "Honeycomb" she had asked, "What does that mean, 'A hank of hair and a piece of bone?'"

"It's just a popular song, it doesn't have to mean anything," Jay offered, and Sister frowned, saying, "But words should mean something." But when Lena suggested that the worldly theme could be "spiritualized" by making it a garden of the Virgin Mary, Sister was satisfied.

Though Chloe had enjoyed planning and creating for the banquet, now the very thought of it irked her. If she couldn't have the real thing, she didn't want a farce in its place. "Just give me a night off to read a book," she thought, but she dared not express her negativity, not now, after everyone had worked so hard. "Either you're going to the prom, or you're not," Chloe thought bitterly, and no fancy banquet with girls dating girls can change that!

She looked for the same disgust in the other girls, but all she saw were smiles and sweet acceptance of the festivities. "When I gave up boys, I didn't give them up for girls," she complained as she crossed the campus.

A wind stirred the apple orchard, sending petals fluttering to the ground like snow. Chloe ambled toward it. She was not eager to go inside the villa. The fresh air caressed her cheeks like a kiss. The sun, sinking in the west, winked at her through the boarders' trees. Breaking off an apple blossom she looked into its pink and yellow center and sniffed deeply of its fragrance. An ache stirred deep inside her. The plaintive chirp of a robin not yet nested down for the evening came to her ears.

At the sound of a car winding up the hill, she stepped behind a bush. Two boys in white coats sat in the front seat of a white convertible. They each wore a flower on their lapel. From the boarders' quarters two girls emerged, floating down the steps of the entrance like apple blossoms toward the car. From where she stood, Chloe could not see their fancy hairdos or their dainty purses, and yet she saw all; their tiny waists and their billowing skirts; their pleasant laughter as they settled into the seats next to the boys. A spasm of hatred gripped her. "Why did the boarders have to live on the Heights, too? Without them, no one would even be thinking about the prom. And there would be no banquet to appease them for what they were missing." Chloe turned to go inside the villa, tossing the twig behind her. It was naked and bare. She had squeezed and crushed its petals until they were no more.

In the hallway of the semi-darkened villa and partway up the stairs, the aspirants were told to line up two-by-two. "How transformed they all looked with makeup and fancy hairdos," Chloe thought. With lipstick even the plainest girl looked pretty. Skinny Aimee didn't look so shapeless, and Jay's boyish features showed a soft femininity. Lucy's white dress with silver threads running through it shimmered as she stood waiting for the march to begin.

But how much more complete would Lucy have looked in a prom dress, with a boy beside her instead of that lanky girl with the close-cropped hair who was leaning against her arm a little too heavily.

The recreation room, sealed off since Wednesday, would soon be opened to reveal the secret theme. While delicious smells of roast beef and spices mingled with whiffs of perfume, the girls, wobbling on high heels, complimented each other while guessing excitedly what this year's theme might be.

Everyone was smiling. But Chloe burned with self-hatred. "She was a stubborn, ungrateful child! Why was she never content? Why could she not be gracious and compliant like Lena Betters?" While she scolded herself someone yelled, "Smile for the picture!" and her "date" moved a little closer to her. Chloe blinked as the flash went off.

* * *

"Dear Mom, Dad, and everybody,

"Today is Pentecost Sunday. It's a lovely, bright and sun-shiny day, and our glee club is giving a spring concert, and we are singing seven songs. My favorites are "Consider the Lilies," by Topliff and "Assumpta Est Maria" by Aichinger. I wish you lived close enough to come and hear us.

"Our banquet last Thursday night was simply out of this world. The theme was "Honeycomb" and we sprayed chicken wire gold to look like a honeycomb, and we had bees hanging from strings. (Fake, of course) A big statue of Mary stood in the middle of a gorgeous fountain full of sparkling stuff that really looked like sprays of water. The rest of the room was like a garden, with big hollyhocks and roses and morning glories that we made from paper! (Sister Ruth helped with the art-work.) We had fake birds and bees everywhere. It felt like a real garden, almost.

I guess the prom was a success too. It was held at the Moose Lodge and their theme was "Some Enchanted Evening." You can read about it in the *Heights' Herald*. (The boarders had to be back by one o'clock. We were in bed by ten.)

"A little old nun (about fifty-eight) died today. Pray for her, though I think she's in heaven. Could I have a dollar please? I'm quite broke. *Thank you!* I can hardly believe I'll be home soon for summer! J.M.J.

Love and prayers,

Chloe"

* * *

"Good-bye!" Have a good summer!" "See you next fall!" Once again smiles and positive words masked the aspirants' fears about persevering through summer. Since it was anathema to voice their concerns to each other, they tried to read them in each other's eyes. As the girls packed and carted and stashed suitcases, they cast knowing glances at one another that spoke louder than words. They hugged long and hard. Some would not be back. It was always so, though they could not guess who. Something would happen to weaken their resolve or to change them, and no one in the villa would ever hear the whole true story.

But Chloe felt confident. Settled. It was a good way to start a summer. This time no forbidden date would upset her equilibrium. She must watch that her own brothers and sisters didn't lure her into activities she might regret. But she had her stomachaches to help her there!

At home, as always, the shock of the noise and clutter and work greeted her. While the mayhem set her back, the surprise was never as bad again as it had been her first Christmas home so long ago. Now she knew what to expect. After a day, she felt at home again. Slowly she and Michelle got reacquainted. But their friendship had a distant quality to it, the distance of two sisters headed in opposite directions in their lives. Brent bore a suspicious air around Chloe, as he had ever since she first said she wanted to become a nun. Owen, the oldest, was friendly and kind, and always grateful for an extra cook around the house.

It was the little ones who loved Chloe best. And she adored each one of them with their bright clear eyes, cute faces, and surprising words. Even with all the work they generated, they made her happy. And this year's baby was already four months old, smiling with his whole body in the crib. He was named Joey, after Daddy. Mr. Polowski had finally agreed to name a baby after himself. Once again the score was even—seven girls and seven boys. Chloe secretly hoped that the score would *never* change.

When Brent mentioned to Chloe that Max was going steady with a girl he knew from Chester High, Chloe was glad to note only a slight twinge of pain in her stomach. She was over him. She was going steady with Jesus, and that was enough. Being faithful to Jesus, she looked forward to letters from her fellow aspirants. Letters postmarked "Blue Earth, Minn." and "New Prague, Minn." and "Bismarck, N.D." gave her the sense of being in touch with a bigger world beyond her daddy's farm. Though those small towns seemed as distant to her as foreign countries, she knew someone who lived in them; Kay and Mabel and Lena, all living lives very much like hers. They wrote to each other of babysitting and gardening and pesky brothers and how hot the summer was. If they were town kids they wrote about swimming and going to the movies and being bored. If they were farm girls they wrote about picking rocks or driving the tractor or pulling thistles.

Obedient to instructions, they didn't discuss their doubts or struggles. Any allusion to difficulty with staying faithful to their vocation was glossed over with the oft-repeated phrase, "Just think, next year we'll be seniors! I can't wait!"

Summer sped by for Chloe, and as usual, she saw little of Lucy, except at church on Sunday. Gladys too, remained a distant but loyal friend, still determined to enter the convent after graduating from Chester High. Kay Wakely from Blue Earth wrote saying she was helping a friend with a paper route. Chloe wrote back, "Sounds fun! Wish I lived in town and could do something exciting." Often Chloe, even with all her brothers and sisters around her, felt lonely on the farm, especially in the evenings after Owen, Brent, and Michelle had driven into town to be with their friends. Instead, she climbed up to the low part of the barn and sat looking toward the lights of Chester, wishing it weren't so far away.

The last week of summer, Michelle asked Chloe to come to a dance with her. "Since Kenny's been drafted, I have nowhere to go anymore, and I'm so bored!" she wailed. "Daddy said I could have the car, so let's make a ladies' night out", she urged. "Call your friends, Lucy and Gladys, and see if they'll come too. Tell them we'll be home by midnight." Chloe agreed with alacrity.

The dance hall was hot and the music loud. Five different boys asked Chloe to dance, and she danced with each one just once, refusing any second invitations, just as the villa's rules required of her. Lucy too, whirled about the dance hall, her lovely curls growing wet with perspiration. But Chloe noticed that she wasn't so careful about the rules. She saw her out there dancing with the same guy at least three times. Gladys didn't like to dance, but her pretty smile attracted boys to their booth. Michelle had slipped a pint of Seagram's into her purse, and the girls mixed a bit of it in their 7 up. Chloe liked the grown-up taste.

Upon leaving the dance hall, a tall, black-haired boy stopped Chloe, blocking the doorway with his arm. They had danced together. His huge expressive eyes looked bright and wild as he smiled at her with an eager, hungry mouth. After she had refused to dance with him a second time, she noticed him slouching by the bar, a drink in his hand. Of course she wanted to dance with him again, but she was determined not to compromise her vocation now, with summer almost over. It felt good to feel safe, her conscience clean.

"Going home with the ladies?" he asked, "I've got a car. I'll take you home."

"Don't leave him in the dark, sisters, tell him!" Michelle said, weaving a bit as she swung the boy's arm away from the doorway like a hinge.

"Tell me what?" he called after her.

"They're all gonna be nuns," she said, waving her hand in the direction of the three aspirants. "They're spoken for, get it?"

"Nuns!" He stepped back, staring. The girls laughed as they swung their purses, wobbling on their high heels and climbing into the big blue station wagon.

"I hope you girls didn't mind me telling him, "Michelle said as she slid behind the wheel, "but he looked like he needed an explanation."

"Tomorrow morning he'll think he dreamt it." Lucy said.

"Or drunk it," Chloe said, chuckling and lolling her head back on the car seat while the station wagon rumbled home along the wide, dark, and empty roads. The humid air rushing in through the windows fanned her hot face. "It was so much better to be riding home without a boy next to you," Chloe thought smugly. "Who needs a boy putting his arm around you and kissing you anyway, when it just gives you a stomachache?"

CHAPTER 29.

Senior

The trees on the Heights were turning colors early this year. Their flamboyant hues glowed like a girl's last fling before entering the convent. The red brick buildings of Mater Dei stood out in sharp relief against the bright blue sky.

Chloe was happy. She had come through the summer unscathed and was back at the villa as a senior. It was a great accomplishment. Just one more summer stood between her and Entrance Day. Then she wouldn't be a child anymore, at the mercy of childish whims and worldly temptations. She pitied the freshmen, new and bewildered. They seemed to her like little beetles just beginning a great and arduous climb.

One freshman, however, had a different air about her. Pauline Bedarf, a petite but muscular girl with alert brown eyes, sat at Chloe's table in the refectory. She did not seem to be in awe of her new surroundings. Instead, she looked boldly about as though she had the right to question or even to doubt. Pauline's aplomb intrigued Chloe.

Already one freshman had left, a puny pale girl who had not stopped sniffling from the minute she had arrived. No one would miss her. Chloe tried to guess who would be next to leave. It was her way of preparing for the shock. When Sister rang the little silver bell in the dining room to announce a new rule or procedure, Chloe watched the new girls' faces for signs of unrest or disgust. And on Saturdays, when the girls wore their own clothes, it was easy to see who was rich and who was poor, who was spoiled and might miss the coddling of home, and who was perhaps more ready for the rigors of villa life. From these clues Chloe thought she was ready for the next face that would vanish from the villa's tight embrace.

One evening after supper, as the aspirants filed out of their dining hall on their way to visit the chapel, Sister Damien tapped Chloe on the shoulder. "Meet me in the new sewing room please," she said.

The new sewing room Sister referred to was a large semicircular room across campus, in what had been the old novitiate. It had been given over to the aspirants' use this year because of overcrowding at the villa. The aspirants totaled ninety-six this year. Comfortably furnished with couches and wicker chairs, the spacious room with a terrazzo floor overlooked the convent roof and part of the chapel. It resembled a porch, with tall floor-length windows all around it.

When Chloe arrived three other seniors were seated with Sister Damien at a little table: Lena, Mabel, and Jay. "An odd combination," Chloe thought, trying to guess the purpose for this special call. Jay and Lena Betters had been elected class officers, but she and Mabel Sappe were not. Mabel, with her thick glasses on her round face, had a lot of the comedienne in her. But she was not frivolous about her vocation. She had an old sister in the convent that was her shining light.

"Girls," Sister began, looking from one senior to the other, "Pauline Bedarf wants to go home." Chloe's hand flew to her mouth. The light from Sister's eyes leaped into hers as she comprehended the threat of a vocation on the brink. "But why were *they* being told? Such things were strictly Sister's battles, fought in the privacy of her office, made known to the girls only after the battle was lost and the girl gone." "I've talked with her for hours but she insists on leaving. I've begged her to stay just one more week, but she won't listen."

Chloe glanced at her classmates. Jay looked casual, her lean body relaxed but not slouching, her short-cropped hair stylishly framing her classic features. Sweet-faced Lena's cheeks glowed bright pink, her lips already moving in silent prayer. Mabel, with her frizzy hair, took the news in stride, showing interest, but no emotion.

"She did agree, after much conversation, to meet with a few seniors, just to talk things over. I chose you four because each of you has something special to offer this confused little girl." Sister paused. "But I will understand if you say you'd rather not do this."

"But if she won't listen to you?" Chloe exclaimed, leaving the rest unsaid. Sister pursed her lips. "It is an unusual step, but this girl is worth it. She came to us highly recommended, and I strongly believe that if she can get over this first barrier, she will be a great asset to the villa. Her vocation hangs in the balance, girls." Sister looked weary, but her impeccable habit, starched, neatly fitting, without spot or wrinkle, seemed to hold her up, giving her strength in this hour. "I've done all I can. She's out of my reach. But maybe she'll listen to you girls. It's worth a try, definitely."

Chloe's heart melted at Sister's humility. Her love for a soul seemed greater than her pride. The mistress of aspirants was asking them to do what she could not. In a rush of love and pity for Sister Damien, Chloe exclaimed, "Thank you, Sister, for the trust you put in us." Her heart was pounding high in her throat. Sister squeezed her shoulder. Jay, her arms folded, narrowed her eyes in a calculating way, but said nothing. Lena's hands were clasped before her tightly. "What do you want us to say?" Mabel asked, her gray eyes blinking behind her thick glasses.

"I'm leaving that up to you. But *whatever* is said stays here. Is that understood?" The seniors nodded. "And *whatever* the results, you are not to feel responsible. The ultimate responsibility lies with Pauline."

The four looked at each other. Jay cocked her head as though sizing up a basketball court, and said, "I'll do my best." Lena nodded, looking extremely pious. Mabel, lifting one shoulder, said "I'll meet with her, but I'm not sure what good we'll do."

Chloe wet her lips before speaking. "Pauline sits at my table, so I'd like to try," she murmured, trying not to swell with the pride that was filling her.

Sister left, saying that she would send Pauline in after they had some time to pray and plan their strategy. Jay took immediate leadership. Chloe knew Jay had been chosen for her cool head. No doubt Lena was chosen for her spirituality. "And herself? Why was she chosen? Maybe to see how it felt to be on the other end of the argument for once?" Mabel was a mystery. Her blank face offered nothing as the four of them, seated around the highly polished table, talked and prayed.

When Pauline entered, her pert nose turned slightly up as her brown eyes slid around the room, warily.

"Sit down please, Pauline," Jay said, motioning to a chair. "Sister tells us that you don't like it here."

"That's right," Pauline said, her eyes darting nervously from one senior to the next. She clasped her hands together on the table.

"Pauline," Lena began, her sweet smile in place, "We've all been lonesome, so we know how you feel."

"I'm not lonesome. You don't know how I feel."

"I mean, it's hard at first, for everybody. We think quitting after just two weeks is a big mistake." Lena's voice rolled like a melody.

"I'm not quitting. I came here to try it out. I tried it, and I don't like it. I want to go home. Why is everyone trying to make me stay?"

"We're not saying you have to stay," Chloe interjected, "we're saying two weeks isn't long enough for you to know all you need to know to make such an important decision."

"I know enough," Pauline said, holding Chloe's gaze until Chloe felt compelled to look away. She couldn't think of one more word to say. Lena stepped into the vacuum, speaking spiritual inspiration and ending with an urgent plea for Pauline to give the villa a "decent try."

"And what's a 'decent try?'"

"Two months."

Pauline shook her head.

"Okay, one month," Jay offered. "Would you stay one month before making a decision? We would all pray for you."

Pauline rolled her eyes up. Chloe cleared her throat. "Pauline, you're a friendly, well-liked girl. You show real leadership potential, and I think once you …"

"Sister Damien's already told me all about my leadership potential," Pauline said, cutting Chloe a look that left her bereft.

"But you're not … I mean what don't you like …" Chloe stumbled, not finding words. Lena laid a soft hand on her and arm, and took over. Then Jay spoke, calmly, rationally, her thin red lips explaining all the reasons for staying. But the girl's sure look didn't waver, and her chin stayed set. It struck Chloe that this young girl was not afraid of the four seniors. Nor was she afraid of Sister Damien.

"I won't like it any better in a month. I want to go home now. Why is everyone saying I *have* to stay?" she demanded.

"Because you might be throwing away the greatest opportunity of your life," Chloe interjected.

"Is that what you really think, or is that what somebody else has told you?" Pauline demanded. Chloe felt undone. After that she stopped talking, letting the others drone on; Lena's tender accents, Jay's choice phrases, Mabel's irrelevant remarks seemed as so much babble to little Pauline.

At one point Mabel, looking at her watch, asked, "How long is this supposed to take?" and the seniors blushed, eying each other across the polished table like children suddenly caught in a game they were playing all wrong. Chloe had stopped listening. Her mind had drifted, and she felt far away from this failed rescue mission, as though she watched across a great chasm as others tried to keep a lone sheep from plunging to its death. She watched in fascination as the young girl's bright brown eyes widened and narrowed, hardened and softened in her fight. Chloe wanted to know how Pauline had become so brave.

As the meeting wore on, Pauline's answers didn't come as swiftly as before, nor were her words as hostile. "Was she weakening?" With her finger Chloe followed a dark, crooked scratch in the wood. What was Jay saying, "Just a week, that's all we ask," and Pauline was replying, "I suppose I could do that."

They were smiling as they pushed away from the table. Chloe blinked as though coming out of a trance. Pauline was standing, thanking them for their time. "I'll tell Sister of my decision," she said as she left the sewing room. Meanwhile the sun had set, and the eastern sky held pale pink hints of glory bursting on the other side of the world.

"Wow! We did it!" Mabel whispered as the door closed. The seniors hugged each other, smiling broadly at their unexpected victory, faces glowing with disbelief. "It's a miracle!" Chloe said weakly while Lena murmured, "Thank you, Mary!" Jay looked quietly out the window at the convent roof below them.

The next day after the noon meal Sister summoned the four seniors again, pulling them out of the line and ushering them into a corner of the hallway. "Pauline went home today," she told them, her eyes a flat green.

"But she said she'd stay!" Chloe cried out.

"I sent her home," Sister announced.

The four stiffened. "Sent her home?" Mabel echoed, "But we had an agreement."

"Yes, you did. But she wasn't committed. When she said, 'the seniors talked me into it,' I marched her straight to the phone and told her to call her parents."

"But why?" Chloe asked, nearly choking.

"Because that remark revealed her true spirit, Chloe. Do you see how an attitude like that could infect the whole villa?"

"She had spunk," Chloe blurted out. Sister's eyes flickered in irritation. "Spunk is not admirable when it resists God's grace," she admonished. "If I would have allowed her to stay, we both would have been living a lie."

That night at supper Chloe looked at Pauline Bedarf's empty chair pressed tightly up against the table, her place setting gone. Tonight Pauline was home, in her own kitchen, eating supper with her mom. Was she telling her about the seniors? Were her brown eyes laughing as she talked? Chloe envied her. By tomorrow her chair here would be moved, and her name erased from every list. Chloe wished with all her heart that she could have known her better.

For the next few days Chloe felt as if she were mourning a death. Even the aspirants' Friday night hike through the flaming woods couldn't cheer her. On Sunday she went to see Sister Damien. "Sister, you said something the other day about living a lie. Sometimes I feel like

I'm living a lie, living here instead of at home, where I am needed. I feel like I'm dishonoring God."

"Chloe, I expected fallout like this. Satan won a victory with Pauline, and now he's after you." Sister lifted Chloe's chin till her eyes met Sister's clear gaze. "Chloe, you couldn't live a lie if your life depended on it. Now promise me you'll stop comparing yourself to Pauline. You are as different from her as day is from night," she said.

"Yes, Sister," Chloe answered, her eyes suddenly brimming from the compassion emanating from Sister's voice. Once again Sister had dispelled her doubts, waved her hand and calmed her fears. But like a river suddenly dropping out of sight and rumbling far beneath the surface of the earth, Chloe's feelings and questions, her half-formed thoughts and unfinished arguments raged on unseen, murmuring, gathering strength, cutting new paths in the hidden recesses of her subconscious mind.

CHAPTER 30.

Concerning Jenny

Sister's sharp shake of the bell cut the dining room chatter like a sharp knife. Every eye turned toward her in the immediate silence.

"Girls," she said, "one of our freshmen has just received some very sad news. Jenny Schneider's mother died of a stroke this morning."

A little cry escaped, a gasp, as though all the girls felt the blow as one.

"Naturally, the family is in deep shock, and Jenny has gone home to be with her father. She is the youngest in a large family, and the others are all grown and married. I promised Jenny we would pray that she will be a comfort to her father. Please carry on with the dishes."

Slowly the dining hall stirred, hands moving delicately over the dishes as though one clash or jar might wake someone. Lena's lips moved in prayer as she tied an apron about her tiny waist and submerged the glasses into the soapy water. Chloe took up the dishtowel and waited.

Chloe knew Jenny Schneider, a quiet, sober-faced girl whom Chloe had half-expected to leave, since she often looked homesick and forlorn. Now, Chloe was sure the girl would leave. She had a perfect excuse.

But two weeks later Jenny was back; stricken, long-faced and pale, but evidently ready to carry on. Chloe's heart went out to her. When Sister, during instructions, encouraged the seniors to be kind to her, Chloe decided to make Jenny her personal mission. The first time she spoke with her, she discovered that Jenny, despite her long sad face, had a beautiful smile. It thrilled her to see the brooding face transformed by just a few words from her. Chloe could see Jenny blossom under her attention. She helped Jenny with her English compositions and drilled her in Latin nouns. She hailed Jenny at recreation hour as she would a peer. Soon they were fast friends.

But after a while, something about their friendship began to bother Chloe. Jenny was growing too affectionate. At first Chloe reminded herself that a girl bereaved of her mother would crave special attention. Such grief as hers needed touching for comfort. So it was that Jenny reached for Chloe's hands the minute she saw her, and seemed to need to caress and squeeze her fingers. Grief also might excuse the exuberant way she ran, breathless and admiring, toward Chloe every evening as soon as Chloe made her appearance. But the behavior made Chloe uncomfortable. She felt embarrassed. "But was it excessive? Had she said or done things to encourage this adulation? Or worse, was she herself beginning to think of Jenny too much?" True, she did find herself searching for Jenny's blonde head in a crowd, hoping they could talk. She even felt a tiny thrill inside her when she saw her. Such a thing had never happened between herself and Kay. Had this friendship, born of good will, developed into a "particular friendship?"

One Saturday evening, as the smells of roast chicken drifted deliciously up to the sewing room, the seniors sat darning their socks and mending their uniforms under Sister Agnitha's watchful eye. Suddenly, Sister Damien called Chloe out of the sewing room. She blushed and rose, sure that a scolding was inevitable because she and Jenny had spent the last three hours of recreation together. And Chloe had enjoyed it immensely. Jenny's face, turned adoringly toward her, seemed charged with an effluence of emotion that made Chloe feel alive. Of course they had not been alone. Others were always around, joining in as they walked and talked or jumped rope or played a game of hopscotch. But it was plain to anyone, Chloe was sure, that they made up the core of the camaraderie.

Now she felt relieved to have a chance to discuss this situation with Sister. She entered Sister's presence feeling guilty. But instead, to her surprise Sister was full of praise for her and the way she was befriending Jenny in her grief.

"Do you think we're together too much?" Chloe asked.

"Heavens, no! The girl simply thrives under your attention. I think I can safely say that she is still here because of you. Her father says she thinks the world of you."

"But that's just it, Sister. She thinks too much of me, too often, and I worry that she is becoming too attached-"

"Nonsense! Chloe, there is nothing for you to worry about. Jenny's going through a very difficult time. She's lost her mother! Think of it. She's a bit immature perhaps, but then again, she is the baby in her very large family. Chloe, you're doing just fine."

Chloe relaxed under Sister's complete trust in her. Jenny was just a child who liked to hold hands. Chloe's guilt about the relationship eased, and she stopped trying to avoid her. Then, one evening as they were walking hand in hand toward the cemetery, they met Jay and Angie Zimms walking by. As they passed, something, a blink, a flicker in Jay's casual glance as she said "Good evening," pierced Chloe's complacency. She felt a warning somewhere in her psyche and, suddenly, she couldn't smile anymore. She felt ashamed and wanted to run from innocent Jenny, still smiling and swaying and talking happily at her side. Chloe's stomach turned to liquid. Jay had seen through her. She felt exposed. Now all her first alarms repeated themselves. Something was not right, even if Sister couldn't see it. She knew what was happening inside of her; the way she melted with Jenny's looks of admiration; the way Jenny's whole being glowed as she bounced toward her from across the campus, her eyes bright with anticipation. But worst of all, she worried about the way Jenny groped for her hand in the darkened gym when they all watched a movie, and how she couldn't pull away. She liked it but she also hated it. It tore at her insides, churning and sinking and walloping her around. But because she dared not hurt the grieving child, she sat enduring Jenny's massaging motions, trembling with the riot of conflicting emotions dancing through her body.

The next evening she determined to avoid Jenny. She ran toward the girls forming softball teams and begged to play. Jay raised an eyebrow, since Chloe was not known for liking sports. The game bored her greatly, but she endured it, standing in the field, waiting for a hit, not letting herself even look for Jenny's whereabouts. The next day she got permission to work in the *Heights' Herald* staff room during recreation. Safe again. On the third evening she joined Angie's jump-rope contest, even though it gave her a headache. Puffing and counting, jumping as though her feet had springs, she glimpsed Jenny's sad face in the crowd and lost count. "Out!" the girls shouted, and she stepped away from the swinging rope, pretending intense interest in the contest. Jenny moved closer. A nervous tic jerked Chloe's lip as she felt the girl's presence beside her. "I miss you!" she whispered plaintively and Chloe's heart flip-flopped. Jenny clearly didn't understand about the necessity of separation. Instead, she took it as a personal rebuff. That night as Chloe opened her history book, a note was folded in it. Heat flushed through her body as she read it.

> "Are you mad at me? Please, please don't do this to me.
> You are the dearest friend I have ever had. Talk to me!
>
> Love, Jenny."

Chloe looked around. “Oh, the bitter gall of it! Receiving love letters from a girl!” The faint throbbing in her body disturbed her. “But what to do about it? Jenny was just a kid, loving her like she was a big sister, oblivious to the turmoil she was causing her. Right?” It was up to her to handle this maturely. She wrote back that she was sorry, she hadn’t realized, she didn’t mean to neglect her, but with every word she felt trapped. She didn’t want to answer her. She crushed the note and refused to look up at the terrible face moping across from her in study hall.

When, at breakfast on Friday Sister announced that Father Schlick had invited the seniors for an evening hike in the woods that would end with a bonfire, Chloe tried not to look too eager as she clapped and smiled. Then, to pacify Jenny and soothe her own conscience, she dashed off a note to Jenny, against her better judgment.

CHAPTER 31.

Graduation

"Dear Momma, I'm sending home my graduation announcements in a package. I'd gladly address them myself, but I don't have everybody's address. Only four tickets per graduate are allowed, 'cause the chapel is not that big. (My friend, Jenny, wants one, but I told her I have too many relatives.)

"On Tuesday we walked over to the postulancy to try on our new postulant dresses. What a thrill to swish around in those long black skirts! Mom, will you please send up three dozen fabric name-tapes, right away? Sister Amadis, the mistress of postulants, says we need to start sewing them onto our new postulant's clothes for next fall."

* * *

It was two-thirty, the last day of school. A shrill bell, like metal scraping on a grindstone, pierced Mater Dei Academy and pandemonium broke loose. For once not even the aspirants heeded the nuns' calls for order, but rushed headlong for the doors, spilling into hallways, pounding down stairs and rushing out into the brilliant May afternoon.

Shouting and laughing, the students gave themselves up to the bliss of the moment, the last day of school and the sheer joy of going home.

Because Graduation was on Sunday, the senior aspirants had to remain on campus until then. But the boarder and day student seniors could leave for the week-end and return on Sunday. A rare weekend was in store for the senior aspirants. As the only girls on campus, they would have Sister Damien's undivided attention. Oh joy! Not to have all the other girls pushing and talking, but just them alone with Sister—for an entire weekend.

For a while the Heights resembled an anthill, with girls swarming in all directions, hauling suitcases and boxes in a mad dash to load their belongings into their car as fast as they could. Car doors slammed snugly one after another as though saying, "There! That's it! Let's go!" Motors rumbled to life, cars pulled away and white hands fluttered out of open windows waving glad good-byes.

Chloe greeted old Mr. Schneider, standing near his car. His tragic face lit up. Behind him, Jenny, down in the mouth, lugged a suitcase. Seeing Chloe she brightened, thrust her suitcase at her father and ran toward her, throwing her arms around her and hugging her tightly. "I'm going to miss you Chloe, I really, really am. Promise you'll come to see me this summer, please!" she begged.

"I'll miss you too," Chloe answered, squirming in her embrace. Jenny finally loosened her arms, but stood close, her hips and shoulders touching Chloe's. Chloe moved away. Jenny followed. "All packed?" Chloe asked, gently pushing Jenny along, her arm around her waist to keep her from grabbing her hands. Jenny nodded, her head bowed. "I'll miss you so much!" she whispered. And again, that strange warm feeling flowed through Chloe, so wrong, yet so pleasant. As Jenny hugged her again, Chloe held herself rigid.

"Jenny really likes you," her father said, his Adam's apple bobbing as he turned to dab at his eyes. While Jenny massaged her hand, Chloe suffered it, knowing that soon the young pathetic girl would be gone for the summer.

"I can never thank you enough," the old man said, blinking his watery eyes, "for befriending my Jenny." Chloe smiled, wondering how long it took someone to get over the death of a spouse. It seemed to her that Mr. Schneider's grief had not lessened one bit since his wife's death eight months ago. Finally they drove away, Jenny gazing back at her like a sad puppy. Chloe felt relief, which in turn, made her feel guilty.

Gradually it happened that the last car was gone. The ten senior aspirants remained, searching each other out. They stood alone, the faint smell of gasoline still hanging in the air. Sunday seemed a long way off.

"Well! When does the fun begin?" Angie asked, laughter dancing in her merry eyes. "Why hadn't a weepy freshman attached herself to Angie instead?" Chloe thought bitterly. "Angie was far friendlier and vivacious that she was. But maybe she was too smart to let a freshmen girl hold her hand! Was there something about her that had drawn Jenny to her in this unnatural way?"

"Hey, why so glum?" Angie asked, poking Chloe.

"Oh nothing. Where's Sister Damien?" Chloe responded, suddenly longing to see her. A red convertible roared onto campus, radio blaring, girls laughing. Day student, Milly Haatch, sat at the wheel.

"Graduation gift from her father," Angie explained. "He's trying to stop her from entering the convent."

Last week the academy had buzzed with the news that day student, Milly Haatch, planned to enter the convent in the fall. She had proudly shown her acceptance letter from Mother Euphemia to everyone. Not even the aspirants had such a letter, but when they asked about it, Sister Damien assured them they didn't need one. They had been accepted years ago. Father Schlick called Milly a "hero."

Milly's car squealed around the boarders' circle, streaked past the villa and sped off down the entrance road, blonde hair flying and horn tooting.

"Wonder how she'll like wearing black?" Chloe remarked acidly.

"Or Grand Silence," Angie added with a laugh as they entered the villa. Their footsteps echoed through the empty building. Sister had promised their last weekend would be one they would never forget.

"Hey, where is everybody?" Angie called. They found Mabel and Lena playing cards in the basement recreation room, a transistor radio playing softly at their feet. Angie joined them while Chloe walked up to her dorm. She felt at a loss. Never before had she had nothing to do. "Where was Sister Damien?" Chloe thought irritably. Lucy was sitting on her bed, something they had not been allowed to do in the four years they had lived at the villa. Spread out around her was a jumble of souvenirs; pins and flowers and napkins that she was pasting into a book. She seemed engrossed in the project.

Chloe looked at her own bed and sat on it gingerly. She had always thought it a silly rule that they could not sit on their own beds. It felt good, wicked but good, and she stayed, leaning over to investigate the contents of her washstand. All was in perfect order, not that it mattered now. There would be no more red-dot days for them. She turned toward Lucy. "Well, they're all gone but us."

Lucy smiled slightly.

"Here we are at the end of the road."

"Huhuh."

Chloe left the dorm thinking she might stroll in the woods. She was free now to do that, wasn't she? Once she had longed to do it. But now? Maybe if she had a good book to take along it would be different, but they had been required to turn in all their books before the last week of school. She glanced into the huge junior dorm. The rows of iron rail beds were stripped down to the mattresses, and the plump pillows lay naked in their pinstriped sacking. The hardwood floors, so shiny and clean this morning, bore dusty footprints along with scraps of paper and bobby pins.

This morning's schedule had been the same as every other morning; rising with the Angelus bell, donning uniforms, praying, meditating, and cleaning. Everything had followed the exact order of the day, right down to reading the "Thought for the Day" before they could speak at breakfast. Such adherence to protocol right up to the last day both annoyed and amazed Chloe. But the day's ending would not be the same. Already those who had fled the Heights were miles away, and by tonight none of them would even be thinking of the villa or its routine of bells and silence beneath Sister's watchful eye. And yet, though they might not give this dorm room a fond thought the whole summer long, most of them would return, as she always had.

Somewhere a shade rattled and scraped against the window sash. The sheer loneliness of the sound sent a shiver through Chloe. She started to go downstairs when a bell rang with the unmistakable shake of Sister's hand. Thrilled with relief, Chloe flew down the stairs. There stood Sister, her back straight, and her face aglow, a beautiful person. Oh, if the villa could be their summer home, with dear Sister Damien as their mom and all of them working together in gardens, doing laundry, helping out around the barns; how safe and sure that would be! No worries about boys and dates and dances; they could all enjoy their last summer as girls ready to enter the convent.

Sister's face held an alert, watchful expression as her small little group of seniors gathered around her. She counted them. "Nine," she said. "Who's missing?" The girls looked around. No one knew. They heard a noise upstairs. "It must be Lucy," Chloe said. They waited, listening to her moving about. An impatient, quizzical look flickered across Sister's face.

"Ring the bell again," Mabel suggested.

"She heard it the first time," Sister remarked. Her wimple rose and fell with a sigh. "Well, here we are, just us! Cozy isn't it?"

The nine seniors smiled shyly.

"It's so quiet," Kay said.

"The girls are always surprised at that," Sister said. "They never expect it to be like this." She raised her voice. "But you'll get used to it. You'll see. It will be the best weekend we've ever had on the Heights."

Lucy's light, quick step was heard on the stairs. She was wearing snug fitting jeans and a Western-style shirt, open at the neck. A blue scarf tied around her neck brought out the blue in her eyes, and she lifted them boldly to meet Sister's gaze, without apology.

Sister nodded stiffly, her eyes taking in Lucy's trim figure, from pointed shoes to soft blonde curls. "I was going to tell you that you may wear what you want these last two days. Please keep in mind, though, that you must wear skirts for benediction tonight. And no sleeveless blouses," she added. "Now that we're all here, let's decide what we want to do with the rest of today. I'm sure you'll all agree on a slumber party tonight because tomorrow you'll want to get to bed early for your *big* day. As you know, there is cleaning to be done. We have to leave the villa in tip-top shape for the sisters arriving for summer school next week. They'll be using your dorms. What do you say about getting the work out of the way first so we can all enjoy ourselves tomorrow?"

The girls nodded vigorously.

"I have to get over to the convent to see some friends before they leave." Extracting her watch from beneath her wimple, she consulted it. "So I'm going to leave you to work out the cleaning schedule. That's the last favor I ask of you as a group, okay?"

At the portent of these words an appreciative sigh escaped the girls. "Yes, Sister Damien," they murmured. Sister's eyes watered as she regarded them sweetly. Chloe felt no tears, but a weight like darkness gathered around her heart.

By the time Sister joined them it was late. The girls had never been left alone for such a long time. After supper they had washed the dishes, cleaned the refectory, packed their suitcases, dressed for bed, and told ghost stories while sipping soda pop. By the time Sister showed up some of them were starting to yawn. Sister arrived carrying a box of what she said were graduation gifts. She gave a little speech about being the first to give them something toward their trousseaus. As each senior opened an identical gift, a pair of black stockings, the others oohed and aahed. Soon it was time to go to bed, and Sister reminded them that keeping the Grand Silence was still the rule.

Saturday morning the seniors rose for seven-thirty Mass, ate breakfast, and did their regular Saturday tasks of making beds and washing their hair. Without the competition of the other girls for sinks and tubs, these tasks were done quickly. Their voices bounced off walls, reminding them that they were the only ones left on campus. They rushed outside to drink in the fresh air and hear the birds sing. There was nothing to do. With the library closed and the usual Saturday activities of mending, studying and instructions cancelled, time stood still.

Now Chloe understood why Sister had, for all these years, filled their weekends with so much activity. Free time was a drag. By noon Chloe had said all her required prayers and, if it had been allowed, she would have said her prayers for the next week, too. But she mustn't start compromising before she even left the Heights! After lunch, a small knot of seniors sat around in the recreation room. No one was talking. They were all tired of saying how much they would miss the villa and how they wished the summer were already over. Kay Wakely was reading a magazine and Mabel Watts was knitting. Lena was playing solitaire. Chloe sank into a stupor of lethargy. She had not felt so strange in all her life. "Cut loose" she described it to herself, "like a boat at sea."

Then Angie Zimms's laughter rang through the hall, and she burst into the recreation room like a ray of sunshine, smiling, her merry eyes squinting with a great idea. "Who's game for putting on our black stockings and walking down to the nearest Dairy Queen?" she asked. Lena Betters looked up from her card game and said it sounded like fun. Jay said she'd go. They begged the rest to come too, saying, "There's nothing else to do this afternoon and I've gotten permission for anyone who wants to go." At that Mabel, Kay, and Aimee rose. Chloe forced herself up and said, much more brightly than she felt, "What're we waiting for?"

After putting on their stockings and shoes the girls set out across the boarders' lawn and started down the two hundred and fifty cement steps, quickly remarking how hot the stockings felt. "I'll never get used to them!" Angie complained. Chloe tried not to think about that. At the bottom of the hill they crossed a meadow to reach the highway, which they followed for a while.

As cars zoomed by them and people stared, Chloe regretted the trek. Some cars honked, and that made Angie laugh. They all walked a little closer together. Chloe laughed too, trying to appear happy and carefree to passers-by. Then a green Chevy full of boys flew by, whistling at them. The girls ignored them. But the boys turned around at the nearest driveway and returned, roaring by the girls with shouts. Chloe, sweating already, now felt even hotter from embarrassment. She did not like being a spectacle. When the car returned a third time it slowed down, nearly stopping. "Hi there, babes! What're your names?"A blond-headed boy looked directly at Chloe and wiggled his ears at her like a clown. Chloe laughed. She would have liked to talk with him. "Wouldn't you like to know!" she answered gaily. The boys sped away, and Chloe announced that she was taking off her stockings. But the others begged her not to, crying out that it would ruin everything. So she trudged on, thirsty and hot, her legs damp with perspiration, and her heart shrouded in a kind of dark and unnamed grief.

The sun finally set on that day. Dusk molted into dark, leaving the girls an hour to get ready for bed. Used to a half hour, all ten were ready in their pajamas and housecoats long before the bell for the Grand Silence rang. Kay and Chloe sat alone in Kay's room, talking.

"I remember last summer, how hard it was to come back," Kay said. "Not that I don't *love* it here. It was just hard to leave home."

Chloe nodded, looking at Kay's long pointed nose and freckled face. She was about to speak when Kay startled her with, "And there was a boy ... we got very close. We really liked each other."

Chloe leaned forward, "A boy? Where did you meet him?"

"He had the paper route on our street." Kay's face softened as she remembered. "I helped him."

Chloe was too surprised to reply. Kay, with her buckteeth, angular body, and breasts smaller than her own, had known a "boy" temptation. She believed it only because she knew that Kay would not lie to her. She waited to hear Kay say that she had brushed her temptation away as casually as one shoos away a fly.

"He still thinks I'm a just a boarder up here. He's waiting for me to come home for the summer."

"Kay Wakely!" Chloe stared, her mouth wide open, and the two girls looked at each other for a long deep moment.

"It's like Sister Damien says, it all looks so easy when we're up here. But once we're home … how hard it is … how soon we forget … when we …" Kay's voice trailed off.

Chloe grabbed Kay's bony shoulders and shook her. "Kay! You'd better come back!" she ordered. Kay pulled away with a shrug. Chloe didn't know what to say. Because her friend was not pretty, Chloe had assumed she was spared temptation. Now she saw how foolish such thinking was. Seeing the misery in Kay's eyes, she said, with more conviction than she felt, "You'll do what's right, Kay. You have to. You're my best friend, and we've been in the villa so for four years and I just won't enter the convent without you!"

Before the lights went out, Chloe slipped her diary from her housecoat pocket and wrote:

> "Dear Mother Mary,
>
> "My last night ever as an aspirant—in the villa. I can't believe it! And next year—your postulant! But what hurtles await us in the world? J.M.J. Help Kay steer clear of that boy! Help us to have good clean fun this summer. That's possible, isn't it?
>
> *Yours,* and your Son's—all summer!

Chloe."

In her dreams, that night, she and Kay walked down a street, delivering papers. But every time they tossed a newspaper a boy jumped out from behind a bush, caught it and threw it back at them. They ran. But no matter where they ran another boy popped up, throwing newspapers after them. Finally Chloe turned and rushed at him yelling, "Go away!" as loud as she could, but he grabbed her and kissed her, pulling her to the ground. As a sweet pleasurable feeling washed over her she heard Kay calling and wrenched herself free. She woke up. It was graduation day.

* * *

> "Dear Graduates," Father Schlick began, his blue eyes scanning his senior girls like beacons as they sat in the hushed chapel.
>
> "The world awaits you. You, boarders, day-students, and aspirants, you have all received an excellent education at Mater Dei. The world needs you. Why, you ask? Because you have been given so much; and as the Scripture says, 'To whom much is given, from him much will be required.' After today the bells and classrooms, the doors and hallways of Mater Dei will no longer have a hold on you. But there is someone who will; someone you have met many times here, in this chapel. And that someone will *never* relinquish His hold on you, because He loves you and has claimed you for His vineyard. He

calls you today to be a leader in bringing others closer to Him.

"No matter where next year finds you, no matter how far, or in what circumstances, you cannot escape this obligation. Christ will wait here for you to give back in some measure all that He's given to you.

"Whether you wear the habit of a Humble Handmaid, the housedress of a mother, or the lead apron of a technician, we will see you shining as stars as you go about doing good. And everything you do, whether good or bad, will be a reflection on Him and on your school, Mater Dei Academy on the Heights."

CHAPTER 32.

Lucy

Chloe had not seen Lucy since they'd come home for summer. Chloe had called her a few times, but the conversations had been slow, with Chloe doing all the talking, so she stopped calling, and Lucy didn't call either. Chloe thought about this as she applied black polish to the boys' shoes at the kitchen table, which was covered with newspaper. It was Saturday night. Momma was stirring a bowl of red Jell-O, and Michelle was combing her hair in the bathroom. Chloe hoped that she might see Lucy if she went to second Mass tomorrow. Since she was an early riser she usually went to first Mass with Daddy and then babysat while Momma went to second Mass.

"Tomorrow I want to go to second Mass," Chloe announced, vigorously buffing a black shoe. "Someone else can go to first Mass with Daddy."

"Yeah, someone else. Why don't you just say me?" Michelle drawled, eyeing Chloe through the bathroom mirror.

"Okay, you," Chloe said.

"I can't. I'm going to be out late tonight."

"Who you going out with? Kenny's in the army!"

"Oh, thanks for the reminder!"

"Girls!" Momma interjected softly, "I'll go to first mass with Dad." And the matter was settled.

The next morning, kneeling in her family's pew between Michelle and little Julie, Chloe glanced toward Fry's pew. There sat Mr. and Mrs. Fry with their three little boys, all scrubbed and clean in their white shirts and ties. But who was that beauty next to them? It was Lucy, her blonde hair all cut and curled in the latest fashion and topped with a white pill-box hat with a touch of netting on it. The sleeveless pink sheath dress she wore was definitely new, with a smart turned up collar that was all the rage. Her slim arms were evenly tanned. While Chloe stared, Michelle leaned over and whispered, "Get a load of her!"

When it came time for Holy Communion the pews emptied out one by one as the faithful filed forward to receive the sacrament. Chloe peeked up to watch Lucy return, eyes downcast, hands folded casually before her. As she swung gracefully into her family's pew, two young men in the side pew nudged each other. Even Grandma Polowski, three pews ahead, turned her stiff neck for a better look.

During the rest of Sunday Mass Chloe tried not to stare, but Lucy was a pretty sight. "Her mom must have dolled her up like that, cause Lucy's her only daughter," Chloe thought. "Still, it is amazing how, in three weeks, She's changed from a girl into a woman."

Chloe had told her mother she didn't want any new dresses this summer. It would be a waste, she said, with her entering the convent in September. But now she was grateful that Momma had insisted on her getting a new dress. "Agatha can wear it next year," Momma had assured her. "She's not your size yet, but with a few tucks here and there, I can make it over for her."

After church, Lucy, a shiny white purse slung over one shoulder, stepped daintily down the church steps in dangerous high heels. She waved briefly to Chloe as she followed her parents straight to their car. Chloe noticed a gaggle of young men watching.

“Those looked like three-inch heels to me,” Michelle murmured to Chloe as they rode home in the rattling station wagon. Owen drove, with Brent seated next to him. The sky was big and round like an enormous blue bowl. Tender green shoots of corn stood out in perfect rows against the black earth, zipping by on either side of them.

“Maybe they’re her mom’s” Chloe whispered.

“Could be,” Michelle said. “But that dress is the latest!”

“It looked good on her,” Chloe said.

“She’d look good in a gunnysack,” Michelle said behind her hand.

“Who’re you whispering about?” Owen asked, cocking an ear, “that Fry girl? If you ask me, she don’t look like she’s going to no convent.”

“Can you blame her?” Michelle said, “With a figure like that?”

“She’ll never be a nun,” Brent said. “I knew it all along.”

“Well, she’s had four years of training and I’ve never heard her say a word against it.” Chloe replied saucily. Silence reigned in the car. “You don’t see her going out with boys, do you?” Michelle shifted in her seat and looked out the window.

“No,” said Brent, “but I don’t know why. She could have anybody she wanted.”

“The girls around here are glad she hasn’t been around,” Michelle said laughingly.

Monday morning Chloe’s bare feet danced over the hot gravel driveway as she raced toward the big mailbox. She reached inside and shuffled through the newspapers and Daddy’s business letters until she spied a small white envelope. She grabbed it hungrily. A spasm of joy shot through her as she saw her name and address neatly typed on the front. Stuffing the other mail back into the mailbox, she headed for the north grove, behind the house. It was less played-in than the other groves, and she wanted to be alone. Ambling toward it, she studied the envelope, noting the three-cent stamp with the round postmark saying "Magnolia." She looked at the return address: "Sister M. Damien. HHOM"

Clasping it close to her heart Chloe could feel Sister's love for her as she hurried through the grove to her favorite place on a large rock pile. No brothers' forts or sisters' playhouses occupied this grove. Neither had Daddy dumped scrap iron or discarded machinery here. It was a thick lonely grove with a few paths where she could walk unhindered. High above the treetops swayed vigorously and free.

Seated on her favorite rock she opened Sister's letter, anticipating the sweet balm of her encouraging words. Though far away, a letter from Sister brought her near to the very woods in which she sat. Her insight and words of encouragement and praise tasted like food and drink to her.

"Dear Chloe..."

The sun brightened the white paper as she read. It was a short letter, not even filling up the page. Chloe felt a bit disappointed, but she read the words over and over, cherishing every nuance, looking for meaning, picturing the kind, loving face of her mistress. She knew Sister cared for and valued her —Chloe Polowski—sitting here on a flat rock far from the Heights on the edge of her daddy's grove. Without Chloe even mentioning it, Sister knew of her lonely nights playing house with the little kids out in the grove while others her age went out in cars, with boys.

> "Every sacrifice you make is worth it ten times over Chloe! You have a great future with the Order! Don't compromise your vocation for a cheap thrill. Don't take a lazy approach to your prayers."

"How had Sister known she had been cutting corners?" All last week she had done her fifteen-minute meditation while carrying her brothers' lunches to them in the field. She told herself she was contemplating God's creation. But she was cheating God. "Shouldn't a bride of Christ give God her undivided attention?"

Chloe leaned back on the wide, warm rock and soaked up the sun. High above her poplar leaves shimmered and shook to breezes only they could feel. She wished summer was over, and she was safe in the convent. But she loved home so much. "Did Gladys and Lucy battle with the same contradicting thoughts? Was God as distant to them as He was to her? Maybe next month, when the three of them got together for the Holy Hour for Perseverance, she would ask them. Surely they were old enough now to discuss their inner struggles. Maybe they could help each other."

Suddenly Chloe had a friend. "Lucy's becoming like one of the family!" Chloe's mother commented one day. And it was true. Lucy Fry had started to visit Chloe in mid-July, riding over with her dad, or finding some excuse to drop in and see Chloe. She came almost once a week, and stayed for an hour or more. Her bright "hello!" included everyone in the family. Chloe was immensely cheered. To her surprise, Lucy didn't seem to mind the Polowski's messy house or the noisy children. Rather, she seemed to enjoy it. She chased the kids, washed the dishes, and swept the kitchen floor. She helped make the boys' lunches and then insisted on walking with Chloe out to the fields with them. Clambering over the rough-plowed fields, in and out of ditches, over fences to the hot, dusty tractors, the two became close friends. Why, it was just the kind of friendship Sister Damien had always said the St. Eli aspirants should cultivate. And this, their last summer, it had finally happened.

Before, Chloe had hated rainy days, when the big boys would hang, thick as flies, in the kitchen, teasing the little ones and making them cry, or fighting with each other, breaking things and generally being in the way; but with Lucy around, tensions melted away. She had a way with the boys that made them laugh. She'd brandish a broom and say, "Lift up those clod-hoppers so I can sweep!" and they'd do it with a smile.

"Lucy says things that I'd get bopped on the head for," Chloe remarked to her mother one day.

"She knows how to handle them," her mother replied. "Don't I always tell you to be nice to them, and they'll be nice to you?'"

"Well, it doesn't work for me!" Chloe retorted. But she was glad it did for Lucy. It made home a more pleasant place to be. Summer wasn't going to be half-bad, Chloe decided. Since Sister's letter, her prayer-time had improved. She rose early most mornings to watch the sunrise. And while she sat on the Chicken coop watching the new day's showy entrance, she meditated. Sometimes she even said her rosary before bedtime. If she missed the sunrise, she walked in the north woods to pray and meditate. She felt closer to God outside, where the breeze and the sun caressed her. Outside, the demands of her vocation didn't seem so bad. Even her unrelenting doubts and questions didn't plague her there. And after she was back in the house with the crying babies and quarreling children, where work lay undone everywhere and her harried mother looked at her with desperate eyes, she felt new strength. She tackled the housework with a will. Everything seemed more bearable after her solitary walk outside.

On the day of the scheduled Holy Hour for Perseverance, Chloe was cleaning her bedroom for the occasion. Sister had sent reminders to the aspirants about it, suggesting that those who lived close to each other make an effort to get together for it. Chloe had invited Lucy and Gladys to join her. Gladys had to babysit, but Lucy said she'd come.

Chloe had hoped Lucy would offer to have it at her house, since her house was so much quieter. It was also air-conditioned. But when Chloe suggested it, Lucy said, "Oh, let's have it at your house, you're so much better at arranging stuff like that than I am."

After mopping and waxing the brown linoleum floor of her bedroom and dusting everything in sight, Chloe built a shrine to Mary. Humming softly, she draped a white embroidered pillowcase over a shoe box and placed a doily over that. On this platform she placed her statue of Our Lady of Fatima that Sister Clarice had given her so long ago. She had picked some daisies that grew in the ditch, along with some Queen Anne's lace and one pink wild rose. This bouquet stood to one side of Mary, while on the other she placed a blue candle.

Stepping back to admire her work, she heard a heavy foot in the hallway. She had thought all the boys were in the field. She grabbed the dust rag and stepped softly in front of her shrine, feeling suddenly embarrassed. There was sharp rap on the door before it opened and Owen stood there, stretching his neck into her room curiously. "You in there?" He asked, his expression tentative.

"Huhuh," she said, relieved to see it was Owen instead of Brent, for Owen had been unusually friendly to her lately, even asking her questions about God.

"Hi! What'cha doin?" he asked, flashing his white teeth at her. "Can I come in?"

"Just cleaning up my room," she said, waving the dust rag toward the other side of the room but not moving from her spot. Owen leaned against the doorframe. "What's that?" he asked, craning his neck to see around her. She stepped aside. "Nothing. We're having a holy hour tonight, and I'm getting ready for it."

"Oh? Who's 'we?'"

"Just Lucy and I. Gladys can't make it, she's babysitting."

He saw the shrine. He narrowed his eyes and cocked his head. "Did you go buy that candle?" he asked.

"Oh no!" Chloe shook her head, relieved that he wasn't ridiculing her. "It's old. I found it in the back of the hutch while I was looking for a doily. Momma thinks it's one that Grandma used to keep handy for when the electricity goes out, you know, a thunderstorm or something."

Owen's small blue eyes gleamed intensely as he stared at the shrine, deep in thought. His young pimply face was sunburned, and a slight rash from his allergies reddened his neck. Chloe was curious about his visit and why he had stopped to chat.

"Are you really going to pray for an hour?" he asked.

She hesitated. She didn't want to brag, but neither could she lie. "Sure, we've done it before." She laughed nervously. "Get's kind of long, though. And it's so hot up here."

Owen's interest was so unusual, and he looked so concerned that Chloe thought perhaps he was about to share some deep thought about his own faith. "Maybe he wanted prayer and didn't know how to ask. Or was he thinking of becoming a priest?"

"You girls from up there, why do you do this?" He asked, crossing his arms like a judge and squinting at her.

"What, pray? All Catholics pray, you know that, Owen."

"Yeah, but here's what I've been wondering. Why can't you be more like other people and have a little fun? How come you'd rather be up here in this hot stuffy room, saying prayers, when you're the best girls around already? You could be outside enjoying the summer air!" Owen made a sweeping gesture with his short hairy arm. Chloe caught her breath at his speech. He was asking the same questions she often asked herself. She remembered Sister's warning that her worst enemies could be those of her own house.

His voice grew solicitous. "I guess I can see it for you ... I mean, you always were like that, religious and stuff, but them other two, it don't fit 'em much. What does Lucy care for holy hours?"

"Well," Chloe tugged at the loops of the crocheted doily, straightening them out, "it's required, for one thing. The others are as much in it as I am. I mean, we're all going to be nuns, and this is one of the things nuns do—they pray." She looked directly into his beady blue eyes. "It isn't as boring as you think." She felt let down. Owen had just come to taunt her, after all.

He backed away from the doorway, glancing from Chloe to the shrine. "Your room looks like a damned church," he said coldly. "Why can't you be more like Lucy? She's so easy going. If it weren't for you, I bet she'd forget all about that stuff up there. God! Don't you ever get sick of it?"

"You don't have to swear!" Chloe said, confused at the sudden turn in her brother's manner. Boys! They were all the same; rude and rough. Especially farm boys! Chloe sat on her bed and listened to Owen's work boots thumping down the steps and out of the house. Then, jumping up she said, "I won't let him spoil things." She went downstairs and made a pan of brownies, taking a plate of them upstairs for Lucy and herself to enjoy after the holy hour.

She had given Daddy thirty cents and asked him to buy two bottles of orange pop for her while he was in town. But when he came home he handed her money back and said, "I bought Kool-aid instead. I don't like to see you get in the habit of drinking that fizzy stuff. You'd be better off drinking milk."

Lucy arrived late for the holy hour. Her dad brought her, saying she should call him when she was ready to come home. She flounced into the house wearing a yellow skirt and a white sleeveless blouse with daisies at the neck. She said nothing about the holy hour but went straight to the parlor, where the TV was blaring. She sat down saying she had to see the rest of this program. Little Gretchen climbed instantly into her lap and examined the daisies on her blouse. Brent and Owen rumbled down the stairs all washed up, shaved and wearing fresh shirts and pants.

"Hi! Going out?" Lucy asked as they passed the parlor.

"Yeah, ya wanna come along?" Brent said, teasingly.

"Where you going?" she asked.

"Depends," he said. "You girls got nothing to do?" Owen's glance flitted over Chloe and rested on Lucy. Chloe waited, watching Lucy.

"Sure. Me and Chloe have plans," she said, "But it won't take us long, will it Chloe?" Lucy set Gretchen down, saying, "Come on Chloe. Let's get this over with. Gee, I hope it's not too hot up there."

CHAPTER 33.

One Hot Summer

Daddy said it was the driest summer in twenty years. Day after day the sun burned on, scorching the corn and the beans in the fields. At least the hard water well had not gone dry, so there was still water for the livestock. Besides that, Michelle's fiancé, Kenny, had not been able to get a furlough all summer. "I live like a nun," Michelle moaned, throwing her arms up and dropping them to her side in an attitude of despair.

"It's not the worst thing in the world!" Chloe remarked. She was ironing a white Sunday shirt from the stack of shirts dampened and rolled up in the wicker basket. It was Saturday night.

"When you've got a diamond ring on your finger, and you're home every Saturday night giving dirty kids a bath, it is!" Michelle complained. A guffaw at the front door stopped their conversation. The boys were home. For the next hour Brent and Owen filled the house with their noise as they ate their dinner of T-bone steak, boiled potatoes and peas from the garden. They turned the radio up and laughed and talked of their plans for the evening.

"Iron that, will ya?" Brent tossed a blue shirt at Chloe as he passed through the living room on his way upstairs. Owen strolled in from the bathroom, still drying his face with a towel which he dropped on the couch. "You girls going out tonight?" he asked pleasantly.

Michelle, two diaper pins in her mouth, shot him a hateful look. She removed the pins from her mouth and jabbed them through the diaper she was putting on the baby's bottom. "You know very well I'm not." she said.

"A little fun never hurt anyone!" Owen said, "You girls should remember that."

Chloe bristled. "Michelle's engaged! You should be proud of her, being true to her man when he's away," she scolded.

"Yeah? And what excuse do you have? Are you a nun already? If you are, then why are you still living here?" Owen sneered.

"I'll be gone soon enough." Chloe replied archly.

"Not soon enough for me," Brent said, coming down from upstairs. His brown arms bulged beneath his clean white T-shirt.

"Yeah, I'm such a terrible sister, ain't I?" Chloe cried, tossing Brent's shirt down angrily.

"Please! Stop arguing!" Momma pleaded from the baby room, which was also the laundry room. The boys scuttled up the stairs, their feet pounding, and their deep male voices rumbling all the way to their room.

"We iron their shirts and cook their meals, and what do they care?" Chloe complained bitterly.

"They work outside for you too," Mother chided.

"For us?" Chloe cried indignantly.

"Yes, for the family," Momma said, setting down a huge basketful of freshly dried diapers. Chloe, offended, stooped to pick up another white shirt, unrolled it, gave it a shake, spread it flat and laid the sizzling hot iron on it. She worked fast, moving the iron back and forth, pressing out the wrinkles, making knife sharp creases in the arms. Owen's words had hurt. It wasn't like him to sneer and speak meanly. He often took her side in an argument. "I'll be glad when I'm living where there aren't any men!" Chloe burst out.

"Oh Chloe, this drought has put everybody on edge," Momma said, smoothing out a diaper against her body with her large rough hands, and folding it into a size that would fit the current baby. Her hair rose in a frizzle around her head like a dark halo. Beads of perspiration stood out on her forehead. A heavy footstep was heard in the kitchen; Dad was home. He stood in the doorway, a glass of milk in his hand. "Dinner ready?" he asked. He looked hot in his blue shirt and black and white striped overalls. "I hear Chester got three inches last night," he said, removing his straw hat. His forehead was white where the sun had not tanned him. The rest of his face was dark brown. "We didn't get a drop. If this keeps up we won't have any harvest to speak of." He burped, holding his hand to his stomach.

Guilt pricked Chloe. A drought plagued the land, and she had skipped her rosary for two days in a row. "How did she expect God to bless the farm if she didn't say her prayers?" She hung the crisp ironed shirt on a hanger and unrolled another, glad to be doing useful work with Daddy watching. As soon as Daddy stepped into the bathroom, Owen and Brent tiptoed down the stairs and out the back door, carefully keeping the screen door from banging. The car spit gravel as they sped away from the farm for a night in town.

"This house is an oven," Chloe cried, pushing on a stubborn window sash, "How come our windows don't open? Who painted them all shut like this?"

"It wouldn't help if they did open, Chloe, the air is so still," Momma said. The baby was fussing. Chloe picked him up. His skin felt hot and sticky. The smaller children lounged listlessly on the old brown couch, too lethargic to even play.

As the drought persisted Daddy grew more and more testy. One hot noon as the family gathered for dinner, he announced, "Okay, the drought's getting worse. If we want to eat this winter, we'd better start cutting back on extras. Mother, no more catsup or jelly for us. We're gonna eat simple for a while. No store-bought bread either. Teach the girls to bake. It's healthier anyway."

The big boys poked each other under the table. Chloe poured milk for the little kids, saying, "Don't spill now," as she set their glasses down before them. Michelle, at the stove, scooped fried potatoes into a bowl while Momma served up the pork chops.

"Let's pray," Daddy said, waving his hands before himself in a casual sign of the cross. They all did the same, mumbling grace followed by the Lord's Prayer. Momma, standing at the stove, crossed herself reverently as they finished. "So, until we get a good hard rain," Daddy continued, sliding himself a pork chop off the plate, "we'd better cut out Saturday-night baths, too."

"What?" cried Michelle.

"You can't mean that!" Momma joined in, setting a plate of fresh sliced tomatoes before him. "We have to be clean for church."

"Well, maybe you're right," he said, reconsidering, "but the little girls can share baths, can't they? And then the little boys?"

"They do that now!" Momma rejoined, "And when they're done, I scoop out the water to flush the toilet with it!"

At this Daddy raised his eyebrows and sawed into his pork chop. Then, glancing up he asked, "Did anyone get the mail?"

Michelle, standing at the counter eating, slipped outside immediately. Momma tossed a few remaining potatoes around in the pan. The boys ate heartily. The kitchen, though hot, was full of good aromas, blown about by the big kitchen fan rattling near the stove. The children picked up their pork chops with their hands and bit off the meat. It was far easier, Chloe realized, for them to eat this way than to struggle cutting the meat with a fork and knife. For once, even the radio was silent. "Daddy must be too discouraged to listen to the farm reports", Chloe thought.

A scream pierced the hot noon air. Momma ran to the door, spatula in hand. Footsteps pounded up the steps and Michelle, never known to run, burst into the kitchen, waving a letter. Her face was flushed. "I'm gonna get married! I'm gonna get married!" She sang, twirling about the hot kitchen. "Kenny's coming home on furlough and I'm gonna get married!" She threw her arms about her mother, and Momma, a bewildered smile on her face, danced with her oldest daughter, holding the spatula high above her head.

"He's getting a week's furlough in August, so we can get married and I can go back with him to Georgia!" Michelle explained breathlessly. Then, suddenly aware of Dad and the boys staring at her, she blushed and ran from the kitchen, shouting as she dashed up the stairs, "I'm gonna get married. Whoopee! I'm gonna get married!"

Daddy, his black hair lifting lightly in the fan's breeze, said, "I hope she's planning to elope, because I don't see how I can afford a wedding."

The boys laughed. Owen, sucking on a juicy bone, said between draws, "Then we'll need a new ladder. The old one's broken."

"A ladder will be a lot cheaper than a wedding," Brent said.

"I'll set it right under her window," Daddy said, his eyes twinkling merrily.

"And I'll hold it!" Owen said. They all laughed uproariously. Even the little ones giggled at the merriment.

"For shame!" Momma stepped forward, shaking her spatula at them. Her black eyes burned like fires beneath her frizzy hair. The boys looked up, surprised. "How dare you joke like that—about your own sister, after she's waited so long, staying home every night? You should be happy for her instead of acting like she don't deserve the best wedding this family can give her."

"We're just having a little fun!" Daddy chided. "Michelle will get the kind of wedding I can afford!"

Momma glared at him before turning back to her stove. The fan clattered on, trying its utmost to make a difference in the sweltering heat. Scraping back his chair, Daddy said, "I hope she knows better than to expect a grand wedding. We're in the midst of a drought you know."

"Sure, take away her biggest dream, the only thing she's talked about since her engagement. If we can't afford to give a decent wedding for our eldest daughter who stayed home to help me with the babies while all her girlfriends ran to the cities for jobs, then I'd like to know why not!"

"Because there's a drought on, that's why!" Daddy thundered, knocking his chair back against the wall as he stood up. His face was dark. The baby in the high chair started to cry and Chloe rushed to quiet him. "And no one, do you hear me? No one is going to tell me what kind of a wedding I can afford to give my daughter!"

Momma's arm dropped to her side. She looked sadly at Dad and turned back to the stove. Chloe fled the hot kitchen with Joey. Upstairs, she tapped on Michelle's door. The heat was even more stifling up here, with the sun streaming in through her painted-shut window. But Michelle lay on her white chenille bedspread as if it were cool satin, rereading her letter from Kenny. "What was all the ruckus about?" she asked.

"Oh, nothing. Everybody's too hot to handle, that's all," Chloe said, kissing and smoothing back Joey's damp hair as she sat down with him next to Michelle. "Read me Kenny's letter, Michelle. When's he coming home exactly? Will I still be here for the wedding?"

"Be here! You'll be my maid of honor!" Michelle cried happily, "If I have to steal you away from Mother Superior herself!" And you'll stand up with Kenny's cousin, Daryl, from the twin cities. He's a dream boat!

CHAPTER 34.

Wedding Woes

Suddenly, because of the wedding, Chloe gained a companion in prayer. Now, evenings, when she slipped out of the house after dishes to amble down through the groves to say her rosary, she heard footsteps pounding behind her. It was Michelle, dangling her blue crystal rosary in her hand and saying, "Let me pray with you!" So Chloe led with the first part of the Hail Mary while Michelle answered with the second part. Chloe liked it. As they prayed they strolled through the shady grove and down the tractor path, along the dry creek bed and around the north grove, past Huffiker's grove on the other side of the gravel road that led back up to the farm. Chloe felt closer to her sister than she had ever felt before. Usually, by the time they got to Huffiker's grove they would be finished with the rosary, and they would climb up Mr. Huffiker's stack of bales and sit down to watch the sun set.

But despite their prayers it didn't rain. Wedding plans inched along, with Momma deciding which of the farm women she would ask to be cooks, and Michelle choosing which of her girlfriends she would ask to waitress. These people would all need gifts; ceramic teapots for the women and bracelets for the girls, they decided. Old Father Black would perform the wedding Mass, naturally, in St. Eli, and the reception would be at the American Legion Hall, a plain, large building that held two hundred guests easily and had a good-sized kitchen.

"It seems like every time I turn around there's another check gone," Daddy growled good-naturedly. Every conversation ended up centering on the wedding. There were so many decisions; bridesmaids dresses, groomsmen's attire, flowers, salads, and vegetable dishes. Details were discussed endlessly.

While Momma and Michelle spent whole days shopping, Chloe stayed home to watch the kids and cook the meals. She didn't mind because she knew she'd still be home for the wedding. She didn't want to miss it. Secretly she decided, "It'll be my going away party." She had seen a picture of Daryl, who would be Kenny's best man, and she was eager to meet him.

With all the wedding talk, the house cheered up and Michelle was transformed. Never one to gush over babies before, she now hugged and kissed them repeatedly until they squirmed to be let go. The usually drab living room now shimmered with the yards of sky-blue organza being measured, cut and sewn into dainty aprons for the waitresses and the cooks to wear. Momma's capable hands tacked on lace, sewed hems, and made bows, while the little girls begged for scraps for their dollies.

One day the two girls sat on Michelle's bed, looking through the bride's book. The waitresses' aprons were finished, stacked in a frothy pile in a corner of Michelle's room. As Michelle thumbed through the well-worn bride's book, Chloe asked, "Where will you live when you're married?"

"I don't know. Where ever the army sends him."

"But won't you miss home? You've never been away before."

Michelle scoffed. "Home? My home will be where *he* is. That's what love is all about."

Chloe immediately compared her own love for God to Michelle's love for Kenny. "Why wasn't divine love as exciting as human love?" She thought of the box of black fabric shoved deep beneath her bed, holding the sewing for her future wardrobe. "Why did she dread pulling it out and working on it?"

"I want my wedding day to be the most beautiful day in my whole life!" Michelle crooned, and she began to talk about her bridesmaids and her flower girl. Eighty close relatives were invited to a sit-down dinner, and later, two hundred more guests were invited to the cafeteria-style supper. As was the custom in St. Eli weddings, free liquor would flow at the bar, at the groom's expense.

Whenever Daddy was in the house the three women avoided talking about the wedding, because he liked to remind them that he had a family to feed. After a shopping trip Momma and Michelle would sneak the packages into the house as if they were contraband and shove them deep into closets or under beds.

One morning, early, before the heat took over, Chloe sat on the front porch snapping beans, wondering idly what would happen to them all if Daddy lost the farm. Would they move to town? Daddy would hate that. Every grown-up in the family would have to get a job. Even her! She bit her lip, thinking that would be a sign from God releasing her from her vocation.

Because the green beans were so puny this year, it took longer than usual to fill a pot for supper. She had already filled one pot for freezing, and now she prepared a second for dinner. It was an unusually peaceful morning. Soft clanks from the kitchen, where Michelle and Momma were working together, drifted to her. The little boys playing in the sandbox made tractor sounds with their mouths as they diligently planted and cultivated their little farms. The big boys were in the fields, and Daddy had gone to Chester for machinery parts. The heat was rising, and Chloe, already sweating in a sleeveless shirt and jeans, wondered how it would feel next summer to wear yards and yards of black wool.

Suddenly a sharp cry rang from the house. "Whaat! Ooohh Nooo! It can't be! Tell me it isn't true! No! No! No! Not for my wedding!" Chloe almost spilled the beans as she jumped up and ran inside the house. "Was it a fire? A burn? A broken leg? Or had the bank foreclosed on their farm?

Momma was standing near the fireplace, one arm resting on the mantle. She looked depleted. The phone hadn't rung. The mailman hadn't come. The radio was not on.

"What happened?" Chloe asked, but her mother turned and went into her bedroom, closing the door. When she emerged later, her dark eyes had lost their sparkle, and she stared dully ahead. Deep in thought, she didn't seem to hear the children clamoring about her. Later, just as Michelle came downstairs, her eyes red from crying, Owen and Brent breezed through the kitchen.

"What's the matter with you? Get a Dear John letter?" they teased.

"Men! You're disgusting!" she said, and flew back upstairs to her room.

The boys looked questioningly at Chloe. She shrugged. "Don't look at me! I don't know a thing," she replied.

"Well, we always knew that!" Brent crowed.

"Yeah, tell us something we don't know!" Owen snickered, looking smugly at his brother.

The next few days Chloe noticed that whenever Daddy entered a room, Michelle left the room. Piqued because they wouldn't tell her, Chloe guessed that it was some little spat that Michelle was blowing out of proportion. "Wedding jitters."

One evening Michelle joined Chloe again on the rosary walk. When they had finished their prayers they climbed up onto Huffiker's stack of bales to sit and enjoy the sunset, as usual. The wide-open sky first glowed orange on the bottom, then gradually changed to pink. Then great luminescent clouds piled one on top of the other became tinged with lavender and shot through with gold, just like a heavenly mountainous scene.

"I saw lightening!" Michelle cried, clapping her hands.

"It's just heat lightening, doesn't mean a thing," Chloe said. "It's like false labor pains."

"Don't talk about that!" Michelle snapped, looking away angrily.

"What is wrong with you?" Chloe cried, exasperated. "Michelle, why won't anybody tell me what's…"

Then suddenly she knew… the crying, the moods, and the secret that had sapped their joy. "Mom's expecting, isn't she?" Chloe said flatly, wondering why it had taken her so long to figure it out.

"Yes, isn't it awful?" Michelle said, holding her head in her hands.

"What's so awful? She's a married woman," Chloe retorted, relieved to know the secret at last.

Michelle glared. "Shows how much you know!"

"It's a human life," Chloe threw up her hands. "Not the end of the world."

Michelle made a sound of exasperation. "The mother of the bride is the first one to march down the aisle! *Everybody* looks at her, and my mom is going to be wearing a maternity top!" Michelle was close to tears.

"But Mom doesn't care about that, does she?

"Of course she does. She's human, unlike you, who just loves to wear black!"

At that Chloe gave Michelle a shove, nearly knocking her off of the bales. "Ooh, ouch!" Michelle cried as she caught herself, "Sure, go and scratch up the bride, a lot you care! I don't even want you in my wedding!"

"I don't even want to *be* in your stupid wedding!" Chloe snapped back as she scrambled down from the stack of bales and ran toward the house.

That night Chloe heard Momma chiding Michelle while they worked in the baby room. Momma's voice was firm, "Listen to me. I have a plan. No one at the wedding will know. I won't wear maternity clothes. I've kept pregnancies a secret before—you'd be surprised how long—and I can do it again. I'll get a loose dress with a full skirt, maybe even a size bigger, with a bolero on top. They're in style now. You'll see, no one will guess. I'll go on a diet, and wear a good girdle. Just for that day it won't hurt anything. I can look better five months pregnant than some of those fat cows who only had four kids!"

Daddy was standing at the counter, measuring out a tablespoon of Milk of Magnesia. He smelled of sweat and grease. "Where's everybody?" he asked pleasantly. Just then Michelle's voice was heard saying, "Men! I hate them! I hate them all!"

Daddy raised his eyebrows. "What's all that about?"

Chloe shrugged. "Wedding jitters."

A few days later, Chloe came in from wandering the groves, and heard her father say in an offended tone, "Chicken? I don't raise chicken, I raise beef."

Michelle sat across from Daddy at the living room table, a pencil posed in her hand, a sheet of paper in front on her. Daddy's checkbook lay on the table before him. "Beef's not as classy as chicken," she said, tossing her dark curls.

"Oh, you're wrong about that. Those city friends of Kenny's will be thrilled to eat some real homegrown beef."

"It's my wedding, and I think I should decide." Michelle said pertly. Chloe held her breath.

"Where are you going to get the chicken?" Daddy asked teasingly, "We don't have but ten chickens on the place, and most of them are tough old hens."

"Herrs," she said.

"Herrs is not gett'n rich off of my wedding," Daddy growled, "I raise beef, and I say we serve beef!"

"Daddy, it is her wedding!" Momma urged softly from the sidelines, walking through the room with an armload of diapers, "would it really cost so much to buy a few chickens?"

Michelle twisted her engagement ring on her finger and looked through the window at the two new silos towering above the farm. "We seem to have plenty money for silos and stuff. Why can't I have something as simple as chicken for my wedding?"

Chloe flinched, but Daddy chuckled softly. Last night it had rained a half an inch, and he had been smiling all day.

"Those silos are necessary for feeding the cattle, and . . ."

"I think I deserve a little something to go my way at this wedding after everything that's happened around here!" Michelle said, sniffing.

"Why, what's happened?" Daddy asked innocently.

Michelle's eyes filled with tears. "The mother of the bride is pregnant, that's what!" she blurted out, dropping her head into her arms and sobbing.

Daddy stood up slowly. "I see," he said, his face dark. A queer light shone in his eyes as he cast them toward the baby room where his wife was working. Chloe tensed. He stepped to the window looking out on his farm, his hands behind his back, the checkbook in his hands. In a calm matter-of-fact voice he said, “If there’s too much happening around here I can take care of that. The wedding’s off. How do you like that? I don’t want to hear another word.” He tucked the checkbook into his back pocket, turned on his heel and left the house. The screen door slammed behind him.

That night when the boys came in for supper, they said, “Dad says the wedding’s off. How come?” No one answered them. The next day Momma told the girls, “Dad’s serious. He says not one more penny until both of you girls apologize to him.”

“Apologize!” Michelle cried, “Never!”

“I didn’t do anything to apologize for!” Chloe protested self-righteously.

Now tempers grew short in the heat and Momma sighed often, as though the child inside of her was too heavy to bear. Tension and sadness had replaced the happy tone. Chloe often slipped off to the woods to rage alone: “I’m glad I’m going to be a nun, if this is all marriage brings!”

Oddly, Chloe suddenly felt that it was time to sew her convent trousseau. She pulled out the box of black fabric from beneath her bed and started planning and cutting. She made two black cotton half-slips and two, long black aprons. She sewed her name tags to eight pairs of black stockings, ten pair of white cotton men’s T-shirts, and ten pair of underwear. Now the living room, instead of being awash in blue organza, was draped in black cloth. It seemed appropriate to the mood. Momma, preoccupied and sad-eyed, went about washing, feeding and changing babies without her usual sweet songs ringing through the house. One sultry afternoon as Chloe sat hemming a cotton half-slip on the sewing machine, Owen strode in, sipping a glass of green Kool-aid.

His lip curled as he surveyed the dark fabric spread about the room. "What's the good of all that black?" he asked.

"It's what nuns wear," Chloe answered curtly.

"But why young girls? It's not natural."

"It's natural for me."

"It don't seem right to me, that's all," he said, looking so forlorn that Chloe was touched at his concern for her. She opened her mouth to say something, but he was gone. The screen door slammed. "I wish it would rain," she said. "I just wish it would rain and rain and rain."

The gloom deepened. Daddy remained silent when he entered the house, except for his loud belches. Even the children knew to pipe down or go play somewhere else when he came inside. Chloe finished her convent wardrobe, folded the items down inside the box and pushed it out of sight again. Mother's waist grew thicker. Dark shadows showed beneath her eyes. Michelle moped about the house, snarling at the little ones who got in her way. She no longer prayed the rosary with Chloe.

Then one night she knocked on Chloe's door. "I did it," she said. She was smiling. Chloe knew what she meant.

"Now you do it," she said.

Chloe shook her head. "I didn't do anything." She protested.

"Come on, do it for me. Please! I'll take you to that dance in Fairview Friday night. I already asked for the car."

"Oh, all right," Chloe said, brightening. She had only been to one dance this summer, and she was allowed two more.

"You're a good sister," Michelle said. Chloe sat frowning while she formulated the words for her apology. They burned in her belly like gall. But she might as well get it over with. Bracing herself, she went in search of her father.

CHAPTER 35.

Dance the Night Away

Chloe stepped out of the hot, sweaty dance hall and took a deep breath of fresh air. She and Michelle had been looking for Lucy all evening, as she had disappeared soon after they had all arrived together, Michelle, Gladys, Lucy and Chloe. Moonlight shone on the hulks of parked cars. The night air reeked of beer and cigarette smoke. Laughter and jukebox music drifted from the Silver Dollar Bar next door.

Chloe strolled away from the music and noise of Ben's Ballroom. She pulled off her heels and walked barefoot past the parking lot and down the quiet streets of Fairview. She passed the sleepy houses, their porch lights lit as if waiting for the dancers to come home. Ahead, the steeple of St. George's Church rose against the moonlit sky. Next to it the graveyard cast shadows on the sloping lawn. At the bottom of the cemetery a smooth, clear lake made a pretty picture in the moonlight. And beyond Chloe knew, but could not see, farmland stretching flat and fertile in all directions, squared off by a grid of gravel roads encasing the land in neat one-square-mile sections. On almost every square-mile section a family farm stood, loving and working their land. She could hear the dry rustling of cornfields desperately needing rain.

Chloe's maternal grandfather had come to Fairview from Belgium long ago, a young man with a dream of owning land. He had rented a farm for years until he was able to buy it. Then he lost it during the depression, but worked to earn it back again. Chloe had heard the story often from Grandpa and Grandma. The same farm was now a little run-down, but it was still the home where Momma had grown up, and where, last Christmas, when the family came to celebrate with the grandparents, Grandma had taken Chloe's hand and pressed a dollar bill into it. "Chloe, a nun can pray her whole family into heaven," she had said.

Hearing a girl's laughter, Chloe shrank against a tombstone, feeling suddenly out of place. A couple strolled by her in the shadows, walking very close to each other before stopping to embrace. As they headed down the hill, their voices drifted back to Chloe with a familiar tone. She knew those voices. All her senses reeled as she took it in. She sat leaning against the tombstone for a long while, spying on them. The boy's stocky figure, the girl's shape, both stood out in the moonlight, confirming their identity.

Chloe stayed crouched against the tombstone until the couple had sauntered back to the dance hall.

Slowly Chloe headed back too. The strains of a polka drifted to her on the hot, humid air. Cars cruising by revved their motors and squealed their tires. One car honked at her. The dance was nearly over. The blue lights on the marquee of Ben's Ballroom blinked, announcing fifteen minutes before closing. People milled about the doorway, talking and jostling one another. Some staggered and talked more loudly than they needed to, their eyes bloodshot from drinking.

"Chloe, where have you been?" Michelle asked, "Have you seen Lucy?"

"Ah, no. Why?"

"She's supposed to ride home with us. She came with us, and she's supposed to go home with us."

In the car Chloe kicked off her high heels and leaned back. After a while Lucy arrived, swinging her purse and waltzing toward the car. "Where were you all night?" Michelle asked.

"Around. My cousins from the cities were here, didn't you see them?" she asked, kicking off her heels and drawing her feet up under her skirt. She leaned her forehead against the window and watched the traffic thinning out as Michelle drove the car toward home. Chloe's heart beat in angry protest at her newly discovered knowledge. She felt betrayed. Lucy's friendship this summer had all been a sham. All those visits to the farm, so eager to help around the house, willing to trek across the fields with lunch for the boys, Chloe now saw in its true light. She felt like a fool. On the long ride home she reviewed it all, Lucy's behavior and Owen's remarks to her. It all made perfect sense. Lucy and Owen were in love, had been in love, but were afraid to tell her.

But was it true love? What about Lucy's vocation? In Sister Damien's words, was she "throwing it all overboard," for a cheap thrill? Chloe stole a glance at Lucy. Her eyes were closed, and there was a quiet look on her face.

CHAPTER 36.

Last Days

To Chloe it seemed no time at all had passed between seeing Daryl's picture and meeting him in person.

"Chloe, this is my cousin, Daryl. Daryl this is Chloe," Kenny said the night of the wedding rehearsal.

"Just like his picture," Chloe thought, smiling up at him as they shook hands. He was a trim young man with a blond crew cut. His blue eyes in his tan face smiled at her in a friendly, easy way that she liked immediately. She knew she was going to enjoy her sister's wedding very much.

During rehearsal, she made frequent prayers of thanks to Mary, the blessed mother, for this gift. After rehearsal old Father Black inspected everyone's baptismal certificates to make sure the entire wedding party was Catholic. Next he disappeared inside the confessional to hear their confessions. Because everyone must receive Holy Communion at the wedding Mass, he gave them this chance to wipe their slates clean.

At last the heavy wooden doors of St Eli Church groaned shut behind them, and the bridal party stood on the church steps smiling at one another. Pink clouds lingered in the western sky like lace lingerie.

"Tomorrow you tie the knot!" Daryl said to Kenny.

"Let's go over to the Jake's Saloon and celebrate," Kenny suggested, "drinks are on me!"

As the jolly group of young people crowded into a booth, laughing and joking about tomorrow, Chloe stole furtive glances at Daryl. Someone mentioned that they were under age and had to drink cokes. So they sat, sipping and grinning at one another while attempting small talk. Chloe wondered what he knew about her. She knew that he was a freshman at the University of Minnesota, played football, and had been the lead in the senior class play last year. "A popular all-around guy from a good family!" was how Michelle had described him to her.

"Can I take you home?" he asked after a while, "We haven't much time to get acquainted before the wedding."

"Sure," Chloe said, her heart singing. She could say yes because for the next twenty-four hours the rules of the villa were suspended; by her. She had decreed that Michelle's wedding was her party too, a gift from God, a last fling before she buried herself in the convent for Him.

Michelle, leaning against Kenny's chest, wore a look of rhapsody. Kenny nodded approvingly as the younger couple rose to leave. as Chloe walked out of Jake's Saloon with Daryl, her blue skirt swishing around her knees, she felt all eyes on her. She laughed for the sheer joy of being, just once, like all the other girls. Daryl opened the door of his blue Thunderbird and she slid to the middle, just as she had seen other girls do. She had never felt as thrilled and happy as she did now, right this moment. The smell of Daryl's cologne, the brush of his shirtsleeve against her arm, was a part of the new rarified air she would breathe for the next two days. Chloe smiled into his blue eyes as she played with the radio dial.

The next morning the wedding day dawned early. Because of the fasting rule for Communion, wedding masses had to be held early. No eleven o'clock or two o'clock weddings such as the Protestants had! Oh no! It had to be an all day affair, from early morning mass to late night dance. The house was jumping. Mrs. Polanski complained that the baby inside of her had picked the past week to have a growing spurt. "I simply cannot wear a girdle!" she wailed, flinging the despised article from her as Chloe entered her parents' bedroom. Her mother began frantically rummaging through her drawers, pulling up nylons and throwing them to the floor, crying that she couldn't find a pair without runs.

"I might have a pair," Chloe said, dashing upstairs. Her head felt light. She was hungry, but she could not eat or drink until she had received Communion during the wedding Mass. To *not* receive communion as a bridesmaid would raise many eyebrows, for it meant you were in mortal sin.

For a moment she recalled last night, when Daryl put his arm around her and held her close, brushing his lips on the top of her hair. Even now, recalling it, feathery echoes of his touch stirred in her. "Was that feeling sin? Since I don't know, it can't be," she decided, putting her conscience at ease. In two days she would enter the convent, put on black, and say good-bye to all such concerns. Finding a pair of nylons for her mother, she started down, and then paused at the boys' room to bang on their door. "Get up you guys!" she shouted. She had heard Brent and Owen stumble in late last night, hours after she was home and in bed. She hoped they had honored Michelle's plea to not get drunk before her wedding so they wouldn't look hung-over.

It was a windy day. Rain had spit fitfully during the night, spattering the drought-stricken fields like a tease. The sky hung low with big soppy clouds. Dad was doing chores and checking machinery. He had hinted yesterday that he might have to work the afternoon of the wedding and skip the reception. It had caused a stir in Momma. Chloe hoped it wasn't true, that it was just Daddy's way of reminding them that not even his daughter's wedding was as important as keeping the farm work going.

Owen and Brent shuffled down stairs, sleepy-eyed and squinting against the daylight. Brent sank into the nearest couch and watched Momma rush about, feeding and dressing the children who were dancing about excitedly in their underwear.

"Remember not to eat anything!" Momma reminded Brent as she stepped over his feet jutting into her path. "Oh, what I wouldn't do for a cup of coffee!" she declared, touching her hand to her throat.

"Me, too!" Brent groaned.

Eventually the big boys were dressed in their suits. They stood before the mantle mirror, combing their hair. One was short and blond, the other tall and dark. "We've got to look our best for our sister's wedding!" Brent said mockingly.

"Yeah, too bad I got such a headache!" Owen groaned.

"Chloe, polish my shoes!" Brent ordered, collapsing on the couch again.

"I polished them yesterday," Chloe snapped.

"Well, do it again!" he said, kicking his shoes toward her. "I can't wear them in the wedding looking like that."

"What did you do with them, play in the mud?" she asked.

"What's it to you?" he snarled, leaning back and closing his eyes. Brent was handsome, with his black hair and fine strong features. "It's too bad he can't be nice, too," Chloe thought. "You polish them," she said, "I don't have time."

"Nope that's women's work," he said, opening one red eye.

"I have my bridesmaid dress on," she retorted, knowing they were losing precious time. She heard her mother's voice wail from one of the back rooms, "Oh where is Dad at a time like this? Why does he have to do those chores so thoroughly the morning of the wedding? It won't hurt those cows to go hungry one day!"

Momma dashed, her dress open in the back, to look out of the window. "The father of the bride shouldn't have to do chores on the day of his daughter's wedding," she whined, turning toward Brent, "Why aren't you boys out there helping him?"

Brent swore and kicked a cardboard box lying at his feet, sending it across the room. "I do plenty of work outside," he said, his voice rising, "and right now I'm waiting for my shoes to get polished so I won't track mud on the wedding runner!"

Momma sprinted back to her bedroom, motioning for Chloe to follow. She lit up a cigarette and inhaled deeply, her hands shaking. "You better polish his shoes," she said. Chloe set her jaw. "Your sister is upstairs crying 'cause she thinks she'll be late for her own wedding. We don't want her to have red eyes. Do it for her, Chloe, please, and then you four older ones can leave. Dad and I will come later with the little ones."

"Okay," Chloe said between clenched teeth. She grabbed Brent's shoes and stomped into the kitchen where she tied an apron around her bridesmaid dress and went to work.

Finally the four were ready. It was almost eight thirty. The wedding was at nine. "Go," Momma begged, shooing them toward the door. "We'll be right behind you." As Michelle sailed through the living room clutching her wedding skirt up from the floor, the children stopped in all their excitement to stare. Momma peered anxiously out toward the barnyard looking for Dad. Peter, the ring bearer in his navy blue suit, was holding hands with Effie, the flower girl, still in her slip. Joey stood in his crib, bawling for attention in the hubbub.

"If you see Dad when you drive by the barn, tell him it's time to come in and get dressed!" Momma called after her departing children. The station wagon's middle seat was draped with a white sheet for

Michelle to sit on. Chloe sat down carefully next to her, adjusting the bride's skirts and holding her beaded purse. Owen drove, with Brent seated next to him.

"I forgot to tell Momma where Warren's shoes are," Chloe cried as the car bolted down the driveway that curved past the barn. But Owen kept driving. The car fishtailed as it leaped onto the gravel road and sped toward St. Eli. The two sisters leaned against each other, steadying themselves.

"Please God, help Mom find the shoes! Mary, mediatrix of all graces, help them get to church on time!" She prayed silently.

Michelle sat very still, her eyes closed, the slightest frown lingering on her smooth white forehead. Dark curls tumbled about her shoulders. Chloe admired how her sister could apply makeup so artfully to accent her eyes and bring out the blush in her cheeks. Her red lips looked exquisite against her fair skin. In her lap her veil rested like a cloud. Michelle's finely tapered hands; perfectly manicured, held the crown, its sparkling beads and sequins glistening like teardrops in her hand. Gradually her frown faded, and the bride looked serene. She was nineteen.

Gravel pinged beneath the car as a cloud of dust hid the farm from view. This is the last time I'll take this wild ride, Chloe thought as Owen swung the car onto the smooth blacktop and pressed the pedal to the floor. His passengers swayed and steadied themselves, saying nothing. When Owen cruised to a halt in front of St. Eli's, guests were already arriving, disembarking from their cars and gawking. Michelle regally gathered up her lacy skirts and bridal train and stepped onto the sidewalk like a queen.

Chloe, carrying the veil, opened the side door to the musty church basement. "Michelle, there's spiders down there," They both peered down into the dark church basement. For many years old Father Black had forbidden any social activities downstairs, so it was dusty from misuse and cluttered with odds and ends of old pews and chairs.

"If you don't need the bathroom, better not even go down there," Chloe warned. So the bride-to-be swept up the side stairs to the "crying room," just off the foyer, where she could wait unseen. It was a small room with pews where mothers with babies stayed during Mass. Large wide windows in the front allowed them a view of the sanctuary. Through the half opened door Chloe saw Momma arrive in the foyer. Her red nylon bubble dress with the black velvet bolero, chosen so carefully with the pregnancy in mind, camouflaged her thickening form nicely. Chloe felt proud of her, and hoped Michelle was happy too.

Shy Effie, demure in her flower-girl dress, exuded all the dignity of her position. Peter, with a solemn air, held the satin pillow. Somehow Momma had scrubbed and dressed and combed all the little ones into a reverential submission. And Warren had his shoes. Daddy, in his new navy blue suit, smiled broadly at the guests as they entered the foyer, shaking their hands and looking perfectly pleased to be the father of the bride.

Aunt Thelma bustled into the crying room just in time to pin on the corsages. As she bent over Chloe she whispered, "I'm so glad you could be here for this!"

Michelle stood quietly waiting, her white veil a diaphanous cloud about her head and shoulders. Finally everything was in place. The hubbub subsided and the younger Polowski children, seated in the front pews, swiveled their heads to watch Momma join them.

The organ music began. The church was filled with people. As Owen escorted Momma down the spotless white runner, the bridesmaids lined up nervously. The wedding had begun. By the time Chloe started down the aisle, Sister Clarice had pulled out all the stops on the pipe organ, and the church fairly vibrated with triumphant wedding music.

Chloe set one foot down hard, commanding it to stop shaking, willing her other foot to follow. "This will be the only wedding I'll ever march in," she thought.

"Not so fast!" someone hissed, and the blue carnations in her hand quivered violently. Slowly, ever so slowly, wobbling and scared, she traversed the long aisle until at last she glimpsed Daryl approaching from the right. She grasped his suited arm in relief, and leaned on his strength as they continued on, through the open gates of the communion railing and up three steps towards the altar. As they genuflected together, Daryl whispered, "So far so good."

Chloe smiled. They parted, stepping to either side to await the coming of the bride.

CHAPTER 37.

"True Love"

At the wedding breakfast Daryl lifted his wineglass to Chloe's lips and said, "To a job well done." She didn't know if it was the sweet red wine or his blue eyes looking into hers that filled her with such delicious joy. But she already knew that she was closer to love than she had ever been before. She felt a little breathless.

Nevertheless, her happy thoughts quivered with qualms. "Was Daryl an eleventh-hour temptation, planted by the devil to break her resolve? Or was he a going-away gift from God?" Chloe shut her eyes tight and decided for the latter.

The American Legion Hall was a plain brick building built on a side street in Delton, one of the many small farm towns situated along Highway 69. The hall was plain and spacious, with a large kitchen and room enough to comfortably seat two hundred dinner guests. The wedding decorations, blue and white crepe paper streamers, were looped gaily beneath the ceiling, wall to wall. Large paper wedding bells hung in every window. The young pretty waitresses stood about like dolls, each wearing a frilly blue apron lovingly sewn by Michelle and Mom. Many girls at the wedding were beautiful, Chloe noticed, yet Daryl didn't seem to see them. When his buddies asked him to play poker uptown with them, he turned them down. That this good-looking, likable guy preferred her company to that of his buddies amazed Chloe beyond measure. Daryl's regard for her, his conversation and his smiles, directed just at her, were like gifts she kept opening. Overcome by her feelings and astonished at this experience, she sipped the liquor and drank in Daryl's attention while she felt herself falling hopelessly in love with him.

Later Chloe could not recall what they had talked about, or what they had done, she just remembered that the afternoon was blissfully short, spun with a rainbow of feelings that didn't stop glowing even though she knew that, like Cinderella's evening, this all must end. But she didn't think about that now. She would enjoy this day, with this boy, to the full. "He's just another boy, like my brothers," she told herself, but his deep blue eyes smiling back at her denied it. His genuine kindness made her feel weak.

In this euphoric state Chloe even thought kindly of Lucy. Instead of despising her, she understood her. Seeing Lucy and Owen openly seated together across the room, she felt happy for them. They were a perfectly matched couple, meant for each other. But to apply that same kindness to her own case was harder. Daryl and she had just met, while Lucy and Owen had known each other for years, and had gone steady secretly all summer. Lucy wore his ring openly now, on a string around her neck, while Owen strutted like a rooster. Chloe was not yet sure how much she meant to Daryl.

In the late afternoon, when the sinking sun winked sideways into the Legion Hall, Daryl suggested they walk uptown for a breath of fresh air. A soft breeze fanned Chloe's flushed face. As they sat on a wooden bench watching the shadows dancing on the grass, the world had never looked more beautiful. With Daryl's arm around her waist, his hand now and then brushing against the slippery organza of her bridesmaid dress, her blood stirred and her head spun. Then, in broad daylight, he kissed her. Her whole body responded with sparks of pleasure and of love. Finally they broke apart and quietly watched the dancing shadows again. His voice sounded husky as he asked, "Did I hear someone say you are going to be a nun?"

"That's what they say!" she remarked lightly, brushing away a wisp of hair from her eyes. His question hung between them like a shroud. "I've been going to a convent school and this will be like a continuation of that," she said. "I'm going to give it a try," she added, feeling like a traitor.

He sighed and nuzzled her neck, sending a thousand sweet messages coursing through her veins. "Seems like you already gave it a try," he said. When she didn't say anything, he said, "You smell so good. What perfume is that?"

"Oh, some Rose stuff of Michelle's." She was glad she was sitting down because she felt weak all over. By eight o'clock the wedding guests, thanks to the free liquor flowing all afternoon, were roaring; men didn't walk, they reeled. Women who, that morning, had entered the church with demure expressions and carefully coiffed hairdos, now bore an air of slovenly disregard for neatness. Young people, glassy-eyed, weaved about with slack grins on their faces. Cars began to leave for Fairview for the dance. As usual, the dance was open to the public, an arrangement that helped the groom pay for the band. At Ben's Ballroom a rotund woman seated behind a small window sold tickets. The gruff policeman whose job it was to stamp the hands of those who had paid their fifty cents, took one look at Daryl's carnation and Chloe's bouquet and waved them inside. The ballroom lights were dimmed. The booths were filled with people waiting for the grand march to begin.

The wedding party gathered in the tiny foyer, waiting for Brent, who had been missing for a while. Michelle's wedding skirt stood out like a lace bell. Her train was neatly gathered to a loop that she held in her hand. She glowed, as though supremely happy. Kenny, at her side, also looked pleased and handsome in his dark suit and bowtie.

The march was to start at 9 p.m. Just before nine, Chloe looked out at the darkening street in search of her brother. Someone said they had seen him staggering uptown around four. But no one had seen him since. Then, just as they were about to start without him, Brent appeared. His tie hung loose and his eyes were bloodshot. But he was present.

"It's about time!" Chloe hissed. He ignored her and took his place in the procession. The groom signaled the band to begin. Wild clapping, whistling and stamping of feet accompanied the music as the wedding party promenaded around the edge of the dance floor. Michelle and her bridesmaids laid their bouquets on the band's platform as they had seen a hundred other brides and bridesmaids before them do. Then their partners took them in their arms to dance the first dance. Camera light bulbs flashed, and whistles pierced the air as they turned and swayed to the music. People streamed into the dance hall, filling the doorway, crowding into the already overflowing aisles between the booths. The air was thick with smoke. This would be a wedding dance the whole county would remember.

Chloe and Michelle exchanged looks of relief. Together they had "accomplished" this wedding against great odds. Chloe felt the victory as much as if it had been her own wedding. Floating in Daryl's arms, she knew there would be no limit to her dances tonight. In her slightly inebriated state, she felt suspended above the reality of the convent, and she dared not look down.

At 3 a.m. it was over for Chloe. She walked into her bedroom, too tired to stand. Looking into the mirror she laughed at herself; her blue beaded tiara with the tiny veil still perched on her head. She kicked off her high heels and moaned with pain as her sore feet, tortured all day by those pointed toes, were at last released. Odd, that she had not noticed it until now. She sat down on her little wooden barrel stool, took her diary and wrote furiously.

"Dear Mary,

I, Chloe Polowski, feel so empty and lost. I don't know where I belong. One more day at home ... and then ... oh Mary, I'm so sick of being good! I wish I could forget about loyalty and perseverance and just be myself. But who am I, really? I look at Owen and Lucy, they are so happy. I'm glad for them. I hope their love is true. I like Daryl. He's smart, good looking, considerate. Please help him find a good wife.

Help me, Mary, to put my whole heart and soul into the *postulancy.* It won't be easy. I want love so bad, Mary, *real genuine love.* I don't even know what love is, but please let me learn it, live it, teach it, give it in its best and fullest way. Love, oh Mary, *love,* I think, is everything. Teach me God's love. Teach me how to love *Him* above all else.

Affectionately,
Clover. (That's what Daryl calls me)"

Exhausted, Chloe reached back to unzip her dress, only to realize that Aunt Zita had applied a tiny safety pin inside the top of her zipper that she could not undo. She tried again and again, but with no success. Her first instinct was to wake Michelle next door, but with a pang she remembered her sister no longer lived here. Not wanting to wake her parents, she lay back on her bed in her bridesmaid dress, the fabric rustling, the waist pinching, too tired to care about any of that now. She knew that, later, this illicit love, this perfidious joy would vanish and leave her bereft. But for now it was worth it to be this happy, to feel this alive.

"I still belong to You, Mary. I still want to be your daughter," she prayed as she fell asleep. "But help me, help me, help me."

It seemed as if the next moment it was daylight, and Daddy was calling from the bottom of the stairs, "Get up sleepy heads! Party's over! There's work to be done." Chloe rolled over. The organza dress, wrinkled and twisted around her waist, cut painfully into her breasts. Slowly she got up, her head throbbing, her mouth dry, her feet aching. Today was her last day at home. Tomorrow night she would sleep in the convent. "Unless I stay home like I stayed in this dress," she thought, looking at her rumpled self in the mirror. "It would be sooo easy. Why is life like that, so easy to do the wrong thing?" Chloe reached back to find the safety pin that had held her prisoner all night. It opened on her first attempt. She unzipped her aqua blue dress and it fell to the floor. She pulled on an old pair of plaid pedal pushers, a shirt, and her tennis shoes for the day ahead: Her last day in the world.

By nine o'clock all able-bodied members of the Polowski family, except Momma, who stayed home with the babies, rode in the blue station wagon to Delton. There the American Legion Hall was just as the partiers had left it, the sidewalk strewn with beer bottles and paper cups, the inside in disarray. Crepe paper streamers lay draped over tables and chairs. The same farm women who had cooked for the wedding had faithfully returned, already clanging pots and pans in the kitchen, preparing the leftover wedding food for the workers' meal.

"Free beer for all workers!" Daddy announced, setting down a heavy wooden case of Grain Belt on the table. Owen and Brent began to fold and stack chairs while Daddy ordered the young kids to pick up trash. The floors were sticky; they would have to be mopped.

Chloe yanked on a blue streamer. It tore in her hand. She moved a metal folding chair and stood on it to retrieve a white paper wedding bell. Someone stepped up lightly behind her, and with one arm around her waist, removed the bell. It was Daryl. She felt weak as she glanced back at him. She couldn't speak. His lips touched her hair, and with his arm still around her, he handed her the bell, asking, "Did you want this?" She felt dizzy. Someone in the hall whistled.

"We could fall," she said, glimpsing Aunt Zita's face through the kitchen opening. At lunchtime the aunts and neighbor ladies served a meal that echoed yesterday's wedding feast; roast beef with gravy, mashed potatoes and peas, four different flavors of Jell-O salads, fruit salads, and rolls. There were even small squares of wedding cake left over. Everyone was in a jolly mood as they rehashed the wedding and gossiped about who had been "three sheets to the wind" last night. Everyone said they were tired, but Chloe didn't think that anyone, except her mother, could be as tired as she was. Her legs felt leaden. She moved as if in a dream, separated from the others, yet seeing and hearing them. She was relieved that no one teased her and Daryl about sitting together for the meal. Instead people accepted it as if it were the most natural thing in the world. Would they also accept it if she quit her high ideals and just stayed home? "Don't love the gift more than the Giver." A quote from the convent warned her.

Lucy and Owen worked together, steering the cart loaded with folding chairs to a corner. Lucy rested a languid hand on Owen's thick arm. They moved about as though they were already one, as though the battle was over, and they were in complete and happy agreement with everything concerning each other. "Did Sister Damien know?" Chloe looked away. Tomorrow, safely ensconced in the convent, she would be on firmer ground from which to ponder God and His ways; from which to overcome Satan.

"Come over to my house after cleanup." Lucy told Chloe, "Others are coming too." Chloe detected a glimmer of sympathy in Lucy's eyes. I should spend my last day home, she thought guiltily. Also, I need sleep. But later, when Daddy stopped at the Fry's farm to drop off Mrs. Fry's roasting pans, Chloe said, "I'll take them in, Dad, and stay a while. This is my last day to see Lucy."

"All right Chloe," he said, studying her, "Just don't overdo it. You have a big day ahead of you tomorrow."

"Yes, Daddy," she said, closing the car door. A big day to return to Mater Dei to study and pray and write cheerful letters home and never dance or drink or wear a pretty dress or kiss a boy again.

"Oh, Chloe, there you are! Thanks!" Mrs. Fry smiled warmly as Chloe entered her farmhouse, the house that Lucy wouldn't have to leave tomorrow, or ever again, until and if she married Owen. As Mrs. Fry put the pans away, Chloe wanted to ask her if she were disappointed in Lucy. "Did she blame Owen?" But Mrs. Fry bustled about her kitchen as if her only concern was getting all her pots and pans back into the right places.

"If tomorrow she rose, fed the kids oatmeal, washed the dishes, baked a cake, cooked dinner, walked in the woods, came back inside and started supper, no one would stop her," Chloe thought. Daddy had to be in the fields and Momma was dog tired. The day would pass deliciously. After supper she would stroll to the edge of Huffiker's grove and watch the pink and golden clouds pile up into surreal mountains against the western sky, knowing that a new and different day was here. Entrance Day would be past. And she would be free.

"You can't. It's too late! You've invested so much. You've struggled and persevered! Think of your vocation, a precious gift. He doesn't give it to everyone. High school is over and you have no girl friends here. Daryl will go back to the cities and you may never hear from him again. You'll be stuck on the farm with the work and the babies, with no way to get out. Don't throw it all overboard now! The best is just around the corner!"

On the back porch Chloe found Daryl reclined in a lounging chair, sound asleep. His sleeping form drew her, making her want to sit beside him and lean her head against him and sleep too. Brazen! Her own thoughts frightened her as she tiptoed past him.

Lucy and Owen sat in the parlor, their heads bent together over a bowl of popcorn. They didn't even see her. Upstairs she found Lucy's younger brother working on a puzzle. She helped him for a while, but felt so limp and tired that she could barely hold up her head. Softly she stepped down the stairs, past the porch door, her heart beating fast. Outside, she determined not to think of him. Wearily she leaned against a tree, closed her eyes and wished the day were over. It had been a mistake to come here. She should be at home, resting.

Just as she decided to lie down somewhere and ease her throbbing head, Daryl appeared on the front steps, looking refreshed and alert. "Want to play catch?" he asked, tossing her a softball.

"Sure," she lied; catching it and throwing it back. She didn't have the energy for this, but activity was safer than sitting near him, wrestling against forbidden feelings all over again. Deliriously happy, terribly tired, she followed him to the large grassy farmyard. His tender smile shone on her like sunshine. She could not believe how he accepted her, didn't criticize or hate her in any way, even when she couldn't throw as well as he did. He loved her, she was sure, and he had almost told her yesterday, but had kept quiet out of respect for her vocation. His consideration only made her love him more.

Her bones leaden, she wound up for the throw. He leaped, caught it, and returned the fire. "Smack!" she caught his return ball, her hands stinging, and sent it sailing back. As the ball flew back and forth Chloe looked toward the sun, low in the west, and asked for the hundredth time if the boy before her was a gift from God or a plant from the devil.

"Oh!" she squealed, jumping for a high ball that sailed past her, over a fence, and into the weeds of the ditch. She streaked to the fence, climbed it, and then heard a rip as her plaid pedal pushers tore on the barbed wire. "Oh no!" she cried, laughing and rolling down the steep ditch, hiding her exposed leg in the tall grass. The rip was five inches long, stopping just short of her underwear. She held it together as Daryl leaped over the fence and landed in the tall grass beside her. "Did you hurt yourself? Let me see." He was perfectly composed as he reached out to touch her leg. A rush of elation mixed with sadness overtook her. It was getting late. The sun was sinking over the Mr. Fry's dried cornfields, weak and sickly in its harvest time.

"Oh, that's too bad!" he said with genuine feeling, "Were they new?" He rested his hand on her knee. Her blood pounded. "No, they were old," she said, "and I won't be wearing them after today anyway."

He looked away. She wanted to reach over and stroke his strong, tan arm. But with a mighty effort she resisted, leaping up. "Let's find that ball before it gets dark," she said. But her heart stayed in the weeds where Daryl rose slowly. Together they searched for the ball, she chattering on, flailing her arms, patting the ground, and crawling about, with him not far behind. Once he stopped, kneeling on one knee, watching her, a puzzled pleading look in his eyes.

"Here it is!" she yelled, picking it up and tossing it toward the yard. He helped her through the fence, holding the barbed wire for her while she crawled through. "Be careful there now," he warned solicitously, and she swallowed hard against this kindness flowing like a sweet balm around her. "Was he kind because he was a city boy? She knew so few boys, just her brothers and their friends, and they were so different from Daryl."

"I've got just the thing for that tear," Daryl said, taking Chloe by the hand.

"What?" she asked, tossing him a puzzled look.

"You'll see," he said, putting his face close to hers, so that she felt herself soaring, like a balloon, up and up. He led her to his car and reached into his glove compartment, removing a roll of masking tape. "I came prepared," he said, smiling and holding it next to her plaid pedal pushers. "Color even matches!" he said, "Your mother will love me." He tore off a long strip and said, "Stand still now. Let me see that leg."

She stood still as he knelt before her and carefully, slowly, wound the tape around her leg. Her legs grew weak. She thought she would melt with pleasure. Tomorrow she would have to confess her sin. She looked down on his blond crew cut, wanting to bend down and kiss it. But instead she looked up at the blue sky above.

Later, as they sat watching the sunset, Chloe wanted to lie back on the grass. But that would be cheapening herself. Again it impressed her how close sin lurked every moment, just a breath away—and after all those years of prayer, too. It was a puzzle to her. She had thought she was stronger than this. "No wonder the world was so bad, if sin was this easy. This was why the world needed convents and seminaries, to keep people good. Otherwise it would be impossible," she was sure.

Just then Owen came looking for her, saying Dad had called and wanted them home for chores. "Hurry now," he said, looking sharply at Chloe.

The house was dark and cluttered and messy. Mother had slept all day, leaving Agatha, a child herself, in charge. The baby was bawling, and the little kids were whining that they were hungry. Walking through the living room, stepping over the debris of broken toys and newspapers, the strong smell of urine emanated from the full diaper pail. The lid was loose. She went to close it when she smelled a worse odor; full diapers tossed in a corner. "Agatha," Chloe scolded, "you're supposed to rinse these out immediately in the toilet, or they smell to high heaven!"

Her skin felt sticky from the heat. No breeze stirred through the old farmhouse with all its windows painted shut. At least her home wasn't tugging at her like a temptation to abandon her vocation too, she thought cheerfully. She was glad for that, at least.

"Chloe, See if you can get a little supper going, okay?" Daddy said, standing in the middle of the stifling living room. "Mother's all worn out, and the kids are hungry. It should be easy with all that food from the wedding we brought home. Just heat that up," he said.

CHAPTER 38.

Postulancy

They would be late for Entrance Day. She could see it now. Momma was washing clothes because "the kids have nothing to wear." Luckily they had a dryer. Momma's belly looked really big now, two days after the wedding. She breathed heavily as she walked.

"It'll take you a while to get over the wedding," Chloe said, putting her arms around her mother and hugging her.

"What a load off my shoulders," Momma said, smiling. Now, with Michelle married, Momma needed her more than ever. Daddy and the boys were already baling alfalfa in the fields. Chloe had heard him roust the boys at five that morning, saying, "Come on now. Make hay while the sun shines!"

For the first time Chloe knew how Michelle must have felt all those years when she, Chloe, had left home. Now it was she who missed her sister and kept expecting her to come down the stairs. Besides that, Daryl's face, his arms, his smile, hovered near her all morning, while a flat empty feeling, like the color of gray, crept over her, preparing her for the denial that lay ahead. But what if she let the day slide by, just rolled on the couch with little Joey who craved attention anyway, and didn't call Daddy in from the fields? He was behind because of the wedding anyway. He'd welcome the extra time. This day would pass the same as any other, one minute at a time, until all the hours had disappeared, and it was too late for her to go.

Chloe said flatly to Momma. "To get there in time for the ceremony we have to leave at eleven." At twelve noon the men hadn't come in from the fields yet. When Dad finally did appear, standing in the kitchen door in his striped bibbed overalls and straw hat, Chloe said passively, "I'll be late."

"I sure wish there was a bus that could take you." Daddy said, "Do you think you could wait until tomorrow? Forecast says it might rain tomorrow, and we could go then so much more easily."

"If I wait until tomorrow, I won't go," she said quietly.

Daddy went to wash up.

In the car at last, Chloe looked back at the farm fast receding from her. On Easter she would be back for one last visit. After that, it would be seven years until she visited again, unless one of her parents died. Even the death of a brother or sister would not permit a home visit. It puzzled her how she could miss home, as messy and hectic as it was. It was her greatest fault, attachment to home. A growing lump in her throat made it almost impossible to swallow. Gravel pinged against the underside of the car as Daddy and Momma stared straight ahead, too exhausted from the wedding of their first daughter to do anything more for their second daughter than deliver her to her chosen destination.

The little girls in the back seat sat as subdued as doves trying not to be noticed. Chloe smiled at their eager faces, then quickly faced the front and watched the scrawny cornfields zip by. Passing by St. Eli Church she thought of Jesus inside, hiding in the small dark tabernacle. He was a prisoner too. He knew how she felt. At the stop sign the car paused, then turned right. They left the school, Pete's Gas and Jake's

Saloon behind. After that there was nothing to look at but the gaunt brown cornfields, their tassels prematurely shriveled, humbly waiting to be picked; that, and the big September sky arching gorgeously all around them.

Then the whole summer, with all its wonderful, terrible longings swept over her, and she began to cry. Silently, big wet tears rolled down her face. She reached down for a white dish towel lying on the floor of the car, a leftover from the wedding, and pressed it to her face. Great sobs heaved up from her soul. The wedding, Daryl, her own wobbly walk down the aisle, Lucy so happy with Owen, Momma pregnant, Michelle gone; it was all too much to take in. Repeatedly she determined to stop crying, resolutely drying her eyes and throwing down the towel. But thoughts and faces and feelings more powerful than her resolve rose, drowning her weak defenses, striking her raw emotions. Again and again she picked up the towel, used it, and threw it down again. A raging flood of pent-up feelings, having surfaced, would not be quelled. It wasn't a cleansing cry, as when she had hugged Daddy at Mater Dei so long ago, or a relieving cry, as when she had once asked Daddy to turn around and take her home, but an exhausting cry that left her feeling shipwrecked and sore inside.

Her parents stared straight ahead, saying nothing. "They must be very tired," she thought, "not to speak to me." They drove through Mazel Run, Fairvew and Delton. Finally in Morgan Town, her mother turned to her and said, "Chloe, if you keep that up, your face will look puffy. What will the sisters think?"

"Yeah," Her father's voice was husky from the long silence. "Don't get all worked up. You're worn out from the wedding and short on sleep."

Chloe didn't reply. After a while her father added, "It's been a hard summer, Chloe. But don't you worry none about us here. We got it rough once in a while, but we always manage to get by somehow." His shoulders rose and fell with a sigh.

"Yes," her mother glanced back at Chloe's tear-drenched face with a tragic look, "we don't do things as smooth and as fancy as some, but like Dad says, we manage. And things will ease up now, with the wedding over. With you and Michelle gone, the younger girls will just have to pitch in more."

Chloe squeezed her eyes tight against more tears. I should be grateful, she thought, for such understanding parents. But instead she felt miserable; evil too. She had flirted with sin and now it was time to pay. When she thought back to her very first trip to the Heights, she felt ashamed. "How disappointed that young eager girl would be with me," she thought; "crying like a baby when I'm finally at the threshold of the convent! I should be thankful my vocation is intact, that I survived and persevered. I'll feel better once I'm back with my friends, on solid ground again. Forcing a smile she turned and spoke cheerfully to the little girls growing restless in the back seat. As they began to chatter happily, Daddy turned on the radio and Momma dozed to the drone of the newscaster.

As they neared Magnolia her mother turned to her and said, "Here Chloe, put on some lipstick." She handed Chloe her shiny gold tube and watched with a sympathetic smile as Chloe applied it to her lips.

"There," she said, "you look much better."

The convent parking lot was nearly empty. Postulants strolled about in the walkway. With a start Chloe realized they were her classmates. "There's Kay!" she gasped, "and Angie!" How different they looked in their long black dresses. As she scrambled from the car Kay flew toward her, squealing with delight, her lanky arms and elbows flying. "You're here! You're here! I was so worried!" Kay cried, hugging her as though her life had just been saved.

"Oh, Kay, I've had such a summer, you wouldn't believe. You look great! Just great!" As classmates gathered around Chloe, all dressed in the same black dress with the neat white collar and the short cape flapping about their shoulders, Chloe felt out of place in her yellow suit and white pumps. She was conscious of her puffy eyes. There stood Aimee, the perpetual twelve-year-old, with her straight hair and plain freckled face, as limp and sexless as a doll. Had she suffered even one trauma this summer? And Mabel, with her grandmotherly ways, looked perfectly at ease in her new garb. Lena Betters, her arms buried in her sleeves, her back erect, presented the perfect picture of a postulant.

"Chloe! Chloe!" It was Gladys from St. Eli, her hair cropped so close that Chloe hardly recognized her. She poked her head into the station wagon saying, "Hello Mr. and Mrs. Polowski. Get over the wedding all right?"

Chloe caught the dour face of Sister Amadis, her new mistress, approaching. She was older than Sister Damien, and her smile looked more like a smirk than a welcome. Her heavy black eyebrows on her long face made her appear stern. She walked with a plodding gait. "You're late," she said, looking Chloe up and down with mournful eyes. "Did you get your sister married off all right?"

"Yes, Sister. And Daddy had to do field work today, to catch up, and so we got off to a late start."

Sister smirked. "Seems like there's always something important going on at your house. But now you can settle down to some peace and quiet. Do you want your dress?" The question hung between them like a dare.

"Oh, yes, Sister!"

"Can I help her?" Gladys asked, taking the suitcase from Mr. Polowski and starting toward the convent. Sister Amadis nodded. Chatting gaily, Gladys guided Chloe through their new quarters. Everything was modern, new and exquisitely clean; with pastel walls and vertical blinds on large, wide windows;

"And here's our very own gymnasium!" Gladys announced, leading Chloe into a large high-ceiling room with a polished wooden floor. Sunshine gleamed down on them through skylights. A piano stood in one corner, next to a dressing screen and a metal clothes rack, on which hung two black gowns.

"This is where we recreate," Gladys said, as though she had lived there a week already. She set the suitcase down on the piano bench and motioned for Chloe to get behind the dressing screen. She obeyed, and Gladys opened her suitcase and quickly began handing black items to her over the screen. Chloe pulled on her black stockings, her black half-slip, her white T-shirt, and the black knit wristlets that covered her arms to the elbows. "Are you ready for the dress?" Gladys asked, coming around to where Chloe stood. She held the precious garment up and dropped it over Chloe's head, patting and pulling until the thick woolen fabric lay in neat pleats all around her waist. The wide stiff belt around her waist was secured the hooks and eyes. Then Gladys, all business, laid the black cape over Chloe's shoulders as if she were a queen. She closed the hook at the throat. "There. You look great!" she said, beaming. Chloe stepped out from behind the screen. She sighed happily. This time yesterday she was sitting on the back steps with Daryl's arms around her, and his lips in her hair. She went over to the metal rack and touched the black gown still hanging there. "Who's is this?" she asked.

"Oh, some girl who never showed up," Gladys replied, stuffing Chloe's street clothes back in to her suitcase snapping it shut. "Let's go, your parents are waiting."

Chloe lingered by the empty dress. A tag pinned to it read: Carolyn Jones. Easing herself onto the piano bench, her elbow struck a discordant note as she rested it on the keys. Some girl had changed her mind at the last minute and stayed home, not giving her vocation even one day's chance. "Who was she? What was she doing now? And how did she feel?" Chloe wondered. "We might have been friends. Or *my* dress might still be hanging here too, if…"

"Come on!" Gladys called. Chloe wanted to muse longer on Carolyn Jones and her aborted vocation. She stood up slowly and said, "I'm sure glad I made it, aren't you?" Then suddenly she remembered the dreaded question the aspirants always asked each other upon returning to the Heights. "Who's missing?"

"Deb." Gladys replied glibly, as though waiting for the question.

"Deb Bach? What happened?" Chloe's stomach was galloping.

"She's marrying an older guy; owns the laundry where she worked this summer."

"Marrying? How old?"

"Past thirty."

"She's crazy."

"He bought her a rock." Gladys paused, waiting for Chloe to digest this. "And Gloria."

Gloria Glacken?" This name fell on Chloe's heart like a hammer. These two girls from the villa, who had sat through the same instructions and shared in the same spiritual practices, would walk no more with her.

"What happened to her?"

"No one knows for sure. She just didn't show up. Someone said she's going with a guitar player who came into her Dad's music store a lot."

With great longing Chloe thought of Sister Damien. Seeing her now would set her world aright. "I can't wait to see Sister Damien," she said.

"She's gone," Gladys said briskly, starting up the stairs.

"What do you mean, gone?"

"She's not mistress at the villa anymore. She's been transferred."

"Whaat?" Chloe's sank to a step and sat down at this news.

"She's teaching downtown at a co-ed school," Gladys said coolly, almost pleased, it seemed, to have all the answers and to see Chloe's response.

"Why didn't she tell us?" Chloe asked.

Gladys shrugged. "Probably just found out herself. They don't get their orders until the end of August sometimes."

Chloe's victory over her temptations felt hollow now. She had persevered for this: To walk the Heights with no hope of meeting Sister Damien coming around a corner? To not hear her sweet voice in greeting, and receive that look that made everything worthwhile? She had returned to be robbed of a great comfort.

"I bet she feels terrible," Chloe said, rising slowly to her feet.

"Actually, no. She said she was ready for a change. Come on, let's go."

Chloe followed dumbly, tripping on her dress. God was stripping her of all that she loved, and it hurt like a whipping. As they stepped out into the dwindling day, her little sisters, Julie and Effie, dashed toward her, then stopped and looked up in awe at the change in their big sister. Shyly they each took one of her hands and led her to their parents. It was five o'clock, time for families to be gone and for the new postulants to enter their new abode. Momma, looking drained and tired, took a picture of Chloe with her brothers and sisters before they all piled into the car. Once again Chloe stood alone, waving good-by; but she wasn't a school girl anymore. She had made it. She felt glad. Surely, after a good night's sleep she would feel much better about everything.

That evening the twenty-two new postulants gathered in their airy new study room with its vertical window shades and smooth, shiny desks. The back half of the room was their "living room, with a fireplace facing a circle of couches and easy chairs, and a coffee table in the center. "If Mom could see this!" Chloe sighed, "She would know I was in a nice place." But from now on, all their living spaces were off-limits to visitors. Though only postulants, their secret life in the convent had begun, and even family could not see beyond the visiting lounge where they would sit and visit with them.

"College starts tomorrow, "Sister Amadis said drily as she handed out textbooks to her new charges. "You will all take the same core classes, as we are a small school with a small staff and can't offer a lot of choices." Turning to Chloe she said, "You may come to my office for your breviary. The others received theirs in the ceremony."

In her office, a wry smile on her lips, Sister Amadis handed Chloe her breviary, a slim black book with purple edges. They would pray from it three times a day, she said. Chloe thanked her. Then Sister removed her glasses and began rubbing them with her hankie. "I hope your tardiness today is not an indication of any hesitation on your part," she said. Her deep-sunk eyes regarded Chloe mournfully.

"Oh, no, Sister!" Chloe responded as earnestly as she could. "It was just getting over the wedding and all—there was so much work, and the men are behind with the fieldwork, and Daddy wanted to get the boys started."

"All right Chloe," her new mistress interrupted, replacing her glasses with a half-smile. "And can I be assured that you will not be seeking more exceptions to the rule now that you're here?"

"Oh, no, Sister!" Chloe shook her head earnestly.

"Very well. Here, wipe that lipstick off of your mouth," Sister Amadis handed Chloe her hankie. Chloe's lips were chapped, and it hurt to rub them with the cotton cloth. Sister watched until she was finished, then, taking her hankie back, smiled a strange, downward curving smile. "Much better." she said.

Chloe knelt in chapel, saying her rosary, her eyes riveted on the altar. She struggled with sleepiness, as, one by one, she pushed the beads through her fingers, praying, "Hail Mary, full of grace, the Lord is with thee ..." She yawned. She was not sleeping well at night, so in the quiet of the chapel she lost the battle to stay awake. Dreaming, she was washing a floor that was curved like a ball, and as she worked she kept sliding off while her pail and her rag kept slipping out of reach. People were watching her, but no one would help. Somehow she finished, but there was another room to clean just like it, and another, and another, each with a rounded floor on which she slipped and slid, falling and getting up again.

Gladys poked Chloe. She awoke and looked sheepishly toward the altar. "When would God help her? But He had. She was a postulant." She hugged herself, liking the warm coziness of her woolen habit. This was what she had always wanted. Joy would come surely, little by little, as the summer memories faded and college work increased. Surely this gray feeling would lift and she would revel in her victory, in this safe harbor from the temptations of the world. She was on her way to becoming a school sister of Mater Dei.

The other postulants appeared to adjust quickly. Jay took charge of basketball practice. Gladys was appointed to be the postulants' barber because she knew how to cut hair. Lena set an example in study habits, and Mabel Sappe, neither exuberant nor negative, commented wryly on her new surroundings in a way that made even the dour mistress of postulants smirk. Kay's face bore a serious, determined look that told Chloe not to ask her any questions.

Almost certain, at first, that Milly Haatch, the former day student, wouldn't last the first week, Chloe was surprised to see her emerge into a calm, studious woman content with her lot. With her face scrubbed clean of lipstick and eye shadow, she looked almost angelic as she grew in kindness and joy. To Chloe, the very sight of Milly filled her with chagrin. This was not what Sister had said would happen. It was she, Chloe, who should be ten steps ahead of Milly, straight from the world. It was she, Chloe, who should feel satisfied and glad that she had reached the shoreline. Had the aspiranture years been for naught?" It was an awful thought.

While Chloe wrestled with these questions, Angie tapped her on the shoulder. "Sister Amadis wants to see you."

"Yes, Sister?" Chloe stood in her office once again, waiting for the sallow-faced mistress to look up from her desk. She held a letter in her hand. The envelope had been opened.

"You received a letter today … from a boy; Daryl Nosbusch. Is he a friend of yours?

Chloe's left leg quivered. "Yes, Sister, I met him this summer."

"What sort of a friend was he?"

Chloe found it hard to talk. She swallowed. "Oh, not close. I met him at the wedding." She said this with a shrug, her heart pounding in her throat so that her voice squeaked.

"I see. Then this letter is not anything that would interest you at this time?" Sister's head was shaking slowly back and forth as she spoke, her starched veil scratching against her wimple in a sad, stifling sound.

"Well, no, I guess not, Sister."

"You guess not? Or you know not? I'm sure you know, if you stop to think about it, that it is highly inappropriate for a postulant to receive a letter from a boy."

"Yes, Sister." Chloe glimpsed her name scrawled on the letter.

"-Of course, it's your letter, and I can't keep it from you, though I strongly recommend that you not read it. Do I have your permission to drop it in the wastebasket?" Sister held the letter over her wastebasket.

"Yes, Sister," Chloe said. She watched the letter drop into Sister's wastebasket. As she turned to go, Sister said, "Please do not mention anything about this to any of your classmates."

"Yes, Sister, I mean, no, Sister, I won't."

Back at her desk Chloe opened a book and pretended to read. Her face burned. Daryl had written to her! How bold. It must mean he liked her. If they had had just a little more time together . . . maybe. What had he said to her? She wanted to know. It had happened so fast, she had not had time to think. She shifted in her seat, almost ready to go back and say she had changed her mind and she wanted to read it. It was her letter, legally. But what would Sister say to that? What dark suspicions would such action kindle in those mournful eyes?

College work, with the stacks of books to read, gradually pulled Chloe away from her worldly distractions. She enjoyed learning and was thankful for time to enrich her mind.

Petite, sporty, upbeat Angie Zimms was suffering from another migraine headache. They had started a few weeks ago and were occurring so often that she spent many days in bed, in a darkened room. Each day a different postulant was assigned to bring Angie her meals. Along with this duty came permission to talk with Angie for a half hour.

"That Milly Haatch doesn't even seem homesick!" Chloe exclaimed to her suffering classmate one noon as she set her tray down carefully by her bed. Angie's crinkly smile wreathed her face. "Doesn't seem fair, does it?" she laughed. "Oh, I wish I could be well, like you, Chloe, so strong."

Chloe smiled. She was glad she looked strong to others, but inside she felt as weak as water. She wanted to say this, but she knew by now that any discussion of personal struggles with a fellow postulant was forbidden. Only Sister Amadis was fit to be a counselor or a confidante.

What did Sister talk about tonight, at lessons?

"Oh, she told a story about a girl who was in the convent once. And then she left because she said she couldn't stand to be lonely. She eventually met a man and got married, and they had a nice wedding, but as they were walking out of the church, the man turned to his wife and said, 'You'll never get me to set foot in a Catholic Church again.'

So the woman went to Mass alone for the rest of her days."

"Oh. That's sad," Angie said. Chloe agreed.

On Sundays the postulants wrote home. Chloe wrote furiously, pouring her heart out on paper. "I never thought keeping silence would be so hard! I thought I liked quiet! But really, Mom, to be limited to speaking just polite greetings all day and to get to talk for just two hours a day is murder! You'd be surprised how many areas in the convent are zoned 'Quiet.' Let me tell you ... every hallway, stairway, and entryway, plus anything near the chapel. And the chapel is in the middle of it all! We barely get started talking, and oops! It's a quiet zone! Even at meals we keep silence while a postulant reads from a spiritual book. I didn't know until now what a *genuine pleasure* it is just to talk. It's freedom, really. And how much I miss it!"

Chloe read what she wrote, and then quietly crushed it in her hands. It had felt good to write it. She began again.

> "Hi Mom, Dad, and all. We sure have good meals here, and the classes are hard, but that's what we're here for, to study and to learn. I'm enjoying the fall weather so. The trees on the Heights have all turned orange and red, and the sunsets are glorious."

"Silence is golden," Sister Amadis often said. Chloe thought back to her days as a student when she had admired the postulants from afar as they strolled across campus, arms tucked deeply into their sleeves. They had seemed the quintessential college students, satisfied, earnest and content. "But underneath had they too roiled against all that silence?" There was no way of knowing.

Chloe marveled how, for so many years, she had talked whenever and to whomever she pleased. Now it was a treat to talk for a half-hour break after supper with fellow postulants. She recalled home with all its noise. Her mother longed for peace and quiet. But would Mom like it here? Sister Amadis said that their silence was meant to be devotional, a quiet speaking with God. But it was so lonely.

One evening in study hall, Sister Amadis flicked the lights off and on for attention. The postulants looked up at her solemn face, her dark eyes woefully sad beneath her black, bushy eyebrows, as, without preamble she said, "I expect none of you will be surprised to learn that Angie Zimms went home today. Anyone could see that she was falling behind in her studies. She plans to see a specialist about her headaches and hopes to re-enter the convent next year. Pray that if this is God's will, she will keep her motivation."

That was all. Chloe's eyes connected with Kay's, and she read there the horror of what they had just witnessed. This casual way of treating the departure of a postulant had never been Sister Damien's way. No expression of grief, no visible angst, just that curt cold announcement. "It must be because we're in college now," Chloe decided, "and older." Vocations here can be kept or rejected. No one was going to "make" you keep it. This fact both scared and strengthened Chloe. She could leave and be a failure, or she could fight the good fight of faith. It was up to her.

Winter snows flew and Chloe and her friends learned how to wear a shawl instead of a coat around their shoulders. The shawl was a black woolen rectangle with no clasp. It had to be held at the neck with one hand. This left one hand free to throw snowballs. Chloe wondered if this was part of a plan to "mature" them by putting away childish things. But every now and then on a bright sunny day when the snow sparkled, an exuberant postulant would drop her cloak and sling some snowballs, and soon all the others were joining in the fun.

The best thing about Christmas in the convent would actually be the day after, which was visiting day. Momma, huge with child, stayed home. But Daddy came, bringing along Agatha, Veronica, Julie, Effie, and Peter. Chloe, flushed with excitement, seated them in the lounge and proceeded to treat them to candy and cookies, popcorn balls and soda pop. She glowed with pleasure to see their round eyes widen at the sight of all the goodies.

One month later, in study hall, Sister Amadis tapped Chloe on the shoulder and whispered, "Your father called and has quite a little surprise for you."

"Oh, what Sister?"

"Twins."

Chloe squealed and jumped with surprise. Sister stood aside saying, "Tell the class your news." There were smiles and congratulations all around, and then they all settled down to study again. Chloe wished she could have talked to her father directly, to hear his voice telling her about the babies. But she musn't wish to be an exception to the rule. Two weeks later Momma's letter came, telling her how surprised she had been on the delivery table, after she had delivered a baby girl, to hear the doctor say, "Mrs. Polowski, you're going to have another baby!"

Gladys knit two pairs of booties for the babies. Kay made a card for Chloe to include in her letter home. The babies were named Ella and Edward.

CHAPTER 39.

Candidature

No one in the study hall guessed, Chloe thought, that just by burying her nose in her cape she was home, holding the twins again, hearing the chaos and the noise of home, smelling the pork chops sizzling on the stove. Easter vacation had come and gone. One brief week at home, and since she was back, Chloe had discovered that her black cape held all the smells of home. She knew she ought to beg to have it dry-cleaned. That was the responsible thing to do. But knowing that her next visit home would only come upon the death of a parent, she put off that action. Then, soon too many weeks had passed, and she was too embarrassed to ask.

"Futuro est bona Qui? The good poison … the bad poison." Chloe glared at the Latin page open before her. She had been hunched over the book for thirty minutes without translating one line. Her paper was full of doodles. Eight months had passed since Entrance Day, and Chloe was now a candidate. This meant that she now wore a partial veil, a short black veil with a starched white edge that circled her head like a hair band, allowing only her bangs to show. It was a thrill to feel it swishing around on her back as she walked. Soon Reception Day would dawn, and she would become a novice. She had been doing so well, studying hard and praying earnestly. Even the silences were easier. She felt some rays of happiness in her routine, giving her confidence that this life did hold some joys and triumphs.

But since Easter vacation, things had gotten harder. Besides the cape, with its memories trapped in its warp and woof, her ballpoint pens grossly hindered her homework. They skipped writing at the most inopportune times. She was constantly rewriting a word, filling in the blanks, or scratching it out, and rewriting it on top. Her papers looked sloppy. Tonight, frustrated, Chloe began to scribble, noting with a sardonic twist of her mouth where the pen wrote and where it didn't. It felt like a deliberate trick to frustrate her. Yesterday, in keeping with the vow of poverty, she had gone to Sister Amadis during the recreation hour and begged for permission to throw away her old pens and to get a new one.

"Let me see them," Sister had said, lifting gloomy eyes to Chloe. She was sitting at a small table. She took the pens, pushed aside the crossword puzzle she had been working on and started drawing circles on the newspaper. The pens didn't write. Undaunted, Sister kept it up, round and round and round, with no visible ink. Sister pressed harder, making grooves in the newspaper. Finally a trace of ink appeared. She continued until the ink flowed freely in dark concentric circles. "Aha!" she crowed, gleaming up at Chloe, "let me try another."

A small knot of candidates had gathered to watch as Sister Amadis, repeatedly succeeded in coaxing ink from the dry pens. Finally, triumphantly, she handed four pens back to Chloe, saying, "These will work now."

But they didn't. It was impossible to write one word of her homework without retracing it or switching pens. Angrily she jabbed her pen at her Latin book. No mark. She jabbed again, pressing harder. She made circles. Sometimes the pen wrote, sometimes it didn't.

She pressed harder and harder until she was striking at the page in a fury of strokes, tearing and ripping through to the pages underneath. Suddenly she felt a "twang" in her heart, as when a string on a guitar suddenly breaks. Breathing hard, she stared at her damaged book, feeling strangely better. Her heart bounded with a sort of trembling shudder. Only a few candidates sat in the library. Lena Betters was blissfully reading a book entitled, *Lost in God*. Kay was bent over a mess of books and papers, deeply engaged. Milly Haatch looked up, blinked, and then returned to her work. Chloe closed her Latin book and opened a novel. But her conscience nagged her. "For shame! To have such a temper after all that you've been though. Where's the virtue? Where's the grace you've earned in the last five years? Has it all been for naught?"

Chloe lay her head down on her arm and let the smells of home engulf her. A sob rose and smothered in her chest. She wished there had never been an Easter break. She had been doing all right before that. Now things had changed. But why? Her visit had been no different than any other time; the noise, the work, and the kids fighting while through it all floated the sweet patient face of Mother struggling under her interminable load. Nothing had changed, except that Michelle was gone, and everyone was older and bigger. Chloe had pitched in as usual, hitching up her black wool dress to scrub the floor, tying on her long black apron when she cooked. She had cleaned out closets and washed down cupboards, baked cookies, held babies, made formula and drank coffee with Mom; loving every minute of it. She had left without a tear. "Why can't I get into the groove again?"

Was it Owen and Lucy's wedding, a day which they had so kindly set to accommodate her home visit? She had not enjoyed it as she had expected. Instead of feeling secure in her convent garb, she had felt dowdy next to the girls in their high heels and bright spring dresses.

The reception had been held on the Fry's farm, the same farm where she and Daryl had played catch not so long ago. But she no longer thought of him. No, it was something else. The atmosphere of the people there, the laughter and the talk, and the way it stopped when she drew near had discouraged her. "I was a fish out of water," Chloe said to herself as she tried, once again, to study her Latin. While the other girls sipped drinks and eyed the boys, she had stood at a distance, talking with the older women. It was awful. Even jolly Uncle Lawrence, who, at other weddings, had teased or complimented her, now tipped his hat respectfully to her before inching away toward where the drinks were served.

Chloe, of course, had not gone to the wedding dance, which suited Momma fine, to have a reliable babysitter for the twins. But after her parents had left for the dance, Chloe sunk into the couch with an odd feeling of abandonment. While the kids tore through the house, she sat and felt sorry for herself. When the twins cried from hunger, she rose tiredly and searched the refrigerator only to discover that the formula was all gone, and no bottles were sterilized. So she set to work boiling the water to sterilize the bottles and nipples. While searching for the right kettles she discovered a half-empty bottle of Mogen David wine tucked in amongst the pans. Gratefully she poured herself a glass of wine. "Ahhh," she said as the sweet red wine soothed her throat, creating a warm place in her stomach. "At least I get this." She sank dreamily back on the couch drinking wine while she waited for the water on the stove to boil. "If I would put on a pair of blue jeans, I don't think I'd ever go back. Why am I so weak and ready to defect? I should have more resolve by now!"

Chloe rose to do her duty, lifting the steaming glass baby bottles with the tongs and setting them on the counter to cool. Both twins were howling by now as she measured and mixed the liquid formula with the boiled water and filled the sterilized bottles, screwing the nipples with their caps on tight and then setting the two bottles in cold water to cool down the milk. As she waited she jounced the howling babies, one in each arm. Finally, she laid the babies down on their sides, both in the same crib, gave them each a bottle held in a bottle holder. "Here's your lukewarm milk," she crooned, to them, "lukewarm, just like me!" As they both sucked eagerly in their cribs, Chloe poured herself another glass of wine and recalled her conversation with Mrs. Pasadag. It was her one bright spot in the day and she wanted to relive it. A corner of her mouth turned up as she recalled the tired woman's face. A farm mother of eight, she held one child on the hip and bulged in front with another on the way. "Sally is in eighth grade, and she wants to be a nun, like you," she said.

"Oh, that's wonderful Mrs. Pasadag. You must be so happy!"

"Yes." The woman said, but she looked aggrieved. "I am. And I don't want to do anything to discourage her. But I … do you? … I mean, does she have to go now, in high school? She wants to go. But I don't want her to leave home yet. Can she still be a nun if she waits until after high school?"

Chloe knew the girl in question; a sweet, pliable girl, just the sort to make a good aspirant. "I was Sally's age when I went to the villa," Chloe said. The mother nodded, her neck taut.

"I went right out of eighth grade."

Mrs. Pasadag nodded again.

"But I was too young. I know it now. You're right to want to keep Sally home. A girl needs her mother at that age. She can always enter the convent later, when she knows more about life and …" Chloe could almost hear Sister Damien gasp; but she saw Mrs. Pasadag's face relax as she spoke. "If Sally has a vocation, God will protect it until she is old enough to enter the convent, after high school." Chloe shuddered inside as she spoke the heretical words. But Mrs. Pasadag looked relieved. For a moment they looked into each other's eyes as if a secret message had been conveyed and understood.

The bell rang, bringing Chloe back to the present. The candidates gathered in chapel for Vespers. Then they filed silently upstairs to their dorms to get ready for bed. "I set Sally free," Chloe said, peeling off her black wristlets and laying them on the dresser, "even if I can't set myself free." Lifting her voluminous black dress up over her head, the smells of home, locked in the woolen fibers, washed over her once again: the bacon she had fried for the boys, and babies she had burped on her shoulder. Sister said that putting on regular clothes while home would be like longing for the "leeks and onions of Egypt." But for her it had worked the opposite way. Keeping her dress on at home had brought all the leeks and onions back with her.

That night Chloe dreamed she was walking in the snow carrying the twins. They were cold and crying. She began to remove her own black clothes and wrap them around the babies until they stopped crying. Then she was wearing just her underwear, walking in the snow. She walked and walked until she saw a cabin. She went inside and there unwrapped the babies who had not stirred or made a sound for a long time. To her horror they were dead, smothered by the black woolen clothes. Her sister, Michelle, shook her head sadly and said, "You should know babies can't take all that black."

Chloe awoke in the dark. "How much black could she take? Was Satan using dreams to sow doubts about her vocation? Why did God permit it?" She could not discuss her dreams with anyone, for Sister said dreams revealed a person's deepest longing and most secret fears.

CHAPTER 40.

Facts of Life

Chloe sat in botany class, staring at a large diagram of a flower as Sister Theresa pointed to its different parts and lectured: "The flower contains the reproductive organs, which produce seeds and fruit. These reproductive organs are the stamen, which is male, and the pistil, which is female. The sex cells are produced through a series of changes involving several divisions of certain cells, including a special division known as meiosis, in which the chromosome number is reduced by one half.

"To bring about fertilization, the sperm cell, which is the pollen grain, must contact the egg cell, which is located in the ovary of the mature pistil. Chloe bent over her notes, trying to ease a stomach cramp that had seized her the moment Sister began to teach. She shifted her position, causing Sister Theresa to frown at her before she went on.

"It does this by sending a pollen tube down to the ovary, which results in the fusion of the egg and the sperm nuclei—which is fertilization. The chromosomes are then doubled to their normal number in the fertilized egg cell. After several divisions the young embryo is formed."

Chloe wrote down "meiosis" in her notebook, thinking, "Here I am, learning about the sex lives of plants, when I don't know the sex life of humans!" Her embarrassing lack of knowledge about the details of human reproduction had become a painful pit in her stomach. Why she had waited so long and not asked Mother when she was home she did not know. Or Daddy could have dropped her off at the library while he shopped at the Farmer's Coop. To ask anyone now was too humiliating. Her heart seemed to be bubbling beneath the layers of wool covering her chest.

Soon she would be shut away in the novitiate for a year, with only spiritual books to read. Her need to know had once again become urgent. She should know, she had to know – and know now! That evening she asked permission to visit the Academy Library.

"For what reason?" Sister Amadis asked, looking askance at her.

"Research for my B-Botany paper," She stammered.

"But our library here covers every subject."

Chloe swallowed, hoping Sister wouldn't repeat her pen experiment of the other night, and personally walk her through the botany books in their library. But instead, to her great relief, Sister nodded, the usual smirk playing about her lips. "Go at seven. Take a companion. Be back in an hour," she said.

"Yes, Sister" Chloe said. Seated, her heart gradually grew quiet. With great relief she learned that Mabel had also asked permission to go to this library. She was not one to pry or ask questions. When they got there, a few boarding students were seated studying. A sister sat behind the front desk. Chloe was glad to note that Mabel's research took her to the opposite side of the library from her.

She tried not to hurry as she began her search in the "500" section. But her hands were clammy and her breath came in shallow gasps as she took down *Earth Life*, scanning its index: "Renal, 33, Rennin, 404, Resects, 218." Glancing nervously around, she reached for another. *Biological Beginnings.* Here, surely! Her heart beat hotly, but outwardly she kept cool. "Relapse, 312, Renascent, 201, Reserpine, 400." No? An alarming thought struck her. "What if the facts of life were banned here—their every reference excised from every book by some little old nun assigned that job late at night when no one could see her?"

She scanned the rows of books. "All useless! Were all facts of life expunged?" One of the boarders glanced at her and smiled, but it only made her tremble and hate herself anew for waiting this long. "Where was the information she needed and craved? Maybe God didn't want her to know. But He created us, so He *must* want us to know how!" Hopefully, she removed a book called, *Nature's Guide* and when she read "Reproduction, human, p. 103," in the index, her chest swelled with her heart's hot beating. With hasty fingers she found it and read: "The human embryo normally requires about 280 days from conception to birth. It takes a sperm and an egg to make a zygote, which becomes a fetus." "I know that!" she thought with such vehemence that the student in uniform glanced at her as though she had spoken the words out loud. Her groin pained her with mysterious stabs as her tension increased. The next two books disappointed her as well, with their few scant sentences. Hungrily she read: "When a person approaches his teen years, conspicuous changes take place that lead toward sexual maturity and the ability to reproduce." That tidbit was all it offered.

Feeling rushed because Mabel might show up at any time saying she was ready, Chloe yanked out books by the handful, any book whose title even hinted at the subject, and, with arms full, carried them to an alcove glowing pink from the setting sun off far away. She sank into an easy chair full of self-loathing. If she had asked Momma, she would have told her.

"When the male passes sperm to the female, desiccation, not only of the male and female gametes, but also of the subsequent embryo, is prevented." Confused, she tried the next book.

"When the ovum is fertilized, it becomes implanted in the mucosa of the uterus, begins embryonic development, and is surrounded by embryonic membranes."

And an ovum is an embryo, which becomes a fetus, which becomes a baby with a soul! Chloe repeated this to herself, exasperated. She had learned that in eighth grade, when Sister Clarice railed against abortion. Soon time would be up. She opened another book.

"The reproductive organs produce sex cells. The female's ovaries are attached dorsally in the coelom, near the kidneys, each supported by a mesentery." Chloe looked forlornly about her, unspeakably sad and angry. Must she wait another year to find out? Replacing that stack of books, she grabbed three more. One book had drawings of the male and female private parts, with each part labeled. "I know that!" she hissed.

One important piece of the puzzle remained missing. *How?* A girl with an armload of books hesitated at Chloe's alcove, but seeing Chloe's face, sidled away. Chloe paged quickly through the rest of the books. The word "sex" jumped out at her, making her lean forward, fists clenched, eyes wide open. She read: "During sexual arousal the male organ becomes engorged with blood and becomes erect. Sexual intercourse occurs when this erect penis is inserted into the female vagina, naturally lubricated by secretions triggered by her sexual arousal. During intercourse sensations of love and excitement increase until there is a climax, a release of sperm from the penis into the vagina. This sperm then quickly makes its way to …"

Chloe's whole body pulsed. Finished reading, she sat back satisfied, her heart slowly growing quiet. So that was it. Intense gratitude toward the writer who had put it so plainly swept through her. She could breathe again. The last puzzle piece was in place, and it made beautiful sense—like everything God did. It was not awful or dirty, as some had hinted; just private. Her only embarrassment was in learning it so late. Softly she closed the book, leaving it on the chair. Relieved and at peace, she took a deep breath and sat still until Mabel came to say she was ready.

That night in the privacy of the bathroom, Chloe reached down to touch herself; a forbidden act, of course. But she needed to know. Then, slowly, shockingly, she realized that she was deformed. She did not have the opening that the book described. She was not normal, not built for sexual intercourse. She leaned against the stall. "Was that why God had called her to be His bride? Was her deformity connected to those stomachaches that came when she saw a boy she liked? Chloe closed her eyes. Brent's mocking words "You're odd!" rang true. She could never marry. But no one need ever know. The news was sad, yet it gave her a strange new strength, a stronghold against temptation. Called and chosen, God was making sure she would not run off. As sacred and as beautiful as the marriage act was, by God's choice it was not for her. Chloe set her jaw. As hard as this news was to take, it felt good to be fully informed on the facts of life.

CHAPTER 41.

Bride of Christ

"We've got one year of college under our belt!" Chloe remarked to Kay as the two inhaled deeply of the fresh spring air. It was May 30, 1960. The schoolgirls were gone for the summer and the unnatural quiet on the Heights unnerved Chloe. It was as if all the real people had left and all that remained were black shells floating gracefully about the campus, just their faces and hands showing they were human. The Heights had changed from a bustling campus to a quiet retreat center.

"And Reception Day is just six weeks away!" Kay replied, her freckled face aglow.

"And we'll get the white veil!" Chloe exclaimed, clasping her hands together. "Do you think the novitiate will go fast?"

Kay shrugged. The novitiate year loomed as a deep, dark mystery. Old nuns said it was a special blessed time, like a honeymoon. But Chloe wondered how she could go a whole year without seeing her parents. It was a year of seclusion, which meant that their only companions would be their fellow novices. The novitiate year seemed to Chloe like a long, dark tunnel. But just as foreboding as that was the eight-day retreat coming in June. "I haven't kept silence for more than a day in my life!" Chloe said worriedly, "I can't imagine keeping silence for eight days!

"Me neither," Kay said. "But maybe if we keep thinking about how we'll see our family for three straight days afterwards, it won't feel so bad." Chloe agreed that that was a comfort.

Meanwhile, as time inexorably marched toward their "wedding day," the candidates busied themselves with summer school, hemming their new habits and doing spring-cleaning. During the recreation hour they pulled weeds and edged sidewalks. Sister Amadis, their mistress of candidates, had declared war on dandelions and so, every lunch hour, she beckoned the future "brides" with a crooked finger to attack them. Her big, sad eyes positively glowed every time a postulant pulled one up by its taproot.

As the day approached, the candidates were called upon to prepare the dormitories for visiting nuns who would also be making the retreat. One hot Saturday as Kay and Chloe labored on the third floor dormitory of the villa, flipping mattresses and making up the beds, Chloe felt a pang in her breast, "like a spring popped," she joked privately to herself. She paused momentarily, but kept on working as the pain subsided. Sweat trickled down her sides beneath her woolen dress. This very dorm where she had spent her first night away from home so long ago looked the same as ever. She wanted to nudge Kay and say, "Remember how that spoiled Kathleen cried after lights were out?" but instead she took a deep breath and kept working in silence. As she raised her arms to spread the sheet, her heart raced and began thumping so that she lunged for the chair and sat down. Kay cut her a concerned look.

"It's the heat," Chloe whispered, fanning herself. Kay took one of the glasses from under a basin and got her a glass of water from the bathroom. Feeling better, Chloe resumed working, but she was worried. This was not the first time her heart had acted strangely. Once while merely sitting in chapel, and once while walking to the cemetery her heart had alarmed her; jerking and hurting like it had a will of its own. After a time, Kay left for her piano lesson and Lena took her place. Together they made a vigorous team. Lena's pink face glistened with sweat. Two red dots marked the center of her cheeks. After a while of turning over mattresses and spanning sheets, Chloe sat down on a bed and murmured softly to Lena, "Why do we have to flip the mattresses every time a new nun sleeps here? Nuns are the cleanest people on earth!"

Lena tilted her head and smiled sweetly, saying nothing. Chloe felt rebuked. Lena suffered too, but how patiently and contentedly! Envy tore at Chloe's heart for Lena's unflappable peace. "Why did things seem so easy for her?" Chloe trembled, troubled at her dislike of work. "Hadn't Daddy always called her his 'good little worker?'?" But here even the city girls showed more stamina than she did. "It wasn't fair," Chloe decided. "Godliness with contentment is great gain." Sister quoted, "but how to get it? Or were the others pretending? Did they rail as much inside as she did?" At these thoughts Chloe's heart ached with a physical pain. Maybe she had heart trouble. Chloe reached beneath her cape and pressed her fist to her heart to ease the pressure growing there.

The next day as the candidates strolled out to the cemetery for their noon walk, Chloe rubbed her hands together and said to Gladys, "I must have grabbed those mattresses too hard yesterday. My hands feel tight and sore, like I have arthritis or something."

"Only old people get arthritis," Gladys said.

"I knew those Rites brothers and Arthur was the worst one!" Mabel joked.

"Maybe its nerves," Chloe mused, clenching and unclenching her fists, "my fingers tingle, like they're on fire."

"Nerves? What would you be nervous about?" Gladys asked.

"Well, not speaking to anyone for eight days, for one thing!" Chloe exclaimed.

Mabel Watts nodded. "We're all nervous about that."

* * *

Eight days later the solemn retreat was over. Reception Day dawned clear and bright. At the first ring of the bell a thrill shot through Chloe. The dreaded retreat was over. Eight days spent in unbroken silence had passed, and she has survived! The long days of prayer and meditation were over. And today was her wedding day. She would receive the white veil of the novice of the Humble Handmaids of Mater Dei.

"Did her jaw still work? If she tried to speak, would any words come out?" Chloe glanced out of the window at the perfect July day. Soon her family would arrive. Or they might be already here, walking into chapel, the little ones excited and Momma, as usual, tired. Chloe admitted that, right or wrong, she was as glad to see her family as she was to receive the veil.

Silently, eighteen candidates in black dresses and capes with little white collars at their necks assembled in the library, speaking to each other only with their eyes. The eight days of silence had so changed and subdued them that their whole demeanor was changed. All signs of girlish vigor or youthful glee had vanished. And in its place was a solemn maturity that governed their steps and controlled their movements. It appeared that these young women were, at last, ready to receive the white veil of the bride of Christ.

Finally, their hour arrived. Silent as ghosts they gathered at the rear of the chapel and waited, subdued and expectant. Chloe's heart pounded beneath the pleated layers of wool lying over her chest. She blinked several times. The chapel was ablaze with lights. The pews were packed with people. Worldly smells of smoke and perfume emanating from them reminded her of the great gulf between them; poor married folks and these virgins now approaching the altar.

The pipe organ from the loft opened with a flourish of glorious notes, breaking the expectant silence. Everyone stood to attention as from the choir loft burst the triumphant song of last year's novices. "Magnificent anima mea Dominum!" Their young female voices soared as one pure tone over the people's heads, past the balconies where the old nuns sat, and toward the brightly lit altar, all its marble statues shining white. For them the year of seclusion was over, and they sounded ready to take their vows and serve the world. Below, the candidates moving in slow procession were prepared to take their place. "Et exsultavit spiritus meus in Deo Salurati meo." They answered, walking two by two down the aisle toward the Bishop, who awaited them in splendid robes.

Chloe scanned the full pews for her family. Just as she passed she glimpsed them, Mom and Dad, Agatha, Veronica, Julie, Effie, Howie, Peter and even Joey! – All squirming and straining to see her. Emotion, like an electric impulse, shook her, filling her with pride and joy and exaltation. Her day was complete. Jenny Dorsey was there too. This was the grandest day of her life—the beginning of her honeymoon with Christ, which would culminate, one year from today, in her Profession Day, when she would take her three vows of poverty, chastity, and obedience. She would also receive her black veil and become a full fledged nun.

The double column of candidates parted, taking seats on two rows of backless stools set up in front of the pews.

"Sancta Dei Genetrix," a group of priests intoned.

"Ora pro nobis," The novices answered in clear round tones.

"Sancta Virgo virginum," the male voices sang.

"Ora pro nobis," the female voices answered.

"Sancte Gabriel,"

"Ora pro nobis."

The ceremony was long, and Chloe's back ached as she sat on the backless stool. Following the litany of the saints, the high Mass was said in Latin. This was followed by benediction and a prayer. From somewhere in the depths of the packed pews a baby cried, and its wail sounded unnatural in this pristine and holy setting. As the Bishop droned on, Chloe's candle dripped profusely, overflowing the paper collar and running down into her hand, where she formed it into a warm ball of wax. Furtively she glanced to her right and her left to see if anyone else had this problem. But their candles seemed to be burning normally, with no excess drips. She squeezed the ball of wax until the Bishop's voice boomed, "What do you desire?" The candidates rose, blew out their candles and laid them on their stools. Chloe rolled her ball of wax beneath her stool before answering with the rest: "Your Excellency, we humbly beg to be received into the congregation of the Humble Handmaids of Mater Dei."

"Are you, however, able to live according to the rules and constitutions of the congregation?" The priests asked in unison.

"Reverend Fathers, we hope, with the grace of God, to be able to live according to them."

The candidates knelt, then stretched out on the floor, face down. Chloe, her forehead resting on her hands, studied a dusty shoe print on the terrazzo floor. It was the size of a man's shoe.

"Lord, you have commanded women to wear the veil as a sign of their submission and modesty."

Far away, Chloe heard scissors snipping. Someone coughed. A pair of shiny black shoes approached, stopping next to her face. After a strand of her hair was cut, the shoes moved on. Rising, the candidates stepped forward to receive their new habits. Father Schlick's eyes burned like blue coals as he placed into each postulant's outstretched arms a fat bundle of black and white clothing.

Chloe walked away dazed with her precious load. At the convent door Mother Euphemia met them, her eyes glittering up at them, for she was short of stature. "Daughters, is it your intention upon entering this convent to take up the cross of Jesus Christ, and to follow Him?"

"This is our intention," they replied. Mother threw open the double doors, and allowed them entrance. As soon as the doors closed behind them, the room burst into a flurry of activity, as nuns assigned to help each postulant rushed forward to do their duty. Their task was to dress a postulant in a novice's garb. While one nun removed Chloe's cape, the other pinned back her hair. As they worked they murmured prayers, pushing and pulling on Chloe as children might dress a doll. "Put on the whole armor of God," Sister George said, placing the starched wimple across Chloe's chest and bending it at its proper creases.

"That you may be able to stand against the wiles of the devil," Sister Alvina lisped, bobby pins in her mouth. Loud scraping noises reverberated in Chloe's ears as her dressers labored to outfit her in the holy habit. Tugging and tying, they wrapped her head up tightly. White wimple flaps covered her ears. A white headband was tied securely around her forehead. She could feel the knots on top of her head that held the wimple flaps in place. Chloe felt like she was a present being wrapped up for Christmas. She tried to move her jaw, but could not. Even swallowing was difficult with the stiff fabric pressing against her neck and throat.

"And take the helmet of salvation," Sister Alvina whispered, lifting the shining white shell of her veil, the crowning glory of the habit, and placing it on Chloe's head. Through a cacophony of sound she endured the nuns' work as they attached the veil with stick pins to her other headgear. Scraping noises surged, scratched and reverberated through her body. Chloe was in shock. For years she had seen nuns walking gracefully, turning, speaking, and looking perfectly comfortable. But the habit was an instrument of torture to her. Her slightest movement registered like thunder. How did one live like this?

Through the flying and rustling fabric Chloe spotted her friend, Kay, staring out from her tight wrappings. Her gray eyes bulged and her nose looked twice as long as before. And whose jowls were those, pushing forward like a gopher's? Mabel's! And there in the corner, Lena, her pink cheeks bright against the white wrapping, was smiling a beatific smile. Finally all the novices were dressed. The room had grown quiet and still. Eighteen brides of Christ, transformed into something not quite human, returned stiffly to the chapel to present themselves to the Bishop, to the professed sisters, to their families and to the world.

"He brought me to His banqueting table." Father Schlick's voice trembled with emotion.

"And His banner over me is love," the new novices squeaked, as they tried, for the first time, to speak from out of their new house, their cell in which they were wrapped and pinned and tied. One by one each veiled head bent to receive a crown of roses.

"Roses represent the flower of your womanhood, so willingly and lovingly offered up to God this day," Father Schlick said, enunciating each word slowly and distinctly. When, at last the service was over, the new novices filed out into the brilliant sunshine to meet their families. Chloe inched toward her mom, feeling bound up like a knight in armor. Julie and Effie smiled shyly at their big sister. As she tried to hug her Mom, Chloe found her arms impeded by the starched wimple. If she lifted her arms the stiff wimple would crumple. Flustered, she stepped back and took her mother's hand in hers, squeaking from out of the chokehold the fabric had on her neck, "Hi Mom and Dad, how do I look?"

"Just great," her father said, smiling and rocking back and forth on his heels.

"Very nice," Momma said with a slight smile.

Little Joey hid behind Peter, coaxing him to say "hello." Veronica stood tall and pretty. Then Jenny Dorsey, smiling her weepy smile that had so irritated Chloe in the past, pressed through the crowd and thrust a bouquet of daisies into Chloe's hands. "Congratulations Sister Ignatius," she whispered, gazing into Chloe's eyes, "You'll always be 'Chloe' to me." She said it with such feeling that for a moment, while their eyes met, the old familiar warmth leapt up in Chloe, of fondness and of love. It was just the two of them for a moment. Then Chloe pulled her eyes away and asked Daddy, "Where are the twins?"

"Owen and Lucy are watching them." He said.

"Oh," Chloe said. "How are they doing?"

"Just great! As much in love as ever!" Mr. Polowski beamed.

"No, I mean the twins." Chloe said.

"Oh, growing like weeds," Mr. Polowski said. "You'll see them next year."

"They'll be walking by then!"

"Yes, I suppose they will."

For three golden summer days the novices, each wearing a crown of roses on her head, strolled about the lawn like brides. Their white veils puffed out behind them as they visited with their families on the impeccable convent grounds dotted with tulips of every color. Great white tents sheltering tables and chairs protected guests from the heat. Big pitchers of ice-cold lemonade stood on the tables, with plastic glasses. For three days the feast went on, and the novices floated freely from family to convent without a thought of rules or decorum or silence. Chloe, despite her discomfort, loved her new habit. She felt complete. When she caught a reflection of herself in a window glass she loved it. "Look at me! I'm a nun!" she rejoiced. The snap of her thick-soled heels on the floor affirmed her standing in the convent. The muffled click of the large wooden beads at her side reminded her that she was still a neophyte in the house of the Lord. This was home. She belonged.

Meanwhile, moving about on the fringes of the festivities, Venerable Sister Georgina, the mistress of novices, regarded her new charges from a distance, watching then like a mother bear her cubs. Ever smiling with her large white teeth, she walked with a slight hitch to the left. Chloe saw her rambling through hallways and lurking at the edge of crowds, always present but saying little. Seeing her bulldog face in the crowd, Chloe felt a chill, as when a cloud passes over the sun. But soon the smiles and hand-holding and admiring glances of her little brothers and sisters banished all concerns, and she enjoyed each day. There would be time enough, after these three glorious days, to get to know her new mistress.

While their families picnicked beneath the tents, the novices took their meals in the brand new novitiate's refectory, built just two years ago in the new million-dollar wing. Everything was modern; the tables and the chairs were trimmed in chrome. Tile covered the walls halfway up. And, as befits a bridal meal, the tables were covered with white linen tablecloths and set with sparkling china, crystal goblets, and gleaming silverware. Fresh flowers adorned each table. And, every day, next to each plate laid a fresh pile of cards and letters from friends and relatives, each one full of congratulations and warm wishes, just as if it really were a wedding. Only there were no gifts.

"Dear Sister Ignatius, Gott and Mary keep you in your holy life wit him," Grandma Polowski had written in her old fashioned scrawl.

"There is no happier year than the one you begin today," Sister Clarice, her eighth-grade teacher, wrote from St. Eli.

"Though we can't speak, we will meet in the hallways!" Lynn, now Sister Mary Jerome wrote.

But there was one letter Chloe ached for: Sister Damien's. When she spied Sister's neat, flowing handwriting on a small white envelope she felt a premonition of satisfaction. Only Sister Damien knew her and all she had been through. Only she could properly comfort and encourage her today.

"Dearest Chloe—'Sister'—now!!! My heartfelt congratulations! I wish I could see you. Chloe, God saw your every sacrifice made along the way, and He is repaying you now a thousand fold. Today is just the beginning of a great journey of joy and service, an adventure with God that will only get better as you mature and deepen your understanding of His will. You deserve every blessing for your faithfulness. The Humble Handmaids of Mary are indeed fortunate to have you."

Chloe silently thanked God for Sister Damien. Just speaking her name was a joy. Chloe whispered it over and over again. Did the other novices feel this way, too? "What had Sister Damien written to them? Surely not the same thing that she had written to her!" In some secret way, Chloe knew that she was special to Sister Damien, her true mother for the four years of high school.

By the first night, Chloe's ears hurt from the rough fabric covering them. Her shoulders too, felt stiff and raw. The top of her head ached where two large knots had lain embedded. "Tie it looser today," she whispered to Sister Alvina, who arrived at 5:15 to dress her the next day. But the nun shook her head and tried to communicate without speaking that her hair might creep out if the earflaps were loose. By the second night Chloe's neck felt rubbed raw. Her ears chafed. "Did all nuns live in pain?" That evening she begged Venerable Sister for lotion, and her new mistress assured her, with a flash of her large white teeth, that she'd get used to it. "Did that mean that the pain would stay and she'd learn to bear it, or that her skin would get tougher and the pain would lessen?" Either way, she gritted her teeth to get through each day. Not a word of complaint did she hear from the others, so she decided that either their habits were more comfortable than hers, or they chose to suffer in silence.

On the last day of their three-day reception, as the red sun sank behind the boarders' trees, Chloe walked with her mother to the car, helping her pack the picnic baskets and blankets in the trunk for the long ride home.

"Chloe, do we have to wait a year before we write to you?" her mother asked, stuffing the large thermos in an open spot.

"Of course not, Mom!" Chloe answered, chagrined at her mother's gross misunderstanding of an elemental detail of her life. "You can write to me any time you want to, but I'll only get the letters once a month. And I'll write to you once a month!"

Weary of the three days' excitement, and wary of the coming year, Chloe longed for one word of praise or a smile from Momma to show that she was proud of her. Now was the time. Maybe this would please mother. She had waited to tell Momma of her prize. Reaching up and touching the rose garland on her head, she said, "Mom, this will be yours to keep next year."

"Oh? What will I do with it?" Momma asked, not even glancing at it.

"Hang it on the wall. It's a souvenir," Chloe said, crushed by her mom's response.

"Oh, that's nice," her mother said absently, staring across the orchard toward the sanatorium. Then she laid her large hand on Chloe's black sleeve. In a tone of imparting an urgent message, she said, "Chloe, I just want you to know you don't have to stay. If ever, this year, you change your mind and want to come home, it's all right." She said it quickly, furtively, with a glance over her shoulder. Chloe heard her quick breath when she was finished.

Chloe stiffened. "Why, now, must Momma speak this way? Would she ever value her vocation? Had nothing about the last three days convinced or impressed her?"

"I mean, don't stay because you think you have to, now that you've come this far," her mother added lamely.

"You're not very encouraging," Chloe said coldly.

"I'm sorry, Chloe," Momma said, hanging her head. "I guess I said the wrong thing again." Just then the children came running ahead of their father, breathless with questions.

"Is it true you can't watch TV or listen to a radio for a whole year?" Julie asked.

"Or read any newspapers or books?" Peter asked, his eyes big with disbelief.

"Yes. But we can read all the spiritual books we want."

"How will you know if the Russians bomb us?" Julie asked anxiously.

"She would hear it," her father interjected, stroking Julie's hair. "Now get in the car, all of you, it's time to go home!"

Little hands waved at the windows. "Good-bye Chloe, I mean, Sister Ignatius, see you in a year!" The children shouted, each trying to drown the other one out, throwing kisses and pleading, "Don't forget our names!"

"Of course I won't," Chloe shouted, shaking her head at such a silly thought. She waved and watched as the big blue station wagon once again disappeared around the curve and began its descent. At the last moment Momma waved, smiling her sad resigned smile that Chloe knew so well.

CHAPTER 42.

Novitiate

With the families gone and the Heights quiet, there remained yet one more event for the new novices: the sealing-in ceremony.

The eighteen novices stood together in the hallway facing Father Schlick. "Sisters," Father said, "tonight begins what can easily be the very best year of your life. Cherish it as a bride does her honeymoon. Remember, 'Many are called, but few are chosen.'"

The novices, their white veils scraping and knocking together, turned to follow Venerable Sister's wide form through a door marked "Convent—Do not Enter" while Father stayed in the hallway. They stopped and turned around to face him. His molten blue eyes burned into theirs as he declared, "A year from now when you emerge from this doorway, you will be new and different; transformed into the very brides of Christ. Be patient with yourselves and with each other, Sisters. Learning to live the vows of poverty, chastity, and obedience will not be easy. But it will be the most rewarding and fulfilling life you can ever know."

The young women reached up to unpin their crown of roses. They then placed them on a mahogany table, above which hung a picture of Mary ascending into heaven.

"By God's grace we will do this," the young women replied to Father Schlick. Venerable Sister pulled the door closed, leaving Father on the outside. The lock clicked.

"Sisters, the lock is on the inside, for you choose a voluntary prison."

"We do so choose for Christ's sake," the novices murmured, reading from their papers. Their sealing-in complete, the novices dispersed to their dorms in silence.

Chloe curled up in her bed, free of the awful headdress with it maddening screeches. Her ears rang. Her head throbbed. The white cotton nightgown felt soft and cozy. It soothed her nerves as she dozed off to sleep. From the darkness their floated toward her a newborn baby, naked, its arms flailing, its legs drawn up to its belly. Someone handed it to her. She took it, and its skin felt like velvet. She awoke with a start, and then fell asleep again.

The next morning there was trash to pick up, dandelions to pluck and laundry to fold. Chloe smelled cigarette smoke in the air, probably from one of the workmen, and was reminded of dear Mom. Next July seemed a long way off.

In time, Chloe grew used to the habit. The scraping of her starched wimple against her stiff veil became less noticeable, and she learned how to tie the knots less tight but still firm. It was an art, she decided, and began to appreciate the warm habit, cozy and comfortable. Seeing her reflection in a window she recognized the garb as a handsome and unmistakable sign of her achievement. At times the veil was cumbersome, flaring out and striking a door jamb with a resounding crack that reverberated through her head. Outdoors it caught the wind and rocked on its moorings like a large bird about to take flight. But, kneeling in chapel, sheltered and hidden inside its arched walls, she felt secure. It was her private cell from which she looked out at the golden doors of the tabernacle and thanked God for her vocation. Casting her eyes down upon her snow-white wimple, starched and stiff across her chest, she felt holy, clean and dedicated.

Through August the heat increased, and the Minnesota humidity pressed down, wilting the starch from the novices' wimples. The walls of their veils sagged inward. In the chapel old nuns hobbled feebly down the aisle. "Did their head knots still hurt?" Chloe wondered. "Did they ever wish, just once, to feel the wind in their hair again?"

On the first mail call Chloe received a letter from Lucy Fry, now Lucy Polowski. She slipped the letter from its envelope eagerly, hoping Lucy was sorry now that she hadn't returned to the convent.

"Dear Sister Ignatius,"

"Congratulations on your reception as a novice. You don't know how badly I wanted to be there with all my classmates! But Owen and I felt it was more important for your parents to be there, and so we offered to babysit the twins. I guess we can't always do what we want, can we? I know your life as a novice must be wonderful and heavenly. I can tell by your letters home, which your mom shows me. Owen and I are getting along just perfect. Owen is so good to me, always helping me. The men are combining oats. The crops look good so far, but we need rain bad or we won't have any corn. Everything is so dry. Could you put a word in for us? We know you do.

"P.S. Dear Sister, we want to tell you a secret. It's wonderful news. We are expecting a baby, we're pretty sure. We're both so happy. Please don't write anything home about this for a while. Thank you. God love you. By the way, I feel just perfect. I couldn't feel better. We miss you around here. Your loving brother and sister,

Lucy and Owen."

Chloe jammed the letter back into its envelope and cast it inside her Latin book. It was nice they were happy, but … she squeezed her left thumb until it hurt. Let Lucy have her dingy farmhouse. Soon it would be full of squalling brats and mess while she, Chloe was getting an education. She, at least, had a future. The habit clothed her in glory. And soon now the abiding joy so often promised her would come, spreading through her like a warm day.

The next evening during recreation Chloe and Lena strolled together toward the cemetery. In the eastern sky, pink clouds were piled high like scoops of ice cream. When they arrived at a fresh gravesite bearing the marker "Sister Joanna," Chloe said to Lena, "If she would have died one month earlier, you could have had her name." Chloe was referring to Lena's desire to have her new name be Sister Joanna. But this old nun, nearly ninety years old, had lingered until time ran out for Lena. No two sisters could bear the same name while alive. So Lena's new name was "Sister Uriah."

"Some lucky novice will get her name next year, I bet," Chloe said, tempting Lena.

"Yes," Lena said, not taking the bait.

"Do you like your name, Sister Uriah?" Chloe persisted.

"I love it," Lena said.

"But it was your third choice," Chloe needled her, for she still rankled at her own given name, her third choice as well. .

"Sister Ignatius, I wouldn't want the name 'Joanna' now if Mother herself let me change. God gave me Uriah, and it means 'The Lord is my light.' Isn't that beautiful?"

"Yes, Sister," Chloe replied, rebuked and humbled by Lena's apparently complete submission to God's will. Perhaps she, too, could learn to like her own name. Silently she repeated it to herself over and over again. "Sister Ignatius, Sister Ignatius, Sister Ignatius." But that didn't help. Her new name was a cross to bear, an irritation to her ears that she must bear for the rest of her days.

CHAPTER 43.

Disillusionment

Little by little, Venerable Sister Georgina, through patient and repetitive teachings, molded her frisky flock of fledging nuns into demure novices. "Your outward decorum must match your inward submission," she instructed them until, eventually, Lena lost her mincing step and Milly her athletic stride. Gladys no longer swung her elbows out when she walked, nor did she gawk at every noise she heard in study hall. Chloe stopped taking the stairs two steps at a time. The novices as a class became so sedate, so alike in their outward demeanor that sometimes Chloe, from a distance, could not tell her own classmates apart.

"Conformity to the Holy Rule helps us die to self and live for Christ."

Chloe blushed now to recall how she had chased her little brothers around the orchard those first days. Venerable Sister must have been mortified. But behind convent walls she had free rein to mold her green novices into nuns befitting the vocation. And she was faithful to the task.

Gradually the discomfort of the habit lessened for Chloe. Her ears toughened up and no longer hurt. Her shoulders had grown used to the starched wimple rubbing on them. The top of her head no longer throbbed from the knots. She learned how to eat and drink without soiling her wimple, and she learned to pass through doorways at a slight angle to avoid the ear deafening crash of a starched veil striking wood.

Each month the novices were expected to meet privately with Venerable Sister. It was Venerable Sister's opportunity to assess her charge's spiritual growth, and it was the novice's chance to discuss anything that troubled her. At one such interview Chloe remarked to her mistress, "It's easier for shy girls to adjust to the novitiate." She was thinking of Aimee Sikes's childish personality and how merely donning the habit had lent her an aura of wisdom and dignity that had little to do with her true self. The habit only served to hide the girl inside.

"Why do you say that, Sister Ignatius?"

"Because those with the most personality have more to curb. So it's harder for them." "And do you have more to curb, Sister Ignatius?"

"Yes, Venerable Sister."

"Is that the fault of the habit, or does the habit merely point out your faults?"

"Well, since the habit requires everyone to act the same, it's the fault of the habit."

"The holy habit is merely God's tool to curb our natural habits."

"But God made us, why does He want to change us?"

"Because Adam fell and lost perfection for us all. Many are called, but few are chosen to walk the narrow way back to perfection. Are you sorry you chose the narrow way, Sister Ignatius?"

"No. Venerable Sister."

"Very well then, take up your cross daily, and follow Him."

"Yes, Venerable Sister."

By the time September came and students swarmed over the campus once again, the novices' outward transformation was complete. They glided instead of walked. They cast their eyes down demurely until greeted. Then they smiled as though they fed on angels' food. One day, as Chloe carried a tray of freshly baked rolls to the aspirants' kitchen, she met two aspirants in a basement hallway. "Praised be Jesus Christ!" the girls murmured, flattening themselves against the wall as though they saw a vision.

"Now and forever more," Chloe answered musically, beaming beatifically as she sailed past them. She heard their awed sighs and felt a rush of gratification. She was special. Her very presence conveyed an aura of holiness accepted as fact. "What did it matter that it wasn't true? That she was still the same ordinary Chloe beneath all the layers? The important thing was that the young were inspired to persevere. Sure, she sinned; constantly. But they were little venial sins of thought and temper that she would master soon, as soon as the promised peace and joy came, vanquishing her irritability and easing her discontent."

In many ways the novitiate resembled the postulancy, except that here they prayed longer, kept silence more and arose earlier than before. Often during the forty-minute meditation before Mass, Chloe, to stay awake, would pull out a favorite snapshot from the cover of her office book and gaze at it intently. It was a black and white photo of the twins standing in their walkers. Her eyes drank in their cute faces and their strong, sturdy legs, remembering how it felt to hold them in her arms.

One day as the novices trooped in from the enclosed garden where they had been engaged in a sedate game of croquet, Venerable Sister stopped them with a solemn look on her large sagging red face and said, "Sisters, there is someone here to see you." Chloe assumed it was a visiting priest or bishop or a high-ranking nun from the motherhouse. For, at times religious dignitaries were allowed to penetrate their hallowed halls so as to look over the new crop of nuns, much like a farmer might like to gaze over his growing corn or his spring calves.

"A former classmate of yours from the postulancy, Angie Zimms, is here and has requested a glimpse of you. She has recovered from her headaches and plans to re-enter the convent in the fall. Since she left because of medical reasons, and because she plans to re-enter, I have given her permission to stand at the doorway as you pass by on your way to chapel. Please do not speak to her. Limit yourselves to the usual spiritual greeting. Nothing more."

A flutter of excitement rose mutely from the novices as they turned in their cumbersome habits toward one another with surprised expressions. Some whispered. Chloe couldn't see over the veiled heads, but she heard a feminine voice up ahead and some cries, like kittens mewing. There she stood in the breezeway doorway, Angie, now a stunningly pretty woman, smiling that same crinkle faced smile that almost hid her eyes from seeing. Tears streamed down her face as she answered each novice's "Praised be Jesus Christ!" with the usual "Now and forever more,"

Angie wore a fitted navy blue suit with red heels. A red scarf fluttered at her neck. She carried a shiny red purse. Her long brown hair fluttered in wisps across her face. Completing the vision was a handsome young man in a suit standing behind her. He had brown hair and a kind face. He kept his eyes on Angie as though to catch her if she fainted from all the excitement.

"Praised be Jesus Christ!"

"Now and forever more!"

The novices, like a flock of big white birds at feeding time, tried to see over each other's heads. A glimpse was all they got as quickly they moved on, filing into chapel without a backward glance. That evening during recreation the novices huddled in little groups, talking. Milly said Angie worked in a bank where she met the young man that was with her. He desperately wanted to marry her, but Angie was determined to enter and start all over as a postulant next year.

“Hmph!” Chloe exploded, “she’s nuts!”

Lena’s eyes fluttered. Kay’s mouth fell open.

“Why do you say that, Sister Ignatius?” Milly asked, tilting her head sideways and squinting at her.

“It’s plain as day. God has given her an ‘out’ and she’s too stubborn to take it. Why can’t she just enjoy what she’s got?”

“That sounds rather simplistic considering all that goes into a vocation,” Milly chided her.

“Vocations aren’t that complicated!” Chloe said, glaring at Milly, the former day student. How she hated her: Milly; who had enjoyed the warmth of home and the thrill of dating all through high school, who now, against all odds, fit in with convent life like hand to glove, was an affront to her. She was proving Sister Damien wrong. Milly was showing Chloe that she, with all her worldly freedom, was better prepared for the convent than an aspirant was. It was a bitter drink to taste.

As Milly opened her mouth to speak, Chloe turned on her heel and walked away.

* * *

“Bless me Father, for I have sinned. My last confession was a week ago. I gave in to my temper five times. I used foul language twelve times. I hated someone. I felt irritated with my sisters fourteen times.”

Father cleared his throat. “My dear sister, it is no sin to experience irritation. Temptations come. They are not evil of themselves. As long as we resist them, we do not sin.”

“Yes, Father. But I give in to them. I hate. I’m jealous.”

"Go on my child." Father sounded weary and sad.

Chloe didn't tell him how, when no one was looking, she had swung a mop against a chair in a fit of rage, or how she had wanted, just once, to slap the pious look from Lena's face.

In his shadowy closet, Father Schlick waved his hand over her in absolution and gave her a penance: five Our Fathers and five Hail Mary's. Then he whispered through the veiled screen at her, "Those we live the closest to are often the hardest to love."

"Then how did people stay married? Was marriage as miserable as community life? Owen and Lucy didn't say so. Michelle and Kenny seemed happy. But she, the bride of Christ, was discontent. Was it a sin to be unhappy?" Instead of enjoying God, she longed for things like the radio and the newspaper. One rainy evening as the novices sat playing board games in the recreation room Chloe said to Kay, "I'd give anything to read a good novel."

"Anything?" Kay asked, raising her eyebrows.

"You know what I mean," Chloe said, feeling guilty. "Spiritual books can be so dry." When Kay didn't nod in agreement, Chloe fell silent, not daring to add that chapel and saying the rosary bored her as well. She looked forward to nothing, and because this was so, she had begun lately a secret game of looking for one bright spot in every day. "Was this anything a person did on her honeymoon? What did it say about her holiness?" She dared not discuss such things with Venerable Sister.

News from the world did arrive. A Catholic, John F. Kennedy, was running for the presidency of the United States. Chloe searched for more news in the laundry, where newspapers were spread on the floor to protect the draping tablecloths from getting soiled. Craning her neck to see over the ironing board, she read the headlines while she ironed.

"Family of Five Die in Fire," "*The Virgin Spring,*" New Ingmar Bergman Film Released."

"Sister Ignatius!" the laundry sister chided, clucking her tongue, "the world is not our business! Holiness is."

"But what was holiness? And how did she get it? And how would she know when she had it?"

One thing didn't bore Chloe; her breviary, or office, as it was called. She loved chanting the verses of Matins and Lauds each day at two o'clock in the chapel, when sunlight beamed down in spears from the high, stained-glass windows. The novices, their veils rustling like angel wings, filled two pews on either side of the church. Then the lead chanter intoned: "O Lord, open my lips."

"And my mouth shall proclaim your praise," the others answered.

"O God, come to my assistance."

"O Lord, make haste to help me."

Then they all bowed forward deeply from the waist, continuing to chant the carefully drawn out vowels: "Gloory bee to the Faather, and to the Sonn, and to the Hooly Ghoost."

Straightening up they finished, "As it waas in the beginning is noow and ever shall bee. Aaaamaann."

The haunting tones of their singing floated upwards to the far reaches of the balconies where old nuns hunched in rockers, half-hidden by pillars. Chloe could hear them shuffle about, coughing and rattling their beads. "They must be thrilled," she thought, "to hear our young voices rising in praise to God."

But almost as soon as she left the chapel, old doubts nibbled at her joy like rats in her father's corncrib. No matter how hard she prayed for contentment her emptiness yawned wider every day. Along with this, there also grew, imperceptibly at first, a tingling in her hands that she had first noticed last spring while turning mattresses. It had increased until now it caused a constant sensation of fire in her bones. Next the steady burning pain, besides being distracting, stirred up fears. "Did she have arthritis in her hands? Or Rheumatism?" Concern nagged at her. "I look forward to eating and sleeping," she thought. "What would Venerable Sister Georgina say if she knew that?" Eventually Chloe traced her unhappiness to one thing: The villa. It had ruined her instead of helping her. This was a conundrum that could not be fixed. Her vocation had hung too long between two worlds, like a towel left flapping on the clothesline through a long, cold winter, and now it wasn't good for anything but to be a rag. But what was she saying? As arguments and comparisons swirled through her head like flies, she struck at them with counter arguments. But they didn't kill the buzz.

She continued her study of her companions. Milly and Gladys had adjusted so well because they had enjoyed their share of living at home and normal public school. Kay, four years at the villa, was doing fine. But she was a different sort of girl than herself. Aimee was a child in woman's garb. Mabel seemed blissfully content, but that was her nature, to follow and not to rail against the life.

"I've put my hand to the plow. I must not look back," she chided herself. "But to stay when I'm unhappy - isn't that madness? I've not said vows yet. But God has called me. I cannot disappoint Him." Some days her moods of heavy introspection lifted. A smile, a kind word, a pertinent line in a spiritual book would be enough to lift her confusion and brighten her outlook. "She did love her vocation. She wanted to be a nun. She must not give up. Peace lay right around the corner. Soon it would wash down on her like gentle rain, feeding her dry roots." She prayed fervently at such times, rubbing and gripping her aching hands.

One morning she awoke with an awful thought sitting like a crow upon her head: "All nuns are liars. Not one of them is happy, but instead of admitting it, each one is foisting this life on the young, pretending it might be good for them. No, there isn't one truly happy nun." Her mouth turned dry at the thought, her body limp. "Was this the truth, or was the devil talking to her?" There were no answers. No sacrifice had any value.

CHAPTER 44.

Love

One night as Chloe rolled back the covers, preparing for bed, she caught her reflection in the black window next to her bed, as clear as a movie. Wearing a long white night gown, she was a pioneer wife climbing into bed with her husband. As she lay down she pulled the blankets up around her shoulders and watched herself. When the lights went out she stared at the moon. Her imagination kept going as she turned toward her husband lying next to her, thinking, "I would make a loving wife." The warmth and tenderness of her young body ached to love and be loved. In her mind's eye she saw her nights stretching endlessly before her into darkness, alone, like this one. What had Father Schlick said about the "marriage act?" "It was one of God's greatest gifts to mankind." The biology book had described it as "highly pleasurable to both male and female." She knew this must be true from her brief encounters with boys. Yet she had renounced it without getting close to it. Chloe sighed. It was easy to imagine Daryl next to her, and to feel his lips on hers again, his strong male arms pulling her close to him. Startled at how easily old feelings flamed to life, Chloe flipped to her stomach in horror while a cold sweat crept up her spine. "How weak I am! How prone to sin! For shame!" Her heart raced, and her body grew rigid as she cast out her wicked thoughts. How close sin always lay ready. Tossing and turning, it took a long while for her to fall asleep, so afraid was she of the tricks her mind might play on her, even in her dreams.

The next morning she awoke with a strange tightness in her chest. It wasn't a cold, just a stiffness that ached when she moved. Her shoulders too, hurt as though she had shoveled snow the day before, or played a hard game of basketball. But she had done neither. Days later she noticed that her chest tightness had settled into one place - her heart. It was becoming sore to the touch. "Did she have heart disease?" In chapel she moved her hand surreptitiously beneath her wimple to press the spot. "Was it a tumor? Was this how God would choose to deliver her from this convent? Through death?"

A few days later Chloe went to her mistress saying, "It feels like I carried something heavy around, like a cross." She smiled at her own silly simile. But Venerable Sister didn't smile. She ran her tongue around her large red lips and said, "Tonight when the supply cabinet is open, beg Sister Patience for rubbing ointment. Tell her I approved it."

That night, behind her dressing screen, Chloe rubbed the pungent ointment onto her neck and shoulders, conscious of the odor emanating out from it. Gladys would be sure to ask about it tomorrow. And she did. At their first opportunity to speak, she asked, "Chloe, what were you doing last night with that ointment?"

"Venerable Sister gave it to me for my sore muscles."

"What are you sore from?"

"Something I did, I guess. Maybe I'm getting old."

Gladys laughed. "Of course you are! We all are."

Chloe didn't use the ointment after that. It didn't help anyway. Instead, the nagging discomfort in her shoulders stayed, and the pain in her chest took up residence as if it owned her. It greeted her upon waking and clung to her all day. But she did get relief at night, when she slept. Again Chloe went to Venerable Sister, and this time Venerable Sister sent her to the convent nurse, Sister Clotildus. After examining her, she sat down across from Chloe and queried, "Sister, are you worried ... anxious about anything?"

Chloe shrugged. "No, Sister."

"It's nothing to be ashamed of. Lots of novices are anxious about taking vows."

"I'm not. I've wanted to be a nun all my life." The nurse dismissed her without any solution, and Chloe left noting that her chest pain spread like hot sauce all over her torso. After that she decided not to mention her discomfort to anyone anymore. "God knew, wasn't that enough?" Yet she made mental notes on her condition. It grew worse on rainy days. It often subsided toward evening. Wearing loose, light clothing, such as her nightgown, helped. In class the novices had learned about a monk named Padre Pio who had received the stigmata from God. His hands and feet bore the wounds of Christ, and they hurt. He considered it both a terrible and a wonderful gift. "Was *this* a gift like that?" She hoped not. More likely it was the devil trying to break her down, get her to leave, forsake her vocation. But she would not let him win.

Upon rising the next morning, Chloe massaged her shoulders behind her screen to allay the tightness already setting in. But it was no use; by the time her wimple was in place across her chest and the veil pinned on her head, pain sat like a victor in her flesh, tightening her neck, weighing down her chest and setting her hands on fire. She was in awe. "Was there no end to Satan's wiles?" The skin on her face felt as taut as if a network of spider webs had stitched itself there overnight. For the third time that morning she felt the need to rub her eyes and massage her cheeks.

That evening Chloe approached Venerable Sister to beg for lotion.

"Are your hands chapped Sister Ignatius?" Venerable Sister asked, taking Chloe's hands into hers and turning them over.

"No, Venerable Sister, my face feels dry."

"Hhmmm. It looks fine to me."

"I know, but it feels funny."

A strange look flickered over Venerable Sister's large face. Then in a conciliatory tone she reached into the cabinet and said, "Oh, all right, here. You can use this sample." She handed Chloe a tiny bottle. "Remember, Sister, lotion is a luxury."

"Yes, Venerable Sister, Chloe said.

"Use it for three days and see if it helps," she said.

After three days Chloe returned the bottle to Venerable Sister. "Thank you, Venerable Sister, for the lotion."

"You're welcome," Venerable Sister said, regarding her closely. "Your face looks fine." Chloe gave her a weak smile and nodded. How could she explain to this old large nun who walked like a gorilla and whose face was filled with wrinkles that her young face and body felt as if she were wrapped inside a cocoon?

CHAPTER 45.

Christmas in the Novitiate

Like a diamond sparkling against black velvet, the silvery tones of a bell pierced Chloe's deep sleep. "Praised be Jesus Christ!" she murmured, sitting up and rolling back her blankets. Someone turned on the light. She blinked. It was Christmas Eve. Maybe today God would heal her. Softly the dormitory stirred to life with the sounds of running water, padding feet, and privacy screens pulled into place around sinks. The novices had twenty minutes in which to get ready for Midnight Mass.

"Expect an austere Christmas in keeping with our vow of poverty," Venerable Sister had warned her charges all during Advent. Chloe hoped that, after Mass, they might have a glass of orange juice before they must return to their beds. "I'm willing," Chloe thought, dropping her woolen dress over her head, "to concentrate on spiritual joys today."

But she couldn't help picturing activity at home. Her family would be riding in the cold car toward St. Eli Church, the tires squeaking on the snow-packed roads; the stars exceptionally bright against the black sky. Veronica would look grown-up in her first long coat and high heels. She remembered her own thirteenth Christmas and how she had wobbled in her heels, fearing she might slip and fall on the ice. That was ages ago. Careful not to dent her starched wimple as she knotted her head flaps, or to prick her finger as she pinned the veil to her white headband, she was ready when the bell summoned them to chapel. Rustling and scraping in their holy garb, the eighteen novices gathered around the organ in the choir loft, their faces still puffy from sleep. Suddenly Chloe realized that not one novice, except Angie, who had left for medical reasons, had left the convent since their Reception Day. She marveled. She had stopped guessing who might leave. "How wonderful if their class might be the first class to keep them all," she thought rapturously.

"Joy to the World, the Lord is come!" As the novices' angelic voices floated over the glittering chapel below, Chloe pressed her hymnbook to her chest, feeling its unremitting ache. A sob caught in her throat. Her fingers flamed invisibly. Though the novices looked and sounded like angels, she felt like a devil. The chapel glowed soft in gold and red tones, like a palace. Banks of red poinsettias graced the steps to the altar. Even the fourteen stations of the cross wore a red bow above each tragic scene of Christ's passion.

"Merry Christmas!" Daddy would boom as he met other farmers and their families walking into St. Eli's, their boots crunching on the frozen snow. Inside, the church would smell of pine, and Grandma Polowski would turn stiffly toward them as if to say, "It's about time!" The first place that drew the eye was St. Joseph's niche, transformed into a Bethlehem scene. Three kings wound their way down from a mountainous route while shepherds below hastened toward the stable. A stand of evergreens dotted with little white lights sheltered the midnight scene traveling on the highest ridge amidst evergreen and rocks. Sheep and their shepherds picked their way down the hillside. And at the bottom, the stable, crude and rugged, was lit up by a star shining on the whole holy family.

Nothing here came close to that. The pews below were filled with nuns, black humps, all in a row. "Who were they, really? Where was the beauty of their lives?" As Chloe struggled to see it, she found far more interesting the folks from downtown Magnolia who filled the back pews, carrying with them the interesting sounds and smells of the world; children's voices, men clearing their throats, women's perfume and the faint smell of liquor. Somewhere down there knelt Milly's folks, probably straining to catch a glimpse of their only daughter. Fiercely opposed to her entering the convent at first, they were now reconciled to her choice. Chloe cut her eyes to Milly. Her face was as blank as if it were wash day. Chloe admired such detachment. If it were her family down there she would hardly be able to contain herself.

Chloe rubbed her cheeks. They felt as tight as if she had washed them with glue. Her mouth felt heavy, as though a weight dragged at its corners. The communion bell rang and the novices filed carefully down the narrow spiral staircase and up the center aisle towards the communion railing, singing "Silent Night," without accompaniment.

Kneeling at the railing, Chloe awaited the moving figure of the priest, accompanied by the altar boy holding the paten. As he held the golden paten under her chin to catch any crumbs, Chloe tilted back her head, held out her tongue, and received the host. "Happy Birthday Jesus!" She said, rising and returning to the choir. She felt all eyes on her. Were people inspired? Spurred on to good works? Or did they see the postulants as young women throwing their lives away? Climbing the winding staircase, Chloe rebuked herself. "What does it matter what they think?" At the top of the staircase her heart gave a stabbing lurch that sent an ugly feeling surging through her, of rage and despair. "Perhaps today I will die of heart trouble. Or the tumor will burst. That would be lovely." With her heart thumping and chunking like an old washing machine, Chloe wanted very much to complain to Jesus, still present inside her. She wanted to stamp her feet and demand an answer.

She wanted to cry. But instead she prayed pitifully, "Help me, help me, help me," with little hope for an answer.

With midnight Mass over, the novices glided down the darkened hallways of the convent on their way to bed. Some, despite it still being Grand Silence, dared to lift their eyes to one another and smile. It was Christmas! Excitement stirred the air. Only Sister Uriah kept her eyes downcast, Chloe noted with disdain. How beautifully her long dark eyelashes rested on her pink cheeks. Chloe grimaced. "If just once Sister Uriah would cuss or swear or lose her temper, just to show she was human, how refreshing that would be." But instead her moist red lips were curved into a satisfied look.

Venerable Sister Georgina motioned for her flock to follow her. She took them down a circuitous route that ended up at the kitchen door. Novices looked expectantly at one another. As Sister opened the door, they gasped. Before them was spread a stunning array of every kind of treat; from cakes and cookies to golden pies and poppy seed rolls. Crystal bowls laden with moist looking fudge and dollops of white divinity gleamed in the candlelight. It was a feast for kings. Even a decanter of wine surrounded by a circle of pretty wine glasses rested on a sideboard.

"Merry Christmas, Sisters!" Venerable Sister boomed.

"Merry Christmas, Venerable Sister!" the novices replied, taken aback by this unexpected feast. Was it for them? If so, it was the exact opposite of the austerity they had been told to expect. They turned in their wide stiff veils to see Venerable Sister's face for an explanation.

"Mother Euphemia has lifted the Grand Silence for half an hour." Venerable Sister's large red mouth hung open in a loose smile as she waved a black sleeve over the feast. "These are gifts from your families and friends. They have showered you with love this Christmas." She stepped back and the novices moved cautiously forward. Their voices, whispers at first, then murmurs, slowly found themselves as they began to sample the delicacies set before them. Chloe, in shock at the opulence, nevertheless bit into a square of walnut fudge. As its sweetness filled her mouth she felt conflicted. She had resigned herself to the sacrifice that Venerable Sister had promised concerning Christmas. Was anyone else troubled by this huge surprise? Mabel's eyes shown over her cheeks, bulging like a gopher's as she stuffed a chocolate covered cherry into her mouth. Lena Betters bit daintily into a poppy-seed bun, explaining to Chloe, "My mom sent these. They are a tradition at our house." Milly Haatch's eyes twinkled at Chloe from over the rim of a crystal wineglass. "Merry Christmas, Sister Ignatius," she said, raising her glass toward her.

"Merry Christmas, Sister Raphael," Chloe answered, searching her eyes for a critique matching hers of this waste. "Was this in keeping with the vow of poverty? Why hadn't they given it to the poor?" There were notes set about bearing good wishes for the novices and saying who had sent what treat. Had Momma sent something? Surely not! For Chloe had written home, as instructed, saying she could receive nothing. But maybe Venerable Sister had added a note to their letters saying that food was all right. Otherwise, how did all these parents know to send these things? Chloe knew that Momma, with her brood of little ones, had been relieved to have one less to think of at Christmas time.

Nevertheless, Chloe scanned the table, reading the calling cards propped up near the plates. "To the hidden brides, from the Haatchs" said the note near the divinity. Chloe spotted a fruitcake, smashed on one side, and her heart beat wildly as she squeezed between two novice's veils to see who had sent it. By candlelight she could tell that it was not her mother's handwriting. Chloe helped herself to a slice just as Kay approached, smiling broadly with her buckteeth protruding. "My sister sent that cake! It's really good?"

"The one with nine kids?" Chloe asked.

"Yes. Isn't she a marvel?" Kay rolled her eyes toward heaven.

"How could she, with all those hungry mouths?" Chloe chided.

"Oh, no," Kay corrected, "she loves to give. It's her way. Do you like it?"

"Yes," said Chloe, licking her lips. But her confusion grew. "How did this indulgence prepare them for their vow of poverty?"

Back in bed Chloe's thoughts drifted homeward, where the kids' stockings would be hanging from the mantel, from one end to the other, each with a handful of hard candy stuck deep in the toes, and one small toy on top, protruding from the stocking. Directly beneath each stocking, on the hearth, would be a larger toy; metal trucks and tractors for the boys and carriages, dolls and dollhouses for the girls. The older kids got new clothes, a B-B gun, or a bike.

Tomorrow, in the midst of their playing, the children would have to tear themselves away from their toys to go to Grandma and Grandpa Polowski's for the noon meal. There, Grandma would cluck over them like a mother hen, urging them to eat, eat more! After that, while the grown-ups played cards, smoked, and drank Hamm's beer; the grandchildren would change into play clothes and run outside, where they stayed for hours.

The older kids would play in Grandpa's barn, where, climbing to the top of the ladder, they would grab a rope attached to a glider at the very top. Then they would push off, hanging while sliding across the vast expanse, screaming and hollering until just the right moment to let go and drop into an enormous mound of hay. They would take turns doing this, over and over again. Then, towards evening, the families would bundle up in their coats and boots, pile into their cars and drive to their other grandparents' farm, where they would enjoy another feast.

Chloe's sore chest complained as she turned over in bed. She was glad that she had written a cheerful letter home. Momma would think she was having a great Christmas.

The next morning the novices attended Mass again, but without receiving Communion, since a person could only receive that sacrament once a day. For breakfast they ate omelets and cinnamon buns thick with caramel and nuts. They drank coffee, cocoa or orange juice, whatever they wanted. At noon the feast surpassed anything Chloe had ever eaten at Grandma's, and they were allowed to talk while eating. Yet there was still more. A surprise awaited them! The recreation doors had been closed and locked since Friday. Now they would be opened. No one knew what to expect. Strains of "Joy to the World" filtered out from behind the doors. When Venerable Sister and Sister Patience each swung the doors open, a collective "Oohhh!" rose up from the novices. A gorgeously decorated Christmas tree reaching to the ceiling sparkled like a vision. A star shone on its top. Beneath it were stacked many presents, gaily wrapped, of all sizes and shapes.

Chloe surmised that they were props, just there for looks. She wished her little brothers and sisters could see this lovely scene. How they'd be jumping up and down. As she drew nearer she saw names on the gifts. Had Venerable Sister gone to this trouble? Surely not. Were they from the Junior Sisters? No. Not likely. Chloe knew that no one from home had sent her anything, for again, the rule had been made clear: only things from the list of acceptable items could be received; white hankies, black scarves, black mittens, pens, or a suitcase. Her parents had sent a black suitcase a month ago, which she had received and stashed away in storage, as Venerable Sister had instructed her to do. Had Venerable Sister retrieved it and asked Sister Patience to rewrap it for under the tree?

"Let's put the chairs in a semicircle around the tree and sit down," Venerable Sister directed. "Sister Uriah, will you please hand out the gifts?" While the novices hurried to obey, Chloe, preoccupied with the question of the gifts, felt her heart revving up to a panic, making it hard for her to smile. An inner trembling had begun in her stomach. Surely, she hoped, someone, Venerable Sister or Sister Patience, had checked that every novice had a gift under the tree.

"Sister Evania!" Sister Uriah's voice sang out as she handed Mabel a pretty box trailing with ribbons. Chloe's hands burned in her lap. Surely no novice would be left out. That would be unkind. But maybe kindness wasn't the main point here. None of the presents looked the shape of a suitcase. Mabel, her present unwrapped, held up a white scarf. The novices ooohed in chorus. Kay (Sister Mary Joseph) opened a box containing an electric razor, blushed, and then cupped her hands over it to hide it. Everybody laughed, including Venerable Sister. Nuns did not shave their arms or their legs. Milly held up a perfume bottle with a puffball at the top. Laughing, she explained that her aunt didn't know a thing about convents.

"Squeeze it!" Mabel challenged, but Milly refrained from releasing the forbidden fragrance into the room. Everyone admired Lena's corn husk doll that her Grandma from Iowa had made and sent. On and on the presents came; colorful towels, childish puzzles, and even a lamp. Gladys received a silver wristwatch, and though nuns didn't wear wristwatches, everyone nodded pleasantly, saying how pretty it was.

Finally, two presents remained beneath the tree. No one had noticed that Chloe had not yet received a present, while some novices held three or more on their laps. "Jay!" Sister Uriah called out, handing her a gift. Then, "Aimee" she called. No more presents remained beneath the towering tree. In the midst of the smiles and laughter, Chloe saw that every novice but her held at least some small gift in her lap. She smiled while her heart beat a muffled protest against the trickery. She felt like a hypocrite, wanting a gift while despising the gifts at the same time. She hoped no one would see her empty lap and make a fuss over her. And yet, they should! They must! Gift opening over, Chloe jumped up and mingled with the others, admiring their gifts, which, one by one, the postulants were piling on top of the ping-pong table.

"What did you get, Sister Ignatius?" Gladys asked.

"Oh, some hankies and white T-shirts," she lied, waving her hand toward the ping-pong table. She had put away childish things. It was all worldly nonsense. Yet a seething rage tore at her against Venerable Sister, against her parents, and against all these smiling numskulls and their smart-alecky relatives who had ignored the rules with their crass and silly extravagance.

Chloe escaped to the bathroom. Alone in the stall, she let her face droop to its natural state. Here she did not have to smile; she could be herself; sad, angry, and confused. She yawned and wished mightily to be able to crawl back into bed and pull the blankets up over her head and sleep. A tear squeezed out of an eye, and she dabbed at it harshly lest it drip on her starched wimple and tell all. She did not understand herself. One moment she balked at opulence, the next she was bawling for a gift. As she flushed the toilet, the noise drowned out a deep sob. How good it felt! If she could go somewhere and cry she'd howl like a pack of dogs; how good that would feel. It positively hurt to swallow. Vigorously she massaged her stiff cheeks, pressing and pushing them into a smile. When she emerged, her smile tightly in place, a burst of laughter exploded from the recreation room.

The novices, their backs to her, were crowded around Milly who held a plastic gun in her hand. She was aiming at a windup rabbit scooting on wheels across the smooth terrazzo floor. Milly pulled the trigger and "ping!" the rabbit turned over, its wheels spinning madly. The novices roared, slapping each other on the back and laughing so hard that they were dabbing tears away from their eyes.

"Me next, Sister Raphael, let me try!" Mabel begged, jumping up and down in genuine excitement. Milly handed her the gun. Sister Evania focused on the rabbit and once again, "ping!" it fell, spinning its wheels. Gladys and Angie doubled up with laughter. Chloe was glad to see her friend from St. Eli so happy. "But how had she achieved it? Not through strict obedience, such as Lena had." Chloe had often observed Gladys ignoring rules, whispering in the hallways, swinging her arms, even talking during the Grand Silence. The only sign of discontent Gladys had ever shown was a cute wrinkling of her pert nose at bathroom duty.

Again the old arguments harassed Chloe until she latched onto the same old culprit: "the villa. Her four years there had done her more harm than good, stunted her growth, ruined her vocation, made her unfit for either the convent or the world." The thought galled her afresh. "Now it was too late. High school was over and she had no girlfriends." She was a wreck around boys. She hadn't the slightest notion of how to act around them. Then there was the matter of her health. With her burning hands and weak heart and shoulders stiff with rheumatism, how would she manage in the world? Better to stay here, where she could do some good, and where she could hide.

The buffoonery over, Milly saw Chloe standing alone, and asked her, "What did you get for Christmas?"

"A suitcase," Chloe replied. "And you?"

"A black scarf and deodorant. The scarf's regulation, so I can keep it."

"You can keep the deodorant too," Chloe said.

"Not for long."

"Why not?"

Milly raised an eyebrow and whispered, "After Christmas, no more deodorant,"

"What? I don't believe you!"

"Sshh. I've known for a while."

"Then how will we ...?"

"Just soap," Milly said, shrugging, "and that's not all." She paused. Venerable Sister's heavy step was heard at the threshold. Her bulky form stopped at the ping-pong table where she surveyed the gifts. "It's time to clear away these things," she said, "any items that are not regulation may be left here to be given to the poor. Tonight you may write your thank-you notes."

Two weeks after Christmas Chloe received a letter from Michelle, saying that she and Kenny and their new baby had stopped by to visit her.

> "It was the day after Christmas, and we were driving right through Magnolia on our way home from Texas. Kenny's out of the army now! I thought for sure they would give us an exception since we didn't make it to your reception last summer. We've been gone for almost two years! But that sister superior was so strict. She didn't even smile. We had little Caroline all dolled up so cute too, all in a pink. I cried. I was so disappointed."

Chloe felt flat and lifeless. "Michelle and Kenny and baby Caroline were here, on the Heights, just yards away from her, and she had not even been told? Were they hoping she would not find out?" How such a visit might affect her, she wasn't sure, but feeling slighted, she took the letter to Venerable Sister. "Couldn't I have just *seen* them, maybe waved at them from the window?" she asked.

"Sister, that would not have done any of you any good. You will see them soon, come June."

"But, Venerable Sister, I thought, I mean, didn't Milly, Sister Mary Charles get to see her brother when he came home from Germany on furlough?"

"Yes, for just a half an hour. It was a hard decision. We didn't make it lightly. Her brother had been gone for three years, and he was home only for a very short time."

"But my brother in law was in the army, and they couldn't afford the trip to see me on my reception."

"They wanted to see you very badly, Sister, and your sister had a hard time accepting the rule. But I would expect you to understand it in light of the vow of obedience that you are preparing to take. This is a wonderful opportunity for you to practice it, don't you agree?"

"Yes, Venerable Sister. Thank you, Venerable Sister." As she walked away, Chloe thought of turning back to ask Venerable Sister what she thought of little Caroline, how cute she was, but, thinking better of it, she kept on walking.

CHAPTER 46.

Sanatorium

A tunnel built underground led from the convent to the sanatorium, where the old and infirm nuns lived. It was a cool passageway, softly lit, with cement sides and a paved floor. The novices, carrying pails and mops, skimmed noiselessly through it on their way to clean. Chloe, shielded from sight by her veil's wide walls, did facial exercises, rolling her eyes to the left and to the right, scrunching up her lips and nose, holding that pose, and then relaxing. The damp air in the tunnel helped her skin feel more elastic. Next she held a grin for the length of ten steps, and then squinted for ten more. On New Year's Day, Chloe had decided to change. She would resist Satan. He would not win. This lethargy would dissipate; she would smile pertly and speak cheerfully. The intense disappointment of Christmas would not squeeze her vocation from her.

But the devil was active. Yesterday, when the novices learned for the first time about "chapter," it had affected her deeply. The very word, "chapter," had all her life been a pleasant word associated with divisions in a book. But now she knew it had a homonym. It meant a discipline of public confession of sin, which included kissing the dining room floor in repentance.

"Now that you are in the second half of your novitiate, it is time for you to learn the disciplines of our order."

It could be borne. It was not torture, or pain, or death. It just took nerve; that was all, to stand at the front of the dining hall, facing the crucifix, your back to the others while you knelt and confessed your sins out loud for all to hear.

"Just your outward sins, the ones that others see, not your inward thoughts," Venerable Sister explained. "And, when you are finished, kneel down and kiss the floor before you return to your seat."

The back of Chloe's head had started to buzz the minute she heard. She had never guessed at such a practice, so it came as a complete surprise. And, as she recoiled from it, she recalled the faces of the nuns she had known; Sister Clarice, her proud eighth-grade teacher, Sister Dorcus, and Sister Damien! All these nuns had submitted to this act of humiliation, for years!

"No wonder convents are off-limits to the world! It would never do for a worldly person to catch them doing that!" Venerable Sister said it would "strengthen their character." But Chloe doubted she had the strength to do it.

At the sanatorium the old nuns' shrunken faces peered up at the novices suspiciously, hobbling about them like curious children, touching their white veils and laughing. Their own veils sagged inward, and their white wimples bore drops of spilled food and drink. One of them reminded Chloe of her Grandma Polowski.

Before starting to work the novices set down their cleaning supplies and sang "O Bone Jesu!" for the nuns. The old nuns swayed and clapped delightedly. One nun in a wheelchair, so humpbacked that she had to twist her neck to look up, never stopped smiling. This nun's veil was soft, not starched, and this gladdened Chloe's heart, to see that a rule could be relaxed when need demanded it. Chloe wanted to talk to that nun. Perhaps, in her great age, she had words of wisdom that might unlock for Chloe the reason for her unhappy life.

Since last summer the novices had not seen or spoken to anyone besides their own seventeen classmates, and of course, Venerable Sister, and Father Schlick in the confessional. Here, as they began to scrub and wash the windows, the old nuns talked to them as if they were oblivious of the rules of the novitiate. They grinned and chatted like happy children. Apparently keeping "devotional silence" all day had long ago been abandoned by these ancient ones.

"You're doing all the talking."

"I'm not stopping you."

"You don't even make sense."

"And you do?"

Mabel giggled at the old nuns' banter, but Chloe puzzled at how, her elders, at the end of a long and disciplined life, could end up sounding like querulous children. "Was this the fruit of a Godly life?" She had hoped that her own life might count for something someday, that she would grow in wisdom and age and grace before God and men.

"You took my colored toothpicks!"

"I never!"

"I can't finish my work without them."

"That's your problem, seems to me."

"I'm telling."

"Go ahead, there's nothing to tell."

Humble Handmaids of Mary were often asked to put aside their talents, sometimes for years, when obedience required it. Often a nun with artistic talent had to wait her whole life long before she could indulge her natural gift. But these nuns had already been "used up," teaching other people's children or cooking and serving other nuns. And now all they were capable of was toothpick art.

As she continued to wash windows and mop the trim boards around the old sanatorium, Chloe saw something else. After years of denying themselves, these nuns were free to be themselves. No rule could hold these bent bodies and broken minds to a regimen of silence. At last they could do as they pleased, with no condemnation.

Chloe, on top of the stepladder, felt a twang in her heart as she reached to wash the window. She clutched her heart and climbed slowly down. It was a sign. She looked about, but no one had noticed her crouching, one hand on her heart as if to keep it from dying. As she bent to retrieve her rag an ocean of pain heaved inside of her. She clamped her mouth shut while wringing out her rag over the pail. The black skirt of an old nun brushed her face. "My papa gave me this last week," she said. A small pink blanket was draped over her thumb, and she was stroking it with a sweet expression on her face. "He brought it out from town."

CHAPTER 47.

Rope

It was raining outside. Heavy rivulets streamed down the library windows, blurring the scene, darkening the room, beating a steady muffled undertone to Venerable Sister's droning voice. Eighteen white humps, each with a pleat falling neatly from the peak of her head, sat listening to Venerable Sister read from the *Holy Rule Book.* Because she sat hunched forward, Sister's large jowls sagged closer and closer to the book as the room grew darker and darker.

At home it often rained on wash day. The house would smell of bleach. "Rugga-rug, rugga-rug" the Maytag washing machine churned its load of clothes as Momma, stripped down to her bra in the summertime heat, lifted dripping laundry from the steaming water with a stick and fed it to the wringer. Sweat glistened on her forehead.

"Somebody's coming!" a child shouted, pointing to a cloud of dust in the distance.

"It's Father Black! Chloe, mind the machine!" Momma yelled as she streaked to her bedroom for a blouse. Daddy frowned. Momma returned buttoning her blouse asking, "Is he here yet?"

Old Father Black could be seen shuffling toward the house, white wisps of hair lifting from the top of his nearly bald head. It was a pastoral call.

"Saints of old, striving for perfection," Chloe jerked awake and clutched her desk. "Would inflict harsh punishments upon their bodies, such as fasting, going without sleep, wearing hair shirts, or sewing bits of glass into their garments."

That scene from home—so vivid. "Was she losing her mind, or had she dozed off?" Yesterday, in the piano room she thought she heard, as plainly as if she were home, Owen's and Brent's voices. "Maybe my heart's not pumping enough blood to my brain. But no. God would not allow this to happen to me on my honeymoon with Him!"

"Today we recognize that suffering exists often in just doing our duty well. Jesus indicated this when He said, "Sufficient for the day is the evil thereof." But for the religious there is a singular, higher calling, a greater responsibility for holiness. Holy Mother Church gives the religious permission to inflict real pain upon their bodies, so that we might "fill up that which is lacking in the sufferings of Christ."

She closed the *Holy Rule Book* to gaze mournfully at her novices. Her large red jowls sagged like a bull-dog's. It was getting dark, and Chloe wished someone would turn on a light. But the vow of poverty required them to do without as much as was possible.

"The Apostle Paul said, 'I beat my body and bring it under subjection, lest having preached to others, I myself become a castaway.' If *he* feared becoming castaway, dear sisters, how much more should we?"

Venerable Sister picked up a rope lying on her desk, a foot long, separated into three strands at the middle. The end of each strand held a large knot. "On Profession Day you will be given a rope like this. It is an instrument of penance to be used by you alone, on yourself alone. You are to tap your bare back lightly, no more than five strikes in a row, and not more than once a day." Venerable Sister struck the palm of her hand twice with the rope. It made a weak and flimsy sound. "It couldn't hurt much," Chloe thought, and yet her poor sick heart, worn and weary from the constant vigilance of guarding her thoughts and feelings, seemed to ache at the sight of it. She felt dull with shock. "How Brent would scoff if he knew nuns beat themselves! What would Mom and Dad say if they knew?"

"Human nature is unrelenting in its depravity. Even here, cut off from the world, sin lurks. Some of you have shared your struggles with me. This is a tool to help you drive temptation from you." Venerable Sister drew the three-stranded cord through her soft, puffy hands. "We would be foolish indeed not to use it."

Dismissed, the novices floated silently as a drifting cloud from the library to the refectory for dinner. The novices stared down at the bound hems of their skirts. Chloe could not face her own revulsion in her classmates' eyes. Yet she hungered for their comments. As soon as recreation hour arrived the novices huddled together to discuss this newest surprise in their lives.

"I had no idea!" Kay said, her eyes wide.

"I've known since Christmas," Milly said.

"It's like something from the Middle Ages," Aimee squeaked.

"You mean the Dark Ages!" Chloe countered.

"Maybe this explains why Sister Jerard was so crabby all the time," Mabel joked.

"They aren't supposed to hurt themselves with it," Milly reminded the others.

"Then what's the use of it, if it doesn't hurt?" Lena asked sweetly.

"Maybe it gets easier after a while. You know—routine." Chloe said this with a shrug, more to banish her own dreadful feelings than to express a conviction. Her chest felt as though ropes were being drawn tightly around it. "How could she not have heard of this before?"

Gladys was standing nearby, listening with a clear untroubled gaze in her brown eyes. It revived Chloe. If her dear friend from St. Eli could take such news calmly, she wanted to be near her; to share in her secret of equanimity. "Want to walk to the cemetery?" she asked.

"Sure!" Gladys said, putting down the pliers with which she had planned to help make rosaries. As they threw their black woolen shawls over their veils and stepped into the rain-washed evening Chloe remarked, "Nuns really do lead *different* lives." She waited hungrily for words of wisdom, even a remark that might cast light on how Gladys was able to accept so well this news about the rope. When none came Chloe fished again, saying, "At least we're all in the same boat." But Gladys seemed unaware that she was leaving her friend in the dark. They both picked up their skirts and walked around a large puddle.

"Did you know St. Eli is having its one hundredth Anniversary this summer? My dad's growing a beard for it." Gladys said. After talking about St. Eli's centennial for a while Chloe tried once more. "That rope business surprised me!" She said bluntly.

Gladys seized Chloe's arm and pointed to the underbrush from which emanated a small scratching sound. They stood very still. A rust-colored bird appeared, kicking backward with both feet in the wet gravel.

"Rufus-sided Towhee," Gladys whispered her face intent. The eastern sky had cleared. Ethereal clouds reflected just a hint of the glorious sunset shining in the west. Suddenly the bird rose in a panic and flew away. "Look! See its white wing bars and its tail spots?" Gladys cried, looking up and pointing.

CHAPTER 48.

January

"Venerable Sister, I think I'm sick," Chloe said at her next spiritual interview. While she explained her symptoms, Venerable Sister's large sympathetic eyes roamed searchingly over her face. All through January Chloe had noticed a growing heaviness in her body, as though she had gained weight. But her cincture belt hung looser than ever on her bony hips. She could put both hands between it and her small flat stomach. If her hands weren't burning, she would have taken the trouble during sewing class to move the hooks and eyes over for a better fit. But the mere thought of sewing through that tough belt made her hands ache more.

The heaviness grew worse when she climbed a flight of stairs. By the time she reached the top she was pulling herself up by the banister. Sometimes she sat down to rest. Her shoulders too, ached steadily. And when working in the kitchen she found the big kettles almost too much to handle.

"My arms feel like lead. I'm always tired. And I puff even when I'm coming *down* the stairs."

"Sister Ignatius, you look angry ... I've noticed ... or maybe sad is a better word," Venerable Sister said. "Are you happy here?"

"Happy?" Chloe gazed at her mistress in profound disappointment. "What kind of guidance was this?" Sister Damien would never have asked such a question. “What had happiness to do with one’s vocation?” But while Venerable Sister waited, her heavy jowls sagging, Chloe considered the word. She had every reason to be happy. This life offered many beautiful things, such as quiet, with time to study and to pray. The meals were delicious, and she got plenty of fresh air and exercise. She slept soundly for eight hours every night. Besides that, she had friends and she was getting a college education! What more could she want? Wouldn’t Momma give her left arm for just one of her peaceful hours? Lately Chloe no longer found the hours of silence onerous. Instead she now preferred silence to the empty prattle of her peers. “Yes, Venerable Sister, I’m happy. I don’t know why I should look sad or be this tired,” she said. “I … I’ve got some kind of sickness … my heart hurts.” Her hands fluttered to the spot beneath her wimple. “My hands burn too.” She looked down at them. “Even my elbows hurt sometimes!” Chloe laughed a light self-deprecating laugh, twisting her hands in her lap.

“You were examined by the nurse, were you not?”

“Yes, Venerable Sister.”

“And she said you were in good health?”

“Yes, Venerable Sister.”

“Then I think we have to go with that, Sister Ignatius, and look elsewhere. Perhaps you do not want this life. Perhaps you want another life, with a husband and children. I’m just asking. I would like you to be entirely truthful about this. Because you should either give yourself completely to this life, holding nothing back, or you should go home.”

Venerable Sister’s words struck Chloe hard. She looked straight into her mistress’s eyes while her mind reeled. Venerable Sister was almost dismissing her. If this was an attack of the devil’s, then she had no one to fight for her but herself. “No, I don’t want a husband or children,” she said flatly.

After that Chloe's muscles seemed to have turned against her; her face refused to smile, pulling her moth down with a force greater than her own will. In chapel it was such an effort to lift her hands in prayer that she let them hang leadenly by her side. "Was this evil lurking in her body something that might be driven out with the rope?" Staring at the white host enthroned in the golden monstrance, she asked woodenly, "Haven't I given myself completely to you?" But she no longer expected an answer from her groom.

Sister Stanislaus had died. None of the novices had known her, but they were told about her last brave days of dying, when no complaint issued from her lips. She was ninety-six. The novices could view the casket in the anteroom off the chapel if they wished. After her noon visit to the chapel, Chloe entered the anteroom where the narrow black casket rested on a metal stand. Sunlight poured in through the arched windows, making all bright. Sister Stanislaus' white face, encased in her habit, looked stern. Her lips were tight together, and her nose jutted up sharply. "How many school children had she terrified, looking down that nose at them? No flowers adorned the coffin, but lush green ferns on pedestals arched their delicate fronds in the sunlight, softening the scene. The walls of Sister Stanislaus' veil were pressed against the edges of her coffin, as if she and the habit barely fit into the narrow box.

Chloe stared at the stillness. The absolute stillness of death intrigued her. Many times in her years at Mater Dei she had viewed a dead nun, and it was always the same; a black rosary entwined in gnarled fingers and the clean white wimple over her chest immaculate and still. Chloe couldn't take her eyes off of it. Though she had often viewed death like this, she had never dared touch it. Glancing about to make sure no one approached, she reached in and touched the dead nun's hand. She drew back, startled. It wasn't the coldness that shocked her. She had expected that. It was the hardness, as if she were touching a statue, or as if Sister had turned to stone.

Chloe turned her attention to Sister's head, where a crown of thorns that she had received on her Profession Day, seventy-five years ago, rested. Among its thorns shone a single gold leaf, signifying her first fifty years, and a ruby marking her seventy-fifth year as a bride of Christ. Chloe stood on tiptoe to see it. She had never seen a young nun in the coffin. But she tried to picture what a novice would look like; young and pretty, with a white veil and a crown of roses on her head. That would be sad but happy too, because all her troubles would be over. Chloe's hand wandered to her sick heart that burned but never burned up. "When would it hurry up and give way?"

CHAPTER 49.

Laundry

April came in like a lamb. Though it had rained all week, on Friday the campus lay quiet and green in the sunlight. The novices could go outdoors without their shawls, and they resembled swans gliding along the sidewalk. As they hastened toward the laundry to work, students looking down from the academy windows rapped madly at the glass, waving and smiling. The novices waved back, smiles lingering on their faces as they entered the steamy laundry. The laundry nuns, their black sleeves pinned up, revealing their naked white arms, looked up with hot, flushed faces at the youthful help.

The novices peeled off their wristlets, rolled up their wide, loose sleeves and tied aprons over their habits. They awaited orders. Six were assigned to the ironing boards along the windows. Three others were directed toward the mangles in the back. Four were stationed on either end of the huge roller press in the middle of the room; two on one side to feed the damp sheets and linens into the rumbling machine, and the other two to catch them, hissing and hot, on the other side, fold them and stack them before the next one came hissing through.

Chloe and Gladys were sent to the folding room, a large, sunny room with a cement floor lined with counters. It was a quieter room. Beneath the counters huge gray laundry carts were parked, ready for loading. Each one was labeled in big letters: ASP, BRDS, CAND, NOV,

CONV, JR.S, INF, SAN, and RECT for the different departments on the Heights. There was even a small cart marked "MEN" for farmer Gene and the two resident priests.

For an hour Gladys (Sister Edwina) and Chloe worked silently; folding white cotton underwear, T-shirts, black cotton slips, and stockings. They read name tags, placing the stacks into appropriate carts. Gladys was quick with names. She knew, without looking at the name charts where each article went. So, while Chloe folded, Gladys sorted. Just as they put the last stack of white towels into the huge cart marked, "CONV," the 10:00 a.m. bell rang for a break. All work stopped, machines cooled down, and the novices were allowed to talk softly to one another and take a drink of water. Chloe reached under her wimple to massage her shoulders.

"What are you doing?" Gladys asked, a quizzical smile playing on her pretty red lips.

"My shoulders are stiff," Chloe remarked, noting how clear Gladys's complexion was this morning, almost translucent. Her brown eyes had a quick lively light in them. Chloe liked her friend from St. Eli, and was sure she would make an excellent nun. Because of her sweet nature, kids would like her. After break, Chloe was directed to an ironing board while Gladys disappeared into the basement for different chores.

From her new station Chloe could see the academy, with its turrets and windows. Students in uniform strolled by on the sidewalks. Chloe started. One was Jenny, she was almost sure. How tall she had grown, and pretty! Chloe had not seen her since Reception Day. Her heart rumbled faster as she watched, praying, "Oh please Mother Mary, let her see me!" Then Jenny did turn and look. Immediately their eyes met and there was no distance between them. Chloe's heart lurched. She felt breathless. She raised her hand in a quick wave, and Jenny leaped and jumped excitedly. Chloe didn't understand the strange magnetism that drew her to the younger girl. She was just glad there was a thick glass between them.

Suddenly Chloe gasped and took up the iron. Too late; she had scorched a blouse. A huge brown blotch in the precise shape of an iron lay stamped upon it. Her knees shook. Her heart, already overwrought, felt as if it were flopping about helplessly like a fish out of water.

Blouse in hand, Chloe sought out Sister Agnitha to beg her forgiveness. She leaned against a pillar for strength, noticing across the wide, green lawn, near the novitiate door, a familiar green Pontiac. But delivery cars parked there all the time, as well as cars waiting to take nuns downtown. She didn't wonder at it long.

"AAch! Sister Ignatius!" short little Sister Agnitha groaned, looking aghast at the blouse. "This is bad, very bad work!" She clucked and wagged her head as she led Chloe to a sink where she told her to scrub out the spot. It took a long time. By the time the great brown scorch was gone, the blouse looked worn and rough.

At noon, in the refectory, Chloe clutched the back of her chair for support while the novices waited for the bell for prayer. Her mouth was dry, and her stomach hurt from hunger. The morning had exhausted her. She felt shaky. "No coffee for you this meal," she chided herself, "You're already too jittery."

A novice stood in front of the dining hall, her back to the others. It looked like Lena, but Chloe wasn't sure. How lonely and vulnerable, how humble she looked, standing beneath the crucifix. "Show off!" Chloe thought irritably, "You would be first!" After the blessing the novices paused. The lone novice dropped to her knees and said in a high wavering voice, "I, Sister Uriah, admit to all my faults, especially that of talking in the corridor. I ask pardon of God and of my sisters."

Then she kissed the floor. Everyone heard the hard, starched veil touch the floor. It grated on Chloe's nerves like a saw. "Kiss it hard, Lena," she mocked as she watched her classmate return to her place, her pink cheeks brighter than ever. How holy she looked … how meek and satisfied and fake and cleansed and forgiven and proud! Once again Lena had gripped a new and odious rule by the horns and wrestled it to the ground. Chloe's jaw tightened. It was she who was proud. It was she, with all her white-hot jealousy, who was the fake!

The bell rang. The novices pulled out their chairs and sat down. The bell rang again, and they unrolled their silverware, spread their napkins on their laps and waited. But before the bell rang allowing them to begin eating, Venerable Sister cleared her throat, and it sounded like gravel beneath a truck. "Sisters, I have an announcement."

A tremor ran through Chloe. Not today. Her scalp flamed beneath her veil. Someone had left. Please no! Her heart would burst, she was sure, with the pain. Faces skimmed across the white china plate before her. Was it Milly? Or Aimee? Or Mabel? Was it Kay? Oh, it couldn't be Kay.

"Sister Edwina went home this morning."

Suddenly the room was still, so still that no one moved or rustled. Chloe was glad she was sitting, because the table was tilting, the room was spinning. Her feeble heart rapped out a weak rat-a-tat-tat of fear and rage and hurt and great disappointment.

"It was not a hasty decision on her part, but something she has been agonizing over for some time. Sister Edwina has a handicapped brother and a crippled mother, but she did not want their needs to influence her decision. That is why she waited this long."

Agonized? Chloe spread her burning fingers out on her skirt while she recalled her friend's calm face.

"None of us like to see our numbers diminish. But in the end it is up to the individual to go or stay. It is between her and God. I promised Sister Edwina we would remember her in our prayers. *Holy Rule* requests that we refrain from mentioning her name or discussing her. This is not condemnation. It is closing ranks with those who are standing true."

Sister shook the little bell. Slowly, as if coming out of a trance, the novices began the business of eating, lifting bowls, handling silverware, pouring water, extra slowly, extra carefully. For Chloe all the motions were mechanical, disconnected from the news still reverberating through her head. The day's reader began "A fire in her heart, the story of Mother Adrian Madonna Levee, founder of the Humble Handmaids of Mary."

Chloe's thighs shook. She squeezed them together. Her stomach started jumping. She feared losing control and becoming a spectacle. Kay handed her a heaping bowl of mashed potatoes and their eyes met. Tears welled up in Chloe's eyes and rolled down her cheeks. She stifled a sound. For the rest of the meal she dared not look at anyone. Stoically she chewed the meatloaf, buttered her bread and put food into her mouth that tasted all the same.

Later, as the novices cleared the tables, filled the dishpans with water, and washed and dried the dishes, Chloe worked quickly, her eyes down. Then, free to leave, the novices sailed down the corridor like ships in flight. In chapel at last, safe inside the privacy of her large side walls, Chloe's tears flowed in hot streams down her cheeks. "Gladys! Gladys! Gladys!" This hurt more than losing Lucy last summer. It felt like a wide-open wound from which was escaping all the joy and hope she had ever known. The bottom had fallen out of her vocation. She had lost a friend; a friend from her hometown, a friend in whom, she realized now, she had found greater comfort and satisfaction than she had realized.

Her throat felt like it had a grapefruit stuck in it. It hurt. She needed to cry freely, but where? She was never alone. At night in the dorm the others lay only a few feet from her. Every moment of the day she was surrounded. Her large white handkerchief was soon soaked with tears.

She recalled Gladys's glee on Entrance Day, when she had so eagerly helped her dress, telling her all the news of the day. A novice knelt down next to Chloe and she guessed from the freckled hands that it was Kay. There *was* kindness in the world. Her friend from villa days knew and empathized with her. Chloe waited for a word or a touch, from Kay. But the novice rose and left without making any contact. Chloe's heart shivered. "Was there no love in the convent?"

Surely, Chloe thought, Venerable Sister knew that Gladys was from her hometown, and she would draw her aside, ask her how she was doing and give her a special word of comfort. But when the day proceeded without this happening, Chloe saw her mistake. Convents didn't recognize worldly connections. Here community mattered, not individual losses. Sisterhood was their life. "But where is the love?" Chloe asked, over and over again.

During Wednesday choir practice, the notes on the page blurred. Chloe lay her hymnbook down in her lap while tears poured down her face. She wasn't able to stop. She dabbed at them listlessly with an already-soaked handkerchief. Then she gave up and let the tears drip down her chin and onto her wimple. She didn't care. Twice Sister Maurice, the choir director, glanced anxiously at her, but said nothing. Her authority extended only to music. Beyond that she was not allowed to speak to the novices.

Chloe's condition troubled her. "Why did Gladys's leaving hurt so much? Why couldn't she even think of her without a flood of tears rushing from her eyes?" The two of them had not exactly been fast friends. But something like a dam had broken inside her that she could not stop. All her inner resources had broken loose, and her feelings were tumbling out madly in a flood.

No one commented on Chloe's red eyes. Every time she went to the bathroom, tears flowed. She chided herself. Her sisters were right to ignore her. This grief was unreasonable and selfish. They hurt, too. Nevertheless, she raged against their coldness.

Finally, puzzled at her sisters' behavior toward her, Chloe concluded that Venerable Sister was flushing her out. "She knows I'm sick, and she wants me to leave before I get worse. She has told the others not to coddle me. There are enough old, sick nuns in the sanatorium without having a dying novice too. I should leave ... follow Gladys out of here. Let them all stay. Cruel brides! But that would be playing right into the devil's hands. He's the one who would win. I'll not give in! No. They expect it. Or do they?"

After three days, Chloe stopped crying. She felt empty and hollow inside, as if waking from a long illness. More tired than ever, she frequently felt the need to stop what she was doing and take a deep breath. The burning sensation in her hands made her think of Moses' bush that burned but never burned up. It made her think of hell.

One morning Chloe awoke with sleep still dragging at her like a veil. All through Mass she rubbed her eyes, blinked, and massaged her cheeks, trying to feel awake. During cleaning, her arms moved heavily, as if lead ran in her veins. Listlessly she moved the dust mop on the clean terrazzo floors. I need fresh air, she thought, throwing on her woolen shawl and taking the mop outside.

While shaking it, she noticed a cigarette, still lit, glowing on a wooden bench. A maintenance man must have left it; or a priest. Her mother always said a cigarette relaxed her. She glanced up at the convent windows, their shades half drawn. No one was looking. *Holy Rule* forbad nuns to watch from windows. Pulling her black shawl down to cover her white veil so that she would look like a full fledged nun on the outside, she picked up the cigarette, put it to her mouth and inhaled. She coughed and inhaled again. The white smoke curled upward, its aroma transporting her to other places and times when people smoked; to Momma. "I could be thrown out for this," she thought dispassionately, and coughed again. She felt light-headed. When she saw two nuns approaching from far away, she dropped the cigarette and ground it out with her toe. Amused, she imagined herself confessing in the dining hall "I took two puffs on a cigarette today. I humbly beg pardon for my indulgence."

"Who am I?" Chloe wondered, hurrying inside: "a good novice enduring temptation or a bad novice revealing her true character?"

CHAPTER 50.

Begging Day

Begging Day arrived. The fifteen novices, hardened survivors of a year of solitude, floated noiselessly behind their heavy-footed mistress who led them down new hallways deep in the inner sanctums of the convent. At last Venerable Sister stopped and pointed them into a high-ceilinged classroom. Her big sad eyes, pools of deep blue in her red, rough face, regarded them woefully. "Please be seated," she said in her deep man's voice. Then she disappeared. In the silence that followed Chloe glanced up at the long windows lining one wall. Brown shades that rolled up from the bottom blocked the outdoors from view. Only at the top could they glimpse the blue sky. Vows were two months away. Joy fluttered through Chloe's stomach, followed by fear. Today each novice must kneel before Mother Euphemia and beg to be admitted into the order. Why did she tremble so? Her dream was finally within reach.

The novices had brought books to read while waiting. While she read, Chloe kept one eye on the closed door at the front of the room. It led to an inner chamber where Mother Euphemia waited, along with Venerable Sister Georgina and Reverend Sister Rose Sharon, the secretary of the order. Chloe mentally rehearsed the protocol: kneel before the three nuns and humbly beg to be admitted into the order of the Humble Handmaids of Mary. "It is just a formality," Venerable Sister had assured them, "No one needs to be the least bit afraid. You have all proven yourselves to be good and faithful novices."

A low murmur emanated from behind the door, filling Chloe's brain with bubbles. She couldn't concentrate. Her heart cowered inside of her, hiding, from what? Those nuns were kind old mothers glad to welcome new daughters into their order. This was a high and happy moment; one last door to pass through to reach her long-sought goal. But every time another novice disappeared behind the door Chloe's stomach tightened up like a fist. She did not feel well.

The three vows of poverty, chastity, and obedience that the novices would take in June would be binding upon them for three years. During that time they would be junior sisters, continuing their education and helping in Catholic schools in downtown Magnolia. Then they would repeat their vows for another three years. After that final vows would be pronounced. Chloe knew this. She needn't fear. She could always back out. But no! Venerable Sister had said "Though your lips say three years, in your heart you should say 'forever.'"

The door opened. It was her turn. Like a pheasant startled by a hunter in her daddy's cornfield, Chloe's heart flew into her throat, banging furiously in panic. Woodenly she moved, rising and passing through the door. She found herself in an empty room. It appeared to be a large office lined with bookshelves. An empty chair and a desk stood in the middle of the room on a threadbare carpet. Confused, Chloe glanced to her right, where, in another room far away, three nuns sat waiting. How straight and stiff their chairs looked. Chloe's knees swayed as she approached them. She knelt down before them, folded her hands, and looked up at the three. Venerable Sister's florid face, Mother Euphemia's beady, black eyes and Reverend Sister Rose Sharon's pale, wrinkled face gazed soberly back at her.

"Mother Superior, Venerable Sister, Reverend Sister Rose Sharon, I, Novice Ignatius, humbly beg to be admitted to the order of the Humble Handmaids of Mary."

"Sister Ignatius," Mother Euphemia asked in a nasal tone, "Are you willing to accept any burden, bear any cross, and perform any duties that your holy vocation might ask of you?"

"Yes, by the grace of God, I am, Mother."

"Novice Ignatius, you have declared your determination to become a member of the order of the Humble Handmaids of Mary. What are your reasons for so requesting this favor, and what are you ready to give in return?"

At the word "favor," something lifted from the top of Chloe's head like the lid on a boiling pot. She could not speak. Planned and practiced words escaped like so much steam. Bereft, she searched for a response, but remained mute. As the moments ticked by she began to doubt that she had a mouth. She wanted to touch it to assure herself. As she knelt, instead of words, a sudden storm of unchecked feelings battered her soul. "I'm sick, I hate it here, and don't think I'm going to beg to join your order, when all I want to do is get the hell out of here and never see your faces again!"

"Had she said that?" Six eyes bored into her skull while the silence thickened. No one moved. Arms stayed tucked out of sight. Noses stayed pointed. She dared not open her mouth for fear the wrong words might come howling out. She felt frozen, like Lot's wife turned to a pillar of salt. In the awkward, interminable, deafening silence Mother Superior turned to Venerable Sister with a quizzical look, her veil making a scratching sound. Venerable Sister leaned forward, "Chloe, can you think of a reason why you want to be a sister?"

This helped. Chloe swallowed. She wet her lips. "I want to serve God," she said slowly, "and bring little children to love Him. And I'm willing to give God my life for that."

The nuns relaxed. Mother Superior withdrew her arms from her sleeves and took up a sheet of paper, cleared her throat and read: "Novice Ignatius, are you convinced that this life is the only life for you, and are you prepared to follow your vocation as a Humble Handmaiden of Mary wherever it will lead you, no matter how odious, no matter how far, no matter how ill-equipped you may feel you are for the task ahead?"

Again Chloe fell mute, her throat pounding. A simple yes was needed. "Why couldn't she say it?"

Mother Superior leaned forward. "Novice Ignatius, do you want me to repeat the question?"

"Yes, Mother Euphemia."

The bare wooden floor seemed to tilt as the words flowed from Mother's mouth and marched around Chloe's head. But she kept silent. An evil insolence had gripped her and she refused to answer. Soon it would be over. It was close to suppertime and there were still many novices to be interviewed.

"Novice Ignatius, is there anything about this life in our convent that you fear might be too hard for you, or that you would not do if asked, even if your talents must be renounced and set aside for the greater good of the order?"

"No, Mother Euphemia." Her mouth was again working properly. She answered the next questions calmly and quickly. Dismissed, she stood up, smiled crookedly at her superiors, and left. They did not return her smile.

That evening at recreation hour, anxious novices shared their accounts of the interview. "And then Mother gave me this sweet little smile,"

"Venerable Sister was so helpful."

"They laughed when I said …"

"So," thought Chloe, "they had not made fools of themselves as she had." An acute sense of loneliness possessed her. While her peers babbled, guilt, like a gooey poison spread through her, sinking to her toes. She had ruined everything. The old evil that she could not conquer had risen up and ruined her, had bitten off her sweetest, ripest, grandest fruit of all.

After that day Chloe couldn't pray. She didn't laugh. Tears no longer wet her eyes. Her vocation, once the most precious and beautiful gift she had, was dead, and God wasn't doing a thing to resurrect it. "Why should He?" She didn't even care about it anymore. "She should leave. But to whom would she go? This life was all she knew. Mom and Dad and the little girls would be disappointed. No more would she be an inspiration to others. How was she to act in a world that had never been her home? She would be a nineteen-year-old with a fourteen-year-old psyche; a misfit, an oddity, an old maid in St. Eli." Thoroughly dismayed, Chloe concluded that she must stay.

With great effort she denied thoughts of leaving. Her heart felt weak from the strain. She must quiet herself, follow the predictable rules of the novitiate, and regain her equilibrium. Her chest felt sore to the touch, as if her heart was infected. She pressed there often during the day, amazed that it neither grew worse nor better, but sulked like an angry child refusing to be comforted. At night, undressing behind her wooden screen, she checked the area. "Was that a lump? Had the tenderness spread?" In bed she lay and felt the beating of her heart gently shake the bed.

When not preoccupied with her heart, Chloe rued her burning hands. They made all work a misery. Sometimes the fiery pain teased her, traveling to her elbows and sitting there to taunt her. Oddly, she saw flashes of hope. God was merciful. Soon He would pluck her from this purgatory and take her to heaven. Or He would end this dark night of the soul with a sudden revelation, as he had for St. Theresa of Avila. But her conscience condemned such prideful hope. She was no saint. Such a foolish bride she was! "She might as well leave, if that's all the spiritual progress she had made by now." At such thoughts as these, her heart, like a dying watchdog, roused and whimpered anxious warnings to her soul.

"Dear Chloe, (Sister Ignatius),

I suppose you thought I went and died some place. But I'm still here. I've been very busy. I suppose this summer I'll be even *more busy*, with a garden. First time I'll ever have my own garden. I'm not too crazy about it. You know how I never liked working outside. But it'll save on the grocery bill.

Mrs. Derek Hoffman died. She was only 28. She had cancer. Two kids too! I saw Gladys at the funeral. What a surprise to hear she was out! She seems no different, still loves to gossip. She was wearing a real pretty dress. Short too! She didn't even stop to talk to her Aunt Clare in her wheelchair. Clare was hurt, she told me.

Momma gave me a little white baby cap. It was yours. I starched it up and it looks so cute on Caroline. Every time I put it on her I think of you. I hope she is still little when I see you next, whenever that will be.

Good-bye. Kenny will be home soon for supper.

Love always,

Your sis,

Michelle."

Chloe jammed the letter into the folds of her habit and strode down the hallway to the library. She yanked out her chair and sat down, trembling. "My baby cap!" she said, opening her Latin book and pressing her fist down the center of the book until the binding cracked. The book lay flat and submissive before her. She seethed. "Why was she upset? What did she care about a baby cap or Gladys's short dress? This life was what she wanted, so why this rage storming her throat like gall?"

"Ssstt!" Someone tapped at her veil. Mabel's eyes smiled at her from behind her thick glasses. "Sister! Your book's upside-down!" she whispered with a smile. Chloe turned her book around and smiled back at Mabel. Then Mabel reached over and squeezed Chloe's hand. It was a quick, spontaneous movement, full of feeling and a special kind of caring; and totally unexpected, coming from Mabel. Long after the two had returned to their private study, Chloe felt sister's touch like a healing balm. Before now she had not thought much of the importance of touch. Here months went by without any touching. Their entire habit prevented hugging, and it would be silly to shake hands. Even a pat on the back was awkward with the veil stiffly arching over the shoulders so.

Maybe she was one of those people who couldn't live that way, without touch. At home there had always been a baby or a child to hold. And the little boys were always wrestling one another. "Even fighting is a form of touching," she thought. "A shove from Brent might be better than nothing," she thought ruefully.

CHAPTER 51.

Road Home

The first of May, 1961, Chloe awoke before the 5:00 a.m. bell, remembering that it was Recollection Sunday, a day of silence. All day. No distractions to relieve the nagging pain already griping her neck like a vice. "Praised be Jesus Christ!" she said with the others, rolling back her blankets and falling to her knees by her bed. "Oh Jesus, through the immaculate heart of Mary I offer you my prayers, my works, my joys and sufferings of this day …"

Behind her privacy screen Chloe massaged her neck and shoulders as best she could to alleviate the growing tightness. Her burning hands already flamed. "Why?" She asked bitterly, dropping her woolen dress over her head and shoulders. "Am I not happy? Why do I hurt all over?" She laid her starched wimple around her shoulders just so, tied the head flaps, and pinned her arched veil to her headband, loving it and hating it at the same time.

"Jesus! All for Jesus!" she clenched her teeth against the strong urge to undo her pins and let the veil slide to the floor. Sorely tempted, she hurried from the dorm and down the stairs. Above the staircase she saw, or thought she saw, a black beam suspended above her head. She blinked, and it was gone. A chill ran through her. "What new terror was this? Was she going mad? Was it an assault from Satan? Or was it God's final test? If it were that, how tragic to give up now!" At the bottom step

Chloe turned a corner, nearly colliding with Venerable Sister, clumping along at great speed herself. Rearing back and apologizing, Chloe felt her mistress's eyes boring through her with unspeakable sadness.

"Oh God! I'm your intended! Help me!" She squared her shoulders. She would fight this demon, this battle ... whatever, whoever it was making her want to scream. She would not turn back. God wanted her to be faithful. She was chosen, and as such she rejoiced in all her trials. But despite her brave attempt at right thinking, she entered the chapel in a dark mood, her heart reminding her with each painful beat, of its strange malady. Kneeling, she stared at the altar coldly, with no more words to say.

Later, in the rumbling boiler room, as Chloe and Kay hung the dish towels on racks to dry, Chloe tried to catch Kay's eyes, longing to say just a few words. But Kay, intent on doing her duty, brushed her hands and hurried from the noisy room. "I just wanted to laugh with you again!" Chloe cried silently after the receding figure of her tall erect friend, her pure white veil billowing righteously behind her.

"Kay was practicing for the vow of obedience. There was no talking today. And yet, hadn't Jesus said that the spirit of the law was above the letter of the law?" But there she went again, rewriting holy rule for her own comfort. Outside, Chloe strolled to the cemetery, the noon sun warm on her back. Far ahead, the white veils of the other novices puffed out like sails against the blue sky; each alone ... each struggling with ... what? Professed nuns too, young and old, strolled by, their faces inscrutable. "Did they too wrestle with demons? Or had pronouncing vows and receiving the black veil put a stamp on their commitment, vanquished their doubts, and nailed down their flesh?" She wanted to ask an old nun shuffling toward her on the gravel road, "Will vows free me?"

She laughed, a sharp sarcastic snort, and the old nun regarded her with a beatific grin and passed on. "What did she think? That this young novice was enjoying a private joke with God? But what had Chloe thought? That this old nun was enraptured with Him! They could each be misreading the other." Chloe squeezed, twisted and rubbed her aching hands together as she ambled along alone.

The white marble slabs in the cemetery stood upright and even, in exact lines, some so old and weathered that their dates were barely discernable. "Sister Mary Obadiah, 1850–1920, R.I.P.", "Sister Mary Albert, 1872–1957, R.I.P." If she would die now her stone would read: "Novice Mary Ignatius," 1941–1961. Girls would stand here telling stories of her life. "But when would she die? So far no one even knew she was ill."

Traces of russet tinged the bare woods sheltering the cemetery, a harbinger of buds about to burst. A playful breeze ruffled the trees. It smelled like spring. Chloe had often missed walking through the groves at home. Long ago, in eighth grade, Sister Clarice had promised her that she would be able to roam the woods at Mater Dei. But it had not been so. Maybe now she might roam free, before she took the vow of obedience. Walking to the edge of the hill, she remembered the organized hikes led by Sister Damien. The old beaten path was still there where today's aspirants plunged down, laughing and clinging to saplings to keep themselves from falling, just as she and Kay had. Sister Damien's sure stride, as she led the way, was never broken.

Glancing about to see that no one was in sight, Chloe stepped onto the path and descended, gripping branches for support as she went down. Her heart complained. "Rat-a tat-tat." But she ignored it. "If you're going to fail me, do it now, here, outside in God's sweet nature while I do something outlandish." Branches scraped against her stiff veil. Her long woolen skirt dragged twigs and leaves with it. Her thick heels sunk into the soft ground. On she went, until she stood at the valley floor, her heart thumping, and her fingers burning. Sunlight fell in splotches on the thickly mulched ground, where tiny ferns unfurled their heads up through the leaf layer. Above her the naked tree branches clicked in the breeze. "Oh Lord, your kindness reaches to the heavens," Chloe recalled from her breviary.

When she was a freshman Sister Damien had led them on their first hike to a meadow. There she had made all the girls sit in a circle, where they sang a child's song, "Rinky Dinky Doo, that's what we learn in the school, Yahoo!" That was the day she had decided to leave. And she had told Jesus about it, and He had agreed. "What had taken her so long?" Her heart lay very still, listening to her thoughts. "Why had she not obeyed? 'Strong bulls of Bashan surround me,' the psalmist wrote. Sister Damien would never let me go. But that hadn't stopped Pauline Bedarf."

Chloe saw a small creek and went to sit by it on a rock. Birds twittered madly above her head. She watched how the water kept on moving no matter what; circling rocks, carrying twigs, dropping down ledges until, with all obstacles overcome, it ran away to parts beyond. "I wanted to do good," she thought. But it was impossible. As holy as her habit might make her look, it only cloaked her true self, her sin. It was a lie. There was no change; none. "So why ask something of herself that God Himself knew was impossible? I'll think about these things later," she said, standing up. Suddenly she was in a great hurry. Climbing back up the hill she felt like an old person, her whole body aching and complaining. But in her mind's eye she saw the bright tiny fern, unfurling its tender head up through the dead leaves. It gave her hope.

Reaching the novitiate, Chloe pulled open the heavy door and trudged up the back steps to the second floor. Puffing heavily she knocked at Venerable Sister's door.

"Come in," a voice boomed.

As Chloe stepped inside, Venerable Sister looked up with big wet eyes, reminding Chloe of a gentle bulldog. "Venerable Sister, I've decided that I can't go on," she blurted out, holding her hands over Sister's desk as if to show her their fire. "My hands hurt all the time, and there's something wrong with my heart!"

"Sit down, Sister," Venerable Sister rumbled, holding Chloe's gaze intently. "Are you ready to put your cards on the table, Sister Ignatius? Tell me all that you have been thinking."

Their talk centered for a while on Chloe's thoughts and feelings. Then they moved to her hopes and dreams. With each sentence that she spoke, her precious vocation, like a huge inflated ball, received a pin prick and grew a little smaller. Venerable Sister received Chloe's words as if she were praying to hear them, as if she had hoped that this young woman in religious garb would realize she was play acting. Chloe took a deep breath. At last, it appeared, she could speak to her Mistress her truest heart without receiving in return a challenge, an argument, or any threat from God concerning duty or breaking her parents' hearts.

The whole interview was topsy-turvy, and yet, it felt so right. Instead of convincing Venerable Sister, it seemed that Venerable Sister was convincing her.

"In the end, Sister," Venerable Sister said, "You have to want the life."

Chloe didn't want the life anymore. Was this how it would end, not with a bang, but a whimper?

CHAPTER 52.

Home

"Oh Lord, open my lips," the cantor began.

"And my mouth shall proclaim your praise," the novices replied, their voices rising sweetly like a flock of birds to the vaulted ceiling.

"Oh Lord, make haste to help me," the cantor chanted.

Bending deep at the waist, the novices answered in deep round tones, "Gloory bee to the Faather, and tooo the Sooon and too the Hooly Ghooost." They straightened up. "As it waas in the begiiinning is noow and ever shall bee; woorld without ennnd, Amennnn."

"One thing I have asked of the Lord, this will I seek," Chloe chanted with the rest, "that I may dwell in the house of the Lord all my days."

"But it's not working out that way," Chloe said to Jesus as tears blurred the flickering candles with the white marble statues that she loved. She saw herself as a zealous thirteen-year-old, running over the plowed earth toward Daddy, her application in her pocket. She saw the shy freshman wanting to go home; the earnest sophomore keeping holy hour, the busy junior, loving journalism class, and the torn senior nestled in Daryl's arms. She saw the crown of roses that would never grace Momma's parlor walls. She, Chloe Polowski, would be just like any other Catholic.

But I'm not sad, she conceded; just tired of trying. She was glad it was over. She had not guessed at the freedom there was in giving up. All her worries and doubts and trepidations for the future had collapsed and slunk away like bad animals. Nor did God condemn her. He who knew all had watched the hard fruit of her vocation ripen, grow soft, and drop to the ground where it had rotted and died. His sunshine still shone, beckoning her on. "To what? How could she please Him now?"

"I'll think about that when I'm home," she thought, noticing how the word "home" no longer stirred up the rich old excitement. Now it was a refuge to which she could slink like a sick dog to rest and lick her wounds.

On Monday, as requested by Venerable Sister, Chloe wrote to her parents asking them to come get her on Friday. She handed her letter to Venerable Sister, unsealed as usual, and Venerable Sister said she would include a note explaining that Chloe was leaving in good standing. Then, like a pregnant mother who knows the child within her is already dead, Chloe performed her usual duties about the convent with no joy or expectation, but merely to pass the time. By next week, nothing she did that week would matter to anyone, least of all to her.

Thursday dawned, her last full day in the convent. She dropped the wool serge dress over her head, cinched the wide stiff belt and stopped to hear the soft rattle of her wooden beads. She tied the wimple flaps tight behind her head with a kind of joy in the performance, a private goodbye show for herself. Lastly she set the veil on her head and anchored it. Complete, she left the dorm dressed as a Humble Handmaiden novice for one last day. By tomorrow night she would be just a farm girl in blue jeans, that is, if Momma hadn't made over all her clothes for the younger girls by now.

That night she peeled off her black wristlets and placed them on her dresser. How humble they looked; mute reminders of a simple life. She set her black oxfords neatly beneath her bed, eyeing them fondly even though they pinched her feet. She had liked their ring of authority on wooden floors. She rolled down her black stockings and removed them, unpinned her white veil and hung it on her screen. Next the headband and wimple came off, making their familiar raspy sounds as she folded them neatly. As she hung her black dress on a hanger she buried her face in its soft, warm folds. Tomorrow it would be dry-cleaned and hung in the sewing room closet for some future girl; for nothing here was wasted. Nothing here was owned.

In bed, Chloe lay in the moonlit room staring at her veil. The Venetian blinds at the window cast black stripes on its whiteness, making it resemble a prison gown. A tear welled up and rolled down her cheek onto the crisp white pillow. There were things she would miss. She wished, once more, that she could have loved the life. Tomorrow at noon, she would be gone, and Venerable Sister would make a terse announcement in the dining room. After that no one would speak her name. All trace of her vocation would be erased.

Though she had heard nothing from home since her letter, she knew her parents would be there in the morning. Chloe felt empty, as empty as the starched round veil now hanging on her screen. "I have fought the good fight, I have finished my course, I have kept the faith." "Who wrote that? St. Paul?" She drifted to sleep, jerked awake once, then fell back to sleep again.

On Friday morning, Father Schlick strode toward the altar, his shiny vestments flapping about his knees to say Mass. He made his usual vigorous sign of the cross, and then said: "Lord have mercy."

"Christ have mercy," the nuns repeated.

"Lord have mercy. Christ have mercy."

"Christ have mercy."

"Christ have mercy." The priest approached the altar for Mass.

After breakfast, Chloe slipped up to her dormitory to gather her few belongings: toothbrush, toothpaste, hankies, and towels. She hoped there were no name-tagged items of hers still in the laundry for the others to see and be stung by. Venerable Sister had asked her to act normal. So, during liturgy class Chloe took notes just as if she would if she were going to be here for the exam. Though she felt lightheaded and shaky and her hands burned with invisible flames, she raised them to answer questions. None of this struck her as insincere, just obedient. After lunch, as the novices finished up the dishes and left the refectory, Venerable Sister signaled to Chloe. "Your parents are here," she murmured, "waiting in the convent lounge. Get your things from your desk. Try not to leave anything behind."

At the words "Your parents are here," Chloe went limp. Without her doing anything to hurry it, time had brought the moment. Her knees trembled as she walked to the study room and with shaking hands removed her breviary, her ethics notes, her missal and her *Imitation of Christ*. She wanted these. She also wished to keep one personal item, like her headband or a wristlet. But that would be stealing. She thought of leaving a note for Kay, but the very idea made her hands protest in pain.

Venerable Sister and she walked in silence down a hallway, stepped quickly into the elevator reserved only for the aged, and watched the gate clang shut. Chloe was curious, and wanted very much to talk, but the rule of silence restrained her.

"How are they? How do they look?" she blurted out.

A flicker of annoyance passed over Venerable Sister's face. "They're fine. Your mother looks a bit worried, but I'm sure you can put her mind at ease," she said drily.

"Dad was so proud of me," Chloe said.

"I've talked to them, explained things," she said. "They understand this is the will of God."

"The will of God." How strange that the very words that had been used to keep her here were now used to ease her going. Chloe frowned at the mystery of it. A tiny laugh bubbled up inside of her.

It was a shock to see them sitting there, just as she had remembered them. Time had stood still for them. They arose, Daddy smiling and reaching out his hand, Momma clutching her purse, looking ready to cry or to laugh, depending on how Chloe appeared to them. Dad wore a brown corduroy jacket, his black pants, and his Sunday shoes. Momma had on a green dress and her scuffed black flats shaped, over time, to her bunions. Her same black speckled coat lay across the back of the couch. Neither one looked crushed or brokenhearted. That was a relief. They didn't look anxious. Just a curious, searching expression played on Momma's face, as if she were watching for signs of suffering, or craziness, perhaps. Dad, very matter of fact, smiled and nodded like he was closing a business deal. He took out his billfold to pay for the last of Chloe's dental work. Chloe sat down briefly with her parents, feeling that it was proper to let them view the body as it had been clothed for the last ten months.

"Well, now that we have that out of the way, I think we should be moving along," Venerable Sister rumbled. "I must join the novices in twenty minutes," she said, reaching under her wimple to retrieve and glance at her watch.

Chloe jumped up, ready to obey, already feeling the distance, the curtain dropping between her and Venerable Sister. Her mother handed her a brown paper bag containing her clothes. She looked inside; the black velvet skirt she had thought so smart when she was a junior, the red and black striped blouse of shiny polished cotton that Sister Damien had looked askance at three Christmases ago. nylons, a pair of worn pumps. Momma tilted her head apologetically. "I really had to hunt to find anything of yours around. I've made over most of your clothes for the younger ones or I've given them to …" Her voice trailed off.

"All she needs is something to go home in," Venerable Sister said briskly. "Come along Sister, you can undress in here." Chloe had not thought of where she might change. Of course it wouldn't be in her dorm; Canon Law forbade a lay person behind convent doors. And soon she would be a layperson, perhaps was one already. She followed Venerable Sister down to a basement storage room. It was dark and cool. Black trunks and suitcases belonging to nuns were stacked neatly on wooden shelves. Sister Patience appeared, smiling her usual doll-like smile and saying nothing but, "I'll guard the door." Chloe knew it was not her privacy she was guarding, but the chance of an unsuspecting novice passing by.

She unpinned her veil and looked for a place to hang it. The door stood ajar so she could have some light, so with a little leap she hung it on the top. She worked quickly, pulling off her headband and untying the wimple flaps. The air felt suddenly chilly. She laid the stiff white wimple on top of a trunk, first feeling the surface for dust. No. Someone must clean in here, for just such a time as this, the secret divestiture of a departing novice. She chuckled to herself. The rest of her costume followed. Nervously she ripped open the package of nylons and pulled the flimsy things on. How unnatural they felt. Momma had remembered a garter belt! And a slip. There was even an old bra, limp and gray. But of course she had one on already. Did Momma think they didn't wear bras in the convent? Slowly she buttoned up her shiny blouse. It pulled across her breasts. She slouched to keep it from gaping. Momma must have shortened the skirt, for she was sure she had never worn it this short. It barely covered her knees. She felt embarrassed to have Venerable Sister see her with so much leg exposed. At least the blouse had long sleeves.

"What shall I do with the habit?" she whispered to Sister Helena, who looked straight at Chloe's eyes as if trying hard not to see her in secular clothes.

"Just leave it. I'll take care of it as soon as you're gone."

She wished for a mirror. Rounding her shoulders and tugging at her skirt she walked toward her mother, feeling half dressed. Her ears and neck felt cold. No warm heaviness swished around her ankles anymore.

"That fits you fine yet," her mother said, looking her up and down, her gaze lingering on her hair. "You haven't gained or lost. You're just the same"

"I don't feel the same." Chloe giggled nervously, glancing around the windowed room awash in sunshine. The polished oak floor shone. This had been their visiting room when they were Postulants and Candidates. Here she had sat visiting her family, sitting on the lovely sofas, and smooth tight chairs situated around a shiny coffee table holding a bouquet of flowers.

"I guess we can go," Daddy said, smiling.

"Come, Chloe," Momma said, taking her arm and steering her toward the door, giving her a little squeeze. "You won't need a coat. I brought mine, but it's' really too warm for a coat." It was the middle of May, 1961.

The car seat felt stiff and cold as Chloe slid onto the front seat next to her father. The motor started. The radio announced, "Cedric Adams and the Noon Time News … in Berlin, Germany yesterday another man was shot and killed by border guards trying to stem the flow of refugees from East to West Berlin. And in Tanganyika, East Africa, good news; nine million blacks are experiencing their first week of self-government. Meanwhile, in our own nation, Citizen Richard Nixon says we must become accustomed to living in a time of crisis. The forces of Communism are determined to conquer the entire world. This week it was Laos. Last week it was Cuba. Next week …" Momma clicked the radio off.

Chloe, seated between her parents, stared at the dusty hood of the blue station wagon as it nosed its way down the curved road away from Mater Dei Heights. Her mother lit up a cigarette. Chloe rubbed her eyes. She felt tired enough to sleep for a week. But she sat stiffly upright, her flaming hands in her lap. "Wait till they hear I have arthritis! I won't be much use to them on the farm," she thought.

As they headed into Magnolia the traffic flowed thickly, and people filled the sidewalks. Chloe felt as if she had returned to earth from another planet. "Did any of these people from Magnolia ever look up at those buildings on the top of the hill and wonder what went on there?" "Did you say you wanted to stop and do some shopping for her?" Daddy spoke to Momma as though Chloe were not there.

"Not here. Not in this town," Chloe said. "People know me here—day students." Little children in shirtsleeves played in their driveways as if it were summer. Chloe shivered. She felt like a dead body being transported to another place. She had no form. Whatever she had been was still back in the shadows of the trunk room. Whatever she would be waited somewhere down the road, around the bend, at the farm and beyond.

Her mother began to talk, telling her the cute things the twins did or said, and what the new baby was like. She talked about whom the married ones were arguing with now, and why. Chloe listened listlessly, as from a great distance. Momma was talking a different language of petty, worldly things that she had forgotten. She would have to re-learn it, sooner or later, she supposed. Timidly, out of a sense of duty, she asked her father, "How are the crops this year?"

This set Daddy prattling about farm prices and the weather. Just as he was decrying the high cost of farming, Momma exclaimed, "Do you have to go into that now? She doesn't want to hear about that. It's so depressing." She exhaled, filling the car with smoke. Chloe loved the smell, for it told her she was home.

"She asked, so I was just telling," Daddy said meekly.

"All she asked was how the crops were. You don't even have the crops in yet."

"That's what I was saying. It's been so wet, this is the first good day we've had to plant."

Tiredly, Chloe gazed out at the rich black fields spreading out on either side of the road to the blue horizon. "Was this the way it was then? Just as when she had read an engrossing novel, would close the book and look up, surprised to find herself in this room, in this house, with this family. Her years at Mater Dei were like a story. And now it was finished."

She lifted her head and took a deep breath. She was free! Though she felt old, she was still young. She shivered again and rubbed her elbows.

"You all right?" Daddy said, glancing at her.

"Yes," she said, nodding. "My elbows burn sometimes, and my hands."

"Oh, I get that too," Daddy said. "It comes from tension."

"It'll be good to get home and see everybody." Chloe said.

Her mother took her hand in her lap and stroked it. "You'll have to tell us all about it," she said, "when you're ready and feel like talking.

The End

Afterword

Chloe's (my) return home was, as always, a big change from life in the convent. But this time I was home for good. Gradually, as I helped with the work, I lost my lethargy and regained my joy. For a time all I wanted was to work near Momma, in the kitchen, the garden, and with the babies. Their soft cuddly selves became for me a healing therapy. I felt needed and loved again.

My hands and heart continued to ache, especially when I did close work, such as sewing or writing. But slowly these symptoms faded and disappeared. Listening to the radio again was a treat. I loved modern songs and my favorite television show was a half hour drama in the middle of the day called "Loretta Lynn."

Eventually I ventured out to "Ben's Ballroom" with my parents to meet people. It was there, at one of the dances, that I met my future husband, Don.

There no longer is a high school at "Mater Dei." The buildings are used by the order for the convent, the aging sisters, and various ministries.

In the ensuing years I began to read the Bible. I also read about Martin Luther's life and how God used him to bring revival, known formally as the Reformation, in 1517. I identified with Luther's struggles as a priest, trying to please God by penance and good works, and rejoiced with his discovery in Romans 1:17: *"The just shall live by faith."*

I thank God for Luther's life and writings that helped free sinners like me from the bondage of works righteousness into the *"glorious liberty of the children of God."* (Romans 8:21)

Eventually I heard a preacher explain the Bible's doctrine of predestination and election. I learned that God has always had a chosen people which make up His Church; and how my soul is saved by God's mercy—alone—not by any good work or decision on my part. No one can earn heaven through sacrifice or by giving money. God's gift of faith freed me from guilt and the need to prove myself "good enough" for Him. Instead of a relationship with God based on what *I* did for Him, I was given a saving relationship built on what *He* has done for me in Jesus Christ.

"And you, being dead in your trespasses and the uncircumcision of your flesh, He has made alive together with Him, having forgiven you all trespasses, having wiped out the hand- writing of requirements that was against us, which was contrary to us. And He has taken it out of the way, having nailed it to the cross." Colossians 2:13–14 (NKJ)

"Oh Lord, You have searched me and known me. You know my sitting down and my rising up; You understand my thought afar off. You comprehend my path and my lying down, and are acquainted with all my ways. For there is not a word on my tongue, but behold, O Lord, You know it altogether. You have hedged me behind and before, and laid Your hand upon me. Such knowledge is too wonderful for me; it is high, I cannot attain it." Psalm 139:1–6 (NKJ)

8444893R0

Made in the USA
Charleston, SC
11 June 2011